Victor's Triumph

E. D. E. N. Southworth

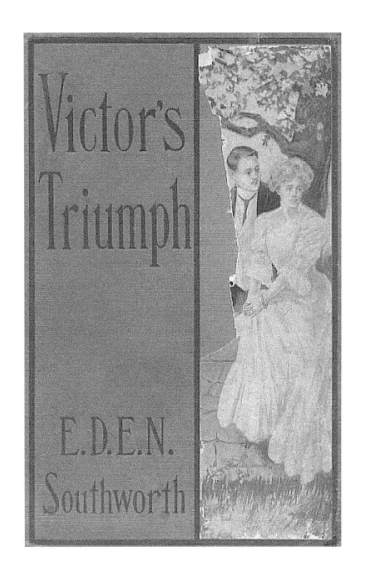

Victor's
Triumph

E.D.E.N.
Southworth

VICTOR'S TRIUMPH

SEQUEL TO

A BEAUTIFUL FIEND

BY

Mrs. E. D. E. N. SOUTHWORTH

AUTHOR OF "TRIED FOR HER LIFE," "THE LOST HEIRESS,"
"ALLWORTH ABBEY," ETC., ETC.

CHAPTER I.

SAMSON AND DELILAH.

> Thus he grew
> Tolerant of what he half disdained. And she,
> Perceiving that she was but half disdained,
> Began to break her arts with graver fits—
> Turn red or pale, and often, when they met,
> Sigh deeply, or, all-silent, gaze upon him
> With such a fixed devotion, that the old man,
> Though doubtful, felt the flattery, and at times
> Would flatter his own wish, in age, for love,
> And half believe her true.
>
> —TENNYSON.

As soon as the subtle siren was left alone in the drawing-room with the aged clergyman she began weaving her spells around him as successfully as did the beautiful enchantress Vivien around the sage Merlin.

Throwing her bewildering dark eyes up to his face she murmured in hurried tones:

"You *will* not betray me to this family? Oh, consider! I am so young and so helpless!"

"And so beautiful," added the old man under his breath, as he gazed with involuntary admiration upon her fair, false face. Then, aloud, he said: "I have already told you, wretched child, that I would forbear to expose you so long as you should conduct yourself with strict propriety here; but no longer."

"You do not trust me. Ah, you do not see that one false step with its terrible consequences has been such an awful and enduring lesson to me that I could not make another! I am safer now from the possibility of error than is the most innocent and carefully guarded child. Oh, can you not understand this?" she asked, pathetically.

And her argument was a very specious and plausible one, and it made an impression.

"I can well believe that the fearful retribution that followed so fast upon your 'false step,' as you choose to call it, has been and will be an awful warning to you. But some warnings come too late. What *can* be your long future life?" he sadly inquired.

"Alas, what?" she echoed, with a profound sigh. "Even under the most propitious circumstances—*what?* If I am permitted to stay here I shall be buried alive in this country house, without hope of resurrection. Perhaps fifty years I may have to live here. The old lady will die. Emma will marry. Her children will grow up and marry. And in all the changes of future years I shall vegetate here without change, and without hope except in the better world. And yet, dreary as the prospect is, it is the best that I can expect, the best that I can even desire, and much better than I deserve," she added, with a humility that touched the old man's heart.

"I feel sorry for you, child; very, very sorry for your blighted young life. Poor child, you can never be happy again; but listen—*you can be good!*" he said, very gently.

And then he suddenly remembered what her bewildering charms had made him for a moment forget—that was, that this unworthy girl had been actually on the point of marriage with an honorable man when Death stepped in and put an end to a foolish engagement.

So, after a painful pause, he said, slowly:

"My child, I have heard that you were about to be married to Charles Cavendish, when his sudden death arrested the nuptials. Is that true?"

"It is true," she answered, in a tone of humility and sorrow.

"But how could you venture to dream of marrying him?"

"Ah, me; I knew I was unworthy of him! But he fell in love with me. I could not help that. Now, could I? *Now, could I?*" she repeated, earnestly and pathetically, looking at him.

"N-n-no. Perhaps you could not," he admitted.

"And oh, he courted me so hard!—so hard! And I could not prevent him!"

"Could you not have avoided him? Could you not have left the house?"

"Ah, no; I had no place to go to! I had lost my situation in the school."

"Still you should never have engaged yourself to marry Charles Cavendish, for you must have been aware that if he had known your true story he would never have thought of taking you as his wife."

"Oh, I know it! And I knew it then. And I was unhappy enough about it. But oh, what could I do? I could not prevent his loving me, do what I would. I could not go away from the house, because I had no place on earth to go to. And least of all would I go to him and tell him the terrible story of my life. I would rather have died than have told that! I should have died of humiliation in the telling—I couldn't tell him! Now could I? *Could I?*"

"I suppose you had not the courage to do so."

"No, indeed I had not! Yet very often I told him, in a general way, that I was most unworthy of him. But he never would believe that."

"No; I suppose he believed you to be everything that is pure, good and heavenly. What a terrible reproach his exalted opinion of you must have been!"

"Oh, it was—it was!" she answered, hypocritically. "It was such a severe reproach that, having in a moment of weakness yielded to his earnest prayer and consented to become his wife, I soon cast about for some excuse for breaking the engagement; for I felt if it were a great wrong to make such an engagement it would be a still greater wrong to keep it. Don't you agree with me?"

"Yes, most certainly."

"Well, while I was seeking some excuse to break off the marriage Death stepped in and put an end to it. Perhaps then I ought to have left the house, but—I had no money to go with and, as I said before, no place to go to. And besides Emma Cavendish was overwhelmed with grief and could not bear to be left alone; and she begged me to come down here with her. So, driven by my own necessities and drawn by hers, I came down. Do you blame me? *Do* you blame me?" she coaxed, pathetically.

"No, I do not blame you for that. But," said the old man, gravely and sadly, shaking his head, "why, when you got here, did you turn eavesdropper and spy?"

"Oh, me!—oh, dear me!" sobbed the siren. "It was the sin of helplessness and cowardice. I dreaded discovery so much! Every circumstance alarmed me. Your arrival and your long mysterious conversation with madam alarmed me. I thought exposure imminent. I feared to lose this home, which, lonely, dreary, hopeless as it is to me, is yet the only refuge I have left on earth. I am penniless and helpless; and but for this kind family I should be homeless and friendless. Think if I had been cast out upon the world what must have been my fate!"

"What, indeed!" echoed the old man.

"Therefore, I dreaded to be cast out. I dreaded discovery. Your visit filled me with uneasiness, that, as the day wore away, reached intense anxiety, and finally arose to insupportable anguish and suspense. Then I went to listen at the door, only to hear whether your conversation concerned me—whether I was still to be left in peace or to be cast out upon the bitter cold world. Ah, do not blame me too much! Just think how I suffered!" she said, pathetically, clasping her hands.

"'Oh, what a tangled web we weave
When first we practice to deceive!'"

murmured the old man to himself. Then, aloud, he said:

"Poor girl, you were snared in the web of your own contriving! Yet still, when I caught you in that net, why did you deny your identity and try to make me believe that you were somebody else?"

"Oh, the same sin of helplessness and cowardice; the same fear of discovery and exposure; the same horror of being cast forth from this pure, safe, peaceful home into the bitter, cold, foul, perilous world outside! I feared, if you found out who I was, you would expose me, and I should be cast adrift. And then it all came so suddenly I had no time for reflection. The instinct of self-preservation made me deny my identity before I considered what a falsehood I uttered. Ah, have you no pity for me, in considering the straits to which I was reduced?" she pleaded, clasping her hands before him and raising her eyes to his face.

"'The way of the transgressor is hard,'" murmured the minister to himself. Then he answered her:

"Yes, I do pity you very much. I pity you for your sins and sufferings. But more than all I pity you for the moral and spiritual blindness of which you do not even seem to be suspicious, far less conscious."

"I do not understand you," murmured Mary Grey, in a low, frightened tone.

"No, you do not understand me. Well, I will try to explain. You have pleaded your youth as an excuse for your first 'false step,' as you call it. But I tell you that a girl who is old enough to sin is old enough to know better than to sin. And if you were not morally and spiritually blind you would see this. Secondly, you have pleaded your necessities—that is, your interests—as a just cause and excuse for your matrimonial engagement with Governor Cavendish, and for your eavesdropping in this house, and also for your false statements to me. But I tell you if you had been as truly penitent as you professed to be you would have felt no necessity so pressing as the necessity for true repentance, forgiveness and amendment. And if you had not been morally and spiritually blind you would have seen this also. I sometimes think that it may be my duty to discover you to this family. Yet I will be candid with you. I fear that if you should be turned adrift here you might, and probably would, fall into deeper sin. Therefore I will not expose you—for the present, and upon conditions. You are safe from me so long as you remain true, honest and faithful to this household. But upon the slightest indication of any sort of duplicity or double dealing I shall unmask you to Madam Cavendish. And now you had better retire. Good-night."

And with these words the old man walked to a side-table, took a bed-room candle in his hand and gave it to the widow.

Mary Grey snatched and kissed his hand, courtesied and withdrew.

When she got to her own room she threw herself into a chair and laughed softly, murmuring:

"The old Pharisee! He is more than half in love with me now. I know it, and I feel it. Yet, to save his own credit with himself, he pretends to lecture me and tries to persuade himself that he means it. But he is half in love with me. Before I have done with him he shall be wholly in love with me. And won't it be fun to have his gray head at my feet, proposing marriage to me! And that is what I mean to bring him to before a month is over his venerable skeleton!"

And, with this characteristic resolution, Mary Grey went to bed.

CHAPTER II.

LAURA LYTTON'S MYSTERIOUS BENEFACTOR.

There never was a closer friendship between two girls than that which bound Laura Lytton and Emma Cavendish together.

On the night of Laura's arrival, after they had retired from the drawing-room, and Electra had gone to bed and gone to sleep, Laura and Emma sat up together in Emma's room and talked until nearly daylight—talked of everything in the heavens above, the earth below, and the waters under the earth. And then, when at length they parted, Laura asked:

"May I come in here with you to dress to-morrow? And then we can finish our talk."

"Surely, love! Use my room just like your own," answered Emma, with a kiss.

And they separated for a few hours.

But early in the morning, as soon as Emma was out of bed, she heard a tap at her chamber door, and she opened it to see Laura standing there in her white merino dressing-gown, with her dark hair hanging down and a pile of clothing over her arms.

"Come in, dear," said Emma, greeting her with a kiss.

And Laura entered and laid her pile of clothing on a chair, discovering in her hand a rich casket, which she set upon the dressing-table, saying:

"Here, Emma, dear, I have something very curious to show you. You have heard me speak of some unknown friend who is paying the cost of my brother's and my own education?"

"Yes. Haven't you found out yet who he is?" inquired Miss Cavendish.

"No; and I do not even know whether our benefactor is a he or a she. But anyhow he has sent me this," said Laura, unlocking the casket and lifting the lid.

"A set of diamonds and opals fit for a princess!" exclaimed Emma, in admiration, as she gazed upon the deep blue satin tray, on which was arranged a brooch, a pair of ear-rings, a bracelet and a necklace of the most beautiful opals set in diamonds.

"Yes, they are lovely! They must have come from Paris. They are highly artistic," answered Laura. "But look at these others, will you? These are barbaric," she added, lifting the upper tray from the casket and taking from the recess beneath the heaviest cable gold chain, a heavier finger ring, and a pair of bracelets. "Just take these in your double hands and 'heft' them, as the children say," she concluded, as she put the weight of gold in Emma's open palms, which sank at first under the burden.

"There; what do you think of that?" inquired Laura.

"I think they are barbaric, as you said. Well intended, no doubt, but utterly barbaric. Why, this gold chain might fasten up the strongest bull-dog and these bracelets serve as fetters for the most desperate felon! Where on earth were they manufactured?" inquired Miss Cavendish.

"In some rude country where there was more gold than good taste, evidently. However, Emma, dear, there is something very touching, very pathetic, to my mind, in these anonymous offerings. Of course they are almost useless to me. I could never wear the chain or the bracelets. They are far too clumsy for any one but an Indian chief; and I can never wear those lovely opals unless by some miracle I grow rich enough to have everything in harmony with them. And yet, Emma, the kindness and—what shall I say?—the humility of this anonymous giver so deeply touches my heart that I would not part with even a link of this useless chain to buy myself bread if I were starving," murmured Laura, with the tears filling her eyes, as she replaced the jewels in their casket.

"And you have no suspicion who the donor is?"

"None whatever. These came to me through Mr. Lyle, the agent who receives and pays the money for our education."

"What does your brother say to all this?"

"Oh, it makes him very uneasy at times. He shrinks from receiving this anonymous assistance. It is all Mr. Lyle can do now, by assuring him that in the end he will find it all right, to induce him to continue to receive it. And, at all events, he declares that after he graduates he will not take another dollar of this anonymous fund—conscience money or not—but that he will begin to pay back in bank, with interest and compound interest, the debt that he is now incurring."

"I think that resolution is highly to his honor," said Emma Cavendish.

"And he will keep it. I know Alden," answered Laura.

And then the two girls hastened to dress themselves for breakfast. And very well they both looked as they left their room.

Laura wore her crimson merino morning-dress, with white linen cuffs and collar, a costume that well became her olive complexion and dark hair and eyes.

Emma wore a black cashmere trimmed with lusterless black silk, and folded book-muslin cuffs and collar. And in this dark dress her radiant blonde beauty shone like a fair star.

They rapped at Electra's door to bring her out.

She made her appearance looking quite dazzling. Electra had a gay taste in dress. She loved bright colors and many of them. She wore a purple dressing-gown with a brilliant shawl border—a dress for a portly old lady rather than for a slim young girl.

They went down together to the breakfast-room, where they found the languishing widow and the old clergyman *tête-à-tête*.

Mrs. Grey greeted them with a sweet smile and honeyed words, and Dr. Jones with a kindly good-morning and handshake.

And they sat down to breakfast.

This Easter Sunday had dawned clearly and beautifully. The family of Blue Cliffs were all going to attend divine service at Wendover.

So, as soon as breakfast was over, the carriage was ordered, and the young ladies went upstairs to dress for church.

At nine o'clock the whole party set out. Emma Cavendish, Laura Lytton and Electra Coroni went in the old family coach, carefully driven by Jerome. Mrs. Grey went in a buggy driven by the Rev. Dr. Jones.

Who arranged this last drive, this *tête-à-tête*, no one knew except the artful coquette and her venerable victim.

They all reached the church in good time.

The rector, the Rev. Dr. Goodwin, read the morning service, and the Rev. Dr. Jones preached the sermon.

At the conclusion of the services, when the congregation were leaving, Mr. Craven Kyte came up to pay his respects to the ladies from Blue Cliffs.

Miss Cavendish introduced him to Dr. Jones, explaining that he had been a ward of her father, and was once an inmate of Blue Cliff Hall.

Dr. Jones received the young man with courtesy, and in his turn introduced him to Miss Coroni.

Then Emma Cavendish invited him to go home with them to dinner, kindly reminding him of the old custom of spending his holidays in his guardian's house.

With a smile and a bow, and with a warm expression of thanks, the young man accepted the offered hospitality.

And when the party entered their carriages to return to Blue Cliffs, Craven Kyte, mounted on a fine horse, attended them.

But, mind, he did not ride beside the carriage that contained the three young ladies, but beside the gig occupied by Mary Grey and Dr. Jones.

And the very first inquiry he made of Emma, on reaching the house, was:

"Is the Reverend Doctor Jones a married man?"

"Why, what a question!" exclaimed Emma, laughing. "No, he is not a married man; he is a widower. Why do you ask?"

"I don't know. But I thought he was a widower. He seems very much taken with Mrs. Grey," sighed the young man.

"Oh, is that it?" laughed Emma, as she ran away to take off her bonnet and mantle.

And that Easter Sunday Mary Grey found herself again in a dilemma between her two proposed victims—the gray-haired clergyman and the raven-locked youth.

But she managed them both with so much adroitness that at the close of the day, when Craven Kyte was riding slowly back to Wendover, he was saying to himself:

"She is fond of me, after all; the beauty, the darling, the angel! Oh, that such a perfect creature should be fond of me! I am at this moment the very happiest man on earth!"

And later the same night, when the Rev. Dr. Jones laid his woolen night-capped head upon his pillow, instead of going to sleep as the old gentleman should have done, he lay awake and communed with himself as follows:

"Poor child—poor child! A mere baby. And she *is* penitent; sincerely penitent. Oh, I can see that! And to think that she is not nearly so much in fault as we believed her to be! She tells me that she really was married to that man—married when she was a child only fourteen years of age. So her gravest error was in running away to be married! And that was the fault of the man who stole her, rather than of herself. And she is as repentant for that fault as if it were some great crime. And oh, how she has suffered! What she has gone through for one so young! And she has such a tender, affectionate, clinging nature! Ah, what will become of her, poor child—poor child! She ought to have some one to take care of her. She ought indeed to be married, for no one but a tender husband could take care of such a pretty, delicate, helpless creature. She ought to marry some one much older than herself. Not a green, beardless boy like that young puppy—Heaven forgive me!—I mean that young man Kyte. He couldn't appreciate her, couldn't be a guide or a guard to her. And she really needs guiding and guarding too. For see how easily she falls into error. She ought to marry some good, wise, elderly man, who could be her guide, philosopher and friend as well as husband."

And so murmuring to himself he fell asleep to dream that he himself was the model guide, philosopher and friend required by the young widow.

Chapter III.

A GROWL FROM UNCLE JACKY.

The next day, Easter Monday, brought a messenger from Lytton Lodge; a messenger who was no other than Mithridates, commonly called "Taters," once a servant of Frederick Fanning, the landlord of White Perch Point, but now a hired hand of John Lytton's.

Mithridates, or Taters, rode an infirm-looking old draft horse, with a dilapidated saddle and bridle, and wore a hat and coat exceedingly shabby for a gentleman's servant.

He also led a second horse, furnished with a side-saddle.

He dismounted at the carriage-steps, tied the horses to a tree, and boldly went to the front door and knocked.

Jerome opened it, and administered a sharp rebuke to the messenger for presuming to knock at the visitors' door instead of at the servants'.

"If I'd a come to the servants' I'd rapped at the servants' door; but as I have comed to the white folks' I rap at dere door. Here; I've fotch a letter from Marse Jacky Lytton to his niece, Miss Lorrer," said Taters, pompously.

"Give it to me then, and I'll take it in to her," said Jerome.

"Set you up with it! I must 'liver of this here letter with my own hands inter her own hands," said Taters, stoutly.

"Well, come along, for a fool! You're a purty looking objick to denounce into the parlor, a'n't you now?" said Jerome, leading the way.

At that moment, unseen by Jerome, but distinctly seen by Taters, a face appeared at the head of the stairs for an instant, but meeting the eye of Taters turned white as death and vanished.

Taters uttered a terrible cry and sank, ashen pale and quaking with horror, at the foot of the steps.

"Why, what in the name of the old boy is the matter with you, man? Have you trod on a nail or piece of glass, or anything that has gone through your foot, or what is it?" demanded Jerome, in astonishment.

"Oh, no, no, no! it's worse'n that—it's worse'n that! It's no end worse'n that! Oh, Lor'! oh, Lor'! oh, Lor'!" cried Taters, holding his knees and sawing backward and forward in an agony of horror.

"Ef you don't stop that howlin' and tell me what's the matter of you I'm blessed ef I don't get a bucket of ice water and heave it all over you to fetch you to your senses!" exclaimed the exasperated Jerome.

"Oh, Lor', don't! Oh, please don't! I shill die quick enough now without that!" cried Taters, writhing horribly.

"What's the matter, you born iddiwut?" roared Jerome, in a fury.

"Oh, I've seen a sperrit—I've seen a sperrit! I've seen the sperrit of my young mistress! And it's a token of my death!" wailed the negro boy in agony.

"What's that you say—a sperrit? A sperrit in this yer 'spectable, 'sponsible house? Lookee here, nigger: mind what you say now, or it'll be the wus for you! A sperrit in this yer ginteel family as never had a crime or a ghost inter it! The Cavendishers nebber 'mits no crimes when der living, nor likewise don't walk about ondecent after der dead. And der a'n't no sperrits here," said Jerome, with ire.

"Oh, I wish it wasn't—I wish it wasn't! But it was a sperrit! And it's a token of my death—it's a token of my death!" howled Taters.

And now at last the noise brought the three young ladies out of the drawing-room.

"What is the matter here, Jerome?" inquired Mrs. Cavendish. "Has any one got hurt? Who is that man?"

"Ef you please, Miss Emma, no one a'n't got hurt, though you might a thought, from the squalling, that there was a dozen pigs a killin'. And that man, miss, is a born iddiwut, so he is—begging your pardon, miss!—and says he's seed a sperrit in this yer harristocraterick house, where there never was a sperrit yet," explained Jerome, with a grieved and indignant look.

"But who is the man? What is he doing here? And what does he want?" inquired the young lady.

"The man is a born iddiwut, Miss Emma, as I telled you before; that's who the man he is! And he's a making of a 'fernal fool of hisself; that's what he's doing here! And he deserves a good hiding; and that's what he wants!" said Jerome, irately.

Miss Cavendish passed by the privileged old family servant, and went up to the man himself and inquired:

"Who are you, boy? What brings you here? And what ails you?"

"Oh, miss! I'm Taters, I am. And I come to fetch a letter from Marse Jacky Lytton to Miss Lorrer. And I seen a sperrit at the top o'them stair steps. And that's what's the matter of me," cried the boy.

"A spirit! Jerome, do you think he's been drinking?" inquired the young lady in a low, frightened voice.

For an answer Jerome, without the least hesitation, seized Taters by the head, pulled open his jaws, and stuck his own nose into the cavity and took an audible snuff. Then, releasing the head, he answered:

"No, miss, he a'n't been drinking nuffin. His breff's as sweet as a milch cow's. I reckon he must be subjick to epperliptic fits, miss, by the way he fell down here all of a suddint, crying out as he'd seen a sperrit."

"You said you had a letter, boy. Where is it?" inquired Emma.

"Here, miss! Here it is! I'll give it to you, though I wouldn't give it to him there!" answered Taters, with a contemptuous glance toward Jerome.

Emma took the letter, which was inclosed in a wonderfully dingy yellow envelope, and she read the superscription, and then called to Laura, saying:

"Come here, my dear. Here is a letter from Lytton Lodge for you."

Laura Lytton, who, with Electra, had been standing just within the drawing-room door, near enough to observe the group, but not to hear the whole of their conversation, now came when she was called and received her letter.

"It is from dear Uncle Jacky," she said, with an affectionate smile, as she recognized the handwriting.

And then she asked the messenger a multitude of questions, which he was too much agitated to answer coherently, until at length Miss Cavendish said:

"Jerome, take the poor fellow into the kitchen and give him something to eat and drink. There is nothing like beef and beer to exorcise evil spirits. And when he is rested and refreshed we will see him again."

And Jerome took Taters rather roughly by the shoulder and pulled him upon his feet and carried him along the hall through the back door toward the kitchen.

"Will you excuse me now, dear Emma, while I read my uncle's letter?" inquired Laura, as she retreated to the drawing-room.

"Certainly," smiled Miss Cavendish, following her guests.

Laura went into the recess of a bay-window and opened the dingy yellow envelope and read as follows:

"LYTTON LODGE, April —, 18—.

"MY DEAR NIECE:—I think my nephew, Alden, has a more correcter ideer of what is jue to kin and kith than what you have shown.

"Alden is spending his Easter holidays along of me and his relations.

"But you haven't been nigh the house since you left it to go to school. You do seem to be so wrapped up in the Cavendishers as not to think anything of your own folks.

"Now I can tell you what it is. The Lyttonses are a great deal older and better family than all the Cavendishers that ever lived. I don't care if they was governors of the state.

"I have heard my grandfather, who was a scholar, say that the Lyttonses was landed gentry in the old country long before the Cavendishers followed of their lord and marster William the Conkerer across the channil. And so I don't approve of your sliting of the Lyttonses for them there Cavendishers. Spesherly as you're a Lytton yourself. And if we don't respect ourselves and each other no one a'n't a going to respect us.

"And talking of that, what do you think Hezekiah Greenfield, the landlord of the Reindeer, went and done to me last week?

"Why, he came over and asked me could I supply his tavern with fruits and vegetables during the summer season at the market price, saying—quite as if he was a making of me a kind proposal instead of offering of me a black insult—that he'd rather deal with me, and I should have his money, than any one else, if so be I was willing to do business.

"Now what do you think I answered him?

"Why, I set the bull-dog on him! I did that! And it was good for him as he scrambled up on his horse and made off double-quick, or he'd been torn to pieces before you could say Jack Robinson.

"That'll learn the tavern-keeper to insult a gentleman next time by offering to buy his garden stuff!

"But what I'm writing to you for, my dear, now, is this. I think you ought to come to see us, anyhow. You must come, if it's only for two or three days, to see your old grandmother, and all your relations, and to meet Alden, who is here, as I said. I have sent Taters on horseback with a led horse and a side-saddle for you. Come back along of him to-morrow morning. And give my honorable compliments to the old madam and Miss Cavendish. Because, mind you, I'm not a saying as the Cavendishers a'n't a good, respectabil family; only I do say as they are not so good as the Lyttonses, and they never was and never will be; and they know it themselves, too. Well, your dear grandma, and your dear aunties and cousins, all sends their love to you, with many good wishes. So no more at present from your affeckshunit uncle,

"JOHN LYTTON."

Chapter IV.

THE GHOST SEEN BY "TATERS."

He shuddered, as no doubt the bravest cowers,
When he can't tell what 'tis that doth appall.
How odd a single hobgoblin's nonentity
Should cause more fear than a whole host's identity.

—Byron.

"Emma, dear, I have a letter from Uncle John Lytton," said Laura, gravely, going to the side of her friend.

"I hope they are all well at Lytton Lodge," responded Emma.

"Oh, yes, thank you, they are all quite well; but," added Laura, with a sigh, "Uncle John has written to me to come at once and pay them a visit. And to leave me no excuse, he has sent his servant Mithridates on horseback, with another led horse and side-saddle, to take me to Lytton Lodge."

"Oh, dear! But you need not go, I hope?" said Emma, looking up, with a sigh.

"I must go," answered Laura, with another sigh. "And really I ought to be glad to go to see such kind friends as all my relatives there have been to me. But, you see, Emma, I don't like to leave you for a single day even before I have to return to school."

"Then why do you go at all? Why can you not send an excuse?"

"Dear Emma, would *you* refuse to go if you were in my place?" inquired Laura.

Emma Cavendish could not reply.

"No, you would not," added Laura, "because it would not be right to refuse."

"But, my dear, to perform so long a journey on horseback! It must be over twenty miles. Let me see—it is about nine miles from here to Wendover, and it must be ten or eleven from Wendover to Lytton Lodge," said Emma.

"No; only about eight or nine. The whole distance is not more than seventeen or eighteen miles by the roundabout route. And if I could go as the crow flies it is not more than six miles. Why, you know the eastern extremity of your land touches the western extremity of uncle's."

"So it does. And if, as you say, you could go as the crow flies—that is, straight over mountains and rivers—you could get there in two hours. As it is, it will take you five or six hours, and that is too long for a girl to be in the saddle, especially a city-bred girl, unaccustomed to such exercise."

"I think I can stand it," smiled Laura.

"But you shall not try. If you will go you must take the little carriage. When do you propose to start?"

"To-morrow morning."

"Well, we will send the redoubtable Mithridates back with his steeds, and send you on your journey in the little carriage, under the guardianship of old Jerome, with orders to remain with you during your visit; but to bring you back again, at farthest, on the third day," said Emma, peremptorily.

Laura thanked her friend, but protested against any trouble being taken on her account.

But Miss Cavendish was firm, and the arrangement was made according to her plan.

In the meantime Mithridates, eating beef and bread and drinking home-made sweet cider in the kitchen, recovered some of his composure; though still, with his mouth full of meat and his eyes starting from his head, he persisted that he had seen the spirit of his young mistress. And it was a token of his death.

"G'long way from her', boy! Ef I didn't know as you *wasn't* I should think as you *was* intoxified! There never was no sperrit never seen into this house," said Aunt Molly, indignantly.

"I don't care! I did see her sperrit! So there now," persisted Taters, bolting a chunk of bread and choking with it for a moment. "And— and it's a token of my death."

"Is that the reason you're a trying to kill yourself now, you iddiwut?"

"No; but I seen her sperrit!"

"I don't believe one word of it. You're a making of it all up out'n your own stoopid head! There, now, ef you're done eatin' you'd better go 'long and put up your hosses," said Aunt Moll, seeing her guest pause in his gastronomic efforts.

But Taters hadn't done eating, and did't get done until all the dishes on the kitchen table were cleared and the jug of cider emptied.

Then, indeed, he gave over and went to look after his "beasts."

At the same hour Mary Grey, locked fast in her room, suffered agonies of terror and anxiety. She, too, had seen a "ghost"—a ghost of her past life—a ghost that might have come to summon her from her present luxurious home!

On her way down-stairs to the drawing-room she had been arrested on the head of the middle landing by the sight of a once familiar face and form.

She met the distended eyes of this apparition, and saw at once that he had recognized her as surely as she had recognized him.

And in an instant she vanished.

She darted into her own room and locked the door and sank breathless into the nearest chair.

And there she sat now, with beating heart and burning head, waiting for what should come next.

A rap at the door was the next thing that came.

It frightened her, of course—everything frightened her now.

"Who is that?" she nervously inquired.

"Only me, ma'am. The ladies are waiting luncheon for you. Miss Emma sends her compliments and says will you come down?" spoke the voice of Sarah, the lady's maid.

"Love to Miss Cavendish, and ask her to excuse me. I do not want any luncheon," answered Mary Grey, without opening the door.

Then she sank back in her chair with throbbing pulses, waiting for the issue of this crisis. She was really ill with intense anxiety and dread. She grew so weak at last that she lay down upon her sofa.

Then came another rap at the door.

"Who is that?" she asked again, faintly.

"It is I, dear," answered the voice of Emma Cavendish.

Mrs. Grey arose trembling and opened the door.

"I was afraid that you were not well. I came up to see," said Emma, kindly, as she entered the room.

"I—no, I am not quite well," faltered Mary Grey, as she retreated to the sofa and sat down, with her back purposely to the light and her face in the shadow.

"You really look pale and ill. What is the matter, dear?"

"I—think I have taken cold. But by keeping to my room for a few days I hope to be better. A cold always affects the action of my heart and makes me very nervous," said Mary Grey, in explanation of the tremors for which she could not otherwise account.

Then Emma expressed sympathy and sorrow, and begged the pretended invalid to have some tea and cream-toast, or some wine-whey or chicken-broth.

But Mary Grey declined all these offers, declaring that a cold always took her appetite away.

And again Emma expressed regret.

And, as Miss Cavendish talked, Mary Grey grew more composed.

It was evident, she thought, that Emma as yet knew nothing of that strange rencounter on the stairs.

Presently, Miss Cavendish said:

"I am sorry to tell you that we shall lose Laura Lytton for a few days. Her uncle, Mr. Lytton of Lytton Lodge, has sent a messenger for her. She goes to visit her relations there to-morrow morning."

"Indeed—a messenger?" exclaimed Mary Grey, pricking up her ears.

"Yes; a queer genius, who signalized his entrance into the house by a scene," added Emma, smiling.

"Indeed!"

"Oh, yes! Why, you might have heard the commotion in the front hall! Did you hear nothing of it?"

"No, dear; I have remained shut up in my room ever since breakfast—have not stirred from it," answered Mary Grey, lying without the least hesitation.

"That accounts for your knowing nothing about it. But the absurd fellow raised quite a confusion by suddenly falling down in the front hall in a spasm of terror, declaring that he had seen the spirit of his young mistress on the middle landing of the front stairs."

"An optical illusion," answered Mary Grey, in a low, tremulous tone and with her face carefully kept in the shadow.

"Of course! And it appears that he was once a servant of that reckless and unlucky Frederick Fanning of White Perch Point, who married my mother's sister. And consequently his young mistress must have been that unfortunate cousin of mine," said Emma, with a sigh.

"Does any one know what ever became of that wretched girl?" inquired Mrs. Grey, in a very low tone.

"No; but I gather from the wild talk of the boy that she is supposed to be dead. It was her spirit that he thinks he saw."

"Whatever became of her father and mother?" questioned Mary Grey in the same low tone and still keeping her face in the deep shadow.

"I do not know. I heard that they went to California. I have not heard anything of them since. But, my dear, you are talking beyond your strength. Your voice is quite faint—scarcely audible indeed. Now I advise you to lie down and be quiet," said Miss Cavendish, with some solicitude.

And then she kissed Mary Grey, begged her to ring for anything she might require, and then she left the room.

And Mary Grey heard no more of the ghost. That cloud passed harmlessly over her head.

CHAPTER V.

A VISIT TO LYTTON LODGE.

Early the next morning Miss Cavendish's snug little pony-carriage, with a pretty pair of grays, stood before the front door waiting for Laura Lytton.

Old Jerome sat on the front seat to drive.

Taters, with his own horse and the now useless led horse, was in attendance.

Laura Lytton, dressed for her journey and with traveling-bag in hand, stood with Emma Cavendish in the hall waiting for Mrs. Gray, to whom they had sent a message inviting her to come down and see the traveler off.

But presently the messenger returned with Miss Grey's love and good wishes, and requested that they would excuse her from coming down, as her cold was so severe that she did not dare to leave her room.

"I must go up and bid her good-bye then," said Laura, as she dropped her traveling-bag and ran upstairs.

She found Mary Grey in a fine white merino dressing-gown playing the interesting invalid.

She hastily kissed her, expressed a hope that she might find her better on returning to Blue Cliffs, and then ran out of the room and down-stairs as fast as she could go.

She had already taken leave of every member of the family except Emma Cavendish, who went out with her to the carriage, saw her comfortably seated in it, and kissed her good-bye.

The little cavalcade then set forward.

It was a lovely spring morning. The woods and fields were clothed with the freshest green; the mountain tops beamed in the most beautiful opal tints, and the blue sky was without a cloud.

Laura enjoyed her drive very much.

At Wendover they stopped to rest and water the horses, and then they resumed their journey and went on to Lytton Lodge, where they arrived just about noon.

John Lytton was evidently on the lookout for his niece, for as the pony-carriage drove up, amid the barking of all the dogs and the shouting of all the little negroes, he rushed out of the house, throwing up his arms; and he caught Laura and lifted her bodily from her seat, roaring his welcome.

And Laura, as she returned his honest, hearty greeting, felt a twinge of self-reproach in remembering with what reluctance she had come.

Uncle John took her into the house and set her down in the hall in the midst of all her relations, who had crowded there to welcome here.

"Lor-lor-lor', John! How dare you ma-ma-make so free as that with Laura, and she a young 'oman?" exclaimed old Mrs. Lytton, as, in her well-known faded calico gown and long-eared muslin cap, she came up and kissed her granddaughter.

"Why, because she *is* a young 'oman, of course, and not an old man!" said John, saucily.

"Why, how much you have improved, child!" said Miss Molly Moss, smiling blandly.

"Oh, a'n't she though, neither?" exclaimed Octy and Ulky in a breath, as they seized her hands, the one clinging to her right and the other to her left.

"Come, now, I think you had better let Laura go upstairs and take off her bonnet and things. Dinner's all ready to go on the table. And I reckon her appetite is ready also. And, Jacky, you had better go out and tell John Brooks to put up and feed them horses," said practical

Aunt Kitty, as she took and faced Laura about toward the spare bedroom that was on the first floor.

"Uncle wrote me that my brother was here. But I don't see him," said Laura as she laid off her bonnet.

"No; he and Charley went to Perch Point fishing yesterday, intending to stay all night and come back this morning. I reckon they'll soon be here," said Aunt Kitty.

Laura washed her face and hands and brushed her hair, put on clean collar and cuffs, and declared herself ready to join the family.

Even as she spoke there was the hilarious bustle of an arrival in the hall outside.

And as Laura emerged from the room she was caught in the arms of her brother Alden.

"My darling sister, I am so delighted to see you!" said the young man, kissing her joyously.

"So am I to see you, Alden, dear. But why didn't you accept Mrs. Cavendish's invitation to come and join our Easter party at Blue Cliffs?" inquired Laura.

"My dear, because I thought my duty called me here," gravely replied Alden.

"But for a day or two you might have joined us," persisted Laura.

"No," said Alden. Then turning toward his red-headed fishing comrade he said: "Here's Cousin Charley waiting to welcome you, Laura."

And Charley Lytton, blushing and stammering, held out his hand and said:

"How do you do? I am very glad to see you."

"And now come to dinner," said Aunt Kitty, opening the dining-room door.

They all went in and sat down to as fine a dinner as was ever served in Blue Cliff Hall, or even at the Government House, although this was laid on a rough pine table, covered with a coarse, though clean linen table-cloth, and in a room where the walls were whitewashed and the floors were bare.

"And now," said Uncle Jacky, as soon as he had served the turtle soup around to everybody, "I want you to tell me why you couldn't ride the gray mare, and why you came in a pony-carriage with a slap-up pair of bloods?"

"Why, you know, I am a good-for-nothing city-bred girl, Uncle John, and Miss Cavendish knew it and doubted my ability to ride eighteen or twenty miles on horseback, and so insisted on my having the pony-carriage," explained Laura, soothingly.

"Well, I'm glad it was no worse. I was thinking may be as you despised the old family mare," said John, somewhat mollified.

"Oh, no, uncle! Quite the contrary. I did not feel equal to her," laughed Laura.

"Well, when must we send that fine equipage back—to-night or tomorrow?"

"Neither, Uncle John. It is not wanted at Blue Cliffs just at present. They have the barouche, the brougham and the gig. They can easily spare the pony-chaise. And Emma insisted on my keeping it here until I should be ready to return. And I promised her that I would do it."

"Now I don't like that. That is a patternizing of us a great deal too much. We've got a carriage of our own, I reckon," said John, sitting back in his chair and lifting his red head pompously.

"Now-now-now, John Lytton, don't you be a foo-foo-fool! Carriage! Why, our carriage is all to pieces! A'n't been fit to use for this six months! And sin-sin-since the Caverndishers have been so obleeging as to lend the loan of the pony-shay to Laura, I say let her keep it till she goes back. And while it's a staying here idle I can use it to go and see some of my neighbors," said old Mrs. Lytton, in that peremptory way of hers that did not brook contradiction from any one—even from the master of the house.

CHAPTER VI.

A FLIGHT FROM BLUE CLIFFS.

Laura Lytton staid two days with her relatives at Lytton Lodge, and was just turning over in her mind the difficult subject of breaking the news of her immediate departure to Uncle Jacky, whom she felt sure would bitterly oppose it, when, on the evening of the second day, she received a surprise in the form of a call from Craven Kyte.

The visitor was shown into the big parlor, where all the family, except Alden and Charley, were assembled, and engaged in cheerful conversation around the evening lamp.

He came in bowing, shook hands with everybody, and then took the seat that was offered him and drew a letter from his pocket, saying, humorously:

"In these latter days, when every one has a mission, it seems to me that my mission is to fetch and carry letters. I happened to call at Blue Cliffs this morning and to mention while there that I was going to White Perch Point and should take Lytton Lodge in my way, and would carry any message that was desired to Miss Laura Lytton, who I understood was on a visit there. And then Miss Cavendish requested me to take a letter to you, which she sat down and wrote right off at once. And here it is, miss," he concluded, placing the letter in Laura's hands.

Laura asked leave of her company, and then opened the envelope and read as follows:

"BLUE CLIFFS, Thursday afternoon.

"MY DEAREST LAURA:—The opportune arrival of Mr. Craven Kyte, on his way to White Perch Point and Lytton Lodge, furnishes me with the means of communicating with you sooner than I could manage to do by mail.

"You will be very much surprised at what I am about to tell you.

"*Mary Grey has left Blue Cliffs.*

"She left so suddenly that I scarcely yet can realize that she has gone.

"My grandmother and myself opposed her departure most earnestly. We used every means in the world but absolute force to keep her here.

"But she would go. She said her health and spirits required the change. You know she was ailing when you left here.

"Well, she has gone to Charlottesville, where she says she has some lady friend who keeps a boarding-house for the students of the University. So if your brother returns to the University he may have an opportunity of renewing his very pleasant acquaintance with her. I do not know when, if ever, she will return.

"Of course this is her home whenever she pleases to come back. But I strongly suspect the pretty little widow has grown tired of our country house.

"You know she has really no resources within herself for enjoyment. She cares nothing for the beautiful scenery surrounding our home, nor for gardening, nor reading, nor visiting and instructing the poor negroes; nor, in short, for anything that makes a remote country place enjoyable. And so she has left us—'It may be for years, and it may be for ever,' as the song says.

"But, my darling, don't *you* desert me just at this time. Come back, according to your promise. I am wearying for you. Tell that excessively affectionate and hospitable Uncle John that I need you so much more than he does. Or show him this letter. All the Lyttons are gallant and chivalrous gentlemen. He is no exception, and he will not oppose my wish, I feel sure. I shall expect you at Blue Cliffs to-morrow evening.

"My grandmother has just directed me to repeat her invitation to Mr. Alden Lytton, and to ask him to accompany you back to Blue Cliffs and make us a visit. I hope he will do so. Mind, I shall expect you both to-morrow evening. Pray present my respects to Mr. and Mrs. Lytton and all their kind family. And believe me, dearest Laura,

"Ever your own

"EMMA.

"*Postscript.*—I have some strange news to tell you which I can not trust upon paper. I also expect a new inmate in the family. I will explain when you come.   E."

Laura folded her letter and put it into her pocket for the present.

"They want you to come back, I suppose," said Uncle John, testily.

"I will show you the letter presently, uncle, so you can read and judge for yourself," said Laura, with a smile.

"Well, all I say is this: if they want you to come back want will be their master. For they can't have you; so there now! I don't mean to let you leave us until you are obliged to go back to school. I don't *that*!" said John, nodding his big red head.

"Did you know Mrs. Grey had left Blue Cliffs?" sorrowfully inquired Mr. Kyte.

"Yes. Emma has written to me about her departure. When did she go?"

"Early this morning. When I got to the house I was very much disappointed at not seeing her, and beyond measure astonished to hear that she had started that very morning to Wendover, to catch the first train to the city, *en route* for Charlottesville. She will be a great loss to the domestic circle at Blue Cliffs, I think."

"And who the mischief is Mrs. Grey?" inquired the sorely puzzled Uncle John.

"She was one of the assistant teachers—the drawing-mistress, in fact—at Mount Ascension. But she lost her situation there. And she became the guest of Emma Cavendish. Afterward she was engaged to Mr. Cavendish. But his death prevented the marriage," Laura explained.

And at this point of the conversation "Mandy" made her appearance at the door and said that supper was on the table.

And old Mrs. Lytton arose and invited the company to follow her to the dining-room.

After supper, as it was a clear, mild, star-lit evening, Mr. Craven Kyte remounted his horse and resumed his journey to White Perch Point.

After his departure, when the family were once more assembled in the big parlor, Laura took her letter out and put it in the hands of John Lytton.

Uncle Jacky read it through, and then quoted a part of it to the family circle.

"'Tell that affectionate and hospitable Uncle John that I need you so much more than he does. Or show him this letter. All the Lyttons are gallant and chivalrous gentlemen.' That's so!" put in Uncle Jacky, nodding his red head. "'He is no exception. And he will not oppose my wish, I feel sure.' Now that is what I call taking a fellow at a disadvantage!" growled John, holding the letter before his eyes and staring at it. "Well, I suppose I must let you go, Laura, seeing she makes such a point of it. But they want Alden, too. And Alden they can't have! Where is the fellow, anyhow? And why wasn't he at supper?"

"He and Charley are down at Uncle Bob's house, getting bait for another fishing match to-morrow. I told Mandy to keep the supper hot for them," answered Aunt Kitty.

And soon after this the little family, who kept very early hours, separated to go to rest.

Laura and her two cousins were the first to leave the room.

Aunt Kitty and Miss Molly followed.

When they were gone old Mrs. Lytton turned upon her son and said:

"Jacky, I ho-ho-hope you a'n't a goin' to be sich a contrairy fool as to stand into the light of your own flesh and blood?"

"Why, what the mischief do you mean, mother? I a'n't a standing into nobody's light, much less my own flesh and blood's!" exclaimed John, raising his red head.

"Yes-yes-yes, you are too! You're a standing into your own dear nephew's, Alden Lytton's, light, in opposing of his going to Blue Cliffs along of his sister to-morrow," complained the old lady.

"Riddle-me-riddle-me-ree! I know no more of what you're talking than the fish of Zuyder Zee!"

"Why-why-why then this is what I'm a talking about. Can-can-can't you see that Emma Cavendish is perfectly wrapped up in Laura Lytton? She's as fon-fon-fond of her as ever she can be. And Emma Cavendish is the most beau-beau-beautiful girl and the richest heiress in the whole state. And Alden Lytton is one of the han-han-handsomest young men I ever saw. And if he goes with his sister to Blue Cliffs—*don't you see?*"

"No, I don't," said honest, obtuse John.

"Well, then, the gal that is so fond of the sis-sis-sister might grow to be equally fond of the handsome bro-bro-brother. *Now do you see?*"

"Oh, I see!" exclaimed John, with a look of profound enlightenment.

"And I hope you won't go and stand into the light of your own dear nephew by raising up of any objections to his going along of his sister to Blue Cliffs," added the old lady.

"*I* stand in the light of my own poor, dear, dead brother's son! 'Tain't likely!" exclaimed Uncle Jacky, with an injured air.

"No, John, I don't think it is. And so, I hope, instead of oppo-po-po-opposing on him, you'll encourage him to go along of his sister to Blue Cliffs to-morrow," said the old lady.

"Mother, I shall do what is right," answered John.

"And lookee here, Jacky! Don't you let on to Alden that any on us have such a thought as him going there to court the heiress, for ef you do, he's so high and mighty he'd see us all furder fust before he'd budge a step to go to Blue Cliffs, sister or no sister. So mind what I tell you, John."

"Mother, I will do all that is right," repeated John, with pompous dignity.

"I only hope as you will. And so good-night, my son," said the old woman, as she lighted her bed-room taper and left the room.

Laura came down-stairs early the next morning, and found her brother alone in the big parlor.

And then she showed him Emma Cavendish's letter.

And when he had read it through, she said, quite piteously:

"Alden, I do want to go back and spend the rest of the Easter holidays at Blue Cliffs, for I love Emma Cavendish better than anybody else in the whole world except yourself. And I hate to disappoint her. But I equally hate to leave you, Alden. So I do wish you would make up your mind to accept Mrs. Cavendish's invitation and accompany me to Blue Cliffs."

"Why-why-why of course he will go, Laura! Do you 'spect your own dear brother is a going to let you go off alone, by your own self, of a journey, when he's invi-vi-vited to go along of you?" exclaimed old Mrs. Lytton, who entered at that moment, and spoke up before Alden Lytton could either accept or refuse.

"Certainly he will. Why, nephew's a gentleman, I reckon, and he wouldn't refuse to escort his own dear sister, when he is requested to do so," added Uncle John, as he strode into the room.

Alden Lytton smiled and bowed.

In truth, now that the secret obstacle to his visit to Blue Cliffs was removed by the departure of Mrs. Grey for an indefinitely long absence, he felt no objection at all to accompanying his sister thither. So, still smiling, he answered:

"Why, you all seem to think that I shall make some difficulty about complying with my sister's wishes. But I shall do nothing of the sort. On the contrary, I shall attend my sister with great pleasure."

"That's you!" exclaimed old Mrs. Lytton.

"Bully boy!" heartily cried Uncle Jacky.

"I thank you, Alden," said Laura, quietly, giving him her hand.

"Yes, that's all very well; but—" began Charley, who had joined the circle.

"But what? What's the matter with you?" demanded his father.

Charley, seeing all eyes turned upon him, and most especially Laura's, blushed crimson and remained silent.

"I had arranged to go with Charley this morning to fish for trout in the Mad River," laughingly explained Alden.

"Oh, well, it can't be helped! You feel disappointed, of course, my boy; but everything must give way to the will of the ladies, Charley. 'All the Lyttons are gallant and chivalrous gentlemen,'" said Uncle Jacky, proudly, quoting the words of Emma's letter. "And we are no exception to the rule. Miss Cavendish is anxious for the society of Laura. Laura wishes the escort of her brother, who has also been invited to Blue Cliffs. We must not oppose the will of the ladies," concluded John, bowing to his niece with pompous deference.

Poor Charley blushed purpler than ever, and holding down his red head—like his father's—he mumbled something about "not wishing to oppose no ladies whatsoever."

"Now, then, what time are you expected at Blue Cliffs?" inquired Uncle Jacky, turning to Laura.

"This evening, uncle. Don't you remember? You read the letter."

"Oh, yes! Well, then, you needn't leave till after dinner, Kitty," he called to his wife, "order dinner for twelve o'clock noon, sharp! I want Alden and Laura, if they *must* leave, to go with full stomachs: do you hear?"

"Why of course, Jacky! Don't we always have dinner at twelve o'clock?" laughingly inquired Aunt Kitty.

"Well, then, mind that to-day a'n't an exception to the rule. Now where's that boy Taters?"

"Here I am, Marse John," said Mithridates, making his appearance with an armful of wood, which he threw upon the fire; for the April morning was chilly.

"Taters," said Uncle John, "you see to having the pony-chaise at the door at half-past twelve precisely to take Mr. Alden and Miss Laura to Blue Cliffs."

"Yes, Marse John."

"And, Taters, you saddle Brown Bill to ride and wait on them. You hear?"

Taters turned dark-gray and staggered to a chair and sat down.

"Why, what's the matter with the fool now?" demanded Uncle John.

"Oh, Marse John, don't send me to Blue Cliffs no more, sir—please don't!"

"Why—why shouldn't I send you there, you idiot?"

"Oh, Marse John, I done see the sperrit of my young mist'ess there; and if I see it ag'in I shall die—'deed I shall, sir!" exclaimed the shuddering boy.

"What the mischief does he mean, Laura? You look as if you understood him," inquired John Lytton.

Laura laughingly told the story of the supposed spirit, adding that it must have been a pure hallucination on the part of the boy.

"Well, anyhow, I'll not send him with you if he's takin' to makin' a fool of himself. It wouldn't do, you know," said John.

"And really, uncle, we need no one at all as an outrider," said Laura.

After an early and substantial dinner, Alden and Laura took leave of their kind relatives and entered the pony-carriage, whose dashing little grays, driven by old Jerome, were to take them to Blue Cliffs.

But we must precede them thither, to find out what it was that had driven Mary Grey from the house in such very great haste.

CHAPTER VII.

A STARTLING EVENT.

What see you in these papers, that you lose
So much of your complexion? Look you how you change!
Your cheeks are paper!—why, what hear you there
That hath so cowarded and chased your blood
Out of appearance?

—SHAKESPEARE.

It was on the evening of the very same day that saw the departure of Laura Lytton for Lytton Lodge that Peter, the post-office messenger of Blue Cliffs, returned from Wendover, bringing with him a well-filled mail-bag.

He took it into the drawing-room, where Miss Cavendish and her guests, the Rev. Dr. Jones, Miss Electra, and Mrs. Grey, were gathered around the center-table, under the light of the chandelier.

Emma Cavendish unlocked the mail-bag and turned its contents out upon the table.

"Newspapers and magazines only, I believe. No letters. Help yourselves, friends. There are paper-knives on the pen-tray. And in the absence of letters, there is a real pleasure in unfolding a fresh newspaper and cutting the leaves of a new magazine," said the young lady, as she returned the empty bag to the messenger.

But her companions tumbled over the mail still in the vain hope of finding letters.

"None for me; yet I did hope to get one from my new manager at Beresford Manors," muttered Dr. Jones, in a tone of disappointment.

"And none for me either, though I do think the girls at Mount Ascension might write to me," pouted Electra.

"And of course there are none for me! There never are! No one ever writes to me. The poor have no correspondents. I did not expect a letter, and I am not disappointed," murmured Mary Grey, with that charming expression, between a smile and a sigh, that she had always found so effective.

"Well, there is no letter for any one, it seems, so none of us have cause to feel slighted by fortune more than others," added Emma Cavendish, cheerfully.

But Peter, the post-office boy, looked from one to the other, with his black eyes growing bigger and bigger, as he felt with his hand in the empty mail-bag and exclaimed:

"I'clar's to de law der was a letter for some uns. Miss Emmer, 'cause I see de pos'marser put it in de bag wid his own hands, which it were a letter wid a black edge all 'round de outside of it, and a dob o' black tar, or somethink, onto the middle o' the back of it."

As the boy spoke, the Rev. Dr. Jones began again to turn over the magazines and newspapers until he found the letter, which had slipped between the covers of the *Edinboro' Review*.

"It is for you, my dear," he said, as he passed the missive across the table to Miss Cavendish.

"I wonder from whom it comes? The handwriting is quite unfamiliar to me. And the postmark is New York, where I have no correspondents whatever," said Emma, in surprise, as she broke the black seal.

"Oh, maybe it's a circular from some merchant who has heard of the great Alleghany heiress," suggested Electra.

"You will permit me?" said Emma, glancing at her companions as she unfolded her letter.

And then, as one and another nodded and smiled and returned to their magazines and papers. Emma Cavendish glanced at the signature of her strange letter, started with surprise, gazed at it a second time more attentively, and then turned hurriedly and began to read it.

And as she read her face paled and flushed, and she glanced from time to time at the faces of her companions; but they were all engaged with pamphlets and papers, except Mrs. Grey, whom Emma perceived to be furtively watching her.

The strange letter was written in rather a wild and rambling style of composition, as if the writer were a little brain sick. It ran as follows:

"BLANK HOTEL, New York City, April 27th, 18—.

"MY DEAR MISS CAVENDISH:—Our near blood relationship might warrant me in addressing you as my dear Emma. But I refrain, because you would not understand the familiarity any more than you recognize this handwriting, which must seem as strange to you as my face would seem if I were to present myself bodily before you; for you have never set eyes upon me, and perhaps have never even heard my name mentioned or my existence alluded to.

"And yet I am one of your family, near of kindred to yourself; in fact, your own dear mother's only sister.

"'We were two daughter's of one race,
 She was the fairer in the face.'

Yes, she was literally so. Your mother was a beautiful blonde, as I have been told that you, her only child, also are. I am—or, rather, I *was* before my hair turned white with sorrow—a very dark brunette.

"If you have ever heard of me at all, which I doubt—for I know that at home my once loved and cherished name

"'Was banished from each lip and ear,
 Like words of wickedness or fear'—

but if you ever heard of me at all you must have heard of that willful love marriage which separated me from all my family.

41

"Since that ill-omened marriage an unbroken succession of misfortunes have attended my husband and myself until they culminated in the most crushing calamity of our lives—the loss of our dear and only daughter in a manner worse than death.

"Soon after that awful bereavement our creditors foreclosed the mortgage on our estate at White Perch Point, and sold the place over our heads.

"And my poor husband and myself went out to California, childless and almost penniless, to begin life anew.

"We began in a very humble way indeed. As he was familiar with hotel business he got a place as bar-tender in a San Francisco hotel; and soon afterward I got a place in the same house, to look after and keep in repair the bed and table linen. And we lodged in the hotel, in a small attic chamber, and took our meals in the pantry.

"But we were both utterly broken down in mind and body, as well as in estate.

"He soon sank into a consumption and had to give up his place. I hired a room in a small house and took him to it. I still retained my place at the hotel, because my salary there was the only support we had. But I lived there no longer. I used to go in the morning, make the daily inspection of the linen, and bring home what needed mending; and working all the afternoon and half the night at my husband's bedside.

"But rent and food and fuel, physic and physicians' fees were very costly in San Francisco. And with all my work I fell deeper and deeper into debt.

"At length my poor husband died. And it took the proceeds of the sale of all our little personal effects to pay for the humblest sort of funeral.

"And I was left entirely destitute. Then my courage gave way. I wept myself so blind that I could no longer mend the linen at the hotel, or even see whether it wanted mending. Then I fell sick with sorrow and had to be taken to the hospital.

"At the end of three months I was dismissed. But where could I go? What could I do, broken in health and nearly blind as I was?

"I must have perished then and there but for the timely assistance of a young gold-digger who happened to hear about me when he came up to the city from his distant mining-camp.

"He was a very queer young man, whom his few friends called crazy on account of his lonely and ascetic manner of life, and his lavish liberality.

"He sought me out to relieve my wants. And upon my telling him that all I wanted was to go home to die, he bought me a whole state-room to myself in the first cabin of the 'Golden City,' bound from San Francisco to New York. And then he bought me an outfit in clothing, good enough for a duke's widow. And he gave me a sum of money besides, and started me fairly and comfortably on my voyage.

"I reached New York three days ago. But my strength continues to fail and my funds to waste. I have no power to work, even if I could procure anything to do. And I have not money enough to support me a month longer.

"I do not like to go into an alms-house. Yet what am I to do?

"But why do I write to you? you may naturally inquire.

"Why? Because, although a perfect stranger, you are, after all, my niece, my only sister's only child, my own only blood relation. And 'blood is thicker than water.'

"'I can not work; to beg I am ashamed.'

"I do not, therefore, beg, even of you. I do not so much as make any suggestion to you. I tell you the facts of the case, and I leave you to act upon them, or to ignore them entirely, at your pleasure.

"I do not even know whether I may venture to sign myself your aunt,

KATHERINE FANNING."

Emma Cavendish read this letter through to the end; then she glanced at her companions, who were still all absorbed in the perusal of their journals.

Even Mrs. Grey was now lost in a magazine; but it was *Les Modes de Paris*, and contained plates and descriptions of all the new spring fashions.

So Miss Cavendish, seeing her friends all agreeably occupied and amused, returned to her singular letter and recommenced and read it carefully through to the end once more.

At the conclusion of the second reading she looked up and spoke to the Rev. Dr. Jones, saying:

"Are you reading anything very interesting in that *Quarterly Review*, my dear uncle?"

"Well, yes, my child—an article entitled 'Have Animals Reason?'"

"Reason for *what*?" naïvely inquired Mary Grey, looking up from her magazine of fashion.

Every one smiled except Dr. Jones, who condescended to explain that the subject under discussion was whether animals were gifted with reasoning faculties.

"Oh!" said Mrs. Grey, and returned to her *Modes*.

"You needn't read any more on that subject, grandpa; I can answer that question for you, or any other inquirer. All intelligent animals, whether they go upon two feet or four, or upon wings or fins, have reason just in proportion to their intelligence. And all idiotic animals, whether they go upon two feet or four, or wings or fins, lack reason just in proportion to their idiocy. Lor'! why I have seen human creatures at the Idiot Asylum with less intellect than cats. And I have seen some horses with more intelligence than some legislators. You can't generalize on these subjects, grandpa," said Miss Electra, with an air of conviction.

The Rev. Dr. Jones stared, much as a hen might stare to see her own ducklings take to the water. And then he turned to Emma Cavendish and said:

"Whether animals have reason or not, my dear, *you* had some reason for interrupting me. Now what was it?"

"To ask you to read this, sir," said Miss Cavendish, putting her letter in the hands of her uncle.

He took it and read it slowly through, muttering from time to time:

"Dear, dear, how distressing! Bless my soul alive! Well, well, well!"

And he glanced uneasily at Mary Grey, who fidgeted and flushed under his observation.

At length he finished and folded the letter and returned it to Miss Cavendish, with the inquiry:

"Well, my dear, what are you going to do in the premises?"

"I shall write immediately and ask my aunt to come here and make this her home," answered Emma, promptly.

At these words Mary Grey started, caught her breath with a gasp, and quickly whirled her chair around so as to bring her back to the light and throw her face in deep shadow.

"What's the matter with you?" inquired Electra.

"The light makes my eyes ache; that is all. You know I have not quite got rid of my cold yet," answered the widow in a low, faltering tone that might have attracted the attention of Miss Cavendish had not that young lady's thoughts been engaged with the subject of her letter.

"You will consult your grandmother before making this important addition to the household, I presume?" inquired the old gentleman.

"Yes, of course; but I am certain beforehand of my dear grandma's consent and co-operation in such an evident Christian duty," answered Miss Cavendish.

And then she turned to her young friends, to whom she thought some explanation was due, and she added:

"I have news in this letter that has much surprised and pained me. It is from my aunt, Mrs. Fanning. She has lost her husband, and has suffered very severe reverses of fortune. She is at this time alone in New York City, and in failing health. I shall write for her to come and live with us. And not to leave her a day in suspense, I shall telegraph from Wendover to-morrow morning."

"I'm glad she's coming. The more the merrier," said Electra, gayly.

Mrs. Grey said nothing. She arose as if to leave the room, tottered forward and fell to the floor in a dead swoon.

CHAPTER VIII.

THE SIREN AND THE SAGE.

All started to their feet and rushed to the prostrate woman's assistance.

She was but a slight creature, and Dr. Jones lifted her easily and laid her on one of the sofas.

Electra flew upstairs to bring down a bottle of Florida water.

Emma patted and rubbed her hands.

Dr. Jones bathed her brow with cold water, sighing and muttering to himself:

"Poor girl! Poor unfortunate girl!"

"I take blame to myself," said Emma. "She is evidently much iller than I thought. I ought not to have persuaded her to leave her room so soon after her cold. It is my fault."

At that instant Electra ran in with the Florida water and dashed a liberal portion of it over the head and face of the fainting woman.

The shock and the penetrating odor combined to rouse her from insensibility; and with a few gasps she recovered her consciousness; though her face, after one sudden flush, settled into a deadly paleness.

"My poor dear, how are you?" inquired Emma Cavendish, kindly.

"Dying, I think; dying, I hope! Let some one help me to my room," she murmured.

Dr. Jones at once lifted her in his arms and bore her upstairs, preceded by Electra, who flew on before to show the way to Mary Grey's room, and followed by Emma Cavendish, who still blamed herself for the invalid's supposed relapse.

Dr. Jones laid her on her bed, and was about to leave her to the care of Emma and Electra, when she seized his hand and drew him down to her face and said:

"I wish to speak to you for a moment *now*. Send Miss Cavendish and Miss Coroni out of the room for a little while."

"My dear children, go away for a moment. Mrs. Grey wishes to speak to me alone," said Dr. Jones.

And Emma and Electra softly retired, with the belief that Mary Grey only wished to consult the minister on religious subjects.

As soon as the door was closed behind them Mary Grey seized the old man's hand and, fixing her great black eyes fiercely upon him, demanded:

"*Do they suspect?*"

"No; certainly not."

"Did you drop no word during my swoon that might have led them to suspect?"

"Not one syllable."

"I thank you then!" she exclaimed, with a long sigh of relief.

"But, my child, was that all you wished to talk to me about?"

"That was all, except this: to beg you still to be silent as the grave in regard to my identity."

"My child, your words disappoint and grieve me. I did hope that you asked this private interview with the design to consult me about the propriety of making yourself known."

"Making myself known!" she exclaimed, with a half-suppressed shriek, as she started up upon her elbow and stared at the speaker. "Making myself known!"

"The opportunity, my dear child, is such an excellent one. And, of course, you know that if Mrs. Fanning comes here—as she must; for there is no other refuge open to her—if she comes and finds you here, discovery is inevitable."

"But she will not find me here! She shall not! I could not look her in the face. Sooner than do that, I will hurl myself from the turnpike bridge into the Mad River!" she fiercely exclaimed.

"My child, do not talk so wickedly. It is frightful to hear such things!" cried the old man, shuddering.

"You will *see* such things, if you do not mind. I am quite capable of doing what I said, for I am tired and sick of this life of constant dependence, mortification and terror—an insupportable life!" she wildly exclaimed.

"Because, my poor girl, it is a life of concealment, in constant dread of discovery and the humiliation attending discovery. Change all that and your life will be happier. Trust in those who are nearest to you, and make yourself, your name, your errors, and your sufferings and repentance fully known. Emma Cavendish is the ruling power in this house, and she is a pure, noble, magnanimous spirit. She would protect you," pleaded the old man, taking her hand.

"Oh, yes, she is all that! Do you think that makes it any easier for me to shock her with the story of my own folly, weakness and cowardice? Oh, no, no! I could not bear the look of her clear, truthful blue eyes! And I would not! There; it is useless to talk to me, Doctor Jones! There are some things that I can not do. I can not stay here!"

"My poor, poor child, whither will you go? Stay! Now I think of it, I can send you to my house at Beresford Manors. That shall be your home, if you will accept it. But what excuse can you make for leaving this place so abruptly?"

"You are very kind, Doctor Jones. You are very kind. But a moment's reflection will teach you that I could not accept your hospitality. You have no lady, I believe, at Beresford Manors? No one there except the colored servants? Therefore, you see, it would not be proper for me to go there," said Mary Grey, affecting a prudery that she did not feel, and objecting to the place only because she did not choose to bury herself in a house more lonely, dreary and deserted, if possible, than Blue Cliff Hall itself.

"Then where can you go, my poor girl?" compassionately questioned the old minister.

"I have thought of that. Sudden as this emergency is, I am not quite unprepared for it. This crisis that I feared *might* come *has* come, that is all. Only it has come in a far different manner from what I feared. But the result must be the same. I must leave the house immediately. And you must help to smooth my way toward leaving it."

"But whither will you go, poor shorn lamb?"

"I have planned out all that, in view of this very contingency. I will go to Charlottesville, where I have a lady friend who keeps a boarding-house for the University students. I can stay with her, and make myself useful in return for board and lodging, until I get something to do for a living. That is all settled. I asked you for this interview only to satisfy myself that no hint of my identity had been dropped, and no suspicion of it excited, during my swoon; and, further, to beg you to keep my miserable secret hereafter, as you have hitherto."

"I have satisfied you, I hope, upon all those subjects."

"Yes; and I thank you."

"But still I can not abandon the hope that you will yet heed good counsel and make yourself known to your best friends," pleaded the old man.

But Mary Grey shook her head.

Dr. Jones coaxed, argued, lectured, all in vain.

At length, worn out by his importunities, Mary Grey, to gain her own ends, artfully replied:

"Well, dear, good, wise friend, if ever I *do* gain courage to make myself known to my family, I must do it from some little distance, and by letter, so as to give them time to get over the shock of the revelation, before I could dare to face them. Think of it yourself. How could we bear to look each other in the eyes while telling and hearing such a story?"

"I believe you are right *so* far. Yes, in *that* view of the case it is, perhaps, better that you should go away and then write," admitted Dr. Jones.

"And you will aid me in my efforts to get away at once and without opposition? Tell them that it is better for my health and spirits that I should go away for a while, and go immediately—as it really is, you know. Will you do this?"

"Yes, I will do it, in the hope that your nervous system may be strengthened, and you may find courage to do the duty that lies before you," said the doctor, as he pressed her hand and left the room.

Dr. Jones went down-stairs to the drawing-room, where the young ladies waited in anxious suspense.

Emma Cavendish arose and looked at him in silent questioning.

"There is no cause for alarm, my dear Emma. Your friend will do very well. No, you need not go up to her room. She requires absolutely nothing but to be left to repose. You can look in on her, if you like, just before you go to bed. That will be time enough," explained Dr. Jones, as he took his seat at the table and took up his *Review* again as if nothing had happened to interrupt his reading.

Emma Cavendish breathed a sigh of relief and resumed her seat. She and Electra read or conversed in a low voice over their magazines until the hour of retiring.

Electra was the first to close her pamphlet, as with an undisguised yawn, for which her school-mistress would have rebuked her, she declared that she could not keep her eyes open a minute longer, much less read a line, and that she was going to bed.

Dr. Jones, with as much courtesy as if he had not been her grandfather, arose and lighted her bedroom candle and put it in her hand.

And she kissed him a drowsy good-night and went upstairs.

Emma was about to follow, when the doctor motioned her to resume her seat.

She did so, and waited.

"I want a word with you about Mrs. Grey, my dear Emma. She is very much out of health."

"I feared so," replied Emma Cavendish.

"Or, to speak with more literal truth, I should say that her nervous system is very much disordered."

"Yes."

"She is full of sick fancies. She wishes to go away for a while to get a change of scene."

"I will go with her to any watering-place she desires to visit, in the season," said Emma Cavendish, readily.

"Yes; but, my dear, she must have this change now, immediately."

"I would go with her now if I could leave my guests. You know I have Electra here, and Laura will return in two days perhaps, with her brother also."

"My good child, she does not ask or need any attendance. She wants to go away by herself for a while. She wants to go to an old lady friend in Charlottesville."

"I have heard her lately speak of such a friend, and of her intention, some day, to visit her."

"Well, she wishes to go now, immediately, but is afraid to mention her desire lest it should meet with opposition, which she has no nerve to contest."

"Dear uncle, how strange that she should feel this way! Why, she is not a prisoner here! And if she wishes to leave us for a short or a long time she can do so."

"Of coarse she can, my dear; but she is full of sick fancies. And my advice to you is that you let her go at once. To-morrow morning, if she wishes."

"Why certainly, Uncle Beresford! I have neither the power nor the will to prevent her."

"So let it be then, my dear. And now good-night," said the doctor, taking his candle to leave the room.

Thus the matter was settled.

But the next day old Mrs. Cavendish, Electra, and, in fact, the whole house, were thrown into a state of consternation at the announcement of Mrs. Grey's immediate departure.

When or how she had managed to get her personal effects together, whether she had kept them packed up for the emergency, or whether she had sat up all night to pack them, I do not know; but it is certain that by seven o'clock that morning she had three enormous Saratoga trunks packed, strapped and locked ready for the wagon that she asked for to take them to the railway station.

It was not until her luggage was in the wagon, and the carriage was waiting for her at the door, and she herself in her traveling-suit and hat, that she went to bid the old lady good-bye.

Mrs. Cavendish had been informed by Emma of the intended abrupt departure of Mary Grey, and she had begun to oppose it with all her might.

But Emma endeavored to convince her that the change was vitally necessary to Mary Grey's health and strength.

So now when the traveler entered the old lady's room the latter feebly arose to her feet, holding on to the arm of her chair, while she faltered:

"Mary—Mary, this is so sudden, so shocking, so sorrowful, that I almost think it will make me ill! Why must you go, my dear?"

"Sweet mother—may I call you so?—sweet mother, I will tell *you* what I did not like to tell dear Emma, for fear it might distress her; she is so sensitive, you know!" murmured the siren, sitting down and tenderly caressing the old lady.

"Tell me then, my love, tell me anything you like," said Mrs. Cavendish, weeping.

"Well, you know that dear old lady friend in Charlottesville, of whom I spoke to you a week or so ago?"

"Ah, yes! The bishop's widow, who is reduced to keeping a student's boarding-house to help support her fifteen children," sighed the ancient dame.

"Yes, and my dear dead mother's dearest friend. Well, I have heard that she is in a dying condition and desires above all things to see me before she departs. That's what shocked me so severely as to make me quite ill. But I never should forgive myself if by any delay of mine she really should depart without having her last wish gratified. Do you blame me for hurrying away?"

"No, no, no, my child—my own lovely child! I do not wonder my poor Charley worshiped you, you are so very good! Go, Mary, my darling! But hurry back as soon as possible."

"Yes, sweet mother, I will. And now, not a word to Emma, or to any one else who might tell her of these distressing circumstances."

"No, no; certainly not! How thoughtful you are, for one so young, my good child! Bend down and take my blessing."

Mary Grey bowed her head.

The venerable lady placed her withered hands upon the bent head, raised her eyes to heaven, and solemnly invoked a blessing on the traitress.

And then Mary Grey arose, kissed her in silence, and left the room.

And thus they parted.

In the hall below she had to part with Emma and Electra.

"We hope you will return to us very soon, dear Mrs. Grey," said Emma Cavendish, as she kissed her good-bye.

"I hope so too, my dear," answered the widow.

"But you will scarcely get back before I return to school, so ours must be a very long good-bye," said Electra, as she also kissed the "parting guest."

"'Tis true, 'tis pity," said Mrs. Grey, between a smile and a sigh.

Dr. Jones then handed her into the carriage, and followed and took a seat by her side, for he was to attend her to the station and see her off on her journey.

CHAPTER IX.

EMMA'S VICTORY.

When Emma Cavendish turned back into the house she went up into the old lady's room with the intention of breaking to her the news of Katherine Fanning's widowhood and destitution, and of her own desire to invite her to come and live at Blue Cliffs.

She found Mrs. Cavendish just finishing her nice breakfast with Aunt Moll in attendance upon her.

"Here, take away the service now," said the old lady, putting down her empty coffee-cup. "And now, Emma, I am very glad you have come. I feel quite low about parting with Mary. What an angel she is!"

"Cheer up, grandma! We shall have another addition to our family circle soon," said Emma, pleasantly.

"Who is coming, my dear?" inquired Mrs. Cavendish, with all the curiosity of a recluse.

"Oh, another lady!" slowly answered Miss Cavendish, to give Aunt Moll time to get out of the room with her breakfast tray.

And when the old woman had shut the door behind her, Emma said:

"Dear grandma, you will be very much surprised to hear who it is that is coming."

And when Mrs. Cavendish looked up surprised indeed, as well as somewhat alarmed, Emma began and told her of the letter she had received from Mrs. Fanning; of her widowhood and destitution, and of her recent arrival in New York.

"All this is very distressing, my dear Emma, but you see in it only the natural consequences of a low marriage," said the old aristocrat.

"But the marriage is broken by death, dear grandma, and the error is atoned for by much suffering," said Emma, gently.

"Well, my dear, what does the poor woman want us to do?" inquired Mrs. Cavendish.

"She asks nothing, grandma. She simply writes to me, her sister's child—"

"Her *half*-sister's child!" haughtily interrupted the old lady.

"It is the same thing, grandma. Her half-sister's child, and her only living relative—"

"Her only living relative?" again interrupted the old lady. "Where is her own misguided daughter?"

"Supposed to be dead, dear grandma. Certainly dead to her," said Emma, sadly.

"Well, go on, child; go on."

"She writes to me, I say, and tells me of her situation—widowed, childless, homeless and utterly destitute in a strange city; but she asks nothing—suggests nothing."

"Well, and what would you do—you, her only living relative?" inquired the ancient dame in a tone approaching sarcasm.

"I would restore to her all that she has lost, if I could. I would give her back husband, daughter, home and competence," said Emma.

"But you can't do it any more than you can give her back her lost caste," interrupted the old lady.

Emma felt discouraged but did not yield her point.

"No, dear grandma," she answered, sorrowfully, "I can not give her back her husband, her child, or her wealth; but I can give my mother's suffering sister a home and a friend."

Madam Cavendish lowered her gold-rimmed spectacles from her cap frills to her eyes, placed her lace-mittened hands on the arms of her chair and looked straight and steadily into the face of her granddaughter.

It was extremely disheartening, and Emma dropped her eyes before that severe gaze and bowed her head meekly.

But Emma, though she was the young girl, was in the right; and Madam Cavendish, though she was an ancient and venerable dame, was in the wrong.

Emma knew this quite well, and in the argument that ensued she lovingly, respectfully, yet unflinchingly, maintained her point.

At length Madam Cavendish yielded, saying, scornfully: "Well, my dear, it is more your affair than mine. Invite her here if you will. I wash my hands of it. Only don't ask me to be intimate with the inn-keeper's widow; for I won't. And that's all about it."

"My dear grandma, you shall never see or hear of her, if you do not like to do so. You seldom leave your two rooms. And she shall never enter either unless you send for her," answered Emma.

"So be it then, my dear. And now let me go to sleep. I always want to go to sleep after an argument," said Madam Cavendish, closing her eyes and sinking back in her arm-chair.

Emma Cavendish stooped and kissed her, and then left the room.

In fifteen minutes after she had written and dispatched to the office at Wendover a telegram to this effect:

"BLUE CLIFFS, April 29th, 18—

"DEAR AUNT:—Come home to me here as soon as possible. I will write to-day.

EMMA CAVENDISH."

And in the course of that day she did write a kind and comforting letter to the bereaved and suffering woman, expressing much sympathy with her in her affliction, inviting her to come and live at Blue Cliffs for the rest of her life, and promising all that an affectionate niece could do to make her life easy and pleasant.

Miss Cavendish had but just finished this letter, when Mr. Craven Kyte was announced.

Emma, who was always kind to the ward of her late father, at once received him and sent for Electra to help to entertain him.

But notwithstanding the presence of two beautiful girls, one the fairest blonde, the other the brightest brunette, and both kind and affable in their manners to him, the young man was restless and anxious, until at length, with fierce blushes and faltering tones, he expressed a hope that Mrs. Grey was well, and made an inquiry if she were in.

Electra laughed.

Emma told him that Mrs. Grey had gone for change of air to Charlottesville, and would be absent for some time. She also added—although the young man had not once thought of inquiring for Miss Lytton—that Laura had likewise gone to visit her uncle's family at Lytton Lodge.

The foolish young victim of the widow's false wiles looked very much disappointed and depressed, yet had sense enough left him to remember to say that, as he himself was on the road to Perch Point and should take Lytton Lodge on his way, he would be happy to convey any letter or message from the ladies of Blue Cliffs to Miss Lytton.

Emma thanked him and availed herself of his offer by sending a letter, as we have seen.

And then she went about the house, attended by old Moll, selecting and arranging rooms for her new-expected guests.

The next afternoon she was quite surprised by another call from Craven Kyte. He was shown into the parlor, where she sat at work with Electra.

"You have come back quickly; but we are glad to see you," she said, as she arose to shake hands with him.

"Yes, miss," he answered, after bowing to her and to Electra; "yes, miss, I reached Perch Point last night, and I left it early this morning. In going I called at Lytton Lodge and delivered your letter, miss."

"The family at the lodge are well, I hope."

"All well, miss. And as I passed by the gate this morning the man Taters, who was at work on the lawn, told me that Mr. Alden and Miss Laura Lytton would leave for this place at noon."

"Then they will be here to-night," said Electra.

"Yes, miss."

"Will you stay and spend the afternoon and evening with us, Mr. Kyte? Shall I ring and have your horse put up?" inquired Miss Cavendish.

"No, thank you, miss. I must get back to Wendover to-night. Fact is, I'm on the wing again," said the young man, stammering and blushing. "Business of importance calls me to—to Charlottesville, miss. So if you should have a letter or a message to send to—to Mrs. Grey I should be happy to take it."

Emma Cavendish and Electra Coroni looked at each other in comic surprise.

"Why, you must be an amateur postman, Mr. Kyte! To fetch and carry letters seems to be your mission on earth," laughed Electra.

"So it has often been said of me, miss. And if you or Miss Cavendish have any to send, I should be happy to take them," answered the young man, quite seriously.

"I have none," said Electra.

"Nor I, thank you," added Emma; "but you may, if you please, give my love to Mrs. Grey, and tell her we shall feel anxious until we hear of her safe arrival and improved health."

"I will do so with much pleasure," said Mr. Kyte, rising to take leave.

As soon as the visitor had left them the two young ladies exchanged glances of droll amazement.

"As sure as you live, Emma, the business of importance that takes him to Charlottesville is Mrs. Mary Grey! He's taken in and done for, poor wretch! I shouldn't wonder a bit if he sold out his share in the fancy dry-goods store at Wendover and invested all his capital in college fees and entered himself as a student at the University, for the sake of being near his enchantress," said Electra.

"Poor boy!" sighed Emma, with genuine pity.

And before they could exchange another word, the sound of carriage-wheels at the gate announced the arrival of Alden and Laura Lytton.

CHAPTER X.

THE FALSE AND THE TRUE LOVE.

Did woman's charms thy youth beguile,
And did the fair one faithless prove?
Hath she betrayed thee with a smile
        And sold thy love?

Live! 'Twas a false, bewildering fire:
Too often love's insidious dart
Thrills the fond soul with wild desire,
        But kills the heart.

A nobler love shall warm thy breast,
A brighter maiden faithful prove,
And thy ripe manhood shall be blest
        In woman's love.

   —MONTGOMERY.

Emma Cavendish, with her cheeks blooming and eyes beaming with pleasure, ran out to meet her friends.

Alden and Laura Lytton, just admitted by the footman, stood within the hall.

Miss Cavendish welcomed Laura with a kiss and Alden with a cordial grasp of the hand.

"I am so delighted to see you, dear Laura; and you also, Mr. Lytton," she said, leading the way into the parlor.

"Well as I like my kind relatives at Lytton Lodge, I am very glad to get back to you, Emma, dear, and that is the truth," answered Laura, as she sank into an arm-chair and began to draw off her gloves.

Alden said nothing. He had bowed deeply in response to Miss Cavendish's words of welcome, and now he was thinking what a bright and beautiful creature she was, how full of healthful, joyous life she seemed, and wondering that he had never noticed all this before.

But he had noticed it before. When he first saw Emma Cavendish in her father's house in the city he had thought her the most heavenly vision of loveliness that had ever beamed upon mortal eyes; and he would have continued to think so had not the baleful beauty of Mary Grey glided before him and beguiled his sight and his soul.

But Mary Grey was gone with all her magic arts, and the very atmosphere seemed clearer and brighter for her absence.

"As soon as you have rested a little come up to your room, Laura, and lay on your wraps. Tea will be ready by the time we come down again. And, Mrs. Lytton, your old attendant, Jerome, will show you to your apartment," said the young hostess, as she arose, with a smile, to conduct her guest.

They left the drawing-room together.

And while Laura Lytton was arranging her toilet in the chamber above stairs, Emma Cavendish told her the particulars of Mary Grey's departure, and also of the letter she had received from her long-estranged relative, Mrs. Fanning.

They went down to tea, where they were joined by Electra and the Rev. Dr. Jones.

Miss Cavendish presented Mr. Lytton to Dr. Jones. And then they sat down to the table.

Alden Lytton's eyes and thoughts were naturally enough occupied and interested in Emma Cavendish. He had not exactly fallen in love with her, but he was certainly filled with admiration for the loveliest girl he had ever seen. And he could but draw involuntary comparisons between the fair, frank, bright maiden and the beautiful, alluring widow.

Both were brilliant, but with this difference: the one with the pure life-giving light of Heaven, and the other with the fatal fire of Tartarus.

After tea they went into the drawing-room, where they spent a long evening talking over old times—*their* "old times" being something less than one year of age.

And every hour confirmed Alden Lytton's admiration of Emma Cavendish.

The next day Alden Lytton was invited upstairs to the old lady's room and presented to Madam Cavendish, who received him with much cordiality, telling him that his grandfather had been a lifelong personal friend of hers, and that she had known his father from his infancy up to the time that he had left the neighborhood to practice law in the city.

And after a short interview the ancient gentlewoman and the young law student parted mutually well pleased with each other.

"A fine young man—a very fine young man indeed; but more like his grandfather, as I remember him in his youth, than like his father, whom I could not always well approve," said the old lady to her confidential attendant, Aunt Moll, who had closed the chamber door after the departing visitor.

"Dunno nuffin 'tall 'bout dat, ole mist'ess, but he monsus hansume, dough—umph-um; a'n't he dough? And a'n't he got eyes—umph-um!"

Alden went down-stairs.

"The most interesting old lady I have ever seen in my life, with the balsamic aroma of history and antiquity about her and all her surroundings," he said, as he joined the young ladies in the drawing-room.

"Balsamic aroma of *what*?" inquired Electra, who had no taste for poetry and no reverence for antiquity. "Young man, it was the dried 'yarbs' she keeps in her closet that you smelled. Besides, antiquity has no other odor than that of mold and must."

Alden blushed, laughed and looked at Emma Cavendish.

"You must not mind my cousin Electra, Mr. Lytton. She is a privileged person among us. By the way, Laura has told you, I presume, of our relationship," said Emma, pleasantly.

"Oh, yes!" returned young Lytton, with a smile and a bow. "And I am happy to have this opportunity of congratulating you both."

"Thanks," said Miss Cavendish, with a vivid blush.

"I believe there was some talk about a picnic party to the top of Porcupine Mountain, was there not?" inquired Electra, to cut short all sentiment.

"Yes, my dear, and the horses are ordered for eleven o'clock. It is half-past ten now, and we will go and put on our hats and habits," replied Miss Cavendish, playfully rising and breaking up the conference.

The party of young friends remained one week longer at Blue Cliffs, every day deepening and confirming the admiration and respect with which the beauty and the excellence of Emma Cavendish inspired Alden Lytton. But yet he was not in love with her.

Every morning was spent by the young people in riding or driving about through the sublime and beautiful mountain and valley scenery of the neighborhood.

And every evening was passed in fancy work, music, reading or conversation in the drawing-room.

And so the pleasant days of the Easter holidays passed away, and the time for study and for work commenced.

Laura and Electra went away from Blue Cliffs on the same day — Laura escorted by her brother Alden, and Electra by her grandfather, the Rev. Dr. Jones.

As the party were assembled in the front hall to take leave of their fair young hostess before entering the large traveling carriage that was to take them to the Wendover railway station, Emma Cavendish went up to Alden Lytton and placed a letter in his hand, saying, with a frank smile:

"As you are going direct to Charlottesville, Mr. Lytton, I will trouble you to take charge of this letter to our mutual friend, Mrs. Grey, who, you know, is now staying in that town. Will you do so?"

"Certainly—with great pleasure," stammered Alden in extreme confusion, which he could scarcely conceal, and without the slightest consciousness that he was telling an enormous falsehood, but with full assurance that he should like to oblige Miss Cavendish.

"I hope it will not inconvenience you to deliver this in person, Mr. Lytton," added Emma.

"Certainly not, Miss Cavendish," replied Alden, telling unconscious fib the second.

"For, you see, I am rather anxious about our friend. She left in ill health. She is almost a stranger in Charlottesville. And—this is the point—I have not heard from her, by letter or otherwise, since she left us; so I fear she may be too ill to write, and may have no friend near to write for her. This is why I tax your kindness to deliver the letter in person and find out how she is; and—write and let us know. I am asking a great deal of you, Mr. Lytton," added Emma, with a deprecating smile.

"Not at all. It is a very small service that you require. And I hope you know that I should be exceedingly happy to have the opportunity of doing any very great service for you, Miss Cavendish," replied Alden, truthfully and earnestly.

For in itself it was a very small service that Miss Cavendish had required of him, and he would have liked and even preferred another and a greater, and, in fact, a different service.

"Many thanks," said Miss Cavendish, with a frank smile, as she left the letter in his hands.

Then the adieus were all said, and promises of frequent correspondence and future visits exchanged among the young ladies. And the travelers departed, and the young hostess re-entered her lonely home and resumed her usual routine of domestic duties.

She was anxious upon more than one account.

More than a week had passed since the departure of Mary Grey, and yet, as she had told Alden Lytton, she had never heard even of her safe arrival at Charlottesville, and she feared that her *protégée* might be suffering from nervous illness among strangers.

More than a week had also passed since she had telegraphed and written to her Aunt Fanning in New York. But no answer had yet come from that unhappy woman. And she feared that the poor relative whom she wished to succor might have met with some new misfortune.

However, Emma had hoped, from day to day, that each morning's mail might bring her good news from Charlottesville or New York, or both.

And even to-day she waited with impatience for the return of Jerome, who had driven the traveling-carriage containing the departing visitors to Wendover, and who might find letters for Blue Cliffs waiting at the post-office.

Emma could not be at rest all that day, partly because she missed her young companions, whose society had made the lonely house so cheerful, and partly because she half expected news with the return of Jerome.

She wandered up and down the deserted drawing-room, and then went upstairs to the chambers just vacated by her young friends, where she found Sarah, the chamber-maid, engaged in dismantling beds and dressing-tables preparatory to shutting up the "spare rooms" for the rest of the season.

All this was very dreary and dispiriting.

She left these apartments and would have gone into the old lady's room, only that she knew her grandmother was at this hour taking the first of her two daily naps.

As she turned to go down-stairs she glanced through the front hall window and caught a glimpse of the traveling-carriage, with Jerome perched upon the box, slowly winding its way around the circular avenue that led to the house.

Chapter XI.

A SURPRISE.

She ran down-stairs briskly enough now, and ran out of the front door.

"Any letters to-day, Jerome?" she inquired.

"No, miss," answered Jerome, shaking his head.

"Oh, dear, how depressing!" sighed Emma, as she turned to go into the house.

But a sound arrested her steps—the opening of the carriage-door. She turned and saw Jerome standing before it and in the act of helping some one to alight from the carriage.

Another moment and a tall, thin, dark-eyed woman, with very white hair, and clad in the deepest widow's weeds, stood before Miss Cavendish.

By instinct Emma recognized her aunt. And she felt very much relieved, and very much rejoiced to see her, even while wondering that she should have come unannounced either by letter or telegram.

As for Jerome, he stood wickedly enjoying his young lady's astonishment, and looking as if he himself had performed a very meritorious action.

"Miss Emma Cavendish, I presume?" said the stranger, a little hesitatingly.

"Yes, madam. And you are my Aunt Fanning, I am sure. And I am very glad to see you," answered Emma Cavendish.

And she put her arms around the stranger's neck and kissed her.

"Dat's better'n letters, a'n't it, Miss Emmer?" inquired Jerome, grinning from ear to ear, and showing a double row of the strongest and whitest ivories, as he proceeded to take from the carriage various packages, boxes and traveling-bags and so forth.

"Yes, better than letters, Jerome. Follow us into the house with that luggage. Come, dear aunt, let us go in. Lean on my arm. Don't be afraid to lean heavily. I am very strong," said Emma; and drawing the poor lady's emaciated hand through her own arm she led her into the house.

She took her first into the family sitting-room, where there was a cheerful fire burning, which the chilly mountain air, in this spring weather, made very acceptable.

She placed her in a comfortable cushioned rocking-chair and proceeded to take off the traveling-bonnet and shawl with her own hands, saying:

"You must get well rested and refreshed here before you go up to your room. You look very tired."

"I am very weak, my dear," answered the lady, in a faint voice.

"I see that you are. I am very sorry to see you so feeble; but we will make you stronger here in our exhilarating mountain air. If I had known that you would come by this train I should have gone to the railway station in person to meet you," said Emma, kindly.

Mrs. Fanning turned her great black eyes upon the young lady and stared at her in surprise.

"Why, did you not get my letter?" she inquired.

"No," said Emma. "I anxiously expected to hear from you from day to day, but heard nothing either by letter or telegram."

"That is strange! I wrote to you three days ago that I should be at Wendover this morning, and so, when I found your carriage there, I thought that you had sent for me."

"It was very fortunate that the carriage was there, and I am very glad of it; but it was not in fact sent to meet you, for, not having received your letter, I did not know that you would arrive to-day. The carriage was sent to take some visitors who had been staying with us, and were going away, to the railway station. It is a wonder Jerome had not explained this to you. He is so talkative," said Emma, smiling.

"I never talk to strange servants," gravely replied the lady. "But I will tell you how it happened. I really arrived by the earliest train, that got in at Wendover at five o'clock in the morning. There was no carriage from Blue Cliffs waiting for me at the railway station, and, in fact, no carriage from any place, except the hack from the Reindeer Hotel. So I got into that, and, having previously left word with the station-master to send the Blue Cliffs carriage after me to the Reindeer when it should come, I went on to the hotel to get breakfast and to lie down and rest. But when half the forenoon had passed away without any arrival for me, I began to grow anxious, fearing that some mistake had been made."

"I am very sorry you had to suffer this annoyance, immediately upon your arrival here too," said Emma, regretfully.

"Oh, it did not last long! About noon the landlord, Greenfield, rapped at my door and told me that the Blue Cliffs carriage had come, and that the ostler was watering the horses while the coachman was taking a glass of beer at the bar."

"Jerome had doubtless taken our visitors to the station, and called at the Reindeer to refresh himself and his horses."

"Yes, I suppose so. Almost at the same moment that the landlord came to my door to announce the carriage, I heard some one else, under my window, saying to the coachman that there was a lady here waiting to be taken to Blue Cliffs; and I went down and got into the carriage with bag and baggage. Jerome, if that's his name, very gravely, with a silent bow, put up the steps and closed the door and mounted his box and drove off."

"But you must have left some baggage behind."

"Yes, three trunks; one very large. Mr. Greenfield, of the Reindeer, promised to send them right after me in his wagon."

While they had been speaking, Emma Cavendish had touched the bell and given a whispered order to the servant who answered it.

So now the second footman, Peter, appeared with a waiter in his hands, on which was served tea, toast, a broiled squab and glass of currant jelly.

This was set upon a stand beside Mrs. Fanning's easy-chair.

"I think that you had better take something before you go upstairs," said the young hostess, kindly, as she poured out a cup of tea.

Consumptives are almost always hungry and thirsty, as if nature purposely created an unusual appetite for nourishment in order to supply the excessive waste of tissue caused by the malady.

And so Mrs. Fanning really enjoyed the delicate luncheon set before her so much that she finished the squab, the jelly, the toast and the tea.

When she had been offered and had refused a second supply, Emma proposed that she should go up to her room, and she took her at once to the beautiful corner chamber, with its southern and eastern aspect, that had been fitted up for her.

Here she found that her traveling-trunks, which had already arrived from Wendover, were placed.

And here, when she had changed her traveling-dress for a loose wrapper, she laid down on a lounge to rest, while Emma darkened the room and left her to repose.

Miss Cavendish went straight to the old lady's apartment.

Mrs. Cavendish was sitting in her great easy-chair by the fire, with her gold-rimmed spectacles on her nose and her Bible lying open on her lap.

As Emma entered the room the old lady closed the book and looked up with a welcoming smile.

"I have come to tell you, my dear grandma, that Aunt Fanning has arrived," said Emma, drawing a chair and seating herself by the old lady's side.

"Yes, my dear child; but I'll trouble you not to call her Aunt Fanning," said Madam Cavendish, haughtily.

"But she *is* my aunt, dear grandma," returned Emma, with a deprecating smile.

"Then call her Aunt Katherine. I detest the name of that tavern-keeper whom she married."

"Grandma—grandma, the man has gone where at least there can be no distinctions of mere family rank," said Emma.

"That's got nothing to do with it. We are *here* now. Well, and when did Katherine arrive, and where have you put her? Tell me all about it."

Emma told her all about it.

"Well," said the old lady, "as she is here, though sorely against my approbation—still, as she is here we must give her a becoming welcome, I suppose. You may bring her to my room to-morrow morning."

"Thank you, grandma, dear; that is just what I would like to do," replied the young lady.

Accordingly, the next morning Mrs. Fanning was conducted by Emma to the "Throne Room," as Electra had saucily designated the old lady's apartment.

Madam Cavendish was dressed with great care, in a fine black cashmere wrapper, lined and trimmed with black silk, and a fine white lace cap, trimmed with white piping.

And old Moll, also in her best clothes, stood behind her mistress's chair.

The old lady meant to impress "the tavern-keeper's widow" with a due sense of reverence.

But the gentlewoman's heart was a great deal better than her head. And so, when she saw the girl whom she had once known a brilliant, rich-complexioned brunette, with raven hair and sparkling eyes and queenly form changed into a woman, old before her time, pale, thin, gray and sorrow-stricken, her heart melted with pity, and she held out her hand, saying, kindly:

"How do you do, Katie, my dear? I am very sorry to see you looking in such ill-health. You have changed very much from the child I knew you, twenty-five years ago."

"Yes," said Mrs. Fanning, as she took and pressed the venerable hand that was held out to her. "I have changed. But there is only one more change that awaits me—the last great one."

"Moll, wheel forward that other easy-chair. Sit down at once, my poor Katie. You look ready to drop from weakness. Emma, my child, pour out a glass of that old port wine and bring it to your aunt. You will find it in that little cabinet," said Madam Cavendish, speaking to one and another in her hurry to be hospitable and to atone for the hard thoughts she had cherished and expressed toward this poor suffering and desolate woman.

And Mrs. Fanning was soon seated in the deep, soft "sleepy hollow," and sipping with comfort the rich old port wine.

"Yes, Katie," said the old lady, resuming the thread of the conversation, "that last great change awaits us all—a glorious change, Katie, that I for one look forward to with satisfaction and desire *always*—with rapture and longing *sometimes*. What will the next life be like, I wonder? We don't know. 'Eye hath not seen—ear heard,'" mused the old lady.

The interview was not a long one. Soon Emma Cavendish took her aunt from the room.

"You must come in and see me every day, Katie, my dear," said the old lady, as the two visitors left.

And from that time the desolate widow, the homeless wanderer, found loving and tender friends, and a comfortable and quiet home.

CHAPTER XII.

ALDEN AND HIS EVIL GENIUS MEET AGAIN.

Meanwhile the visitors that had left Blue Cliffs that morning traveled together until they reached Richmond.

The train got in at ten o'clock that night.

There was no steamboat to Mount Ascension Island until the next day.

So the party for that bourne were compelled to spend the night at Richmond.

Alden, although he might have gone on to Charlottesville that night, determined to remain with his friends.

The whole party went to the Henrico House, where they were accommodated with adjoining rooms.

The next morning they resumed their journey, separating to go their several ways. Alden saw the two young ladies safely on the steamboat that was to take them to Mount Ascension, and then bade them good-bye, leaving them in charge of the Rev. Dr. Jones, who was to escort them to the end of their journey.

He had barely time to secure his seat for Charlottesville, where he arrived on the afternoon of the same day.

The letter he had to deliver to Mary Grey "burned in his pocket." He could not have done otherwise than promise to deliver it in person, when fair Emma Cavendish had requested him to do so. And now, of course, he must keep his word and go and carry the letter to her, although he would rather have walked into a fire than into that false siren's presence.

It is true that his love for her was dead and gone. But it had died such a cruel and violent death that the very memory of it was full of pain and horror, and to meet her would be like meeting the specter of his murdered love. Nevertheless he must not shrink from his duty; he must go and do it.

Before reporting at his college, he went to a hotel and changed his clothes, and then started out to find Mary Grey's residence. That was not so easily done. She had omitted to leave her address with her friends at Blue Cliffs, and Emma's letter was simply directed to Mrs. Mary Grey, Charlottesville.

True, Charlottesville was not a very large place; but looking for a lady there was something like looking for the fabulous needle in the haystack.

Still, he had formed a plan of action to find her. He knew that she pretended to great piety; that she was a member of the Protestant Episcopal Church, and that wherever she might happen to sojourn she would be sure to join the church and make friends with the clergy of her own denomination.

So Alden bent his steps to the house of the Episcopal minister at Charlottesville.

He found the reverend gentleman at home, and received from him, as he had expected to do, the address of Mrs. Grey.

"A most excellent young woman, sir—an earnest Christian. She lost not a day in presenting her church letter and uniting herself with the church. She has been here but ten days, and already she has taken a class in the Sunday-school. A most meritorious young woman, sir," said the worthy minister, as he handed the card with Mrs. Grey's new address written upon it.

To Alden, who knew the false-hearted beauty so well, all this was surprising.

But he made no comment. He simply took the card, bowed his thanks, and left the house to go and seek the home of Mrs. Grey.

Among many falsehoods, the woman had told one truth when she had informed Emma Cavendish that she had a lady friend at Charlottesville who kept a students' boarding-house. She had met this lady just previous to engaging as drawing-mistress at Mount Ascension. And by her alluring arts she had won her sympathy and confidence. She was staying with this friend at the time that Alden sought her out.

He now easily found the house.

And when he inquired of the negro boy who answered the bell whether Mrs. Grey was at home, he was answered in the affirmative and invited to enter the house.

The boy opened a door on the right hand of the narrow entrance passage, and Alden passed into the parlor and found himself, unannounced, in the presence of his false love.

There was no one with her, and she was sitting at a table, with drawing materials before her, apparently engaged in copying a picture.

Hearing the door open and shut, she lifted her head and looked up.

Seeing Alden Lytton standing before her, she dropped the pencil from her fingers, turned deathly pale and stared at him in silence.

Alden, if the truth must be told, was scarcely less agitated; but he soon recovered his self-command.

"I should apologize," he said, "for coming in unannounced; but I did not know that you were here. I was shown into this room by the waiter, supposing that I was to remain here until he took my card to you."

She neither moved nor spoke, but sat and stared at him.

"I have only come as the bearer of a letter to you from Miss Cavendish—a letter that I promised to deliver in person. Here it is," he said, laying the little packet on the table before her.

Still she made no answer to his words, nor any acknowledgment of his service. She did not even take up Emma's letter.

"And now, having done my errand, I will bid you good-afternoon, Mrs. Grey," he said, bowing and turning to leave the room.

That broke the panic-stricken spell that held her still.

She started up and clasped her hands suddenly together, exclaiming:

"No, no, no; for pity's sake don't go yet! Now that you are here, for Heaven's sake stay a moment and listen to me!"

"What can you possibly have to say to me, Mrs. Grey?" coolly inquired the young man.

"Oh, sit down—sit down one little moment and hear me! I have not got the plague, that you should hasten from me so," she pleaded.

It was in Alden's thoughts to say that moral plagues were even more dangerous and fatal than material ones; but the woman before him looked so really distressed that he forbore.

"I know that you have ceased to love me," she went on in a broken voice. "I know, of course, that you have ceased to love me—"

"Yes, I am thoroughly cured of that egregious boyish folly," assented Alden, grimly.

"I know it, and I would not seek to recover your lost, lost love; but—"

Her voice, that had been faltering, now quite broke down, and she burst into tears and sobbed as if her heart was breaking.

And her grief was as real as it was violent; for she had loved the handsome young law student, and she mourned the loss of his love.

Alden sat apparently unmoved, but in truth he was beginning to feel very sorry for this woman, but it was with the sorrow we feel for a suffering criminal, and totally distinct from sympathy or affection.

Presently her gust of tears and sobs exhausted itself, and she sighed and dried her eyes and said:

"Yes, I know that all love is quite over between us."

"Quite over," assented Alden, emphatically.

"And it is not to renew that subject that I asked you to stay and listen to me."

"No," said Alden, gently, "I presume not."

"But, though all thoughts of love are forever over between us, yet I can not bear that we should live at enmity. As for me, I am not your enemy, Alden Lytton."

"Nor am I yours, Mrs. Grey. You and I can live as strangers without being enemies."

"Live as strangers! Oh, but that is just what would break my heart utterly! Why should we live as strangers? If all love is over between us, and if we are still not enemies, if we have forgiven each other, why should we two live as strangers in this little town? Why may we not meet at least as the common friends of every day?"

"Because the memory of the past would preclude the possibility of our meeting pleasantly or profitably."

"Oh, Alden, you are very hard! You have not forgiven me!"

"I have utterly forgiven you."

"But you cherish hard thoughts of me?"

"Mrs. Grey, I must regard your actions—the actions that separated us—as they really are," answered Alden, sadly and firmly, as he arose and took his hat to leave the room.

"No, no, no; *don't* go yet! You *must* hear me—you *shall* hear me! Even a convicted murderer is allowed to speak for himself!" she exclaimed, with passionate tears.

Alden sighed and sat down.

"You must regard my actions as they really are, you say. Ah, but the extenuating circumstances, the temptations, the motives—aye, the motives!—have you ever thought of them?"

"I can see no motive that could justify your acts," said Alden, coldly.

"No, not justify—I do not justify them even to myself—not justify, but *palliate* them, Alden—palliate them at least in your eyes, if in no others."

"And why in my eyes, Mrs. Grey?"

"Oh, Alden, all was planned for your sake!"

"For *my* sake? I pray you do not say that!"

"Listen, then, and consider all the circumstances. I loved you and promised to be your wife at that far distant day when you should come into a living law practice. But I was homeless, penniless and helpless. I had lost my situation in the school, and I had no prospect of getting another. The term of my visit to Emma Cavendish had nearly expired and I had nowhere to go. Governor Cavendish loved me with the idolatrous love of an old man for a young woman, and besought me to be his wife with such insane earnestness that I thought my refusal would certainly be his death, especially as it was well known that he was liable to apoplexy and that any excitement might bring on a fatal attack. Under all these circumstances I think I must have lost my senses; for I reasoned with myself—most falsely and fatally reasoned with myself thus: Why should not I, who am about to be cast out homeless and penniless upon the wide world— why should not I secure myself a home and save this old man's life for a few years longer by accepting his love and becoming his wife? It is true that I do not love him, but I honor him very much. And I would be the comfort of his declining years. He could not live long, and when he should come to die I should inherit the widow's third of all his vast estates. And then, after a year of mourning should be over, I could marry my true love, and bring him a fortune too. There, Alden, the reasoning was all false, wicked and fatal. I know that now. But oh, Alden, it was not so much for myself as for others that I planned thus! I thought to have blessed and comforted the old man's declining years, and after his death to have brought a fortune to you. These were my motives. They do not justify, but at least they palliate my conduct."

She ceased.

Alden did not reply, but stood up again with his hat in his hand.

"And now, Alden, though we may never be lovers again, may we not meet sometimes as friends? I am so lonely here! I am, indeed, all alone in the world. We may meet sometimes as friends, Alden?" she asked, pathetically.

"No, Mrs. Grey. But yet, if ever I can serve you in any way I will do so most willingly. Good-afternoon," said the young man.

And he bowed and left the room.

As he disappeared her beautiful face darkened with a baleful cloud. "No fury like a woman scorned," wrote one who seemed to know. Her face darkened like a thunder-storm, and from its cloud her eyes shot forked lightning. She set her teeth, and clinched her little fist and shook it after him, hissing:

"He scorns me—he scorns me! Ah, he may scorn my love! Let him beware of my hate! He will not meet me as a friend, but he will serve me willingly! Very well; he shall be often called upon to serve me, if only to bring him under my power!"

Chapter XIII.

MARY GREY'S MANEUVER.

> She'd tried this world in all its changes,
> States and conditions; had been loved and happy.
> Scorned and wretched, and passed through all its stages;
> And now, believe me, she who knew it best,
> Thought it not worth the bustle that it cost.

—MADDEN.

Mary Grey now set systematically to work. Partly from love or its base counterfeit, partly from hate, but mostly from vanity, she determined to devote every faculty of mind and body to one set object—to win Alden Lytton's love back again and to subjugate him to her will.

To all outward seeming she led a most blameless and beneficent life.

She lived with the bishop's widow, and made herself very useful and agreeable to the staid lady, who refused to take any money for her board.

And although the house was full of students, who boarded and lodged and spent their evenings there, with the most wonderful self-government she forebore "to make eyes" at any of them.

She now no longer said in so many words that "her heart was buried in the grave," and so forth; but she quietly acted as if it was.

She put away all her mourning finery—her black tulles and silks and bugles and jet jewelry—and she took to wearing the plainest black alpacas and the plainest white muslin caps. She looked more like a Protestant nun than a "sparkling" young widow. But she looked prettier and more interesting than ever, and she knew it.

She was a regular attendant at her church, going twice on Sunday and twice during the week.

On Sunday mornings she was always sure of finding Alden Lytton in his seat, which was in full sight of her own. But she never looked toward him. She was content to feel that he often looked at her, and that he could not look at her and remain quite indifferent to her.

She was also an active member of all the parish benevolent societies, a zealous teacher in the Sunday-school, an industrious seamstress in the sewing-circle, and a regular visitor of the poor and sick.

Her life seemed devoted to good works, apparently from the love of the Lord and the love of her neighbor.

She won golden opinions from all sorts of men, and women too. Only there was one significant circumstance about her popularity— *she could not win the love of children*. No, not with all her beauty and grace of person, and sweetness and softness of tone and manner, she could not win the children. Their sensitive spirits shrank from the evil within her which the duller souls of adults could not even perceive. And many an innocent child was sent in disgrace from the parlor because it either would not kiss "sweet Mrs. Grey" at all, or would kiss her with the air of taking a dose of physic.

But all the people in Charlottesville praised the piety and, above all, the prudence of Mrs. Grey—"Such a young and beautiful woman to be so entirely weaned from worldliness and self-love and so absorbed in worship and good works!"

All this certainly produced an effect upon Alden Lytton, who, of course, heard her praises on all sides, who saw her every Sunday at church, and who met her occasionally at the demure little tea-parties to which both might happen to be invited.

When they met thus by chance in private houses he would bow and say, quietly:

"Good-evening, madam;" a salutation which she would return by a grave:

"Good-evening, sir."

And not another word would pass between them during the evening.

But all the young man observed in her at such times was a certain discreet reserve, which he could but approve.

"She seems to be much changed. She seems to be truly grieved for the past. Perhaps I have judged her too harshly. And yet what a base part that was she proposed to play! may be that she herself did not know how base it was. Such ignorance would prove an appalling moral blindness. But then, again, should she be held responsible for her moral blindness? It sometimes requires suffering to teach the nature of sin. A child does not know that fire is dangerous until it burns itself. *Her* suffering must have opened her eyes to the 'exceeding sinfulness of sin.' For her own sake I hope it is so. As for myself, it does not matter. I have ceased to regard her with any other feeling than pity and charity. And although she would become a saint I could never love her again," he said to himself one night, after passing an evening with her at one of the professor's houses.

And his thoughts reverted to that lovely maiden whose golden hair formed an appropriate halo around her white brow, and whose pure soul looked frankly forth from her clear blue eyes.

He was not in love with Miss Cavendish, he said to himself, but he could not help feeling the difference between radiant frankness and dark deceit.

One evening, about this time, they met at a strawberry festival, held in the lecture-room of the church, for the benefit of the Sunday-school.

While the festival was at its height a thunder-storm came up, with a heavy shower of rain. But the company at the festival cared little about that. They were housed, and enjoyed themselves with light music, fruits, flowers and friends. And before the hour of separation the storm would probably be over, and carriages, or at least water-proof cloaks, overshoes and umbrella's, would be in attendance upon every one.

So they made merry until eleven o'clock, when the storm was passing away with a steady light rain.

Every lady who had a carriage in waiting offered to give Mrs. Grey a seat and to set her down at her own door.

Mary Grey thanked each in succession and declined the kind offer, adding that she expected some one to come for her.

At last nearly everybody had left the room but the treasurer of the festival, who was counting the receipts, and the sexton, who was covering the tables, preparatory to closing for the night.

Alden Lytton had lingered to make a quiet donation to the charity, and he was passing out, when, he saw Mary Grey standing shivering near the door.

As he came up to her she stepped out into the darkness and the rain.

He hastened after her, exclaiming:

"Mrs. Grey! I beg your pardon! Are you alone?"

"Yes, Mr. Lytton," she answered, quietly.

"And you have no umbrella!" he said, quickly, as he hoisted his own and stepped to her side. "Permit me to see you safe to your door. Take my arm. It is very dark and the walking is dangerous. The sidewalks are turned to brooks by this storm," he added, as he held his umbrella carefully over her.

"I thank you very much, Mr. Lytton; but indeed I do not wish to give you so much trouble. I can go home quite well enough alone. I have often to do it," she answered, shrinking away from him.

"It is not safe for you to do so, especially on such a night as this. Will you take my arm?" he said; and, without waiting for her answer, he took her hand and drew it through his arm and walked on with her in silence, wondering at and blaming the heartlessness of the ladies of her circle who had carriages in attendance, and had, as he supposed, every one of them, gone off without offering this poor lonely creature a seat, leaving her to get home through the night and storm as she could.

As they walked on he felt Mary Grey's arm trembling upon his own, and involuntarily he drew it closer, and, in so doing, he perceived the tremor and jar of her fast-beating heart, and he pitied her with a deep, tender, manly pity.

"I am afraid you feel chilled in this rain," he said, by way of saying something kind.

"No," she answered, softly, and said no more.

They got to the door of her dwelling, and he rang the bell and waited there with her until some one should come.

"I am very much indebted to you, Mr. Lytton," she said, softly and coolly; "but I am also very sorry to have given you so much trouble."

"I assure you it was no trouble; and I beg that you will not again attempt to go alone at night through the streets of Charlottesville," he answered, sadly.

"But why?" she asked. "What harm or danger can there be in my doing so?"

"Ladies never go out alone at night here. Many of the wild students are on the streets at night and are not always in their senses."

"Oh, I see! Well, I will try to take care of myself. I hear the page coming to open the door. Good-night, Mr. Lytton. You have been very kind. I thank you very much," said Mrs. Grey, coldly.

He touched his hat and turned away just as the door was opened.

Alden Lytton went back to the college with somewhat kinder thoughts of Mary Grey.

And Mrs. Grey went into the house and into the back parlor, where the bishop's widow was waiting up for her.

"Why, my dear, your shoes are wet through and your skirts are draggled up to your knees! Is it possible you walked home through the rain?" inquired the lady.

"Yes, madam; but it will not hurt me."

"But how came you to walk home when Mrs. Doctor Sage promised faithfully to bring you home in her carriage?"

"Oh, my dear friend, the storm came up, and so many people were afraid of wetting their feet that I gave up my seat to another lady," answered Mary Grey.

"Always the same self-sacrificing spirit! Well, my dear, I hope your reward will come in the next world, if not in this. Now go upstairs and take off your wet clothes and get right to bed. I will send you up a glass of hot spiced wine, which will prevent you from taking cold," said the hospitable old lady.

Mary Grey kissed her hostess, said good-night, and ran away upstairs to her own cozy room, where, although it was May time, a bright little wood fire was burning in the fire-place to correct the dampness of the air.

"Well," she said, with her silent laugh, as she began to take off her sodden shoes, "it was worth the wetting to walk home with Alden Lytton, and to make one step of progress toward my object."

And the thought comforted her more than did the silver mug of hot spiced wine that the little page presently brought her.

A few days after this she met Alden Lytton again, by accident, at the house of a mutual friend. Alden came up to her and, after the usual greeting, said:

"I have received a short note from Miss Cavendish inquiring of me whether I had delivered her letter to you, and saying that she had received no answer from you, and indeed no news of you since your departure from Blue Cliffs. Now if I had not supposed that you would have answered Miss Emma's letter immediately I should certainly have written myself to relieve her anxiety on your account."

"Oh, indeed I beg her pardon and yours! But I have sprained the fore-finger of my right hand and can not write at all. Otherwise I am quite well. Pray write and explain this to Emma, with my love, and my promise to write to her as soon as my finger gets well," said Mary Grey.

And then she arose to take leave of her hostess, and, with a distant bow to Alden Lytton, she left the house.

Two days after this she received a very kind letter from Miss Cavendish expressing much regret to hear of her disabled hand, and affectionately inquiring of her when she should return to Blue Cliffs, adding that Mrs. Fanning had arrived, and was then domiciled at the house; and, though a widow and an invalid, she was a very agreeable companion.

This letter also inclosed a check for the amount of the quarterly allowance Emma Cavendish wasted upon Mary Grey.

"For whether you abandon us or not, dear Mrs. Grey, or wherever you may be, so long as I can reach you I will send you this quarterly sum, which I consider yours of right," she wrote. And with more expressions of kindness and affection the letter closed.

This letter was a great relief to Mary Grey's anxiety; for now that this worshiper of mammon was sure of her income she had no fears for the future.

But she dared not herself answer the letter. While Mrs. Fanning should remain at Blue Cliffs, Mary Grey must not let her handwriting go there, lest it should be seen and recognized by Frederick Fanning's widow.

But the next day was Sunday, and Mrs. Grey went to church, taking Emma's letter in her pocket.

Usually she avoided Alden Lytton on these occasions, refraining even from looking toward him during the church service or afterward, for she did not wish him to suppose that she *sought* his notice.

But now she had a fair and good excuse for speaking to him; so when the service was over and the congregation was leaving the church she waited at the door of her pew until Alden passed by, when she said, very meekly and coolly:

"Mr. Lytton, may I speak with you a moment?"

"Certainly, madam," said Alden, stopping at once.

"I have a letter from dearest Emma, but I can not answer it. Ah, my poor crippled finger! Would you be so very kind as to write and tell my darling that I have received it and how much I thank her? And here; perhaps, as you are to acknowledge the letter for me, you had better read it. There is really nothing in it that a mutual friend may not see," she said, drawing the letter from her pocket and putting it into his hand.

"Certainly, madam, if you wish me to do so; certainly, with much pleasure," answered Alden Lytton, with more warmth than he had intended; because, in truth, he was beginning to feel delight in every subject that concerned Emma Cavendish, and he was now especially pleased with having the privilege of reading her letter and the duty of acknowledging it.

"Many thanks! You are very kind! Good-morning," said Mary Grey, with discreet coolness, as she passed on before him to leave the church.

"Step number two! I shall soon have him in my power again!" chuckled the coquette, as she walked down the street toward her dwelling.

For Mary Grey had utterly misinterpreted the warmth of Alden Lytton's manner in acceding to her request. It never entered her mind to think that this warmth had anything to do with the idea of Emma Cavendish. She was much too vain to be jealous.

She did not really think that there was a man in the world who could withstand her charms, or a woman in the world who could become her rival.

And certainly her personal experience went far to confirm her in that vain theory. Therefore she did not fear Emma Cavendish as a rival.

And while she did not dare to write to Blue Cliffs, she did not hesitate to make Alden Lytton the medium of communication with Emma Cavendish.

Her other lover, the counterpart of Alden Lytton, had not appeared since he had called on her on his first visit to Charlottesville.

But he wrote to her six times a week, and she knew what he was doing—he was trying hard to settle up his business at Wendover, with the distant hope of removing to Charlottesville and opening a store there.

CHAPTER XIV.

IN THE TOILS.

Affairs went on in this way for one year longer. Emma Cavendish continued to write regularly to Mrs. Grey, telling her all the little household and neighborhood news. Among the rest, she told her how Mrs. Fanning, by her gentleness and patience, was winning the affections of all her household, and especially of Madam Cavendish, who had been most of all prejudiced against her; and how much the invalid's health was improving.

"She will never be perfectly well again; but I think, with proper care, and under Divine Providence, we may succeed in preserving her life for many years longer."

Now, as Mary Grey could not venture to return to Blue Cliffs, or even to write a letter to that place with her own hand, so long as Mrs. Fanning should live in the house, the prospect of her doing either grew more and more remote.

She could not plead her sprained finger forever as an excuse for not writing; so one day she put on a very tight glove and buttoned it over her wrist, and then took a harder steel pen than she had ever used before, and she sat down and wrote a few lines by way of experiment. It was perfectly successful. Between the tight-fitting glove and the hard steel pen her handwriting was so disguised that she herself would never have known it, nor could any expert ever have detected it. So there was no possible danger of any one at Blue Cliffs recognizing it as hers.

Then, with this tightly-gloved hand and this hard steel pen, she sat down and wrote a letter to Emma Cavendish, saying that she could no longer deny herself the pleasure of writing to her darling, though her finger was still so stiff that she wrote with great difficulty, as might be seen in the cramped and awkward letters, "all looking as if they had epileptic fits," she jestingly added.

When Miss Cavendish replied to this letter she said that indeed Mrs. Grey's hand must have been very severely sprained, and that she herself would never have known the writing.

After this all Mrs. Grey's letters to Miss Cavendish were written by a hand buttoned up in a tight glove, and with a hard steel pen, and continued to be stiff and unrecognizable.

And in all Emma's answers there was surprise and regret expressed for the long-continued lameness of Mary Grey's right hand.

One day Emma communicated a piece of neighborhood gossip that quite startled Mary Grey.

"You will be sorry to hear," she wrote, "that our excellent pastor, Dr. Goodwin, has had a paralytic stroke that disables him from preaching. The Rev. Mr. Lyle, formerly of Richmond, is filling the pulpit."

Mary Grey was very much interested in this piece of news, that her own old admirer should be even temporarily located so near Blue Cliffs, with the possibility of his being permanently settled there.

She had not heard from this devoted clerical lover once since she had left Mount Ascension. She did not understand his sudden withdrawal, and she had often, with much mental disquietude, associated his unexpected estrangement with her own unceremonious dismissal from her situation as drawing-mistress at that academy.

It is true that when they corresponded, in answer to his ardent love-letters, she would write only such kind and friendly notes that could never have compromised her in any way, even if they should have been read in open court or published in a Sunday newspaper.

And he had sometimes complained of the formal friendliness of these letters from one for whom he had truly professed the most devoted love, and who had also promised to be his wife—if ever she was anybody's.

But Mrs. Grey had artfully soothed his wounded affection without departing from her prudential system of writing only such letters as she would not fear to have fall in the hands of any living creature, until suddenly he ceased to write at all.

At the time of this defection she had been too much taken up with her purpose of winning the affection of the wealthy and distinguished statesman, Governor Cavendish, to pay much attention to the fact of the Rev. Mr. Lyle's falling away.

But in these later and calmer days at Blue Cliffs and at Charlottesville she had pondered much on the circumstance in connection with her simultaneous dismissal from her situation at Mount Ascension; and she thought all but too likely that Mr. Lyle had, like Mrs. St. John, learned something of her past life so much to her disadvantage as to induce him to abandon her.

And now to have him so near Blue Cliffs as Wendover parish church seemed dangerous to Mary Grey's interests with the Cavendish family.

Sometimes the unhappy woman seemed to think that the net of Fate was drawing around her. Mrs. Fanning was at Blue Cliffs. Mr. Lyle was at Wendover. What next?

Why, next she got a letter from Emma Cavendish that struck all the color from her cheeks and all the courage from her soul.

Miss Cavendish, after telling the domestic and social news of the week, and adding that the Rev. Mr. Lyle was now settled permanently at Wendover, as the assistant of the Rev. Dr. Goodwin, whose health continued to be infirm, wrote:

"And now, dearest Mrs. Grey, I have reserved the best news for the last.

"Laura Lytton and Electra have left school 'for good.' They will arrive here this evening on a visit of some months.

"Next week we are all going to Charlottesville, to be present at the Commencement of the Law College, when Mr. Alden Lytton expects to take his degree.

"Aunt Fanning, whose health is much improved, will accompany us as our chaperon, and the Rev. Mr. Lyle will escort us.

"So you see, my dear Mrs. Grey, though you will not come to us, we will go to you.

"But we will form quite a large party. And I know that Charlottesville will receive an inundation of visitors for the Commencement, and that there will be a pressure upon all the hotels and boarding-houses. Therefore I will ask you to be so good as to seek out and engage apartments for us. There will be four ladies and one gentleman to be accommodated; we shall want at least three rooms—one for Mr. Lyle, one for Aunt Fanning and myself, and one for Laura and Electra. We want our rooms all in the same house, if possible; if not, then Mr. Lyle can be accommodated apart from the set; but we women must remain together.

"Please see to it at once, and write and let me know.

"By the way: after Mr. Lytton takes his degree he will make us a short visit at Blue Cliffs, after which he will go to Richmond to commence the practice of law, where *he* thinks the prestige of his father's name, and *I* think his own talents, will speedily advance him to fame and fortune.

"But what am I telling you? That of which you probably know much more than I do; for of course Mr. Lytton must have informed you of his plans.

"We confidently hope to persuade you to accompany us when we go back to Blue Cliffs. Our summer party will be such a very pleasant one: there will be Laura, Electra, Mrs. Grey and Aunt Fanning among the ladies, and Mr. Lyle, Mr. Lytton and Dr. Jones among the gentlemen. I shall have your rooms made ready for you."

There was much more of kind and affectionate planning for the summer's work and pleasure. But Mary Grey read no further.

Dropping the letter upon her lap, she clasped her hands and raised her pale face toward heaven, murmuring:

"She is coming here. I dare not meet her. I must go away again. I am hunted to death—I am hunted to death! I was hunted from Blue Cliffs, and now I am hunted from Charlottesville! Where shall I go next? To Richmond? Yes, of course, to Richmond! And there I will stay. For there is room to hide myself from any one whom I do not wish to see. And in a few weeks *he* will go to Richmond to settle there permanently. But I will go some few weeks in advance of him, so that he will never be able to say that I followed him there!"

Having formed this resolution, Mary Grey then set about, immediately to engage lodgings for the Blue Cliffs party.

She knew that her hostess, the bishop's widow, had one vacant room: that would accommodate two of the ladies, and therefore she resolved to make a virtue of her own necessities and give up her own room for the accommodation of the other two.

She proposed this plan to her hostess, who at first opposed the self-sacrifice, as she called it. But finally, being persuaded by Mary Grey, she yielded the point, and fervently praised the beautiful, unselfish spirit of her young guest, who was ever so ready to sacrifice her own comfort for the convenience of others.

Mary Grey then wrote to Miss Cavendish, telling her of the arrangement, and then explaining:

"You must know, my dear girl, that my health is not improved. For the last twelve months it has been growing steadily worse. My nervous system is shattered. I can not bear noise or tumult or excitement. I dread even to meet strangers. Therefore I think I shall go away and stay during this carnival of a Commencement. I hope that you and Laura will occupy my vacant chamber. The chamber adjoining is already vacant, and I have engaged it for Mrs. Fanning and Electra. I know I have paired your party off differently from *your* pairing; but then I like the thought of having you and Laura in my deserted chamber. I think I shall go to some very quiet village far from the bustle of company. Forgive me for not remaining to meet you, and set me down as very, *very* nervous; or, if that will not excuse me in your eyes, set me down as *crazy*; but never, *never* as ungrateful or unloving.

MARY.

"P.S.—Mr. Lyle must find accommodations at the hotel."

Having finished, sealed and dispatched this letter, Mary Grey went to work and packed her three great trunks for her journey. That kept her busy all the remainder of the day.

The next morning she dressed herself and went to call upon her friends and bid them good-bye. They were very much surprised at the suddenness of her departure; but she explained to one and all that she rather wished to avoid the crowd, bustle and confusion of Commencement week, and had therefore determined to leave town for a few days, and that her rooms with the bishop's widow would be occupied in the meantime by her friend Miss Cavendish, of Blue Cliffs, and her party.

This made an impression upon all minds that "sweet Mrs. Grey," with her spirit of self-sacrifice, had left town at this most interesting period for no other reason than to give up her quarters to her friends.

Lastly, Mary Grey went to her pastor and obtained from him a letter to the pastor of St. John's Church in Richmond.

Furnished with this, she would obtain entrance into the most respectable society in the city, if she desired to do so.

On the third day from this, Mrs. Grey left Charlottesville for Richmond.

CHAPTER XV.

AN OLD FACE REAPPEARS.

What the Carnival is to Rome, and the Derby is to London, the Commencement week of its great University is to the little country town of Charlottesville.

It is looked forward to for weeks and months. A few days previous to Commencement week the little town begins to fill. The hotels and boarding-houses are crowded with the relatives and friends of the students and professors, and even with numbers of the country gentry, who though they may have no relative at the University yet take an interest in the proceedings of Commencement week.

Emma Cavendish and her friends were therefore peculiarly fortunate in having had comfortable apartments pre-engaged for them.

It was late on the evening of the Monday beginning the important week that they arrived at Charlottesville, and proceeded at once to the house of the bishop's widow.

They found the house hospitably lighted up, and open.

Their hostess, a dignified gentlewoman, received them with great cordiality, and rather as guests than as lodgers.

She showed the ladies to the two communicating rooms on the first floor that they were to occupy—large, airy, pleasant rooms, with a fresh breeze blowing from front to back. Each room had two neat white-draped single beds in it.

"If you please, Mrs. Wheatfield, which of these was Mrs. Grey's apartment?" inquired Emma Cavendish.

"This back room overlooking the flower-garden. But as the front room was unoccupied she had the use of that also, whenever she wished it," answered the bishop's widow.

"I was very sorry to hear from her by letter that she would not be able to remain here to receive us," said Miss Cavendish.

"Ah, my dear, I was just as sorry to have her go away! A sweet woman she is, Miss Cavendish," answered Mrs. Wheatfield.

"Why did she go? Is her health so very bad, Mrs. Wheatfield?"

"My dear, I think that her malady is more of the mind than of the body. But I believe that she went away only to give up these rooms to you and your friends, because there were no other suitable rooms to be obtained for you in Charlottesville."

"I am very sorry to hear that; for indeed I and my companions would rather have given up our journey than have turned Mary Grey out of her rooms. It was really too great a sacrifice on her part," said Emma Cavendish, regretfully.

"My dear, that angel is always making sacrifices, for that matter. But I do think that *this* sacrifice did not cost her much. Love made it light. I feel sure she was delighted to be able to give up her quarters to friends who could not in any other way have been accommodated in the town," said the bishop's widow, politely.

"I am sorry, however, not to have met her," murmured Emma Cavendish.

"And now, ladies, here are the apartments. Arrange as to their occupancy and distribution among yourselves as you please," said the hostess, as she nodded pleasantly and left the room.

The ladies had brought but little luggage for their week's visit, and it had already arrived and was placed in their rooms.

They washed, dressed their hair, changed their traveling-suits for evening-dresses and went down into the parlor, where they found Alden Lytton—who had walked over from the University to meet his sister—in conversation with Mr. Lyle.

There was quite a joyous greeting. But Alden had to be introduced to Mrs. Fanning, who had changed so much in the years that had passed since their last meeting that the young man would never have known her again.

But every one remarked that when the lady and the student were introduced to each other their mutual agitation could not be concealed. And every one marveled about its cause.

Alden Lytton found fair Emma Cavendish more beautiful than ever, and he now no longer tried to deny to himself the truth that his heart was devoted to her in the purest, highest, noblest love that ever inspired man.

"Do you know, Mr. Lytton, where Mrs. Grey has gone? She did not tell me in her letter where she intended to go; I believe she had not then quite made up her mind as to her destination," said Miss Cavendish.

"I was not even aware of her departure until I learned it from Mrs. Wheatfield this evening," answered Alden Lytton.

"Then no one knows. But I suppose we shall learn when we hear from her," said Emma, with a smile.

Then Alden produced cards for the Commencement, with tickets inclosed for reserved seats in the best part of the hall, which he had been careful to secure for his party. These he gave into the charge of Mr. Lyle, who was to attend the ladies to the University.

And then, as it was growing late, the two gentlemen arose and took leave.

They left the house together and walked down the street as far as the corner, where Alden Lytton paused and said:

"Our ways separate here, I am sorry to say. I have to walk a mile out to the University. Your hotel is about twenty paces up the next street, on your right. You will be sure to find it."

And Alden lifted his hat and was about to stride rapidly away when Mr. Lyle laid his hand on his arm and said:

"One moment. I did not know our paths parted so soon or I might have spoken as we left the house. The fact is, I have a very large sum of money—ten thousand dollars—sent me to be paid to you as soon as you shall have taken your degree. It is to be employed in the purchase of a law library and in the renting and furnishing of a law office in the best obtainable location. I wish to turn this money over to you as soon as possible."

"It is from my unknown guardian, I presume," said Alden, gravely.

"Yes, it is from your unknown guardian."

"Then we will talk of this after the Commencement. I hardly know, Mr. Lyle, whether I ought to accept anything more from this lavish benefactor of ours. I may never be able to repay what we already owe him."

"You need have no hesitation in accepting assistance from this man, as I have often assured you. But, as you say, we will talk of this some other time, when we have more leisure. Good-night!"

And the gentlemen separated: Alden Lytton striding westward toward the University, and Mr. Lyle walking thoughtfully toward his hotel.

His room had been secured and his key was in his pocket, so that he possessed quite an enviable advantage over the crowd of improvident travelers who thronged the office clamoring for quarters, and not half of whom could by any possibility be accommodated.

As it was long after the minister's usual hour for retiring, he walked through the crowded office into the hall and up the stairs to his room—a very small chamber, with one window and a single bed, both window and bed neatly draped with white.

Mr. Lyle sat down in a chair by the one little table, on which stood a bright brass candlestick with a lighted spermaceti candle, and took from his pocket a small Bible, which he opened with the intention of reading his customary chapter before going to bed, when a rap at his door surprised him.

"Come in," he said, supposing that only a country waiter had come with towels or water, or some other convenience.

The door opened and a waiter indeed made his appearance. But he only said:

"A gemman for to see yer, sah!" and ushered in a stranger and closed the door behind him.

Mr. Lyle, much astonished, stared at the visitor, whom he thought he had never seen before.

The stranger was a tall, finely-formed, dark-complexioned and very handsome man, notwithstanding that his raven hair was streaked with silver, his brow lined with thought, and his fine black eyes rather hollow. A full black beard nearly covered the lower part of his face.

"Mr. Lyle," said the visitor, holding out his hand.

"That is my name, sir; but you have the advantage of me," said the minister.

"You do not know me?" inquired the stranger in sad surprise.

"I do not, indeed."

"I am Victor Hartman!"

CHAPTER XVI.

THE RETURNED EXILE.

Danger, long travel, want, or woe,
Soon change the form that best we know;
For deadly fear can time outgo,
And blanch at once the hair;
Hard time can roughen form and face,
And grief can quench the eyes' bright grace;
Nor does old age a wrinkle trace
More deeply than despair.

—SCOTT.

"Victor Hartman!" exclaimed Mr. Lyle, in a tone of astonishment and joy, as he sprang from his chair and grasped both the hands of the traveler and shook them heartily—"Victor Hartman! My dear friend, I am so delighted—and so surprised—to see you! Sit down—sit down!" he continued, dragging forward a chair and forcing his visitor into it. "But I never should have known you again," he concluded, gazing intently upon the bronzed, gray, tall, broad-shouldered man before him.

"I am much changed," answered the stranger, in a deep, mellifluous voice, that reminded the hearer of sweet, solemn church music.

"Changed! Why, you left us a mere stripling! You return to us a mature man. To all appearance, you might be the father of the boy who went away," said the minister, still gazing upon the stranger.

"And yet the time has not been long; though indeed I have lived much in that period," said the traveler, in the same rich, deep tone, and with a smile that rendered his worn face bright and handsome for the moment.

"Well, I am delighted to see you. But how is it that I have this joyful surprise?" inquired the minister.

"What brings me here, you would ask; and why did I not write and tell you that I was coming?" said Hartman, with an odd smile. "Well, I will explain. When I got your letter acknowledging the receipt of the last remittance I sent to you for my children, I learned for the first time by that same letter that my boy would graduate at this Commencement, and hoped to take the highest honors of his college. Well, a steamer was to sail at noon that very day. I thought I would like to be present at the Commencement and see my boy take his degree. I packed my trunk in an hour, embarked in the 'Porte d'Or' in another hour, and here I am."

"That was prompt. When did you arrive?"

"Our steamer reached New York on Thursday noon. I took the night train for Washington, where I arrived at five on Friday morning. I took the morning boat for Aquia Creek, and the train for Richmond and Charlottesville. I got here about noon."

"And you have not seen your *protéges*?"

"Yes, I have seen my boy pass the hotel twice to-day. I knew him by his likeness to his unfortunate father. But I did not make myself known to him. I do not intend to do so—at least not at present."

"Why not?"

"Why not?" echoed Hartman, sorrowfully. "Ah, would he not shrink from me in disgust and abhorrence?"

"No; not if he were told the awful injustice that has been done you."

"But if he were told, would he believe it? We have no proof that any injustice has been done me, except those anonymous letters and the word of that strange horseman who waylaid me on my tramp and thrust a bag of gold in my hands, with the words, 'You never intended to kill Henry Lytton, and you never killed him. Some one else intended to kill him, and some one else killed him.'"

"Have you ever heard anything more of that mysterious horseman?"

"Not one word."

"Have you no suspicion of his identity?"

"None, beyond the strong conviction that I feel that he himself was the homicide and the writer of the anonymous letters."

"Well, I can not tell you why, but I always felt persuaded of your innocence, even before the coming of those anonymous letters, and even while *you* were bitterly accusing yourself."

"You knew it from intuition—inward teaching."

"May I ask you, Hartman, *why* after you discovered that you had nothing to do with the death of Henry Lytton, you still determined to burden yourself with the support and education of his children—a duty that was first assumed by you as an atonement for an irreparable injury you supposed you had done them?"

"Why I still resolved to care for them after I learned that I had nothing to do with their great loss? Indeed I can not tell you. Perhaps—partly because I sympathized with them in a sorrow that was common to us all, in so far as we all suffered from the same cause; partly, I also think, because it was pleasant to have *some one* to live for and work for; partly because I was so grateful to find myself free from blood guiltiness that I wished to educate those children as a thank-offering to Heaven! It was also very pleasant to me to think of this boy at college and this girl at school, and to hope that some day they might come to look upon me with affection instead of with horror. And then I took so much pride in talking to my brother miners about my son at the University and my daughter at the Academy! And then, again, your letters—every one of them telling of the progress my children made and the credit they were doing me. I tell you, sir, all this was a great comfort to me, and made me feel at home in this strange, lonesome world," said the exile, warmly.

"Hartman, you have a noble soul! You must have made a very great pecuniary sacrifice for the sake of these young people," said the minister, earnestly.

"No, sir; no sacrifice at all. That was the strangest part of it; for it seemed to me the more I gave the more I had."

"How was that?"

"I don't know how it was, sir; but such was the fact. But I will tell you what I do know."

"Yes, tell me, Hartman."

"You may remember, Mr. Lyle, that when I told you I was going back to California I explained to you that I knew a place where I felt sure money was to be made."

"Yes, I remember."

"Well, sir, the place was a gully at the foot of a certain spur of the mountains, called the Red Cleft. Now, at that time I knew very little of geology. I know more now. Also, I had had but little experience in mining; and, moreover, whenever I mentioned Red Ridge I was simply laughed at by my mates. I was laughed out of giving the place a fair trial. But even after I left the Gold State the idea of the treasure hidden in the gully at the foot of Red Ridge haunted me day and night, something always prompting me to go back there and dig. Sir, it was intuition—inward teaching. When I went back to California I made for Red Ridge. Sir, when I first went to Red Ridge I dug there eight weeks without finding gold. That was the time my mates laughed at me. When I next went back—the time I now speak of—I worked four hours and then struck—struck one of the best paying mines in the Gold State. It is worked by a company now, but I have half of all the shares."

"You have been wonderfully blessed and prospered, Hartman."

"Yes," said the traveler, reverently bowing his head; "for their sakes, I have."

"And for your own, I trust, Hartman."

"Mr. Lyle—"

"Well, Hartman."

"May I ask you a favor?"

"Certainly you may."

"You addressed all your letters to me under the name of Joseph Brent."

"Yes, certainly—at your request."

"Continue, then, to call me Joseph Brent. That name is mine by act of legislature."

"Indeed!"

"Yes, and I have a still better claim. It was the name of my grandfather—my mother's father. It was also the name of his eldest son, my uncle, who died recently a bachelor, in the State of Missouri, and left me his farm there, on condition that I should take his name. I was more anxious to have his name than his estate. So I applied to the legislature, and the name that I had borrowed so long became my own of right."

"So I am to introduce you to my young friends as Mr. Joseph Brent?"

"Yes, if you please. Let the name of poor Victor Hartman sink quietly into the grave. And do not let them know that I was Victor Hartman, or that Joseph Brent was ever their benefactor," said the exile, gravely.

"I will keep your counsel so long as you require me to do so, hoping that the time may speedily come when all shall be made as clear to these young people as it is to me."

"Now when will you introduce me to my children?"

"To-morrow, after the ceremonies are concluded. But, my friend, it is a little strange to hear you call these grown-up young people your children, when you yourself can be but little older than the young man."

"In years, yes. But in long experience, suffering, thought, how much older I am than he is! You yourself said that, to all outward appearance, I might be the father of the boy who went away two years ago."

"Yes, for you are very much changed—not only in your person, but in dress and address."

"You mean that I speak a little more correctly than I used to do? Well, sir, in these two years all the time that was not spent in work was spent in study. Or, rather, as study was to me the hardest sort of work, it would be most accurate to say all the time not spent by me in manual was spent in mental labor. I had had a good public-school education in my boyhood. I wished to recover all I had lost, and to add to it. You see, Mr. Lyle, I did not want my boy and girl to be ashamed of me when, if ever, we should meet as friends," said Hartman, with his old smile.

"That they could never be. Any other than grateful and affectionate they could never be to you—if I know them."

"I believe that too. I believe my children will love me when they understand all."

"Be sure they will. But, Hartman—by the way, I like the name of Hartman, and I hope you will let me use it when we are alone, on condition that I promise never to use it when we are in company."

"As you please, Mr. Lyle."

"Then, Hartman, I was about to say that when I hear you speak of Henry Lytton's son and daughter as your boy and girl, the wonder comes over me as to whether you never think of marriage—of a wife and children of your own."

"Mr. Lyle, since my mother went away to heaven I have never felt any interest in any woman on earth. I have been interested in some girls, but they happened to be children: and I could count them with the fingers of one hand and have a finger or two left over. Let me see," said Hartman, with his odd smile. "First there was Sal's Kid."

"Sal's Kid?" echoed the minister, who had never heard the name before, but thought it a very eccentric one.

"Yes, Sal's Kid—a wild-eyed, elf-locked, olive-skinned little imp, nameless, but nicknamed Sal's Kid, who lived in a gutter called Rat

Alley, down by the water-side in New York. I used to be fond of the child when I was cook's galley-boy, and our ship was in port there. I haven't seen her for ten years, yet I've never forgotten her. And I would give a great deal to know whatever became of Sal's Kid. Probably she has gone the way of the rest. They were all beggars, thieves, or worse," added Hartman, with a deep sigh.

"And the next?" inquired the minister, with a wish to recall his visitor from sorrowful thoughts.

"The next girl that interested me," continued Hartman, looking up with a bright smile, as at the recollection of some celestial vision, "was as different from this one as the purest diamond from a lump of charcoal. She was a radiant blonde, with golden hair and sapphire eyes and a blooming complexion. In the darkest hour of my life she appeared to me a heavenly messenger! They were leading me from the Court House to the jail, after my sentence. I was passing amid the hooting crowd, bowed down with despair, when this fair vision beamed upon me and dispersed the furies. She looked at me with heavenly pity in her eyes. She spoke to me and told me to pray, and said that she too would pray for me. At her look and voice the jeering crowd fell back in silence. I thought of that picture of Doré's where the celestial visitant dispersed the fiends. I have never, never seen her since."

"And you do not know who she was?"

"Her companions called her 'Emma.' That is all I know."

"The third girl in whom you became interested?"

"Is my child Laura Lytton, whom I have never seen. During the weeks I was in Mr. Lytton's law office I never once beheld his son or daughter."

"Then personally you are a stranger to both?"

"Yes, personally I am a stranger to both. But to-morrow I hope to know them, although I can not be perfectly made known to them. Remember, Mr. Lyle, I do not wish them to know that I was ever Victor Hartman, or that Joseph Brent was ever their benefactor."

"I will remember your caution. But I will hope, as I said before, for the time when they shall know and esteem you as I know and esteem you."

"Your confidence in me has been, and is, one of my greatest earthly supports," said Hartman, earnestly, as he arose to bid his friend good-night.

Long after his visitor had left him, Mr. Lyle sat at his window in an attitude of deep thought.

The unexpected meeting with Victor Hartman had deprived him of all power or wish to sleep.

He sat at the window watching the crowd that thronged the village streets with his outward eyes, but reviewing all the past with his inner vision. It was long after midnight before he retired.

CHAPTER XVII.

VICTOR MEETS "HIS CHILDREN."

The next morning revealed the full measure of the crowd that filled the little country town to overflowing. And the road leading from the village westward to the University was crowded with foot-passengers, horsemen and carriages of every description.

Those who had no reserved seats set out early, to secure the most eligible of the unreserved places.

The ceremonies were to commence at twelve noon.

Our party, consisting of Emma Cavendish, Laura Lytton, Electra Coroni, Mrs. Fanning, Mrs. Wheatfield and Dr. Jones occupied the whole of the third form from the front.

They were in their places just a few moments before the overture was played.

The hall was crowded to overflowing. Not only was every form filled, but chairs had to be set in the space between the audience and the orchestra, and also in the middle and side aisles, to accommodate ladies who could not otherwise be seated; while every foot of standing room was occupied by gentlemen.

Mr. Lyle had given up his seat next to Laura Lytton in favor of a lady, and had explained to his party that he had a friend from San Francisco who was present and with whom he could stand up.

And he went away and took up his position in a corner below the platform, beside Victor Hartman, but entirely out of the range of his party's vision.

I will not weary my readers with any detailed account of this Commencement, which resembled all other college commencements in being most interesting to those most concerned.

There was an overture from a new opera.

Then there was an opening oration by one of the learned professors of the University, which was voted by the savants to be a masterpiece of erudition and eloquence, but which the young people present found intolerably dull and stupid. And when the great man sat down a storm of applause followed him.

Then ensued the usual alternation of opera music and orations.

And the young people listened to the opera music, and yawned behind their fans over the orations.

And the savants gave heed to the orations, and closed their senses, if not their ears, to the music.

At length the time for the distribution of the diplomas arrived, and the names of the successful graduates were called out, and each in turn went up to receive his diploma and make the customary deep bow, first to the faculty and then to the audience.

Then followed the offertory of beautiful bouquets and baskets of flowers from friends to the graduates. But the most beautiful offering there was a basket of delicate silver wire filled with fragrant pure white lilies sent by Emma Cavendish to Alden Lytton.

Laura Lytton, in a patriotic mood, sent a bouquet composed of red, white and blue flowers only.

The other ladies of the party sent baskets of geraniums.

The valedictory address was delivered by Alden Lytton, who had, besides, taken the highest honors of the college.

His address was pronounced to be a great success. And his retiring bow was followed by thunders of applause from the audience.

There were several proud and happy fathers there that day; but perhaps the proudest and the happiest man present was Victor Hartman.

With tearful eyes and tremulous tones he said, as he grasped Mr. Lyle's arm:

"My boy pays me for all—my boy pays me for all! He is a grand fellow!"

The people were all going out then.

"Come," said Mr. Lyle, himself moved by the generous emotion of Victor. "Come, let me introduce you to your boy."

"No, not now. Let me go away by myself for a little while. I will see you an hour later at the hotel," said Hartman, as he wrung his friend's hand and turned away.

Mr. Lyle joined his party, with whom he found the most honored graduate of the day, who was holding his silver basket of lilies in his hand and warmly thanking the fair donor.

Mr. Lyle shook hands with Alden and heartily congratulated him on his collegiate honors, adding:

"We shall see you on the Bench yet, Mr. Lytton."

Alden bowed and laughingly replied that he should feel it to be his sacred duty to get there, if he could, in order to justify his friend's good opinion.

"But what have you done with your Californian, Mr. Lyle?" inquired Laura Lytton.

"Sent him back to his hotel. By the way, ladies, he is a stranger here. Will you permit me to bring him to see you this evening?"

"Certainly, Mr. Lyle," promptly replied Emma Cavendish, speaking for all.

But then she gave a questioning glance toward her aunt, the chaperon of the party.

"Of course," said Mrs. Fanning, in answer to that glance. "Of course the Reverend Mr. Lyle's introduction is a sufficient passport for any gentleman to any lady's acquaintance."

Mr. Lyle bowed and said:

"Then I will bring him at eight o'clock this evening."

And, with another bow, he also left the party and hurried off to the hotel.

That evening, at eight o'clock, the three young ladies were seated alone together in the front drawing-room of their boarding-house. Their elderly friends were not present.

Dr. Jones was dining at the college with Alden Lytton and his fellow-graduates.

Mrs. Fanning, fatigued with the day's excitement, had retired to a dressing-gown and sofa in her own room.

Mrs. Wheatfield was in consultation with her book concerning the next day's bill of fare.

Thus the three beauties were left together, and very beautiful they looked.

Emma Cavendish, the "radiant blonde, with the golden hair and sapphire eyes and blooming complexion," was dressed in fine pure white tulle, with light-blue ribbons.

Electra, the wild-eyed, black-haired, damask-cheeked brunette, was dressed in a maize-colored silk, with black lace trimmings.

Laura Lytton, the stout, wholesome, brown-haired and brown-eyed lassie, wore a blue *barége* trimmed, like Electra's dress, with black lace.

The room was brilliant with gas-light, and they were waiting for their friends and visitors.

Dr. Jones had promised to return, and bring Alden with him, by eight o'clock at latest. And Mr. Lyle had promised to come and bring "the Californian."

The clock struck eight and with dramatic punctuality the bell rang.

The next moment the little page of the establishment opened the drawing-room door and announced:

"Mr. Lyle and a gemman."

Chapter XVIII.

AN INTRODUCTION.

The three young ladies looked up, to see Mr. Lyle enter the room, accompanied by a tall, finely-formed, dark-complexioned man, with deep dark eyes, and black hair and full black beard, both lightly streaked with silver, which, together with a slight stoop, gave him the appearance of being much older than he really was.

Mr. Lyle bowed to the young ladies, and then, taking his companion up to Emma Cavendish, he said, with old-fashioned formality:

"Miss Cavendish, permit me to present to you my friend Mr. Brent, of San Francisco."

"I am glad to see you, Mr. Brent," said the young lady, with a graceful bend of her fair head.

But in an instant the Californian seemed to have lost his self-possession.

He stared for a moment almost rudely at the young lady: he turned red and pale, drew a long breath; then, with an effort, recovered himself and bowed deeply.

Miss Cavendish was surprised; but she was too polite and self-possessed to let her surprise appear. She mentally ascribed the disturbance of her visitor to some passing cause.

Mr. Lyle, who had not noticed his companion's agitation, now presented him to Laura Lytton and to Electra Coroni.

To Laura he bowed gravely and calmly.

But when he met the wild eyes of Electra he started violently and exclaimed:

"Sal's—" then stopped abruptly, bowed and took the chair that his friend placed for him.

He sat in perfect silence, while Emma Cavendish, pitying, without understanding, his awkwardness, tried to make conversation by introducing the subject of California and the gold mines.

But Victor Hartman replied with an effort, and frequently and furtively looked at Emma, and looked at Electra, and then put his hand to his head in a perplexed manner.

At length his embarrassment became obvious even to unobservant Mr. Lyle, who longed for an opportunity of asking him what the matter was.

But before that opportunity came there was another ring at the street door-bell, followed by the entrance of Dr. Jones and Alden Lytton.

The last-comers greeted the young ladies and Mr. Lyle, and acknowledged the presence of the stranger with a distant bow.

But then Mr. Lyle arose and asked permission to introduce his friend Mr. Brent, of California.

And Dr. Jones and Mr. Lytton shook hands with the Californian and welcomed him to Virginia.

Then Alden Lytton, who had some dim dreams of going to California to commence life, with the idea of one day becoming Chief Justice of the State, began to draw the stranger out on the subject.

Victor Hartman, the unknown and unsuspected benefactor, delighted to make the acquaintance of "his boy," and, to learn all his half-formed wishes and purposes, talked freely and enthusiastically of the Gold State and its resources and prospects.

"If all that I have heard about the condition of society out there be true, however, it must be a much better place for farmers and mechanics, tradesmen and laborers, than for professional men."

"What have you heard, then, of the condition of society out there?" inquired Victor.

"Well, I have heard that the climate is so healthy that the well who go there never get sick, and the sick who go there get well without the doctor's help. And, furthermore, that all disputes are settled by the fists, the bowie-knife, or the revolver, without the help of lawyer, judge or jury! So, you see, if all that is told of it is true, it is a bad place for lawyers and doctors."

"'If all that is told of it is true?' There is not a word of it true! It is all an unpardonable fabrication," said Victor Hartman, so indignantly and solemnly that Alden burst out laughing as he answered:

"Oh, of course I know it is an exaggeration! I did think of trying my fortune in the Gold State; but upon reflection I have decided to devote my poor talents to my mother state, Virginia. And not until she practically disowns me will I desert her."

"Well said, my dear bo—I mean Mr. Lytton!" assented the Californian.

He had begun heartily, but ended by correcting himself with some embarrassment.

Alden looked up for an instant, a little surprised by his disturbance; but ascribed it to the awkwardness of a man long debarred from ladies' society, as this miner seemed to have been.

Gradually Victor Hartman recovered his composure and talked intelligently and fluently upon the subject of gold mining, Chinese emigration, and so forth.

Only when he would chance to meet the full gaze of Electra's "wild eyes," or catch the tones of Emma's mellifluous voice, then, indeed, he would show signs of disturbance. He would look or listen, and put his hand to his forehead with an expression of painful perplexity.

At ten o'clock the gentlemen arose to bid the young ladies good-night.

It was then arranged that the whole party should visit the University the next day and go through all the buildings on a tour of inspection.

When the visitors had gone, Electra suddenly inquired:

"Well, what do you think of the Californian?"

"I think him very handsome," said Laura, "but decidedly the most awkward man I ever saw in all the days of my life. Except in the matter of his awkwardness he seems to be a gentleman."

"Oh, that is nothing! One of the most distinguished men I ever met in my father's house—a gentleman by birth, education and position, a statesman of world-wide renown—was unquestionably the most awkward human being I ever saw in my life. He knew very well how to manage men and nations, but he never knew what to do with his feet and hands: he kept shuffling them about in the most nervous and distracting manner," said Emma Cavendish, in behalf of the stranger.

"Somehow or other that man's face haunts me like a ghost," mused Electra, dreamily.

"So it does me," quickly spoke Emma. "I feel sure that I have met those sad, wistful dark eyes *somewhere* before."

"I'll tell you both what. Whether you have ever met him before or not, he *thinks* he has seen you. He seemed to me to be trying to recollect *where* all the evening," said Laura Lytton, with her air of positiveness.

"Then that might account for his awkwardness and embarrassment," added Emma.

"But he is certainly very handsome," concluded Electra, as she took her candle to retire.

Meanwhile the four gentlemen walked down the street together to a corner, where they bade each other good-night and separated—Dr. Jones and Alden Lytton to walk out to the University, and Mr. Lyle and Victor Hartman to go to their hotel.

"What on earth was the matter with you, Victor?" inquired Mr. Lyle, as they walked on together.

"What?" exclaimed Hartman, under his breath, and stopping short in the street.

"Yes, what! I never saw a man so upset without an adequate cause in all my life."

"Don't let us go into the house yet," said Victor; for they were now before the door of the hotel. "It is only ten o'clock, and a fine night. Take a turn with me down some quiet street, and I will tell you."

"Willingly," agreed Mr. Lyle; and they walked past the hotel and out toward the suburbs of the little town.

"Mr. Lyle, I have seen them both!" exclaimed Victor, when they were out of hearing of every one else.

"Both? Whom have you seen, Hartman?" inquired the minister a little uneasily, as if he feared his companion was not quite sane.

"First, I have seen again the heavenly vision that appeared and dispersed the furies from around me on that dark day when I passed, a condemned criminal, from the Court House to the jail," replied Victor Hartman, with emotion.

"Hartman, my poor fellow, are you mad?"

"No; but it was enough to make me so. To meet one of them, whom I never expected to see again in this world, would have been enough to upset me for a while; but to meet both, and to meet them together, who were so widely apart in place and in rank, I tell you it was bewildering! I felt as if I was under the influence of opium and in a delightful dream from which I should soon awake. I did not quite believe it all to be real. I do not quite believe it to be so yet. Have I seen that celestial visitant again?" he inquired, putting his hand to his head in the same confused manner.

"Now, which one of these young ladies do you take to have been your 'celestial visitant,' as you most absurdly call her?"

"Oh, the fair, golden-haired, azure-eyed angel, robed so appropriately in pure white!"

"That was Miss Emma Cavendish," said Mr. Lyle, very uneasily; "and you talk of her like a lover, Hartman—and like a very mad lover too! But oh, I earnestly implore you, do not become so very mad, so frenzied as to let yourself love Emma Cavendish! By birth, education and fortune she is one of the first young ladies in the country, and a bride for a prince. Do not, I conjure you, think of loving her yourself!"

Victor Hartman laughed a little light laugh, that seemed to do him good, as he answered:

"Do not be afraid. I worship her too much to think of loving her in the way you mean. And, besides, if I am not greatly mistaken, *my boy* has been before me."

"Alden Lytton?"

"Yes, sir. I saw it all. I was too much interested not to see it. My boy and my angel like one another. Heaven bless them both! They are worthy of each other. They will make a fine pair. He so handsome; she so beautiful! He so talented; she so lovely! His family is quite as good as hers. And as for a fortune, his shall equal hers!" said Victor, warmly.

"Will you give away all your wealth to make your 'boy' happy?" inquired Mr. Lyle, with some emotion.

"No! The Red Cleft mine is not so easily exhausted. Besides, in any case, I should save something for my girl She must have a marriage portion too!"

"You really ought to have a guardian appointed by the court to take care of you and your money, Victor. You will give it all away. And, seriously, it grieves me to see you so inclined to rob yourself so heavily to enrich others, even such as these excellent young people," said Mr. Lyle, with feeling.

"Be easy! When I have enriched them both I shall still have an unexhausted gold mine! By the way, parson—parson!"

"Well, Hartman?"

"I saw something else beside the love between my angel and my boy. I saw—saw a certain liking between my girl and my friend."

If the bright starlight had been bright enough Victor Hartman might have seen the vivid blush that mantled all over the ingenuous face of Stephen Lyle.

"I certainly admire Miss Lytton very much. She is a genuine girl," said Mr. Lyle, as composedly as if his face was not crimson.

"And I see she certainly admires you very much. She evidently thinks you are a genuine man. So, my dear friend, go in and win. And my girl shall not miss her marriage portion," said Hartman, cordially.

Mr. Lyle was beginning to feel a little embarrassed at the turn the conversation had taken, so he hastened to change it by saying:

"You told me that you had met them *both* whom you never had expected to see again in this world. One was Miss Cavendish, your 'heavenly vision;' who was the other?"

"Can you be at a loss to know? There were but three young ladies present. My own girl, whom I went to see and did expect to meet; Miss Cavendish, whom you have just identified as one of the two alluded to, and the brilliant little creature whom you introduced by a heathenish sort of name which I have forgotten."

"Miss Electra?"

"Aye, that was the name; but however you call her, I knew her in Rat Alley as Sal's Kid."

"What!" exclaimed Mr. Lyle, stopping short and trying to gaze through the darkness into the face of his companion; for Mr. Lyle had never happened to hear of the strange vicissitudes of Electra's childhood.

"She is Sal's Kid, I do assure you. Her face is too unique ever to be mistaken. I could never forget or fail to recognize those flashing eyes and gleaming teeth. And, I tell you, I would rather have found her again as I found her to-night than have discovered another gold mine as rich as that of Red Cleft."

"Hartman, you were never more deceived in your life. That young lady, Electra Coroni, is the granddaughter of Dr. Beresford Jones, and is the sole heiress of Beresford Manors. She was educated at the Mount Ascension Academy for Young Ladies in this State, from which she has just graduated."

"Whoever she is, or whatever she is, or wherever she lives now, when I knew her she was Sal's Kid, and lived in Rat Alley, New York. And she knew me as Galley Vick, the ship cook's boy."

"Hartman, you have certainly 'got a bee in your bonnet!'"

"We shall see. She almost recognized me to-night. She will quite know me soon," answered Victor, as they turned their steps toward their hotel.

CHAPTER XIX.

VICTOR AND ELECTRA.

Heaven has to all allotted, soon or late,
Some lucky revolution of their fate;
Whose motions, if we watch and guide with skill—
For human good depends on human will—
Our fortune rolls as from a smooth descent,
And from a first impression takes its bent;
But if unseized, she glides away like wind,
And leaves repenting folly far behind,
Now, now she meets you with a glorious prize,
And spreads her locks before her as she flies.

—DRYDEN.

The next morning at the appointed hour the Rev. Mr. Lyle and Victor Hartman left their hotel together and went to Mrs. Wheatfield's, to escort the ladies to the University, where Dr. Jones and Alden Lytton were to meet them and introduce them to the president. The two gentlemen found the young ladies already dressed and waiting.

Miss Cavendish explained that her aunt did not care about seeing more of the University than she had already seen, and preferred to remain in the house with the bishop's widow and rest that day.

And so, under the circumstances, they—Miss Cavendish and her young friends—had decided not to have a carriage, but to take advantage of the fine morning and walk the short mile that lay between the village and its great seat of learning.

Nothing could have pleased their escorts better than this plan.

And soon they—the party of five—set out upon the pleasant country road that led out to the University.

Emma Cavendish and Laura Lytton led the way, and by Laura's side walked the Rev. Mr. Lyle. Electra dropped a little behind, and was attended by Victor Hartman.

They talked of the fine morning and of the beautiful country, of the grand Commencement of the preceding day and of the University they were going to see; but they talked in an absent-minded manner, as if, indeed, they were both thinking of something else.

This lasted until they were half-way to the place, when at length Electra turned suddenly upon Victor and said:

"Do you know, Mr. Brent, that your face seems a very familiar one to me?"

"Indeed!" said Victor, bending his head nearer to her.

"Yes, indeed! Your face struck me as being familiar the first moment I saw you, and this impression has grown deeper every moment we have been walking together; and now I *know* of whom you remind me," answered Electra; and then she paused and looked at him.

He made no remark.

"You do not care to know who that was, it seems," she said.

"Oh, yes, I do, I assure you, Miss Coroni, if you please to tell me!"

"Then you remind me of a poor lad whom I once knew and liked very much in New York, when I was as poor as himself," said Electra, meaningly.

"It is very kind of you to remember the poor lad after so many years and so many changes," replied Victor.

"I wonder if that poor lad ever thinks of *me*, 'after so many years and so many changes?'" murmured Electra, musingly.

"I don't know. Tell me his name, and then perhaps I can answer your question. I have roamed around the world a good deal and seen a great many different sorts of people. Who knows but I may have met your poor lad? Let us have his name," said Victor, gravely.

They were both, to use a household phrase, "beating about the bush."

"Oh, he was too poor to own a name! But he was cook's boy on board a merchantman, and they called him 'Galley Vick.' I never knew him by any other name. Did you ever see him at all?"

"Oh, yes, I've seen him! A good-for-nothing little vagabond he was! No, I don't suppose he ever dares to think about such a fine young lady as you are. But he cherishes the memory of a poor little girl he once knew in Rat Alley, New York. And only the day before yesterday, when I happened to be with him, he was saying how much he would give to know what had become of that poor little girl."

"Yes, it was very nice of him to remember her," said Electra, musingly.

"You say that you knew the poor lad in New York. Perhaps, as they were so much together, you may have known the poor little girl also?" said Victor.

"I can not tell you unless you give me her name. There were so many poor little girls in New York," answered Electra, shaking her head.

"*She*, like the boy, was too poor then to own a name. They called her 'Sal's Kid.' I never knew her by any other name," answered Victor.

And then their eyes met, and both laughed and impulsively put out their hands, which were then clasped together.

"I knew you at the very first sight, Vick," said Electra, giving full way to her feelings of pleasure in meeting her old playmate again.

"And so did I you. Heaven bless you, child! I am so happy and thankful to find you here, so healthy and prosperous. You were a sickly, poor little thing when I knew you," said Victor, with much emotion.

"I was a famished poor little thing, you mean, food has made all the difference, Victor," laughed Electra.

"My name is Joseph Brent, my dear," said Hartman, who almost trembled to hear the old name spoken.

"Ah, but Sal's Kid knew you only as Galley Vick. I thought Vick was the short for Victor. But it seems you really had a name all the time as well as I had, though neither of us suspected we possessed such an appendage."

Hartman bowed in silence.

"And now I suppose you would like to know how it happens that you find poor little ragged, famished, sickly Sal's Kid, who used to live in Rat Alley among thieves and tramps, here—well lodged, well dressed and in good company?"

"Yes, I really would."

"Well, it was 'all along of' a grandfather."

"A grandfather!"

"Yes, a grandfather. I really had a grandfather! And I have him still. And you have seen him, and his name is Dr. Beresford Jones. And, moreover, I had a great-grandfather back of *him*; and also forefathers behind *them*, and ancestors extending away back to antiquity. In fact, I think they ran away back to Adam!"

"I dare say they did," answered Victor, with a smile; "but tell me about that grandfather."

"Well, you must know that he was wealthy. He owned Beresford Manors. He had one child, 'sole daughter of the house.' She married a poor young Italian music-master against her father's will. Her father cast her off. Her husband took her to New York, where they fell by degrees into the deepest destitution. They both died of cholera, leaving me to the care of the miserable beings who were their fellow-lodgers in the old tenement house. I believe I was passed from the hands of one beggar to those of another, until my identity was lost and my real name forgotten. But I do not clearly remember any of my owners except Sal. And I was called 'Sal's Kid.'"

"It was then I knew you," said Victor.

"So it was. Well, you know all about that period. It was soon after you went to sea that Sal's husband, being mad with drink and jealousy, struck his wife a fatal blow and killed her."

"Horrible!"

"Yes, horrible! I have heard since that the man died of *mania-à-potu* in the Tombs, before his trial came on."

"And you?"

"I was taken by the Commissioners of Charity and put into the Orphan Asylum at Randall's Island."

"And how did your grandfather ever find you there, where your very name was lost?"

"You may well ask that. My name was lost. I suppose, hearing me called Sal's Kid, they mistook that for Sal Kidd. Any way they registered my name on the books of the Island as Sarah Kidd."

Victor laughed at this piece of ingenuity on the part of the authorities, and again expressed wonder as to how her grandfather ever found her.

"If I were a heathen, I should say he found me by chance. It looked like it. You see, he had met with misfortunes. His wife—my grandmother—died. And he was growing old, and his home was lonely and his life was dreary. And so he relented toward his poor daughter, and even toward her husband."

"But too late!" put in Victor.

"Yes; too late. He relented too late," sighed Electra. "He went to New York, where they had been living when he had last heard of them, and after making the most diligent inquiries he only learned that they had been dead several years, and had left an orphan girl in great destitution. Well, he advertised for the child, offering large rewards for her discovery."

"But in vain, I suppose?" said Victor.

"Ah, yes, in vain, for I was at Randall's Island, registered under another name."

"The case seemed hopeless," said Victor.

"Entirely hopeless. And then, partly from his disappointment and partly from seeing so much of suffering among children, he became a sort of city missionary. It was in his character of missionary that he went one day to an examination of the pupils of the girls' school on Randall's Island. There he saw me, and recognized me by my striking likeness to my mother. Indeed he has since told me that I am a counterpart of what my mother was at my age."

"And your face is such a very peculiar and, I may say, unique face, that the likeness could not have been accidental, I suppose," observed Victor.

"That is what he thought. Well, without saying a word to me then of his recognition, he commenced with the slight clew that he had in his hands and pursued investigations that in a few days proved me to be the child of Sebastian and Electra Coroni. Then he came to the Island and took me away, and put me to school at Mount Ascension. There I made the acquaintance of the young lady friend that I am now staying with. Miss Cavendish is my cousin. Last month I graduated from Mount Ascension. And on the first of next month I am going to Beresford Manors, to commence my new life there as my grandfather's housekeeper. And, Victor—I beg your pardon!—Mr. Brent, I hope that you will come and visit us there," concluded Electra, with a smile.

"But how would your grandfather, Dr. Beresford Jones of Beresford Manors, take a visit from a poor adventurer like me?" inquired Victor.

"He will take it very kindly; for he also will ask you to come," said Electra.

Victor bowed and walked on in silence.

Electra spoke again:

"I have told you without reserve how it was that I was so suddenly raised from extreme poverty to wealth, and now—"

She paused and looked at her companion.

"And now you want to know how I came by my fortune?" smilingly inquired Victor.

"Yes, of course I do," answered Electra.

"The explanation is short and simple enough. I became suddenly rich, as some few other poor vagabonds have, by a fortunate stroke of the pick—by a California gold mine," quietly answered Victor.

"Oh!" exclaimed Electra.

And she stopped and put him away from her a step, and stood and stared at him.

Victor laughed. And then they went on, for their companions were at the gates of the University, waiting for them to come along.

They entered the beautiful grounds occupied by the extensive buildings of the University, and where several of the professors, as well as a few of the students who had not yet left for the vacation, were taking their morning walks.

The visitors were soon met by Dr. Jones and Alden Lytton, who came up together to welcome them.

After the usual greetings, Alden introduced his party to several of the professors, who received them with great courtesy, and attended them through the various buildings, pointing out to them the most notable objects of interest, and entertaining them with the history, statistics and anecdotes of the institution.

They were taken into the various libraries, where they saw collected vast numbers of the most valuable books, among which were a few very unique black letter and illuminated volumes of great antiquity.

They were then led into the several halls, where were collected costly astronomical and chemical apparatus.

And finally they visited the museum, filled with cabinets of minerals, shells, woods, fossils, and so forth.

And after an interesting but very fatiguing tour of inspection, that occupied four hours, they were invited to rest in the house of one of the professors, where they were refreshed with a dainty lunch, after which they returned to the village.

And the evening was spent socially in Mrs. Wheatfield's drawing-room.

CHAPTER XX.

A SURPRISE.

In the course of that evening they were surprised by a visit. It was from Mr. Craven Kyte, who came to call on Miss Cavendish.

He was invited into the drawing-room and introduced to the whole party.

Mr. Kyte was in the deepest state of despondency.

He told Miss Emma that a few days previous he had received a letter from Mrs. Grey, saying that she was about to leave Charlottesville for a little while, in order to give up her rooms to Miss Cavendish and her party, and that she did not know exactly where she should go, but that she would write and tell him as soon as she should get settled.

"And since that, Miss Emma, I have not heard one word from her, nor do I know where she is, or how she is, or how to find out," concluded Mr. Kyte, in the most dejected tone.

"How long has it been, Mr. Kyte?" inquired Miss Cavendish.

"Five days," answered the young man, as solemnly as if he had said five years.

"That is but a short time. I do not think you have cause to be anxious yet awhile," said Emma, with a smile.

"But you haven't heard from her yourself even, have you, Miss Emma?" he anxiously inquired.

"Certainly not, else I should have told you at once," replied Miss Cavendish.

"For mercy's sake, you never came all the way from Wendover to Charlottesville to ask that question, did you, Mr. Kyte?" inquired irrepressible Electra, elevating her eye-brows.

131

The lover, who had so unconsciously betrayed himself, blushed violently and stammered forth:

"No—not entirely. The fact is, for more than a year past I have been watching and waiting for an opportunity to change my business from Wendover to Charlottesville. And I came up partly about that also. But as a—a friend of Mrs. Grey, I do feel anxious about her mysterious absence and silence."

"I assure you, Mr. Kyte, that Mrs. Grey is quite capable of taking excellent care of herself," added plain-spoken Laura Lytton.

"Come, Mr. Kyte, cheer up! We are going on a pilgrimage to Monticello to-morrow and you must join our party," said Miss Cavendish, kindly.

But Mr. Kyte excused himself, saying that he could not leave his business long, and must start for Wendover the next morning.

And soon after this he took leave.

The next day was devoted by our party to a pious pilgrimage to the shrine of classic Monticello, once the seat, now the monument of Thomas Jefferson.

The whole party, young and old, gentlemen and ladies, went.

The bishop's widow forgot her housekeeping cares and took a holiday for that day.

And even Mrs. Fanning, who did not care to see the great University, could not miss the opportunity of a pilgrimage to that mecca.

The party was a large one, consisting of five ladies and four gentlemen.

And so it required two capacious carriages and two saddle horses to convey them.

They formed quite a little procession in leaving the village.

In the first carriage rode Mrs. Fanning, Emma Cavendish, Electra and Dr. Jones.

In the second carriage rode Mrs. Wheatfield, Laura Lytton and Mr. Lyle.

Alden Lytton and Victor Hartman rode on horseback, and brought up the rear.

Their way lay through the most sublime and beautiful mountain and valley scenery.

Monticello is built upon a mountain, some three miles south of the village.

Perhaps there is no private dwelling in the whole country occupying a more elevated site, or commanding a more magnificent panorama of landscape, than Monticello.

It is a fine country house of great architectural beauty and strength, built upon a lofty and slightly inclined plain, formed by grading the top of the mountain.

It commands a stupendous prospect, bounded only by the spherical form of the earth. And standing there, with the earth beneath and the heavens all around, one fully realizes that we live upon a great planet rolling in its orbit through immense space.

Our party spent a long summer's day up there in the sunshine, and then, after eating the luncheon they had brought with them, they set out on their return to the village, where they arrived in time for one of Mrs. Wheatfield's delicious early teas.

The remaining days of the week were passed in walking, riding or driving to the most interesting points of the neighborhood.

On Saturday morning they took leave of the bishop's widow and set out for Richmond, *en route* for Wendover and Blue Cliffs.

They reached the city late on the same night, and took up their old quarters at the Henrico House.

They staid over the Sabbath, and went to hear Mr. Lyle preach, morning and evening, to his old congregation.

On Monday morning the whole party resumed their journey, and arrived at Wendover early in the afternoon of the same day.

There the party were destined to divide.

There were carriages from Blue Cliffs waiting by appointment at the railway station to meet Miss Cavendish and her friends; and there was the hack from the Reindeer Hotel for the accommodation of any other travelers who might require it.

Mrs. Fanning, Emma Cavendish, Laura Lytton and Electra, attended by Dr. Jones and Alden Lytton, entered their carriages to go to Blue Cliff Hall.

Mr. Lyle and Victor Hartman took leave of them at their carriage doors, saw the horses start, and then set out to walk together to the bachelor home of Mr. Lyle, where Hartman was to be a guest.

CHAPTER XXI.

AT THE PARSONAGE.

Mr. Lyle lived in a pretty white cottage, covered nearly to the roof with fragrant creeping vines, and standing in the midst of a beautiful flower-garden.

Here he lived his bachelor life quite alone but for the occasional sight of the old negro couple that were waiting on him—Aunt Nancy, who did all his housework, and Uncle Ned, who worked in the garden.

He found the faithful old couple prepared to receive him and his guest.

A tempting repast, combining the attractions of dinner and tea, was ready to be placed upon the table just as soon as the gentlemen should have made their toilets after their long journey.

Mr. Lyle led his guest into a fresh, pretty room, with white muslin curtains at the vine-clad windows and a white dimity spread on the bed, and white flower enameled cottage furniture completing the appointments.

"This is a room for a pretty girl rather than for a grim miner," said Victor Hartman, looking admiringly around the little apartment.

"I call it the 'Chamber of Peace,' and that is why I put you in it," said Mr. Lyle.

After they had washed and dressed they went down together to the cozy little dining-room, where they did such justice to the tea-dinner as made Aunt Nancy's heart crow for joy.

And when that was over they went into the snug little parlor and sat down to talk over their plans.

It was then that Mr. Lyle informed Victor Hartman that he was doing all the work of the parish during Dr. Goodwin's hopeless indisposition, and that he had been doing it for the last twelve months.

"You will succeed him here as rector, I presume?" said Victor.

"I presume so; but I do not like to speak of that," gravely replied Mr. Lyle.

"No, of course you do not. And I really beg your pardon. I should not have spoken myself, only in my girl's interests. You see, I felt a little curious and anxious to know where her future life would be likely to be passed, and I thought it would be a much happier life if passed here, near her dear friend Miss Cavendish, that's all," explained Victor.

"You seem to consider that quite a settled matter," replied Mr. Lyle, a little incoherently, and blushing like a maiden.

"Yes, of course I consider it all quite settled! You, in your earnestness, can not conceal your liking for my girl, and she, in her innocent frankness, does not even try to conceal hers from you. And I heartily approve the match and am ready to dower the bride," said Victor.

"But I have not ventured to speak to her yet," stammered Mr. Lyle.

"Then you may do so just as soon as you please," answered Victor.

"And now about Alden," said Mr. Lyle, by way of changing the conversation.

"Yes, now about Alden. He does not suspect that I am his banker, I hope?"

"No, indeed! I paid him over the munificent sum you intrusted to me for him. He feels—well, I may say painfully grateful, and is confident that he must some time repay you, with interest and compound interest."

"Yes, my boy will certainly repay me, but not in the way he thinks," observed Victor, gravely.

"After a week's visiting with his sister at Blue Cliffs, he will go up to Richmond and select a site for his office and purchase his law library, though I think he will have to go to Philadelphia to do that."

"Yes, I suppose he will," admitted Hartman.

"What are your own plans about yourself, Victor, if I may be allowed to ask?" inquired the minister.

"Well, I haven't any. I came on here to see my boy and girl, and settle them in life as well as I can. I shall stay till I do that anyway. After that I don't know what I shall do. I do not care about going back to California. My business there is in the hands of a capable and trustworthy agent. And somehow I like the old mother State; and now that you lead me to think about it, perhaps I shall spend the rest of my life here; but, as I said before, I don't know."

"By the way, dear Victor, you spoke to me with much simple frankness of my most private personal affairs. May I take the same liberty with you?" inquired Mr. Lyle, very seriously.

"Why, of course you may, if you call it a liberty, which I don't, you know!" answered Victor, with a smile.

"Then, my dear Hartman, how about Miss Electra? I was not so absorbed in my own interests as not to have an eye to yours."

"Ah, Miss Electra! Well, parson, she *was* my little old acquaintance of Rat Alley, when I flourished in that fragrant neighborhood as Galley Vick."

"No!" exclaimed Mr. Lyle, opening his eyes wide with astonishment.

"Yes," quietly answered Victor Hartman. "And it is a wonder that you, who know the family so well, do not know this episode in its history."

"How was I to know, my friend, when no one ever told me? I suppose that few or none but the family know anything about it."

"I suppose you are right," said Victor. "Well, you see, she recognized me, as surely as I did her, at first sight. We had an explanation as we walked out to the University that day."

"But how came the granddaughter of Dr. Beresford Jones ever to have had such a miserable childhood?"

"Well, you see, there was a disobedient daughter, a runaway marriage, a profligate husband, and the consequences — poverty, destitution, early death, and an orphan child left among beggars and thieves! Her grandfather found her at last and took her under his guardianship. That is the whole story in brief."

"Well, well, well!" mused Mr. Lyle, with his head on his breast; then, raising it, he went back to the previous question: "But what about Miss Electra?"

"I have just told you about her," replied Victor.

"Oh, yes, I know! You have told me something about her, but you haven't told me all. Take me into your confidence, Victor."

"What do you mean?" inquired Hartman, in some embarrassment.

"Why, that you and your little old acquaintance seem to be very fond of each other."

Victor laughed in an embarrassed manner, and then said: "Do you know that when we were in Rat Alley, and she was a tiny child and I was a lad, there was a promise of marriage between us?"

"That was funny too! Well, what about it?"

"Nothing. Only, if I dared, I would, some day, remind her of it."

"Do, Victor! Believe me, she will not affect to have forgotten it," said Mr. Lyle, earnestly.

"Ah, but when I think of all I have passed through I dare not ask a beautiful and happy girl to unite her bright life with my blackened one! I dare not," said Hartman, very sadly.

"Nonsense, Victor! You are morbid on that subject. Yours is a nobly redeemed life," said Mr. Lyle, solemnly.

"But—my past!" sighed Victor.

"She had a dark past too poor child! But no more of that. In both your cases

"'Let the dead past bury its dead!
Live—live in the living present,
Heart within and God o'erhead!'

And now it is time to retire, dear Victor. We keep early hours here," said Mr. Lyle, as he reached down the Bible from its shelf, preparatory to commencing evening service.

Then they read the Word together, and offered up their prayers and thanksgivings together, and retired, strengthened.

This week, to which Alden Lytton's holiday visit to Blue Cliffs was limited, was passed by the young people in a succession of innocent entertainments.

First there was a garden-party and dance at Blue Cliff Hall, at which all the young friends and acquaintances of Miss Cavendish assisted, which the Rev. Dr. Jones and the Rev. Mr. Lyle endorsed by their presence, and in which even Victor Hartman forgot, for the time being, his own dark antecedents.

Next Mr. Lyle himself opened his bachelor heart and bachelor home to the young folks by giving them a tea-party, which delighted the hearts of Aunt Nancy and Uncle Ned, who both declared that this looked something *like* life.

But the third and greatest event of the week took place on Friday evening, when Dr. Beresford Jones gave a great house-warming party, on the occasion of his carrying home his granddaughter and sole heiress, Electra Coroni.

Not only all our own young friends, including the reverend clergy and the California miner, but all the neighborhood and all the county were there.

And they kept up the festivities all day and well into the night.

Emma Cavendish and Laura Lytton remained with Electra for a few days only, for Alden Lytton was to leave the neighborhood for Richmond on the Monday morning following the party at Beresford Manors.

And during all this time no word was heard of Mary Grey.

That baleful woman had heard all that had passed at Charlottesville and at Wendover, and her vain and jealous spirit was filled with such mortification and rage that she was now hiding herself and deeply plotting the ruin of those who had been her best friends and benefactors.

CHAPTER XXII.

MORE MANEUVERS OF MRS. GREY.

She, under fair pretense of saintly ends,
And well-placed words of sweetest courtesy
Baited with reason, not unplausible,
Glides into the easy hearts of men,
And draws them into snares.

—MILTON'S *Comus*.

When Mary Grey reached Richmond she went first to a quiet family hotel, where she engaged a room for a few days.

Then she took a carriage and drove to the rectory of old St. John's Church and presented her letter to the rector.

The reverend gentleman received her very kindly and cordially, and glanced over her letter, saying, as he returned it to her:

"But this was not at all necessary, my dear madam. I remember you perfectly, as a regular attendant and communicant of this church, while you were on a visit to the family of the late lamented Governor of this State."

"Yes, sir; but then I was only a visitor at the church, just as I was a guest at the Government House. Now I wish to be a member of the church, as I intend to become a permanent resident of the city," Mary Grey explained, with her charming smile.

The pastor expressed himself highly gratified, and added:

"Your large circle of friends, that you won during your long visit here two or three years ago, will be delighted to hear of this."

Mary Grey bowed gracefully and said:

"The pleasure, she believed, would, like the advantage, be mostly on her own side."

Then she inquired of the rector—with an apology for troubling him with her own humble affairs—whether he could recommend her to any private boarding-house among the members of his own church, where the family were really earnest Christians.

The rector could not think of any suitable place just then, but he begged to have the pleasure of introducing Mrs. Grey to his wife, who, he said, would most likely be able to advise her.

And he rang the bell and sent a message to Mrs. — —, who presently entered the study.

The introduction took place, and the rector's wife received the visitor as cordially as the rector had.

She knew of no boarding-house of the description required by Mrs. Grey, but she promised to inquire among her friends and let that lady know the result.

Soon after this Mrs. Grey took leave.

Many of her former friends were, at this season of the year, out of town, as she felt sure; but some among them would probably be at home.

So, before she returned to her hotel, she made a round of calls, and left her cards at about a dozen different houses.

She then went back to her room at the hotel and spent the remainder of the day in unpacking and reviewing her elegant wardrobe.

There was no sort of necessity for doing this, especially as she intended to remain but a few days at the house; and the operation would only give her the trouble of repacking again to move.

But Mary Grey never read or wrote or sewed or embroidered if she could avoid it, and had nothing on earth else to occupy or amuse her; so her passion for dress had to be gratified with the sight of jewels, shawls and mantles, laces, silks and satins, even though she durst not wear them.

Next day the rector's wife called on her and recommended a very superior boarding-house to her consideration.

It was a private boarding-house, in a fashionable part of the town, kept by two maiden ladies of the most aristocratic family connections and of the highest church principles.

This was exactly the home for Mrs. Grey.

And the rector's wife kindly offered to take her, then and there, in the rectory carriage, to visit "the Misses Crane," the maiden ladies in question.

"The Misses Crane," as they were called, dwelt in a handsomely-furnished, old-fashioned double house, standing in its own grounds, not very far from the Government House.

The Misses Crane were two very tall, very thin and very fair ladies, with pale blue eyes and long, yellow, corkscrew curls each side of their wasted cheeks.

They were dressed very finely in light checked summer silks, and flowing sleeves and surplice waists, with chemisettes and undersleeves of linen cambric and thread lace.

They were very poor for ladies of their birth. They had nothing in the world but their handsome house, furniture and wardrobe.

They depended entirely upon their boarders for their bread; yet their manners were a mixture of loftiness and condescension that had the effect of making their guests believe that they—the guests—were highly honored in being permitted to board at the Misses Cranes'.

But if not highly honored they were certainly much favored, for the Misses Crane kept neat and even elegant rooms, dainty beds and an excellent table.

Presented by the rector's lady, Mrs. Grey was received by the Misses Crane with a lofty politeness which overawed even her false pretensions.

Presently the rector's lady, leaving Mrs. Grey to be entertained by Miss Romania Crane, took the elder Miss Crane aside and explained to her the nature of their business call.

"I think she is just the kind of boarder that will suit you, as your house is just the kind of home needed by her," added the lady.

Miss Crane bowed stiffly and in silence.

"She is, like yourself, of an old aristocratic family, and of very high-church principles; and she has, besides, an ample income, much of which she spends for benevolent purposes," continued Mrs. — —.

Miss Crane bowed and smiled a ghastly smile, revealing her full set of false teeth.

"She is, I should tell you, also entitled to all our sympathy. She has suffered a great disappointment in her affections. She was engaged to be married to the late lamented Governor of the State, when, as you know, he was suddenly struck down with apoplexy, and died a few days before the day appointed for the wedding."

"Oh, indeed!" breathed Miss Crane, in a low, eager voice, losing all her stiffness and turning to glance at the interesting widowed bride elect.

"Yes. And you will find her a most interesting young person—devoted to good works, one of the excellent of the earth. When she was here, two or three years ago—in the same season that she was engaged to our honored and lamented Governor—she was quite famous for her charities."

"Oh, indeed!" again aspirated Miss Crane, glancing at Mrs. Grey.

"I am sure that you will be mutually pleased with each other, and, as she has declared her intention to make Richmond her permanent residence, I should not wonder if she also should make your pleasant house her permanent home," added the lady.

"Much honored, I'm sure," said Miss Crane, with a mixture of hauteur and complacency that was as perplexing as it was amusing.

"And now, if you please, we will rejoin your sister and Mrs. Grey," said the rector's lady, rising and leading the way to the front windows, near which the other two ladies were sitting.

The end of all this was that the Misses Crane engaged to take Mrs. Grey as a permanent boarder, only asking a few days to prepare the first floor front for her occupation.

No arrangement could have pleased Mary Grey better than this, for she wished to remain at the hotel a few days longer to receive the calls of her old friends, who would naturally expect to find her there, as she had given that address on the cards that she had left for them.

So it was finally arranged that Mrs. Grey should remove from the hotel to the Misses Cranes' on the Monday of the next week.

Then the two took leave, and the rector's lady drove the widow back to her hotel and left her there.

The next day Mrs. Grey had the gratification of hearing from the cards she had left at the different houses of her old acquaintances. Several ladies called on her and welcomed her to the city with much warmth.

And on the Saturday of that week she had a surprise.

The Rector of St. John's paid her a morning visit, bringing a letter with the Charlottesville postmark.

"It came this morning, my dear madam. It was inclosed in a letter to me from Mrs. Wheatfield, the esteemed widow of my late lamented friend, Bishop Wheatfield," said the rector, as he placed the letter in her hand.

She thanked the reverend gentleman, and held the letter unopened, wondering how Mrs. Wheatfield could have found out that she was in Richmond.

When the rector had taken his leave, she opened her letter and read:

"CHARLOTTESVILLE, July 15, 18—.

"My dearest Mary:—We have not heard a word from you since you left us.

"All your friends here suffer the deepest anxiety on your account, fearing that you may be ill among strangers.

"Only on Sunday last, when I happened to speak to our minister, after the morning service, I got a slight clew to you; for he told me that you had asked him for a church letter to the Rector of St. John's Parish in Richmond.

"That information gives me the opportunity of writing to you, with some prospect of having my letter reach you, for I can inclose it to the Rector of St. John's, who will probably by this time know your address.

"And now, having explained how it is that I am enabled to write to you, I must tell you the news.

"The great nuisance of the Commencement is abated. It is all over; the students, the visitors and the vagrants have nearly all gone, and the town is empty and—peaceful.

"One set of visitors I lamented to lose. They went on Saturday.

"I mean, of course, your friends from Blue Cliffs. They were all charming.

"I was very much interested in Miss Cavendish.

"And now, my dear child, although I am no gossip and no meddler, as you are well aware, I really must tell you what I would not tell to any other living being, and which I tell you only because I know you to be perfectly discreet, and also deeply interested in the parties of whom I shall take the liberty of writing.

"There are three marriages in prospect, my dear. I see it quite plainly. Our young people are the frankest and most innocent of human beings. They have no disguises.

"Who are to be married? you ask me.

"I will tell you who, I *think*, will be married.

"First, Mr. Alden Lytton and Miss Emma Cavendish.

"Not a prudent marriage for her, because she is a minor, with an immense fortune. And he is a young lawyer, with not a dollar of his own and his way yet to make in the world.

"But what can we do about it?

"With one guardian in her dotage and the other at the antipodes Miss Cavendish is practically, if not legally, her own mistress.

"The only comfort is that the young man in question is rich in *everything else*, if not in money.

"Well, the second prospective marriage pleases me better. The Rev. Mr. Lyle, a worthy young clergyman, is devoted to Miss Laura Lytton.

"The third approaching nuptials interest me least of all, in any manner. A dark, brigandish-looking Californian, of almost fabulous wealth, who is the friend and guest of Mr. Lyle, has evidently fallen in love at first sight with pretty little sparkling Electra Coroni.

"They have all gone down to Wendover together, and the Lyttons are to make a long visit at Blue Cliffs.

"I must not forget to tell you that worthy young man, Mr. Kyte, has been here inquiring after you with much anxiety. He went back to Wendover a day or two before our young people left.

"Now, my dearest Mary, let me hear that you are well, and believe me ever your devoted friend,

"MARIA WHEATFIELD."

Chapter XXIII.

A DIABOLICAL PLOT.

Between the acting of a dreadful thing
And the first motion, all the interim is
Like a phantasma, or a hideous dream;
The genius and the mortal instruments
Are then in council; and the state of man,
Like to a little kingdom, suffers then
The nature of an insurrection.

—SHAKESPEARE'S *Julius Cæsar.*

No language can adequately describe the mortification and rage that filled the bosom of Mary Grey as she read the foregoing letter.

Two of her once ardent worshipers—handsome Alden Lytton and eloquent Stephen Lyle—had forsaken her shrine and were offering up their devotion to other divinities.

They had wounded her vanity to the very quick.

And to wound Mary Grey's vanity was to incur Mary Grey's deadly hatred.

She was always a very dangerous woman, and under such an exasperation she could become a very desperate enemy.

She had felt so sure that no woman, however young and lovely, could ever become her rival, or even her successor, in any man's affections. So sure, also, that no man, however wise and strong, could ever resist her fascinations or escape from her thraldom.

And now that charming illusion was rudely dispelled! She saw herself even contemptuously abandoned by her subjects, who transferred their allegiance to a couple of "bread-and-butter schoolgirls," as she sneeringly designated Emma Cavendish and Laura Lytton.

She was consumed with jealousy—not the jealousy born of love, which is like the thorn of the rose, a defence of the rose—but the jealousy born of self-love, which is like the thorn of the thorn-apple, a deadly poison.

She sat on one of her trunks, with her elbows on her knees and her clutched fists supporting her chin. Her lips were drawn back from her clinched teeth and her black eyes gleamed like fire from the deathly whiteness of her face.

And so she sat and brooded and brooded over her mortification, and studied and studied how she might pull down ruin upon the heads of those hated young people who were loving each other and enjoying life at the cost of her humiliation.

And of course the foul fiend very soon entered into her counsels and assisted her.

"I have one devoted slave—one willing instrument left yet," she muttered to herself: "he would pay any price—yes, the price of his soul—for my love! He shall pay *my* price down! He shall be the means of drawing destruction upon all their heads! Yes, Miss Cavendish, marry Alden Lytton, if you *will*, and afterward look honest men and women in the face if you *can*! Yes, Stephen Lyle, become the husband of Laura Lytton, and then hold up your head in the pulpit—if you dare! Ah, if my plot succeed! Ah, if my plot succeed, how terribly will I be avenged! And it *shall* succeed!" she hissed through her grinding teeth, with a grim hatred distorting her white features and transforming her beautiful face for an instant into demoniac hideousness.

She started up and commenced traversing the floor, as a furious tigress her den.

When she had raged herself into something like composure she opened her writing-case and wrote the following letter:

"RICHMOND, VA., Aug. —, 18—.

"TO CRAVEN KYTE, ESQ.

"*Dear Friend*:—My wanderings have come to a temporary end here in this city, where I expect to remain for some weeks, even if I do not conclude to make it my permanent residence.

"Shall I trouble you to do me a favor? Some time ago I left in the hands of the jeweler at Wendover a little pearl brooch, which I forgot to call for when I left, and have neglected to send for ever since.

"The brooch in itself is of small intrinsic value; but as it is an old family relic I should like to recover it. Will you, therefore, please go to the jeweler's and get it and send it to me in a registered letter by mail? and I shall be very much indebted to you. And if you should happen to come to this city during my stay here I hope you will call to see me; for I should be very glad to see any old friend from Wendover.

"Yours truly,

M. GREY."

She immediately sealed this letter, rang for a waiter, and dispatched it to the post-office.

This letter had been written for but one purpose—to bring Craven Kyte immediately to Richmond, without seeming especially to invite him to come.

She always wrote her letters with an eye to the remote contingency of their being produced in court or read in public.

This letter to Craven Kyte was a sample of her non-committal style— it compromised no one.

When she had sent it off she began to pack up her effects, in preparation for their removal, on Monday morning, to the Misses Cranes'.

Even after that work was done she could not be still. Like an uneasy beast of prey, she must needs move to and fro.

So she put on her bonnet, called a carriage and drove out to the rectory to spend the evening.

But though she was received in the most friendly manner she could not enjoy the visit. She was absent and distracted during the whole evening.

She returned late to a restless bed. And then she got up and took laudanum to put her to sleep. And this was not the first time she had had to resort to the same dangerous narcotic.

No more rest for Mary Grey!

Remorse sometimes begins *before* the commission of a contemplated and determined crime; repentance never. That is one difference between the two.

On Sunday morning, to keep herself actively employed, as well as to win "golden opinions," Mrs. Grey dressed herself plainly, but very becomingly, and went early to the Sunday-school at old St. John's, to offer herself as a teacher.

She was soon appointed to the temporary charge of a class of little girls, whose regular teacher was then absent on a summer tour of the watering places.

Afterward she attended both morning and afternoon services, and went to a missionary meeting in the evening.

Still, after all the fatigues of the day, she was unable to sleep at night, and again she had recourse to the deadly drug.

On Monday morning she paid her week's bill at the hotel and removed to the Misses Cranes'.

She was received with lofty politeness by the two maiden ladies; and she was put in immediate possession of her apartment—a spacious chamber, with a balcony overhanging the front flower-garden.

She had scarcely finished unpacking her effects and transferring them from her trunks to the bureaus and wardrobes of the chamber, before a card was brought to her by the neat parlor-maid of the establishment.

The card bore the name of Mr. Craven Kyte.

"Where is the gentleman?" inquired Mrs. Grey.

"In the drawing-room, madam," answered the maid.

"Ask him to be so kind as to wait. I will be down directly," said Mrs. Grey.

The girl left the room to take her message, and Mrs. Grey began to change her dress, smiling strangely to herself as she did so.

She gave a last finishing touch to the curls of her glossy black hair, and a last lingering look at the mirror, and then she went down-stairs.

There, alone in the drawing-room, stood the one devoted lover and slave that she had left in the whole world.

He came down the room to meet her.

"You here! Oh, I'm so delighted to see you!" she said, in a low tone, full of feeling, as she went toward him, holding out both her hands.

He trembled from head to foot and turned pale and red by turns as he took them.

"I am so happy—You are so good to say so! I was almost afraid—I thought you might consider it a liberty—my coming," faltered the poor fellow, in sore confusion.

"A liberty? How could you possibly imagine I would consider your coming here a liberty on your part? Why, dearest friend, I consider it a favor from you, a pleasure for me! Why should you think otherwise?" inquired Mary Grey, with her most alluring smile.

"Oh, thanks—thanks! But it was your letter!"

"My letter? Sit down, Craven, dear, and compose yourself. Here, sit here," she said, seating herself on the sofa and signing for him to take the place by her side.

He dropped, trembling, flushing and paling, into the indicated seat.

"Now tell me what there was in my harmless letter to disturb you," she murmured, passing her soft fingers over his forehead and running them through the dark curls of his hair.

"Nothing that was *meant* to disturb me, I know. It was all kindness. You could not write to me, or to any one, otherwise than kindly," faltered the lover.

"Well, then?" inquired Mary Grey, in a pretty, reproachful tone.

"But I felt it was cold—cold!" sighed the young man.

"Why, you dearest of dears, one must be discreet in writing letters! Suppose my letter had expressed all my feelings toward you, and then had fallen into the hands of any one else? Such mistakes are made in the mails sometimes. How would you have liked it?" she inquired, patting his cheeks.

"I should have been wild. But it would only have been at the loss of your letter. As for me, Heaven knows, I should not mind if all the world knew how much I adore you. On the contrary, I should glory in it," added the lover.

"But a lady feels differently. She only lets her *lover* know how well she loves him; and not always does she even let him know," softly murmured the beautiful temptress, as she lightly caressed his raven curls. "And now tell me the news, dear Craven. How are all our friends at Blue Cliffs?" she archly inquired.

"I only want to tell you how much I adore you," whispered the lover, who was beginning to recover his composure.

"That would be a vain repetition, darling, especially as I know it all quite well," murmured Mary Grey, with a smile, and still passing her hand with mesmeric gentleness over his hair.

"Aye; but when will you make me completely happy?" sighed the poor fellow.

"Whew!" smiled Mary Grey, with a little bird-like whistle. "How fast we are getting on, to be sure! Why, a few minutes ago we were afraid that we were taking a liberty in coming here to call on our lady-love at all! And now we are pressing her to name the day! See here, you impatient boy, answer me this: When did I ever promise to 'make you happy' *at all*?" she inquired, in a bantering tone.

"But you gave me hopes—oh, do not say that you never gave me hopes!" he pleaded, turning red and pale and trembling from head to foot as before.

"Well, I don't say it; for I know I promised if ever I should marry living man I should marry you. I repeat that promise now, dear Craven," she added, gravely and tenderly.

"Ah, Heaven bless you for those blessed words! But when—*when* will you make me happy? Oh, if I possess your love, when—*when* shall I possess your hand?" he pleaded.

And then, as if suddenly ashamed of his own vehemence, he stopped in confusion.

"You have won my love, you petulant boy!" she answered, archly. Then, dropping her voice to its tenderest music, she murmured: "What would you do to win my hand?"

"Anything—anything under the sun!" he answered, wildly, and forgetting all his embarrassment. "Whatever man has done to win woman would I do to win you—more than ever man did to win woman would I do to win you! I would renounce my friends, betray my country, abjure my faith, *lose my soul* for you!"

"Words, words, words! You talk recklessly! You know you would not do the least one of these dreadful deeds for me," answered Mary Grey, laying her hand on his lips.

"Try me!"

Chapter XXIV.

THE PRICE OF A SOUL.

I love you, love you; for your love would lose
State, station, heaven, mankind's, my own esteem.

—Byron.

He spoke these two words with such a desperate look, in such a desperate tone, that Mary Grey was half frightened; for she saw that he was in that fatal mood in which men have been driven to crime or death for the love of woman.

This was the mood to which she wished to bring him, and in which she wished to keep him until he should have done his work; and yet it half frightened her now.

"Hush—hush!" she murmured. "Be quiet! There are people in the next room. They may hear you. And I am sure they should do so they would take you for a lunatic."

"But—do you believe me? Do you believe that I would defy the universe in your service? Do you believe me? If not, try me!" he aspirated, vehemently.

"I *do* believe you. And some day I *will* try you. You have won my love; but he who wins my hand must first prove his love for me in a way that will leave no doubt upon the fact."

"Then I am safe, for I am sure to prove it," he said, with a sigh of intense relief.

She looked at him again, and knew that he spoke as he felt. Yes, for her sake he would "march to death as to a festival."

"Now, then, will you be good and quiet and tell me news of my old neighbors at Wendover and Blue Cliffs?" she archly inquired.

"I do not think I can. I wish to sit here and look at you and think only of you. It would be a painful wrench to tear away my thoughts from you and employ them upon anything else. Let me sit here in my heaven!" he pleaded.

"Yes, love; but remember I am very anxious to know something about my dear friends, whom I have not heard from for a month. Can not you gratify me?" coaxed Mary Grey.

"I can not fix my mind upon them long enough to remember anything. You absorb it all," he answered, dreamily gazing upon her.

"But if I ask you questions surely you can answer them," said Mary Grey, who, though very anxious for information later than that afforded by Mrs. Wheatfield's letter, was not ill-pleased at the devotion which baffled her curiosity.

"Yes, I will answer any question you ask. That will not be so much of a wrench," he said.

"Then how is my dear friend, Emma Cavendish?" inquired the traitress.

"Well and happy, at Blue Cliffs," answered the lover.

"Is it true, as I hear, that she is to marry—" Mary Grey hesitated for a moment before her choking voice could pronounce his name—"Mr. Alden Lytton?"

"Yes, I believe so. Everybody says so."

"When?"

"As soon as he gets established in his profession, I suppose."

"Tell me about him."

"Well, he is coming here on the first of the month to find an office and fit it up. And then he is going on to Philadelphia to select books for a law library."

"Ah, he is coming here and he is going on to Philadelphia. Yes, yes, yes, yes! That will do," murmured Mary Grey, to herself.

"What did you say?" inquired Craven Kyte.

"I said that it was a good plan; but it will take money," answered Mrs. Grey.

"Yes, that it will. And he has got it. That mysterious guardian of his has sent him ten thousand dollars to begin with."

"A round sum! When did you say he was coming here?"

"On the first of next month; or, perhaps, before the end of this month."

"Good! Very good!"

"Good for what?" innocently inquired Craven Kyte.

"Good for his professional prospects, of course! The sooner he begins the better, isn't it?"

"Oh, yes; certainly!"

"And when does he go to Philadelphia?"

"Just as soon as he has selected his law office and set painters and glaziers and paper-hangers and upholsterers and such to fit it up. For no expense is to be spared, and the young lawyer is to set up in style. For such is the wish of his guardian."

"You know this?"

"Yes, I know it. One knows everything that anybody else knows in a small village like Wendover."

"You do not know when Mr. Lytton and Miss Cavendish are to be married?"

"No, because I do not think they know themselves. But the people say it will be as soon as the young gentleman gets settled in his practice."

"Good again! The delay is favorable," muttered Mary Grey to herself.

"What did you say?" again inquired the ingenuous young man.

"I say the delay is wise, of course."

"Oh, yes; certainly!" assented Mr. Kyte.

"And now tell me about the others," said Mrs. Grey.

But her lover took her hand and gazed into her face, murmuring:

"Oh, my love, my life, let me sit here and hold your thrilling little hand and gaze into your beautiful eyes, and think only of you for a moment!"

She put her hand around his head and drew it toward her and pressed a kiss upon his forehead, and then said:

"There! Now you will go on for me, will you not?"

"I would die for you!" he earnestly exclaimed.

"I would rather you would live for me, you mad boy!" she answered, smiling archly.

"I will do anything for you."

"Then answer my questions. Is it also true that Mr. Lyle and Miss Lytton are to be married?"

"Oh, yes! That is certain. Their engagement is announced. There is no secret about that."

"When are they to be married?"

"Well, there is a slight obstacle to their immediate union."

"What is that?"

"An old school-girl compact between Miss Cavendish and Miss Lytton, in which they promised each other that they would both be married on the same day or never at all."

"A very silly, girlish compact."

"Very."

"Why do they not break it by mutual consent?"

"Because mutual consent can not be had. Miss Cavendish indeed offers to release Miss Lytton from her promise; but Miss Lytton refuses to be released. And although her clerical lover presses her to name an earlier day, she will name no other than the day upon which Miss Cavendish also weds, be that day sooner or later."

"So it is settled that they will be married upon the same day?"

"Quite settled."

"How do you know?"

"Everything is known in a little country town like Wendover, as I said before."

"They will be married the same day. Better and better. If I had arranged it all myself it could not be better for my plans," muttered Mary Grey to herself.

"What did you say?" inquired Craven Kyte.

"I say I think, upon the whole, the arrangement is a good one."

"Oh, yes; certainly!" admitted the young man.

"Where are you stopping, Craven?" softly inquired Mrs. Grey.

"Oh, at the same hotel from which you dated your letter! I thought you were there, and so I went directly there from the cars. When I inquired for you—I hope you will pardon my indiscretion in inquiring for you," he said, breaking off from his discourse.

"Oh, yes, I will pardon it! But it was a very great indiscretion, you thoughtless boy, for a handsome youth like you to be inquiring for a young widow like me at a public hotel. Now go on with what you were talking about."

"Well, when I inquired for you they told me you had left this very morning, and they gave me your present address."

"That was the way in which you found me?"

"That was the way I found you. But, before starting to come here, I engaged my room at that hotel; for, after it had been blessed by your dear presence, it had quite a home-like feeling to me," said the lover, fervently.

"How long do you stay in the city, Craven, dear?" sweetly inquired the siren.

His face clouded over.

"I must return to-morrow," he said. "It was the only condition upon which our principal would consent to my leaving yesterday. He is going North to purchase his fall and winter goods, you see, and wants me to be there."

"How long will he be absent?"

"He says only four days, at the longest."

"And when does he go?"

"By the next train following my return."

"Then he will be back again at his post by Saturday evening?"

"Yes; in fact, he intends to be back by the end of the week, and that is the very reason why he is so anxious to get away to-morrow night."

"Craven, dear, when your senior partner gets back do you think you will be able to return here for a few days?"

"Do you really wish me to come back so soon?" exclaimed the lover, his face flushing all over with pleasure.

"Yes; but don't cry out so loud—that's a dear! I repeat, there are people in the next room. But you have not yet answered my question."

"Oh, yes, I can return here as soon as my partner gets back! He promised that I should take a week's holiday then. So, if he gets back on Saturday evening, expect to see me here on Sunday morning, in time to wait on you to church."

"Stop; not so fast, my dear! You can take your week's holiday at any time, I suppose?"

"At any time this month or next."

"Very well. Now, dear boy, I want you to promise me two or three things."

"I will promise you anything in the world you wish."

"Then listen. Every time I write to you I will inclose within my letter another letter, sealed and directed to me, which you must stamp and post at the Wendover post-office. Will you do that for me?"

While she spoke the young man gazed at her in unqualified amazement.

"Will you do that for me?" she repeated.

"I solemnly promise to do that for you, although I am all in the dark as to what you would be at," earnestly answered Craven Kyte.

"I thank you, dearest dear," cooed the siren, caressing him tenderly.

"I would do anything in the world for you," he answered fervently. "I would die for you or live for you!"

"Well, secondly, I want you, when you go back, to keep an eye on Mr. Alden Lytton. Find out, if possible, the day that he comes to this city. And precede him here yourself by one train. Or, if that is not possible, if you can not find out beforehand the day that he is to come, at least you can certainly know when he actually does start, for every passenger from Wendover is noticed. And then follow him by the next train, and come directly from the depot to me, before going to a hotel or showing yourself at any other place. Will you do that for me?"

"I promise, on my sacred word and honor, that I will, although I have not the slightest idea why you wish me to do this," said Craven.

"You are a true knight, worthy of any lady's love! Well, thirdly, and lastly, as the preachers say, I wish you to promise me never to divulge to a human being anything that has been said between us during this interview."

"I not only promise, but I solemnly vow, in the sight of Heaven and all the holy angels, sacredly to observe the silence you require of me, although I feel more and more deeply mystified by all this."

"You must trust in me, my dear, blindly trust in me for the present, and in time you shall know why I require these things of you," she said, very sweetly.

"I trust in you blindly, utterly, eternally!" answered the lover.

"And now, do you know what your reward shall be?"

"Your smile of approval will be my all-sufficient reward!" exclaimed the young man, earnestly.

"Ah, but you shall hear! When you have done these little favors for me, and *one more*, which I will tell you about when you come back from Wendover, then—" she said, pausing and looking at him with a bewildering smile.

"Then? Yes! Then?" eagerly aspirated the young man, gazing at her in rapt admiration and expectancy.

"Then I will give you my hand in marriage. I solemnly promise it."

"Oh, you angel—you angel! You have made me so happy!" fervently breathed the infatuated lover, as he drew her, unresisting, and pressed her to his heart.

At this point there was heard the sound of light footsteps approaching.

And the moment after, several of the lady boarders opened the door and entered the room.

Craven Kyte, always shy of strangers, arose to take leave.

As he did so, he seemed suddenly to recollect something.

He put his hand in his breast-pocket and drew forth a little box, which he handed to Mrs. Grey, saying:

"It is your brooch that you requested me to get from the jeweler."

And then, with a bow, he left her.

Mary Grey went back to her room.

"I shall succeed in ruining them all now!" she said, her dark eyes on fire with anticipated triumph.

CHAPTER XXV.

A VERY DESPERATE GAME.

I have set my life upon a cast,
And I will stand the hazard of the die.

—SHAKESPEARE.

Craven Kyte, the infatuated and doomed instrument and victim of a cruel and remorseless woman, returned to Wendover and resumed his place in Bastiennello's establishment, where he culpably neglected his business, and lived only on the thought of receiving her daily letters and of soon returning to Richmond to be blessed by her promised hand in marriage.

Every morning he was the first man at the post-office, waiting eagerly, impatiently, for the arrival and opening of the mail.

And he was never disappointed of receiving her letter, and—never satisfied with its contents.

Every letter was in itself something of a mortification to him, containing no expression of confidence or affection, no word by which any one might suspect that the correspondent was writing to one she loved and trusted, much less to her betrothed husband.

Every letter began and ended in the most polite and formal manner; never alluded to the matrimonial intentions between the correspondents, but treated only of church services, Sunday-schools, sewing circles and missionary matters, until the young man, famishing for a word of affection, with pardonable selfishness, sighed forth:

"She is a saint; but oh, I wish she was a little less devoted to the heathen, and all that, and a little more affectionate to me!"

But the instant afterward he blamed himself for egotism, and consoled himself by saying:

"She always told me that, however much she loved, she would never write love-letters, as they might possibly fall into the hands of irreverent and scoffing people who would make a mockery of the writer. It is a far-fetched idea; but still it is *her* idea and I must submit. It will be all right when I go to Richmond and claim her darling hand."

And the thought of this would fill him with such ecstasy that he would long to tell some one, his partner especially, that he was the happiest man on earth, for he was to be married in a week to the loveliest woman in the world. But he was bound by his promise to keep his engagement, as well as all other of his relations with the beautiful widow, a profound secret. And though the poor fellow *was* a fool, he was an *honorable* fool, and held his pledged word sacred.

Every letter that came to him also contained another letter, to which it never referred by written word. This inclosed letter was sealed in an envelope bearing the initial "L" embossed upon its flap. And it was directed to "Mrs. Mary Grey, Old Crane Manor House, Richmond."

Craven Kyte would gaze at this mysterious letter in the utmost confusion and obscurity of mind.

"Now, why in the world does she write a letter and direct it to *herself* and send it to me to post privately, by night, at the Wendover post-office? And why did she give me only verbal instructions about it? And why does she avoid even alluding to it in her letter to me? Why is the envelope stamped with the letter L? And why, oh, why does the handwriting so closely resemble that of Mr. Lytton?" he inquired of himself, as his eyes devoured the superscription of the letter. "I can not tell," he sighed. "It is too deep for my fathoming. I give it up. I must blindly do her bidding, trusting to her implicitly, as I do, and as I will."

Then, following her verbal instructions, given him in Richmond, in regard to these mysterious letters, he put it away until dark, and then stole out and dropped it secretly into the night-box at the post-office.

Five days passed, in which he received and re-mailed three of these inexplicable documents.

Then, on Saturday morning, Bastiennello, the head of his firm, returned to Wendover and resumed the control of his business.

On the evening of the same day a van arrived from Blue Cliff Hall, bringing the heavy baggage of Mr. Alden Lytton, to be deposited at the railway station and left until Monday morning, when the owner intended to start for Richmond by the earliest train.

When Craven Kyte heard this he went straight to his principal and claimed his promised leave of absence.

"Why, Kyte, you are in a tremendous hurry! Here I have not been back twelve hours and you want to be off," said Bastiennello, with a shrug of his shoulders.

"It is a case of necessity, sir, believe me," pleaded Craven Kyte.

"And this is Saturday night, the busiest time in the whole week," complained Bastiennello.

"Well, sir, you will not keep open after twelve, will you?"

"Certainly not after eleven."

"Nor will you need my services after that hour?"

"Of course not."

"Then that will enable me to serve here as usual until the hour of closing, and then give me time to catch the midnight train to Richmond."

"Oh, well, if you can do that it will be all right, and I can have no objection to your going to-night," said Bastiennello.

And so the affair was concluded.

The great village bazaar closed at eleven that night.

As soon as he had put up the last shutter, Craven Kyte rushed off to his humble lodgings, stuffed a carpet-bag full of needed clothing and hurried to the railway station to catch the train.

It came thundering along in due time, and caught up the waiting victim and whirled him along on his road to ruin, as far as Richmond, where it dropped him.

It was nearly eleven o'clock in the morning, and all the church bells were ringing, when the train ran in to the station.

Craven Kyte, carpet-bag in hand, rushed for the gentlemen's dressing-room nearest the station, hastily washed his face, combed his hair, brushed his clothes, put on a clean collar and bosom-piece, and fresh gloves, and hurried off to old St. John's Church, which he thought the most likely place on that Sunday forenoon to meet Mary Grey.

The service was more than half over when he reached the church, but he slipped in and seated himself quietly on one of the back seats near the door and looked all over the heads of the seated congregation to see if he could discover his beloved in the crowd.

Yes, there she was, in a front pew of the middle aisle, immediately under the pulpit.

To be sure he could only see the back of her head and shoulders, but he felt that he could not be mistaken.

And from that moment he paid but little attention to the service.

Do not mistake the poor soul. He was not impious. He had been religiously brought up in the family of the late Governor Cavendish. He was accustomed to be devout during divine worship. And on this occasion he wrestled with Satan—that is, with himself—and tried to fix his mind in succession on anthems, psalms, collects and sermon. All to little purpose. His mind went with his eyes toward Mary Grey.

And even when he closed those offending orbs he still found her image in his mind.

At length the sermon was finished and the benediction pronounced.

The congregation began to move out.

Craven Kyte went out among the first, and placed himself just outside the gate to wait until his adored should pass by.

In a continued stream the congregation poured forth out of the church until nearly all had passed out, but still he did not see Mary Grey.

In truth, that popularity-seeking beauty was lingering to bestow her sweet smile and honeyed words upon "all and sundry" who would give her the opportunity.

At length, among the very last to issue from the church, was Mrs. Grey.

She came out chatting demurely with a group of her friends.

Craven Kyte made a single step toward her, with the intention of speaking; but seeing that she did not notice him, and feeling abashed by the presence of strangers about her, he withdrew again and contented himself with following at a short distance until he saw her separate herself from the group and turn down a by-street.

Then he quickened his footsteps, turned down the same street and joined her.

At the same instant she looked back upon him with a smile, saying:

"You clever boy, how good and wise of you to refrain from speaking to me before so many strangers! Now what is the news?"

"The news is—Oh, my dear, dearest, dearest Mary! I am so delighted to meet you!" he exclaimed, breaking suddenly off from his intended communications.

"So am I to see you, darling. But that is no news. Come, this is a quiet street, and leads out of the city. Let us walk on, and as we walk you can tell me all the news," she said, smilingly, resting her delicate hand on his arm.

"I can tell you nothing—nothing yet, but that I love you—I love you!" he fervently breathed, as he drew her arm within his own and pressed her hand to his bosom.

"And I love you," she murmured, in the lowest, sweetest music. And then, after a moment's pause, she added, gayly: "And now tell me what has brought you here so suddenly."

"Did I not promise you that I would be in Richmond this Sunday morning, in time to attend you to church?"

"Yes, you did, but—"

"Well, I could not get in so early as I intended, because I came on by the train that leaves Wendover at midnight. So I did not reach the city until nearly noon to-day. However, if I was not in time to attend you *to* church, I was in time to attend you *from* church. So I kept my promise tolerably well."

"Yes; but, my dear friend, I particularly requested that you would wait at Wendover and watch certain events, and not come to Richmond until something had happened or was about to happen."

"Well then?"

"You gave me your word that you would do as I directed you."

"Yes, certainly I did."

"Then, seeing you here, I am to presume that all the conditions of your engagement have been fulfilled."

"Yes, they have, dear lady mine."

"First, then, as you were not to come here until Mr. Alden Lytton was about to start or had started for this place, why, I am to presume, by seeing you here, that Mr. Lytton is either present in the city or on his way here."

"Mr. Lytton will leave Wendover for Richmond by the earliest train to-morrow. He will be here to-morrow evening," said Craven Kyte, gravely.

"You are absolutely sure of this?" inquired Mrs. Grey.

"As sure of it as any one can be of any future event. His heavy baggage came over from Blue Cliff Hall yesterday evening, and was left at the station to be ready for transportation on Monday morning, when Mr. Lytton intended to take the earliest train for this city."

"Then there can be no mistake," said Mary Grey.

"None whatever, I think."

"You say you have fulfilled all the conditions of our engagement?"

"Yes, dearest, I have indeed."

"How about those letters I inclosed to you to be re-mailed?"

"I received them all, and re-mailed them all. Did you get them? You never acknowledged the receipt of one of them, however," said Craven Kyte, thoughtfully.

"I got them all safe. There was no use in acknowledging them by letter, as I expected to see you so soon, and could acknowledge them so much better by word of mouth. But that is not exactly what I meant by my question, darling. Of course I knew without being told that you had re-mailed all those letters, as I had received them all."

"Then what was it you wished me to tell you, dearest Mary? Ask me plainly. I will tell you anything in the world that I know."

"Only this: Did you post those letters with great secrecy, taking extreme care that no one saw you do it?"

"My dearest, I took such care that I waited until the dead of night, when no one was abroad in the village, and I stole forth then, and, all unseen, dropped the letters into the night box."

"You darling! How good you are! What shall I ever do to repay you?" exclaimed the traitress, with well-acted enthusiasm.

"Only love me—only love me! That will richly repay me for all. Ah, only love me! Only love me truly and I will die for you if necessary!" fervently breathed the poor doomed young man, fondly gazing upon her, who, to gain her own diabolical end, was almost putting his neck into a halter.

"You foolish darling! Why, you would break my heart by dying! You can only make me happy by living for me," she said, with a smile.

"I would live for you, die for you, suffer for you, sin for you—do anything for you, bear anything for you, be anything for you!" he burst forth, in a fervor of devotion.

"There, there, dearest, I know you would! I know it all! But now tell me: Have you kept our engagement a profound secret from every human being, as I requested you to do?"

"Yes, yes, a profound secret from every human being, on my sacred word and honor! Although it was hard to do that. For, as I walked up and down the streets of Wendover, feeling so happy—so happy that I am sure I must have looked perfectly wild, as the people stared at me so suspiciously—I could scarcely help embracing all my friends and saying to them, 'Congratulate me, for I am engaged to the loveliest woman in the world, and I am the happiest man on earth!' But I kept the secret."

"You mad boy! You love too fast to love long, I doubt! After a month or two of married life you will grow tired of me, I fear," said Mary Grey, with mock gravity.

"Tired of you! Tired of heaven! Oh, no, no, no!" he burst forth, ardently.

CHAPTER XXVI.

THE HAUNTED COTTAGE.

She suddenly brought him down to the earth with a homely remark.

"I am tired of walking. And here is a vacant house placarded 'To Let,' with a nice long porch in front. Come, let [us] go in and sit down on one of the benches and rest."

And she drew him toward the little gate that led into the yard in front of the house.

It was a rustic two-story frame cottage, with a long porch in front, all overgrown with honeysuckles, clematis, woodbine and wild roses.

They went in together and sat down on the porch, under the shadow of the blooming and fragrant vines.

Then she turned and looked at him attentively for the first time since they met at the church.

"You look tired," she said, with alluring tenderness. "You look more exhausted than I feel. And that is saying a great deal, for I am quite out of breath."

"I am grieved that you feel so, dearest! It was selfish and thoughtless in me to keep you walking so long," said Craven, compunctiously.

"Oh, it is nothing! But about yourself. You really look quite prostrated."

"Do I, dearest? I am not conscious of fatigue. Though indeed I should never be conscious of that by your dear side."

"Now tell the truth," she said, again bringing him down from his flights. "Have you had your breakfast this morning?"

"Breakfast? I—don't remember," he said, with a perplexed air.

172

"Come to your senses and answer me directly. What have you taken this morning?" she demanded, with a pretty air of authority.

"I—Let me see. I believe I bought a package of lemon-drops from a boy that was selling them in the cars. I—I believe I have got some of them left yet," he said, hesitating, and drawing from his pocket one of those little white packets of candy so commonly sold on the train.

Mary Grey burst into a peal of soft, silvery laughter as she took them, and said:

"An ounce of lemon-drops and nothing else for breakfast! Oh, Cupid, God of Love, and Hebe, Goddess of Health, look here, and settle it between you!"

"But I do not feel hungry. It is food enough for me to sit here and feast upon the sight of your face, your beautiful face!"

"You frenzied boy! I see that I must take care of you. Come, now that we have recovered our breath, we will go on a little further to a nice, quiet, suburban inn, kept by an old maid. I have never been there myself, but I have seen it in driving by with the rector's family. It is such a nice place that the school children go there to have picnic parties in the grounds. We will go and engage a parlor, and have a quiet little breakfast or dinner, whichever you may please, for it shall combine the luxuries of both. Now will you go?" said Mary Grey, rising from her shady seat.

"Of course, if you wish me to do so; but indeed I do not need anything."

"But I do; for I breakfasted at seven o'clock this morning, before going to the Sunday-school. It is now one o'clock. I have been fasting six hours, and as I intend to spend the most of the day with you, I shall miss our luncheon at home; for, you see, we are deadly fashionable at the Misses Cranes'. We lunch at two and dine at six. So come along."

Craven Kyte arose and gave her his arm, and they walked on together until they reached the little cottage, half farmhouse, half hotel, that was so well-kept by the nice old maiden hostess.

The good woman looked rather surprised to see Sunday visitors walk into her house.

But Mary Grey, prayer-book ostentatiously in hand, took her aside, out of the hearing of Craven Kyte, and explained:

"I and my brother walked in from the country to attend church this morning. We have a carriage and might have ridden, only we do not think it is right to make the horses work on Sunday, do you?"

"No, miss, I candidly don't; and that's a fact," replied the good creature.

"Mrs.," amended Mary Grey, with a smile.

"'Mrs.' of course! I beg your pardon, ma'am! But you looked so young, and I may say childish, and I didn't notice the widow's cap before," apologized the hostess.

"Well, as we had no friends in the town—no one with whom we could stop to dinner—I and my brother set out to walk home again. He is an invalid, and is quite exhausted with fasting and fatigue. So perhaps, under the circumstances, you would not mind letting us have a parlor to rest in and a little dinner."

"Of course not, ma'am; for under such circumstances it is clearly my duty to entertain you," answered the good soul, who, under no possible circumstances, would have been false to her ideas of right.

"You are very kind. I thank you very much," said Mary Grey, sweetly.

"Here is a room at your and your brother's disposal, ma'am. No one will intrude upon you here," said the hostess, opening a door that led into a neat back parlor, whose windows overlooked the garden and orchard attached to the house.

"Come," said Mary Grey, beckoning to her companion.

"Dear me! I never saw a brother and sister look so much alike as you two do," remarked the hostess, admiringly, as she showed them into the back parlor.

She left them, promising to send in a nice dinner.

"And coffee with it, if you please," added Mary Grey, as the landlady went out.

"Yes, certainly, ma'am, if you wish it," she answered, as she disappeared.

Mary Grey went to the back window and looked out upon the pleasant garden, verdant and blooming with shrubs, rose-bushes and flowers.

Craven Kyte joined her.

"Did you hear that old lady call us brother and sister?" inquired the young man.

"Yes," answered Mary Grey, with her false smile. "But I did not think it necessary to set her right."

"And she said we looked so much alike," smiled Craven.

"We both have dark hair and dark eyes. And we are both rather thin in flesh. That is the beginning and the ending of the likeness. And her imagination did the rest," explained Mary Grey.

They were interrupted by a pretty mulatto girl, who came in to lay the cloth for dinner.

And this girl continued to flit in and out of the room, bringing the various articles of the service, until, on one of her temporary absences, Craven Kyte exclaimed:

"I would rather have sat and fasted with you under that pretty porch of the old road-side empty house than sit at a feast here, with that girl always running in and out to interrupt us."

"Never mind, dear. As soon as we get something to eat we will go," said Mary Grey, with her sweet, false smile.

In a reasonable time a dainty little dinner was placed upon the table, consisting of broiled chickens, green corn, asparagus and mashed potatoes, with fragrant coffee for a beverage and peaches and cream for dessert.

When they had partaken of this, and had rested a while, Craven Kyte went out and paid the bill. And Mary Grey again drew the landlady aside, out of hearing of her companion, and said:

"We are so much rested and refreshed by your admirable hospitality that my brother and myself think we shall walk back to town and attend afternoon service."

The good hostess smiled approval, but expressed a hope that they would not overdo themselves.

Mary Grey smiled and took leave, and walked off with her captive.

They went on until they came in front of the vacant house with the vine-clad porch.

"Come, won't you rest here a little while?" inquired Craven Kyte, laying his hands upon the latch of the gate.

"Yes, for a little while only," said Mary Grey, consulting her watch. "It is now half-past three o'clock, and service commences at half-past four. And I *must* be at church in time for the commencement of the service. You will go to church with me, of course," she added.

"Of course!" answered Craven Kyte, emphatically.

"I am sorry that I can not ask you to sit with me; but the fact is I have only one seat that I can call my own in a crowded pew belonging to the Blairs. But you can walk with me to church, and join me again after the service," exclaimed Mary Grey.

"I should so much like to sit by your side!" said poor Craven, with a disappointed look.

"Don't you see, my dear, it is quite impossible? The service, however, is short, and I will join you immediately after it."

And as they talked they went in and sat down on the porch.

"This is a pretty little old-fashioned cottage. Don't you think so?" inquired the beauty, as they looked around them.

"Very pretty," agreed her victim, who would equally have agreed to anything she might have proposed.

"Look what a fine luxuriant garden it has behind it, all growing wild with neglect."

"Yes."

"And the orchard back of that. See the trees bending under their loads of ripening apples or peaches."

"Yes. It's a wonder the boys don't go in and steal them."

"No boy would enter there for love or money."

"Why?"

"Because this is the house in which Barnes killed his wife and child, in a fit of insane jealousy; and the place has the terrible reputation of being haunted."

"Oh!"

"Yes; it is said that the ghost of a weeping woman, carrying a weeping child in her arms, is seen to wander through garden and orchard at all hours of the night, or to come in and look over the beds of the sleepers in the house, if any are found courageous enough to sleep there."

"Oh! And that is the reason, I suppose, that the house remains untenanted?" said Craven Kyte.

"Yes, that is the reason why the house, pleasant and attractive as it looks, remains untenanted; and why the garden and orchard, with their wealth of flowers and fruit, remain untouched by trespassers," said Mrs. Grey.

"It is a pity such a pretty place should be so abandoned," mused the young man.

"It is. But, you see, family after family took it and tried to live in it in vain. No family could stay longer than a week. It has now been untenanted for more than a year. I have heard that the owner offers to rent it for the paltry sum of fifty dollars a year."

"For this delightful house!"

"For this haunted house, you mean!" said Mrs. Grey.

"Oh, nonsense! I beg your forgiveness, my dearest, I did not mean that for you, but for the gabies that believe in ghosts!" said Craven Kyte.

"Then you do not believe in ghosts?"

"I!"

"Well, I thought you did not. In fact, I knew you did not. Now I want you to do something to please me," said the siren, laying her soft hand upon his shoulder.

"Anything in this world, you know, I will do to please you."

Chapter XXVII.

WHAT SHE WANTED HIM TO DO.

"Well, I want you to rent this house."

Craven Kyte started with surprise and looked at the speaker.

She went on, however, regardless of his astonishment.

"And I want you to purchase furniture enough to fit up one room for yourself; and I want you to do that the first thing to-morrow. And I want you to lodge here alone, while you remain in Richmond."

He still stared at her in amazement, but with no sign of a wish to disobey her strange commands.

She went on with her instructions.

"You can walk into the city, and take your meals at any restaurant you please; but you must lodge here alone while you stay in the city."

"I will do so," he answered, earnestly, as he recovered the use of his tongue—"I will do anything you tell me. I am entirely under your orders."

"You are the best fellow in the whole world, and I love the very ground you walk on!" exclaimed the traitress, warmly.

He grasped her hand convulsively and pressed it to his lips, and then waited her further directions.

"To reward you I will come out here every morning and spend the whole day with you."

"Oh, that will be heavenly! I should be willing to live in a cave on such delightful conditions!"

"But mind, my dearest one, you must not come to see me at my boarding-house, or try to meet me, or to speak to me, after to-day, anywhere where I am known," added Mrs. Grey, gravely.

"Oh, that seems very hard!" sighed the victim, with a look of grief, almost of suspicion.

"Why should it seem hard, when I tell you that I will come out here every morning to spend the whole day with you?" inquired Mrs. Grey.

"But why, then, can I not go home with you and spend the whole evening in your company at your boarding-house?" pleaded the poor fellow.

"Because we should have no comfort at all in a whole parlor full of company, as there is at the Misses Cranes' every evening. And because we should be talked about in that gossiping boarding-house circle. And, finally, because I should much rather stay with you alone here in this house, where there is no one to criticise us, as late every evening as I possibly can, and let you walk home with me and leave me at the door at bed-time. Now don't you think mine the better plan?"

"Oh, yes, indeed, if you really will spend the evenings with me also!"

"Why, certainly I will! And now let us walk on to church. And mind, you must leave me at the church door and find a seat for yourself, while I go to mine. After church I will come out here with you again and sit with you all the evening. I have no doubt the good woman at the rustic inn down the road will give us tea, as she gave us dinner," said the beauty, as she arose and slipped her hand within her companion's arm.

They left the house together and walked on to the church.

And the programme for the afternoon and evening was carried on according to the beautiful schemer's arrangement.

After the services were concluded they walked out to the suburban inn, where the simple-minded hostess willingly agreed to furnish tea for such a pious church-going brother and sister.

And when they had had this tea, Mary Grey, to beguile the landlady, took her willing captive for a walk further out toward the country; and then returning by a roundabout route, came to the vacant road-side cottage, where, as the September evening was very warm, they sat under the vine-clad porch until ten o'clock.

Then they walked back to the town together.

Craven Kyte took Mary Grey to the gate of her boarding-house, where, as the place was silent and deserted, they paused for a few last words.

"Mind, the first thing you do to-morrow morning will be to go and find the owner of the haunted house and rent it from him," said the widow.

"Yes," answered her white slave.

"And the next thing you do will be to go and buy the furniture necessary to fit up one room for yourself, and have it taken out there and arranged."

"Yes," he answered again, very submissively.

"That will take you nearly all day, I think."

"I will hurry through the business as fast as I can, so that I may see you the sooner. When can I see you to-morrow?" he pleaded.

"At seven o'clock to-morrow evening wait for me at the haunted house. I will come and stay with you there until eleven."

"Oh, that is so long to wait! May I not see you sooner?"

"Impossible! I have a sacred duty to do to-morrow that will engage me all day. But you too will be busy. And we can look forward all day to our meeting in the evening. And after to-morrow we can meet every morning and spend the whole day together," said the traitress, sweetly.

"I suppose I must be content!" sighed the victim.

"Now good-night, dear. And good-bye until to-morrow night," murmured the siren, as she gave her lover a Judas kiss and dismissed him.

Mary Grey hurried into the drawing-room, where the Misses Crane were still sitting up.

"My dear Mrs. Grey, we feared that something had happened to you," said the elder Miss Crane.

"Oh, no! I went to see one of my Sunday-school pupils, whom I missed from my class, and whom, upon inquiry, I found to be ill at home. I have spent the whole day with the sick child, except the hours spent at church. And I must go to see her again to-morrow morning," said the widow, with a patient smile.

"How good you are!" murmured Miss Crane.

Mary Grey shook her head deprecatingly, bowed good-night to the slim sisters and went upstairs to her own room.

Early the next morning Mary Grey, telling her hostesses that she was then going to sit with the sick child, left the old manor-house and walked rapidly to the railway station and took a ticket for Forestville, a village about twenty miles from the city, on the Richmond and Wendover Railroad.

CHAPTER XXVIII.

A HAPPY LOVER.

The lover is a king; the ground
He treads on is not ours;
His soul by other laws is bound,
Sustained by other powers.
Liver of a diviner life,
He turns a vacant gaze
Toward the theater of strife,
Where we consume our days.

—R. M. MILNES.

On that Monday morning Alden Lytton left Blue Cliff Hall with his heart full of joy and thankfulness.

He was the accepted lover of Emma Cavendish. And he was so somewhat to his own amazement, for he had not intended to propose to her so soon.

She was a very wealthy heiress, and he was a poor young lawyer, just about to begin the battle of life.

They were both still very young and could afford to wait a few years. And, ardently as he loved her, he wished to see his way clearly to fame and fortune by his profession before presuming to ask the beautiful heiress to share his life.

But the impulse of an ardent passion may, in some unguarded hour, overturn the firmest resolution of wisdom.

This was so in the case of Alden Lytton.

Up to Saturday, the last day but one of his stay at Blue Cliff Hall, the lovers were not engaged.

Rumor, in proclaiming their engagement, had been, as she often is, beforehand with the facts.

But on that Saturday evening, after tea, Alden Lytton found himself walking with Emma Cavendish up and down the long front piazza.

It was a lovely summer night. There was no moon, but the innumerable stars were shining with intense brilliancy from the clear blue-black night sky; the earth sent up an aroma from countless fragrant flowers and spicy shrubs; the dew lay fresh upon all; and the chirp of myriads of little insects of the night almost rivaled the songs of birds during the day. And so the night was filled with the sparkling light of stars, the fresh coolness of dew, the rich perfume of vegetation and the low music of insect life.

The near mountains, like walls of Eden, shut in the beautiful scene.

Alden Lytton and Emma Cavendish sauntered slowly up and down the long piazza feeling the divine influence of the hour and scene, without thinking much about either.

Indeed, they thought only of each other.

They were conscious that this was to be their last walk together for many months, perhaps for years.

Something to this effect Alden murmured.

He received no reply, but he felt a tear drop upon his hand.

Then he lost his self-control. The strong love swelling in his soul burst forth into utterance, and with impassioned tones and eloquent, though broken words, he told her of his most presuming and almost hopeless love.

And then he waited, trembling, for the rejection and rebuke that his modesty made him more than half expect.

But no such rebuff came from Emma Cavendish.

She paused in her walk, raised her beautiful eyes to his face and placed both her hands in his.

And in this manner she silently accepted him.

How fervently he thanked and blessed her!

Emma Cavendish had always been a dutiful daughter to the doting old lady in the "throne room;" so that night, before she slept, she went in and told her grandmother of her engagement to Alden Lytton.

Now, by all the rules of wrong, Madam Cavendish should have resolutely set her face against the betrothal of her wealthy granddaughter to a young lawyer with no fortune of his own and with his way yet to make in the world.

And if the old lady had been somewhat younger she would probably have done this very thing.

But as it was, she was "old and childish;" which means that she was more heavenly-minded and nearer heaven than she ever had been since the days of her own infancy and innocence.

So, instead of fixing a pair of terrible spectacled eyes upon the young girl and reading her a severe lecture upon "the eternal fitness of things," as illustrated in wealth mating with wealth and rank with rank, she looked lovingly upon her granddaughter, held out her venerable hand, and drew her up to her bosom, kissed her tenderly, and said:

"Heaven bless you, my own darling! This has come rather suddenly upon me; but since, in the course of nature, you must some time marry, I do not know a young gentleman in this world to whom I would as soon see you married as to Mr. Alden Lytton. But, my child, I do not think you ought to be married very soon," she added.

"No, dear grandma, I know that," said Emma, kneeling down by her side and tenderly caressing and kissing her withered hands. "No, dear grandma, I will never leave you—never for any one—not even for him!"

"My darling child, you mistake my meaning. It is not for the selfish purpose of keeping you here near me that I advise you to defer your marriage for a time. It is because I think it is decorous that some months should elapse between the betrothal of a young pair and their wedding. Though, of course, there are some cases in which a short engagement and a speedy marriage become expedient or even necessary. As, for instance, my child, if I felt myself near death now I should certainly wish to hasten your marriage, rather than leave you unprotected in this world."

Emma Cavendish could only kiss her grandmother's hands and thank her through falling tears.

"And now; my child, I must go to sleep. I always want to go to sleep after anything exciting has happened to me. Good-night, and may Heaven bless you, my love!" said the old lady, affectionately, as she dismissed her granddaughter.

While Emma Cavendish was talking with her grandmother, Alden Lytton went into the parlor, where he found his sister alone, sitting by one of the windows, gazing thoughtfully out upon the beautiful night.

He drew a chair to her side, seated himself and, with his arm around her waist, told her of his new-born happiness.

She congratulated him fervently and earnestly; and then, returning confidence for confidence, told him of her engagement to the young minister of Wendover.

For rumor, in Mr. Lyle's and Miss Lytton's case also, had anticipated the facts, and had reported their betrothal all over the country long before it was announced to their nearest friends.

Alden Lytton, with all his approving heart, wished his sister joy in her prospective union with the worthy young clergyman.

And then the two, talking together over their future, decided that they must write at once to their Uncle John Lytton and inform him of their engagements.

Alden undertook to write a letter on the part of both his sister and himself that night.

And, on further discussion, it was decided that at the close of her visit to Blue Cliff Hall, Laura should go to Lytton Lodge to make a visit to her relatives there.

The entrance of Emma Cavendish put an end to the discussion, and was the occasion of new congratulations.

The next morning Madam Cavendish sent for Alden Lytton and Emma Cavendish to come up to her room together.

And she then and there read them a grave and affectionate little lecture upon the duties and responsibilities of an engaged couple, gave them her blessing and dismissed them to go to church.

That Sunday morning every one at Blue Cliffs knew of the betrothal of Mr. Lytton to the young mistress of the Hall.

And on Monday morning all the county knew it just as well as they had known it a month before it happened.

And every one said over once more what they had already said so often—that it was a great pity the daughter of the late Governor Cavendish should be allowed to throw herself and her wealth away upon a penniless young fortune-hunter like Alden Lytton, and all for the want of a proper guardian at hand to restrain her. Old Madam Cavendish, they said, was no better than none at all. And really the Orphans' Court ought to interfere, etc.

But the very bitterest of the malcontents were parents with marriageable sons of their own, any one of which might one day have aspired to the hand of the heiress.

Little cared the happy lovers what their neighbors might think about their betrothal.

They parted that morning, not with tears, but with bright smiles and promises of frequent correspondence.

Alden Lytton stopped in Wendover to take leave of his friend, Mr. Lyle, and to announce the betrothal of Miss Cavendish and himself.

And then, scarcely waiting to receive the congratulations of the minister, he hurried off to catch his train for Richmond.

An hour after this Mr. Lyle had an interview with Victor Hartman, and delighted that poor fellow's soul with the announcement of the betrothal.

And on the same day Mr. Lyle, commissioned by Victor Hartman, went to Blue Cliff Hall and requested an interview with Madam Cavendish.

The old lady, thinking this was the usual pastoral call from the minister, sent word for him to come up to her room.

And there she received him alone, and after the usual greetings opened the conversation herself by informing him of the betrothal of her granddaughter to Mr. Alden Lytton.

"It was upon that very subject that I came to see you, madam, on the part of the young gentleman's guardian," replied the minister, and then and there announced the fact that Mr. Alden Lytton's "guardian" would be prepared to pay down to his ward one hundred thousand dollars on the day of his marriage with Miss Cavendish.

"Emma has money enough," said the old lady; "but that indeed is very liberal. I never could understand about that secret guardian, friend, patron, or whatever you might call him, of the young Lyttons," she added, as if she would have liked some information on the subject.

"No, madam, and I am sorry that I am not yet at liberty to tell you more about him. This, however, I may say, that he is able and willing to keep his word."

And so that interview ended.

CHAPTER XXIX.

ON TO MEET HIS FATE.

Meanwhile, Alden Lytton sped on toward the city. He traveled by the express train, which stopped at but few stations.

About two o'clock in the afternoon the train made its longest pause, at a little station about midway between Wendover and Richmond, where it stopped twenty minutes for dinner.

Many of the passengers left the train to stretch their cramped limbs or to satisfy their hunger.

Alden Lytton got out and went into the waiting-room, when the first form his eye fell upon was that of Mary Grey.

She looked pale, weary and harassed, as she sat alone on one of the benches, with a small carpet-bag at her feet.

Now Alden Lytton's heart was so full of happiness that it expanded with affection for the whole human race, and even warmed with sympathy for this erring woman, who had once possessed and forfeited his faithful boyish love.

And now, in his compassion, he went to her and, smiling very kindly, he said:

"Why, Mrs. Grey! I am so surprised to see you here, and alone too!" he added.

"When, since I left Blue Cliff Hall, have you ever seen me when I have not been alone?" she inquired, with a sad smile.

"True," he answered, gently. "Even in a church, or a crowded parlor, you have still been ever alone. But why should this be so, while you have so many faithful friends? Miss Cavendish I know is—"

She put up her hand to stop him. She turned paler than before, and trembled as with a chill. For she had loved this man *only*, of all that she had fascinated and fooled; she had loved him *utterly*; and even now, when she bitterly hated him, she could not bear to hear her rival's name from his lips.

"'The heart knoweth its own bitterness,'" she murmured, in faltering tones. "Let us talk of something else. I came down here to bring some funds that I had collected from charitable friends for a poor family who were burned out near this village. And now I am going back by this train. Pray pardon my nervousness! But the crowd and bustle and excitement of a railway station always does make me very nervous."

"You need refreshment. Come to the table with me and have something. There is yet plenty of time," he said, kindly, offering her his arm.

He felt so safe and happy in his wisely placed affection and firmly based engagement to Emma Cavendish that he could afford to be very kind to this poor woman, although she had once possessed— and by her conduct forever forfeited—his honest youthful love.

He gave her his arm and led her away to the dining-room, where a crowd was collected at the refreshment table.

There was a whisper between two attendants as they passed by.

"Hush! That is the young fellow she has been waiting here to meet. It is a runaway marriage, bless you!"

This whisper reached the ears of Alden Lytton and Mary Grey.

Alden Lytton paid no attention to it, thinking that it referred to some "levanting" youth and girl who had chosen this station for their escapade.

But Mary Grey smiled grimly to herself as she heard it.

They had barely time to get a cup of coffee each before the warning shriek of the steam engine called the passengers to take their places.

Alden Lytton drew his companion's arm within his own, led her into the ladies' car, put her into a comfortable seat, and took his place beside her.

Purposely suggested by Mary Grey's own calculated actions while waiting at the station, a whisper had got around among the attendants that the lovely young lady in black had come down to meet her lover and elope with him; and from the attendants it had reached the ears of some of the passengers.

And now, as Alden Lytton placed himself innocently enough on the seat beside Mary Grey, the eyes of several of their fellow-travelers turned with curiosity toward them.

Certainly the demeanor of both rather favored the idea of their being a pair of engaged lovers.

Alden Lytton, with his beaming and happy face, and his careful attentions to his companion, wore the look of a successful suitor and prospective bridegroom. Mary Grey, with her pale, pretty face and nervous manner, had as much the appearance of a runaway girl, trembling and frightened at what she was daring.

Meanwhile the train whirled onward, bearing many passengers to happy homes or on pleasant visits; but carrying one among them on to crime and another to disaster.

As they drew near the end of the journey the crowd in the ladies' car was thinned out by the leaving of passengers at the smaller stations, until at length Alden Lytton and Mary Grey were left nearly alone and quite out of hearing of any fellow-traveler.

Then Alden said to her:

"I hope you have some plan of occupation and happiness for your future life."

"Yes," murmured Mary Grey, "I have some little prospect. I have the offer of a very good position in a first-class ladies' college near Philadelphia."

"I hope it will suit you."

"I do not know. I have promised to go on and see the institution and talk with the principal before concluding the engagement."

"That would be safest, of course," said Alden.

"And I should have gone on a day or two since, but the journey, with its changes from steamer to car and car to steamer, is really quite a serious one for me to take alone, especially as I always get frightened and lose my presence of mind in the terrible uproar of a steamboat landing or a railway station."

"Then you should never undertake such a journey alone," said Alden, compassionately.

"No, I know it. But yet I shall have to do so, unless I can hear of some party of friends going on in a few days whom I could join," sighed Mary Grey.

"I am not 'a party of friends,'" smiled Alden; "but I am *one* friend who will be pleased to escort you on that journey, as I am myself going to Philadelphia in a few days."

"*You!*" exclaimed Mary Grey, in well-affected astonishment.

"Yes, madam," replied Alden, with a bow.

"I did not know you ever went North at all," she added, lifting her eyebrows.

"I never yet have been north of Baltimore, strange to say," smiled Alden Lytton; "but I am going in a few days to Philadelphia to purchase a law library, and should be happy to escort you to your place of destination."

"You are very kind to me, and I am very grateful to you. I accept your offer, and will try to give you as little trouble on the journey as possible."

"Oh, do not speak of trouble! There will be none, I assure you," said Alden, pleasantly.

"You are very good to say so, at all events."

"What day would it suit you to go on?" inquired Alden.

"Any day this week—whenever it will be convenient to you. I am the obliged party and should consider your convenience."

"Not by any means! Any day this week would suit me equally. So I beg that you will please yourself alone."

"No."

"Let me be frank with you then and prove how little it really would matter to me whether we go to-morrow or any day thereafter. I have to select and fit up a law office, and I have to select and purchase a law library; and I do not care in the least which I do first," said Alden, with earnest politeness.

"Then, if it really is a matter of indifference to you, I think we will go to Philadelphia on Wednesday morning."

"Very well. I will make my arrangements accordingly. This is Monday night. We have one intervening day. Where shall I call for you on Wednesday morning?"

"You need not call. I will meet you on the Washington boat."

"Just as you please. I will be there."

The engine shrieked its terrific warning, slackened its speed, and ran slowly into the station.

"I will call a carriage for you," said Alden Lytton.

And he left his companion in the waiting-room while he went out and selected a good carriage for her use.

Then he came back, took up her traveling-bag, drew her arm in his own, and led her out to it.

"Where shall I tell the coachman to take you?" he inquired, when he had placed her comfortably in her seat.

"To the Misses Cranes', Old Manor, near the Government House," she answered.

Alden Lytton bowed and closed the door, gave the order to the coachman, and then walked off to his own old quarters at the Henrico House.

The carriage started, but had not gone more than a quarter of a mile when Mrs. Grey stopped it.

The coachman got off his box and came to the window to know her will.

"Turn into the old paper-mill road. I wish to call on a sick friend there before going home. Go on. I will keep a lookout and stop you when we get near the house."

The coachman touched his hat, remounted, and turned his horses' heads to the required direction.

Mary Grey sat close on the left-hand side of the cushion, and drew the curtain away, so that she could look through the window and watch their course.

The night was clear, starlit and breezy after the hot September day.

It was still early, and the sidewalks were enlivened by young people sauntering in front of their own houses to enjoy the refreshing evening air, while the porches and door-steps were occupied by the elders taking their ease in their own way.

But in the next mile the scene began to change, and instead of the populous street, with its long rows of houses and the cheerful sidewalks, there was a lonely road with detached dwellings and occasional groups of people. In the second mile the scene changed again, and there was an old turnpike, with here and there a solitary road-side dwelling, with perhaps a man leaning over the front gate smoking his pipe, or a pair of lovers billing and cooing under the starlit sky.

Mary Grey kept a bright lookout for the "haunted house," and presently she recognized it, and saw a light shining through the little front window under the vine-covered porch.

"He is there, poor wretch, sure enough, waiting for me. I feel a little sorry for him, because he loves me so devotedly. But heigho! If I do not spare myself, shall I spare him? No!" said Mary Grey to herself, as she ordered the coachman to draw up.

He stopped and jumped off his box, and came and opened the carriage door. But it was the door on the other side of the carriage, opposite the middle of the road, and not opposite the house, where she wanted to get out.

"Open the other door," she said.

But the negro's teeth were chattering and the whites of his eyes rolling, in fearful contrast with the darkness of his skin.

"Open the other door and let me out. I want to go into that house," repeated Mrs. Grey, a little impatiently.

"Dat dere house? Oh, laws-a-messy! Bress my soul, missy, you don't want to go in dat house! Dat's de haunted house! And oh, law, dere's de corpse lights a-burnin' in dere now!" gasped the negro, shudderingly, pointing to the dimly-lighted windows under the porch.

"You blockhead, those are the tapers in my friend's sickroom! Open the other door, I tell you!" said Mrs. Grey, angrily.

"'Deed—'deed—'deed, missy, you must scuse ole nigger like me! I dussint do it, missy! I dussint go on t'other side ob de carriage nex' to de ghoses at no price!" said the negro, with chattering teeth.

Mary Grey turned and tried to open the other door for herself, but found it impossible, and then turned again and said:

"Well, stand out of my way then, you idiot, and let me out of *this* door!"

The negro gave way, and she got out of the carriage into the middle of the dusty road.

CHAPTER XXX.

THE SACRIFICE.

At the same moment some one came softly through the cottage gate and looked up and down the road, as if watching for some one else.

As Mary Grey came round the carriage to the front of the house, she recognized in the watcher Craven Kyte, who at the same instant perceived her.

"Wait here for me," she said to the frightened coachman, as she walked rapidly toward the man who was hurrying to meet her.

"My darling! I have been waiting for you so long!" he said, seizing her hand.

"Hush! The coachman might hear you," she whispered. "Let me come in."

He drew her arm within his own and led her into the cottage, and into a cool, well-lighted and tastefully-furnished parlor.

Poor fellow, he had not only put in a few necessary articles of furniture for his own sleeping-room, but he had fitted up a pretty parlor for her reception, and provided a dainty feast for her entertainment.

To do this in time, he had worked like a mill-horse all day long, and he had spent all his available funds, and even pawned his watch and his little vanities of jewelry to raise more purchase-money.

And now he felt rewarded when he saw her look of surprise, which he mistook for a look of pleasure.

There was an Indian matting of bright light colors on the floor, white lace curtains lined with rose-colored cambric at the windows, and a sofa and easy-chairs covered with rose-colored French chintz. There were a few marble-top stands, and tables covered with white crochet-work over rose-colored linings. There were vases of fragrant flowers on the mantle-shelf, and on the window-sills and stands, and every available place.

In the center of the room stood a small table, covered with fine white damask, decorated with a Sevres china set for two, and loaded with a variety of choice delicacies—delicious cakes, jellies, fruits, preserves and lemonade.

"This is a surprise," said Mary Grey, sinking into one of the tempting easy-chairs.

"Oh, I am glad you like it as it is! But oh, indeed, I wish everything here was more worthy of you! If it were in my power I would receive and entertain you like a queen."

"You are so good—so thoughtful! And nothing in the world could be pleasanter than this cool, pretty parlor," said Mary Grey, trying to rouse herself from the abstraction into which she had fallen after her first look of surprise at the decorated room; for, truth to tell, her mind was occupied with graver thoughts than appertained to house or furniture, flowers or fruits.

"And this has been ready for you, my queen, ever since sunset. And here I have sat and waited for you, running out every five minutes to see if you were coming," he said, half reproachfully.

"Well, I am here at last, you impatient boy! I could not come before. I was sitting with a sick friend and could not leave her until she went to sleep," smiled the siren.

"I shall end in being very wickedly jealous of your sick friends, and your poor friends, and your lame friends, and all the other forlornities that take you away from me, and keep you away from me so much," he sighed.

"Ah, but when we are married I shall give up this sort of life! For I know that 'charity begins at home;' and though it ought not always to stay there, yet should it stay there the principal part of its time," smiled the witch.

"Ah, I am so glad to hear you say so, dearest dear! You *will* stay at home for me most of your time then?"

"It will be my delight to do so!"

He caught her hand and kissed it ardently, and drew her slightly toward him, looking at her longingly, as if pleading for a closer kiss.

But she smiled and shook her head, saying, archly:

"Remember—remember, if I come here to see you, you must treat me with some respectful reserve, or I will never come again."

"I will do exactly as you wish. I am your slave, and can do no otherwise than as you bid me," he said, with a sigh.

"That is a good, dear boy!" she answered, patting his cheeks; and then adding, archly, "A few days, you know, and 'the tables will be turned.' It will then be *you* who will have the right to command, and some one else who must obey."

As the Circe murmured these words, his color went and came, and when she ceased he panted out his answer:

"Oh, the thought of ever having you for my own is—too much rapture to be credited! But, Mary, my queen Mary, then and ever I shall be your slave as now!"

"Well, we'll see," she murmured, smiling and caressing him. "But now I am tired and hungry, and you are forgetting the duties of a host."

"I am forgetting everything in looking at your beautiful face. But now, will you let me take off your bonnet and shawl here, or will you go into the next room and do it for yourself, I remaining here until you come back?"

"I will go into the next room, if you please," said Mary Grey.

And he arose and opened the back door of the cottage parlor and held it open for her.

She passed through into a prettily-furnished and well-lighted little bed-room, whose back windows opened upon the fragrant flower-garden.

Here she found everything prepared for her comfort, as if it had been done by the hands of a woman. She took off her bonnet and shawl, brushed her clothes, bathed her face and hands, smoothed her raven ringlets, took a fresh cambric handkerchief from her pocket and saturated it with Cologne from the toilet-table, and then passed out again into the parlor.

Her devoted slave was waiting for her there. And on the table, in addition to the other comforts, there was a little silver pot of rich aromatic coffee.

"Why, have you a cook?" inquired Mrs. Grey, in some disturbance.

"No, darling; I made that coffee myself. Sit down now and try it," smiled the poor fellow.

"You are a jewel!" she said, as all her disturbance disappeared, and she sat down to the table.

He waited on her with affectionate solicitude, helping her to coffee and cream, to chicken salad and pickled oysters; changing her plate and pressing her to try the jellies and the cakes, or the fruit and ices, until she had feasted like a princess.

He, in the meantime, ate but little, seeming to feed upon the sight of her enjoyment. At length she pushed her plate and cup away and declared she could touch nothing more.

Then he arose as if to clear the service; but she stopped him, saying:

"Leave it just as it is and come and sit with me on the porch outside. The night is beautiful, and I want to sit there and talk with you. I have something to propose."

And she ran into the back room for her bonnet and shawl.

He got up and gave her his arm and took her out upon the porch.

And they sat down together on the bench, under thickly overhanging vine-leaves.

"Craven," she murmured, with her head upon his shoulder, "do you really love me as much as you profess to do?"

"Do I really love you?" he repeated, with impassioned earnestness. "Oh, how shall I prove to you how much? Protestations are but words. Show me how I can prove to you how much I love you! Put me to the test! Try me—*try me!*"

She hesitated and sighed—perhaps in pity and remorse for this poor boy, who loved her so devotedly, and whom she was about to require to pay down his honor and his life as the price of her hand.

"Oh, tell me how I can show you the height and depth and breadth—no; I should rather say the immeasurability of my infinite love!" he pleaded, prayerfully.

Again she sighed and trembled—yes, trembled at the contemplation of the wickedness she was about to perpetrate; but she did not draw back from it. She slid her arm around his neck and kissed him softly, and then said:

"Listen to me, Craven, my dearest. This is Monday night, you know."

"Yes," he said, attentively.

"On Wednesday morning I am to start for Philadelphia."

"Oh!" he exclaimed, uneasily.

"Hush! Wait until you hear me out. You must meet me in Philadelphia on Friday morning. And we will be married on Friday noon."

He was struck speechless, breathless, for a few moments with the excess of his delight.

Then he panted forth the words:

"Oh, bless you! Bless you, my queen, my angel! I bless you for this great joy!"

"You must be calm, my dear, and hear me out. You must be punctual, and meet me on Friday morning at ten o'clock, at *this* address," she continued, handing him a slip of paper with the address in question written upon it. "There; now put it into your pocket-book and keep it safe."

"I will—I will, my queen! But why may I not go with you?"

"For reasons that I will explain soon. Till I do, you must trust me."

"I trust you utterly."

"Then please leave here for Philadelphia on Tuesday evening, so as to precede me by twelve hours. And on Friday morning, by ten o'clock, be at the place I have designated, and wait until I join you."

"And we will be married the same day?"

"We will be married at noon on the same day. Now do you understand?"

"My mind is in a delirium of joy, but I understand."

"Now, dearest, you must take me out to the carriage," she said, rising and drawing her shawl around her.

He gave her his arm and led her out to the carriage, which the frightened negro coachman had driven quite to the opposite side of the road from the terrible haunted house.

"Now go on to the Misses Cranes'," she said, after she had taken leave of her victim and settled herself in her seat.

It was nearly twelve o'clock when she entered her boarding-house; but she told her waiting landladies that she had spent the day and half the night with the sick child, and they were satisfied.

CHAPTER XXXI.

A FATAL JOURNEY.

Thither, full fraught with mischievous revenge,
Accursed and in a cursed hour, she hies.

—MILTON.

On that Wednesday morning the fine steamer "Pocahontas" lay at her wharf receiving freight and passengers for Washington and Alexandria.

Her decks were crowded with men, women and children, all either going on the voyage or "seeing off" departing friends and acquaintances.

Among the passengers on the forward deck stood a slight, elegant, graceful woman, clothed in widow's weeds and deeply veiled.

This was, of course, Mary Grey, bound upon her baleful errand.

She had spent the intervening Tuesday with her infatuated instrument, Craven Kyte. But when he pleaded to attend her to the boat and see her off she forbid his doing so on pain of an eternal separation from her.

But she renewed their agreement that he should precede her by twelve hours, and meet her at a designated place in Philadelphia on Friday morning.

And she stayed with him until quite late in the evening, and finally left him comforted with the hope of a speedy meeting and a certain marriage.

For the edification of her landladies, the precise Misses Crane, she trumped up a story that at once explained the necessity of her sudden journey North, and, as usual, redounded to her own credit.

She had received a telegram, she said, from a friend who had just lost her father, and who was in great affliction. And she must go on immediately to comfort that bereaved soul.

The Misses Crane, as usual, thought she was an angel in woman's form, and bade her heaven speed on her benevolent errand.

And now she stood upon the deck of the "Pocahontas," waiting for that traveling companion whom she had fatally beguiled to be her escort.

The boat was getting up her steam, and yet he had not made his appearance.

What if he should not come, after all?

Just as she asked this question it was answered by his rapid approach.

He came up, traveling-bag in hand, happy, smiling, radiant.

"Mrs. Grey, I have been looking for you all over the boat. I feared that I had missed you," he said, gayly, holding out his hand.

"I have been waiting for you here," she answered, with a smile.

"I am glad to find you at last. But will you not come into the cabin? The deck is not a pleasant place while the boat is at the wharf," he said, as he offered her his arm.

She thanked him with a smile, took his arm and let him lead her into the saloon.

It was at that moment empty of other visitors. And those two were tête-à-tête.

He gave her a pleasant seat, placed himself beside her, and then and there he told her of his betrothal to Emma Cavendish.

Of course she already knew all about it. But he was not aware of her knowledge. And his motive in announcing the intelligence to her was evident even to Mary Grey's vanity-blinded mind. It was to set their own relations at once upon a true basis, and prevent all misunderstanding and all false hopes growing out of their long-lost love.

Although she had known all this so well before he spoke of it, yet it required all her powers of self-control and duplicity to listen quietly while he spoke of her rival and to affect a sympathy with his happiness.

Yet she did this so well that he was thoroughly deceived.

"It was all a foolish mistake our fancying we loved each other so much, was it not, Alden, dear?" she inquired, with an arch smile.

"I think so," he answered, quite frankly.

"I am glad to hear you admit that, for now we can understand each other and be good friends, and nothing more," she added, sweetly.

"Yes, good friends always, Mary," he agreed.

He was so happy in his blessed love for Emma Cavendish that he felt kindly toward all the world, and especially toward this "friendless young widow," as he called her.

"But you know, Alden, that it is quite common for young men of earnest souls like yours to take a liking to women older than themselves."

"You are not older than myself, Mary."

"Not in years, perhaps, but oh, ever so much in suffering, and in the bitter knowledge of the world it brings! And thus, for this reason, I was no proper wife for a happy young man like you. No young man should ever marry a widow, and no young girl should ever marry a widower. Our fancied love for each other was a mistake, dear Alden, and I am very glad it was discovered before it was rendered irremediable."

"So am I," replied the young man, quite frankly. "But, dear Mary, I hope you will henceforth look upon me and my dearest Emma as your brother and sister, for we will be truly such in deed as well as in word to you," he added, with grave gentleness.

"I know you will; I feel certain of that. And I thank you from my heart, while I rejoice in your happiness. Yours will be a good, wise and beautiful marriage with Emma, Alden," she murmured, with emotion.

"Yes, I think so too. Thanks be to Heaven!" replied the young man, reverently bowing his head.

The steamer was now pushing off from the wharf amid much pulling, hauling, hallooing and shouting.

You couldn't "hear yourself think," even in the cabin, for a while.

"We are off, I believe," said Mary Grey, at length, when the uproar had subsided and they were moving swiftly and smoothly along.

"Yes. Will you come on deck? It is pleasanter there now," said Alden, rising and offering her his arm.

She took it with a smile and let him lead her up on deck.

And as they promenaded slowly up and down, enjoying the fine September morning and the beautiful river scenery, Mary Grey drew him on to speak of Emma Cavendish.

Of course the young lover desired no better theme.

And in this way, leading him to discourse of his love, listening to him with attention, pretending sympathy with his happiness, she effected several objects important to the success of her demoniac plot. She pleased him with himself and with her. She dispelled his suspicions, if any still lurked in his candid soul, and she kept him always near her, talking with her, and unconsciously attracting the attention of their fellow-voyagers, and leading them to believe that this handsome young man, speaking so earnestly in such low tones to his companion, and the lovely youthful widow, who was listening to him with such rapt attention, were a pair of happy and devoted lovers.

Thus passed the forenoon.

When the early steamboat dinner was ready he took her down to the table, sat beside her, and assiduously attended to her wants.

After dinner, when she was disinclined to walk or to talk, he brought out some newspapers and magazines and sat down beside her on deck and they read together.

At tea-time he took her down to the table again.

And after tea, as the September night was cool on the water, they sat down at one of the cabin tables and played checkers together until it was time to retire.

And thus all day long and all the evening through, in sight of all the people, Alden Lytton unconsciously conducted himself, as Mary Grey intended that he should, like her betrothed lover.

In due time they reached Washington, and crossed the length of the city to take the train for Philadelphia, where they arrived late on Thursday night.

"Have you any preference for one hotel over another?" inquired Alden, as they stood amid the horrible din of contesting hackmen, porters, 'bus-drivers, *et cætera*.

"None whatever," she answered.

"Then we'll go to the Blank House, if you have no objection."

"None. We will go there."

"Here's your Blank House 'bus!" shouted a driver above all the other shouts.

"Oh, don't let us get into that crowded cage! A carriage, please," pleaded Mrs. Grey.

And Alden Lytton, believing her fastidiousness and timidity to be real and not affected, and withal feeling bound to be guided by her wishes, called a carriage and put her into it.

As they were rolling rapidly on their way to the Blank House, Mary Grey shivered and suddenly said:

"Oh, please, when we get to that great rambling hotel do not let them put me away off in a room in a remote part of the house by myself or among total strangers. I always feel so frightened in a great hotel. And I am always sure to lose myself, or do something ridiculous, or get into trouble, whenever I attempt to find my way through the labyrinth of halls and passages between the bedrooms and parlors. Will you please take care of me?"

"I will take the same care of you that I would take of my sister Laura. I will see that you have a room adjoining my own," answered Alden Lytton, unsuspiciously, and smiling indulgently at what he thought her childish cowardice.

When their carriage reached the Blank House he took her up to the reception-room and left her there, while he went to the office and engaged apartments for himself and for her.

And then he came for her, attended by the porter, who loaded himself with their traveling-bags, umbrellas, and so forth, and led the way up two pairs of stairs to a little suite of apartments, consisting of two small chambers, with a small parlor between them.

They entered the parlor first, where communicating doors on the right and left led into opposite chambers.

The porter put down the luggage, received his fee, and retired.

"I hope you like these rooms, Mrs. Grey. The two chambers are exactly alike; but if you have a preference, please take it," said Alden, pleasantly.

"It does not matter the least. I will go in here," answered Mary Grey, opening the right-hand door and disappearing through it, with her traveling-bag in her hand.

She found every convenience for making a clean toilet there. And when she had refreshed herself with a wash and a change of dress, she re-entered the little parlor, where she found supper laid on the table and an attentive waiter at hand.

"I ordered supper here, because I remembered your fastidiousness and thought you would prefer this to the public dining-room," explained Alden.

"Thanks! Oh, I do like it ever so much better! I can not endure the public rooms," said Mary Grey, as she took the seat the obsequious waiter placed for her.

"Anything more, if you please, sir?" inquired the man.

"N-n-no," answered Alden, hesitatingly; for in fact, if he could have found a fair excuse, he would have preferred to have the waiter remain in attendance.

The man bowed and left the room.

Chapter XXXII.

THE SERPENT AT WORK.

One sole desire, one passion, now remains
To keep life's fever still within her veins.
For this alone she lives—like lightning's fire,
To speed one bolt of ruin—and expire.

—Byron.

Alden sat down at the table and began to carve a roasted chicken.

While he was intent upon his task, Mary Grey drew from her watch-pocket a little folded paper. With her eyes upon him, to be sure that he was not observing her, she deftly poured a white powder from this paper into one of the coffee-cups, and then quickly returned the empty paper to her watch-pocket.

Meanwhile he had taken off the liver-wing from the roasted chicken and placed it on a warm plate, which he passed to her.

"Will you have a cup of coffee now, or afterward?" she inquired, as she took the offered plate.

"Now, please. Coffee is the most refreshing of all beverages after a fatiguing journey," he added, as he received the cup from her hands.

It was a very nice supper, yet neither of them seemed inclined to eat.

Mary Grey trifled with her chicken-wing, tasted her milk-toast and sipped a little coffee. She looked pale, frightened and self-concentrated.

Alden Lytton drank his coffee, remarking, with a smile, that it was very, very strong, in fact quite bitter in its strength.

And when he had finished it he pushed the cup away, saying that it had quite satisfied him and deprived him of the inclination to take anything else.

As he said this he looked at his companion, and noticed for the first time the ghastliness of her countenance.

"Mrs. Grey, are you ill?" he inquired, in some alarm.

"No; only fatigued from that railway journey. The train always shakes me into a jelly," she answered, shivering.

"How very delicate you are, poor child! It is a great pity you should ever be called to bear any of the roughness of life. And when my dear Emma and I have a home together we must take care to shield you from all that," he said.

And then he sank into a sudden silence, while she watched him closely.

"Will *you* not take anything?" she inquired.

"No, thank you. That coffee was no doubt very fine; but it was a bitter draught, and it has taken away my appetite for anything else," he answered, with a smile and a half-suppressed yawn.

"Are you not well?" she next inquired.

"Oh, yes; quite well; never better in my life!" he answered, putting his hands on his lips to conceal an irrepressible yawn.

"But you also seem very tired."

"No, only deliciously sleepy, as if I would like to go to sleep and never wake up again," he said, with a laugh and a smothered gape.

"Then do not stand on ceremony with an old friend like me. Bid me good-night and go at once," she said.

"And you?" he inquired.

"I am too tired to go to sleep yet. I shall sit in that rocking-chair and rock gently. That motion will soothe and rest me better than anything else, and after an hour I shall be able to go to bed and go to sleep."

As Mary Grey spoke, Alden Lytton staggered to his feet and tottered toward her, held out his hand and faltered, drowsily:

"I am forced to take your advice. I must retire at once or I shall not be able to reach my room. I never felt so over-powered by sleep in all my life before. Good-night, my dear Mrs. Grey. I hope that you will sleep as well as I am sure that I shall. Good-night."

He pressed her hand, and then, groping like a blind man, he passed into his own room and shut the door behind him.

Mary Grey gazed breathlessly at the closed door for a while, murmuring to herself:

"I doubt if that fellow will be able to divest himself of his outer garments before he falls down headlong in a dead stupor. I have him in my power now—I have him in my power now! At last—at last! Oh, yes! Oh, yes, Miss Cavendish, you will marry him, will you not? And you, Stephen Lyle, how proud you will be to have his sister for your wife and himself for a brother-in-law! But I must cover up my tracks," she added, suddenly, as she went around to his vacated place at the table and took his empty cup and rinsed it out carefully several times, throwing the water into the empty grate, where it soon dried up. Then she poured some of the coffee-grounds from her own cup into the rinsed cup to conceal the rinsing. Finally she drew from her watch-pocket the little white paper from which she had poured the powder into the coffee-cup and she held it in the blaze of the gas-light until it was burned to ashes.

Then she sat down in the rocking-chair and smiled as she rested.

At intervals she bent her head toward the door leading into Alden Lytton's room and listened; but she heard no sound of life in there.

She sat on in the rocker until the striking of a large clock somewhere in the neighborhood aroused her.

It was twelve o'clock.

Midnight!

She arose and cautiously opened the door leading into Alden Lytton's room.

She looked like a thief.

The gas was turned down very low; but by its dim light she saw him sleeping a heavy, trance-like sleep.

She went into the room and to the door leading into the passage and bolted it.

Then she closed every window-shutter and drew down every window-shade and let down the heavy moreen curtains, making all dark.

Then she returned to the parlor, closed the intervening door and threw herself into the rocking-chair and closed her eyes in the vain endeavor to rest and sleep.

But sleep and rest were far from her that night.

The clock struck one.

All sounds even about that busy hotel gradually ceased. The house was still, awfully still, yet she could not sleep.

The clock struck two.

She started up with a shiver, exclaiming:

"I can not sleep; but I can go to bed and lie there."

And she went into her own room and went to bed, but not to rest.

She heard the clock strike in succession every hour of the night, until it finally struck four.

Then, when the people of the house were beginning to stir, she, overcome with fatigue and watching, at length fell asleep.

As usual in such cases of long night watching and early morning sleep, she slept long into the forenoon. When she awoke and looked at her watch she found it was nine o'clock.

She arose in haste and dressed herself.

This was the morning in which she was to meet her unconscious confederate in crime, Craven Kyte.

As soon as she was dressed she went into the parlor, where, it appeared, the waiter with his pass-key had already been before her, for the remains of the last night's supper had been carried away and the room had been restored to order.

She then listened at Alden Lytton's door.

All was dark as a vault and still as death there.

She opened the door cautiously and went in.

He was still sleeping a death-like sleep in the pitch-dark room. She went and looked to the door leading into the passage and found it still bolted.

Then she came out of the room, locked the door between it and the parlor, and so isolated the sleeper from all the house.

Lastly she put on her bonnet and shawl and walked out. She walked down the street for several blocks, and then hailed an empty cab that was passing and engaged it to take her to a certain picture-shop in a distant part of the city.

It was at this shop that she had engaged to meet Craven Kyte that morning at ten o'clock.

A half-hour's rapid drive brought her to the place.

On arriving, she got out, paid and dismissed the cab, and entered the shop.

It was not yet ten o'clock, nor had her intended tool and victim yet made his appearance.

It was also too early for the usual customers of the establishment.

But a polite clerk came forward and placed a catalogue and a small telescope in her hands, that she might the better examine the pictures.

"Thank you. I would like to look at a city directory first, if you please," she said, as she put aside the catalogue and the telescope.

The clerk handed her the required volume.

She turned to the church directory, and looked down its columns until she found what she seemed to be in search of.

And then she marked it with a pencil and closed the book.

At that moment Craven Kyte entered the shop.

On catching sight of her whom he loved and came to meet his face lighted up with joy and he hastened toward her.

But she held up a warning finger to him, and in obedience to its signal he moderated his transports and came to her quietly.

"This is no place to make demonstrations of that sort," she said. "Here, take your pencil and a bit of paper and copy off this address for me," she added, opening the directory and pointing to the name she had marked.

"The Reverend Mr. Borden, number —, —— street," said Craven Kyte, reading the address that he had copied.

"That will do; now come along. We will go straight to that reverend gentleman's house," said Mary Grey.

And they left the shop together.

"Oh, Mary, my love—my love! How tantalizing it is to me to meet you here in public, where I may scarcely take your dear hand, when my heart is nearly breaking with its repressed feelings!" he whispered, in eager tones.

"You impatient boy, you are worse than any spoiled child!" she said, archly.

"Oh, Mary, my love, my lady, you will keep your promise? You will be mine to-day?" he pleaded.

"I will be yours within two hours—upon one condition."

"Name it—name it!" he eagerly exclaimed.

"You must not marry me under your own name, but under that of Alden Lytton."

When she had said this, she stole a glance at him to see how he took it, and she was somewhat abashed by the look of unutterable amazement on the honest face of the young man.

"Come, what do you say to that?" she inquired.

"My dear Mary, what an astounding proposition!" he exclaimed.

"But you will agree to it?"

He was silent.

"You will agree to this, because you love me," she added.

But he continued silent and very sad.

"You will agree to do this for the sake of making me your wife?" she persisted.

"My dearest Mary, it is impossible!" he answered, with a painful effort.

"There! I knew it! Say no more! You professed great love for me once. You were willing to do, dare, or die for me, if necessary. You wished me to put you to the test, to *try* you, as you called it; yet, the very first time I have tested your sincerity, you have failed me, as I foresaw that you would. Good-bye, Mr. Craven Kyte. We part here, and we part forever," said Mary Grey, with cold contempt, as she turned away from him.

"No, no, no—for Heaven's sake, no!" cried the young man, piteously. "Do not leave me so suddenly. Give me time to think. Oh,

I can not part with you! I must—must have you at any cost!" he muttered to himself.

She stopped and contemplated him as with scornful pity.

"Come—come into the square here and sit down. Let us talk this matter over. Pray do! Oh, I can not lose you so!" he pleaded, seizing her hand.

"Well, I will go in and sit on one of those benches for a few moments, and give you the opportunity of recovering your place in my confidence," she said, with a sort of contemptuous pity, as she turned and entered the square.

He followed her immediately, and they sat down together.

Chapter XXXIII.

A WICKED WEDDING.

> Bid me to leap
> From off the battlements of yonder tower
> And I will do it.

—Shakespeare.

"Now tell me what you wish me to do, and why you wish me to do it," said the lover, submissively.

"I have already told you *what* I wish you to do. *Why* I wish you to do it must remain my secret for the present. You must trust me. Oh, Craven," she added, suddenly changing her tone to one of soft, sorrowful pleading, "why will you not trust me, when I am about to trust you with the happiness of my whole future life?"

"I do trust you! I trust you, as I love you, without limit!" answered the poor fellow, almost weeping.

"Ah, you *say* you do, yet you refuse to do as I wish you," sorrowfully replied the siren.

"I refuse no longer! I will do anything in the world you wish me to do with joy, if in that way I can have you for my own," he declared, with tearful emphasis.

"I knew you would. You are a dear, good, true heart, and I love you more than life!" she said, giving his arm a squeeze. "Listen, now."

He became suddenly all devoted attention, as she artfully unfolded to him just as much of her nefarious plan as was absolutely necessary to secure his co-operation in it. The whole of her scheme in all its diabolical wickedness she dared not expose to his honest soul.

She told him now that she had set her mind on a harmless practical joke, to win a wager with Emma Cavendish.

She said that he must so with her to see the Rev. Mr. Borden, rector of St. — — Church, and ask him to perform the marriage ceremony between them, and that he must give his own name as Mr. Alden Lytton, attorney at law, Richmond, Virginia, and give her name as it was—Mrs. Mary Grey, of the same city. And that they must be married under those names.

The young man stared until his black eyes looked big as old Booth's in the last scene of "Richard."

"But why?" he inquired.

"A practical joke, I tell you. Ah, how hard you are to manage! Why can you not trust me through a little mystery like this—a little practical joke like this?"

"I *do* trust you; but I am afraid that it might seem like a practical forgery to be married under another person's name," he replied.

"Nonsense! Do you think that I could be such an idiot as to implicate you in any act that might be construed into forgery, practical or otherwise?" she inquired, with a light laugh.

"Oh, no, certainly you are not the lady to do that!" he admitted.

"Well, then, what next? You look as solemn as a judge or an owl!"

"I am afraid, also, that if I should be married under any other name than my own our marriage itself might turn out to be nothing more than a practical joke instead of a legal union."

"Mr. Kyte!" she suddenly exclaimed, with her eyes flashing fire. "You insult me! Am I the sort of woman that would compromise my good name in a marriage of doubtful legality?"

"Oh, no; certainly you would not! Nor did I mean that. I earnestly beg your pardon!" said Craven, penitently.

"You are a silly gander, and a dear, darling duck of a boy! And I love you! But you must understand that I know what I am about. And you must trust me—you must trust me; and, once for all, you must *trust* me!" she said, archly, giving his arm another squeeze.

"I do—I do! Come; shall we be going? I am on the rack till our wedding is over."

"Yes; but we must take a cab. The distance is a long one."

"There is a cab-stand a couple of blocks from here. I noticed it as I came along. We will take one there, if you please."

She assented, and they walked on to the stand and engaged a cab.

When they were seated in it Craven Kyte ordered the cabman to drive to the rectory of St. —— Church.

Half an hour's driving brought them to their destination.

When the cab drew up to the door of the house, Craven was about to alight, when Mary Grey stopped him.

"Wait," she said.

And taking from her card-case a pencil and a blank card, she wrote upon it the name:

"Mr. Alden Lytton."

"Send that in," she said, handing the card to the bewildered young man.

Craven Kyte took it, looked at it attentively, and then exclaimed:

"Why, that is exactly like Mr. Lytton's own handwriting! If I had not seen you write it I should have taken it to be his autograph."

"Should you? So much the better. But never mind that now. Go and do as I told you."

He alighted immediately and went up to the door of the house. He rang the bell, and sent in the card by the servant who answered it.

After the lapse of a few moments the servant came back with a very favorable message.

Craven Kyte returned to the cab and whispered:

"Mr. Borden is at home and will see us. Come."

And he assisted her to alight.

And they went into the rectory, and were shown by a servant into the study of the rector.

Mary Grey courtesied to the gray-haired, dignified clergyman, who arose to receive her; but she kept her veil down as she took her seat in the chair he placed for her.

Craven Kyte then drew the reverend gentleman aside and spoke to him in a low voice.

Mr. Borden nodded and nodded as the speaker proceeded.

When he had finished speaking, the rector inquired:

"Both of legal age?"

"Both of more than legal age, and both quite independent of others," answered Craven Kyte.

"I merely asked the question because in cases of this kind I prefer that the parties should be of legal age; though were they minors I should feel it to be my duty to marry them all the same, because, I think, when a youth and maiden run away with each other the best thing a Christian minister can do for them is to tie them together for life."

"I am a bachelor of twenty-two years of age, and my chosen wife is a widow of twenty-one. We take this simple method of getting married for economy and convenience, and for no other reason; for there is no one in the world who has either the power or the will to prevent us," said Craven Kyte.

"Very well, Mr. Lytton; I am ready to wait on you. I prefer, however, to solemnize marriage in the church, when possible. There must be witnesses also. And if you have none at hand the sexton and some members of his family can serve."

Craven Kyte winced at the prospect of all these formalities.

"I thought that in the Quaker City marriage was a matter of less form," he said.

"Yes, among the Quakers; but even they must have witnesses. If you and the lady will go into the church I will join you there in a few minutes. You will find the doors open and the sexton in the building, preparing for the usual Friday afternoon service," said the rector.

And Craven Kyte again offered his arm to his companion and led her out of the rectory and into the church.

It was evident from all signs that the interior had just been swept out.

And an old man and a young woman, whom Craven Kyte and his companion rightly guessed to be the sexton and the sexton's daughter, were busily engaged in dusting the pews.

Craven Kyte and Mary Grey sat down upon a front seat before the altar to wait until the rector should make his appearance.

Mr. Borden did not keep them long in suspense. He soon entered, dressed in his surplice, and took his place within the chancel.

The candidates for matrimony advanced and stood before him.

He beckoned the sexton and the sexton's daughter to draw near and stand as witnesses.

And they came up, dusting-brushes in hand, and stood staring while the ceremony was performed.

After the preliminary exhortation and prayers the important questions were put:

"Will you, Alden, take Mary to be your wedded wife, to live together after God's ordinance in the holy estate of matrimony?" and so forth, and so forth, and so forth.

To which Craven Kyte, turning pale at his own unwilling duplicity in answering to a false name, replied:

"I will."

"Will you, Mary, take Alden to be your wedded husband?" and so forth, and so forth.

To which Mary Grey answered firmly:

"I will."

And the ring was placed upon her finger. And her marriage vows were solemnly repeated, the last prayer said, and the benediction pronounced.

It was all over.

"Those whom God hath joined together let no man put asunder."

The newly-married pair were about to turn from the altar, when the rector said:

"Come with me into the vestry for a moment."

And they followed him into the vestry, attended by the two witnesses.

The rector made an entry into a large book, and then called upon the bridegroom and the bride to sign their names.

Again Craven Kyte turned pale as death as he registered the false name under which he had been married.

But his companion wrote her name in firm and steady characters.

Then the sexton and his daughter signed as witnesses.

The rector filled out a blank form, which he also signed and caused to be signed by the two witnesses.

This he put into an envelope and handed to the bride.

Then he bowed to both, as a signal that all the forms had been complied with, and they were at liberty to depart.

"What was that paper the minister gave you, my dearest love?" whispered Craven, as they left the church.

"It was the certificate of marriage which the minister usually—and very properly—gives to the newly-married woman," answered the bride.

"Oh, quite right, my angel!" replied the doomed bridegroom, as he tenderly put her into the cab and took his seat beside her.

And then he clasped her to his honest heart in an ecstasy of love and went off into the most extravagant rhapsodies about his happiness.

CHAPTER XXXIV.

AFTER THE WICKED WEDDING.

"And I no friends to back my cause withal,
But the plain devil and dissembling looks.
I have him, but I will not keep him long."

"Did you tell the coachman where to drive?" inquired the bride, as the carriage rolled rapidly through one of the principal streets of the city.

"Yes, dearest," answered the infatuated bridegroom. "I told him to drive to the Asterick, where I am stopping, and where I have had elegant rooms prepared for your reception. Do you think I could have forgotten anything in which your comfort was concerned?"

"No, I am sure you could not; but—" She hesitated a moment, and then added: "I wanted to go somewhere else."

"My love—my love, you shall go where you please. After we have got to our rooms at the Asterick, and refreshed and rested ourselves, we will consult about where to go and spend a pleasant fortnight together," he answered, affectionately.

"Yes; but I don't want to go to the Asterick just yet."

"Where then? I will go anywhere you wish."

"You know I did not come to this city alone."

"Didn't you, dear? I thought you did."

"No; I came with a party of lady friends. And I left them all abruptly this morning to meet you, without telling them where I was going or when I should be back. I have now been gone two hours. They will be uneasy about me by this time. I must go back there and relieve their anxiety, and also get my traveling-bag."

"Very well, my darling, we will drive there immediately."

"No, no; *you* must not go there! I have not told them anything about my intended marriage, so I don't want them to know anything about it, lest they should be offended. There is a reading-room at the corner of the street near the hotel. Stop there, and I will get out and walk to the house and take leave of my friends, and then return to the reading-room and join you. In the meantime you can send the carriage away, and while waiting for me you can amuse yourself looking over the books."

"But I hate to lose you even for an hour."

"Ah, be reasonable, and remember that it will be but for an hour or less time. And when we meet again it will be to part no more forever—or until death himself shall part us."

"I must submit, I suppose," said Craven, with a sigh.

"Submit? Oh, you crazy boy! You talk as if you were making some painful sacrifice!" she answered, with a light laugh.

"It *is* painful to let you leave me even for an hour."

"Bah! You'll be glad to be rid of me some of these days."

"Never!"

"Bah, I say again! Come, here we are at the reading-room. Stop the carriage."

He did so.

"Let me out here and I will walk on," she said.

"Had you not better let me get out here, and keep your own seat and drive on?" he inquired.

"No. I don't want the carriage to take me to the hotel. The distance is short. I prefer walking. You had better dismiss it, and go into the reading-room and amuse yourself while waiting for me," she said.

He acquiesced, and she got out and walked rapidly on toward the Blank House.

With her thick veil let down, she slipped in through the ladies' entrance with some visitors that just happened to be going there.

She hurried upstairs to her own rooms and unlocked the door of the private parlor.

All within the place was just as she had left it two hours before.

She opened the window-shutters to let in the daylight, and then she went and listened at the door communicating with Alden Lytton's room.

At first all was still. But presently she heard a step about the room, and soon after other motions that proved the inmate to be busy at his toilet.

"He is up and dressing himself. I have not returned one minute too soon," she said, as she seated herself in an easy-chair near the window.

The next moment the door opened and Alden Lytton entered, smiling.

"I do not know how to apologize for my stupid neglect. But I hope you will believe me when I assure you it was inadvertent. The truth is I overslept myself. I can't think what made me do it," he said, actually blushing like a boy at the thought of his involuntary sluggishness.

"You were very much fatigued last night. I am very glad you had a refreshing sleep. I hope you feel the better for it," she answered, with her sweet smile.

"Well, no; not much better. You know there is such a thing as taking too much sleep. I feel quite as if I had taken twice too much—dull and heavy, with a stupid headache. I never was inebriated in my life, but I should think a man that had been so, over night, would feel just as I do this morning."

"Ah, I am sorry! But the fresh air will do you good, no doubt."

"No doubt. And really it is not worth speaking of. I see you have your hat on. You have been taking a walk this fine morning, while I lay like a sluggard, sleeping myself into a headache?"

"No, I have not been out. I put my hat on merely to be ready to start the moment we had breakfasted. For I must go and see the principal of the ladies' school this morning."

"Why, I hope you have not waited breakfast for me all this time!" exclaimed Alden, in a tone of regret.

"I have not waited very long. And if I must confess the fault, I have not been up very long myself."

"Ah!" laughed Alden Lytton. "So somebody else overslept herself!"

"Yes; ''tis true, 'tis pity, and pity 'tis 'tis true!'"

"You must be hungry, however. I will ring and order breakfast directly."

"No, please don't. It will take too much time. For once we will go down in the dining-room and get our breakfast."

"As you please," said Alden Lytton, as he arose to attend her downstairs.

The guests had nearly all left the dining-room, so there were waiters enough at leisure to attend to these late arrivals; and it followed, of course, that they had not long to wait for their coffee and rolls.

They did not tarry over their meal. Both were in a hurry.

"I should have been at the law publisher's two hours ago," said Alden.

"And I should have been at the ladies' school about the same time," added Mary.

"I shall never forgive myself for sleeping so ridiculously long and detaining you," said Alden.

"Say no more about it. We shall only have to hurry over our breakfast to make up for lost time," answered the traitress.

And they soon finished and arose from the table.

"Will you be so good as to order a carriage for me while I run upstairs and get my traveling-bag?" she inquired.

"Certainly," he answered, as he gave her his arm and led her to the foot of the grand staircase.

And as she ran up, he turned and sent a hall porter for the carriage.

And then he waited at the foot of the stairs for her return.

The carriage was announced, and she reappeared about the same time.

She carried in her hand a leather bag and a small silk umbrella, both of which she handed to a porter.

"This looks like a departure," said Alden Lytton, as he gave her his arm to lead her to the carriage.

"It may be a departure," she answered; "and I must take this, perhaps last, opportunity of thanking you for all your brotherly kindness to me. If I should not return by six o'clock this evening, please give up my room."

"I will do so," said Alden Lytton. "And in that case I also shall give up my room, for I think I shall be able to get through with my business to-day. If you should be returning to Virginia I should be pleased to escort you back."

"Thanks! But I rather think that I shall try the school. That will do. I am very comfortable. Thanks, very much!" she added, as she settled herself in the seat where he had placed her.

"Where shall I tell the coachman to drive?" inquired Alden.

"Tell him to call first at the reading-room at the corner of the next street. I wish to look at the directory there before going further."

This order was given to the coachman, who immediately started his horses.

In a very few minutes the carriage drew up before the reading-room door.

Mary Grey—as I still prefer to call her—got out and ran into the room.

Craven Kyte was there, trying to interest himself in a morning paper. As soon as he saw her he dropped the paper and started to meet her.

"It seems to me you have been gone four hours instead of one," he said.

"I have been gone just an hour and seven minutes, you very bad boy!" she answered, playfully. "Now, then, I am at your lordship's service."

"Oh, my beloved, do not speak so to me, even in sport, for you are my queen and I am your subject! Shall we go now?"

"Yes, I have a carriage at the door, with my little luggage in it."

"Come then, love."

They went out together and entered the carriage.

"Drive to the Asterick Hotel," said Craven Kyte to the coachman.

"And tell him to drive slowly, for I wish to talk to you as we go along," she whispered.

"Drive slowly," said Mr. Kyte, giving her order.

"Now, Craven, dear," she said, as they went along, "I wish you to understand that I don't want to stop at the Asterick longer than it will take you to pay your bill and pack your portmanteau."

"Where do you want to go then, my darling? I am ready to go anywhere with you," he replied.

"Then I have a fancy for spending a few days at Havre-de-Grace. It is a very pretty place. We can take the next train and get there in two or three hours."

"Very well, my angel, I will make every effort to catch that train."

"Now, then, tell the coachman to drive fast."

Again Craven Kyte conveyed her orders to the man on the box, who touched up his horses.

And they were whirled rapidly on toward the Asterick Hotel, where they soon arrived.

"Hadn't I better tell the carriage to wait?" inquired Craven Kyte.

"No; send it away. We can pick up another one in a moment," answered his companion.

Craven Kyte paid and discharged the carriage, and they went into the house.

He took his companion up into the private parlor he had engaged for her, and he pressed her to partake of some refreshments while he packed up his portmanteau and paid his bill.

But she declined the refreshments and said she would wait, keeping herself closely veiled all the time.

He hurried through his business as fast as he could, and soon rejoined her.

He took her down to the cab he had engaged, and which was already packed with their luggage.

A half-hour's rapid drive took them to the railway station, which they reached only in time to buy their tickets, check their baggage and take their seats before the train started.

It was the express. And they were soon whirled through the country to the town where the bride chose to spend her honeymoon.

CHAPTER XXXV.

HER CRIME.

They took rooms in a pleasant hotel in the town, and after an early tea they strolled down to the water-side to look at the small shipping.

It was a delicious evening in September. The sun had just set, and the whole expanse of water was aflame with the afterglow.

A refreshing breeze had sprung up, and the river was alive with pleasure boats of every description, from the sail- to the row-boat.

And there were more boats for hire, at the service of any who might wish to amuse themselves upon the water.

"Take a boat. Craven, and let us go out for a row. The evening is so delightful, the sky and the water so beautiful," said the bride, coaxingly.

"I would like to do so, my angel; but, to tell the truth, I am a very inexperienced oarsman, and I can not swim at all," answered the poor fellow, apologetically.

"Are you afraid then, Craven?" she asked, with exasperating archness.

"No, love, not for myself, but for you. If by my awkwardness any accident should happen to you I think I should run raving mad," he answered, earnestly.

"Oh, well, never mind me! There is no cause for fear whatever, as far as I am concerned. I can row like a squaw and I can swim like a duck. And I think I could do so ever since I could walk. At least, I certainly do not remember the time when I could not swim," said the lady, laughingly.

"What a wonder you are—in everything!" exclaimed the lover-bridegroom, in a rapture of admiration.

"No wonder at all. I was brought up on the water-side, and was always a sort of amphibious little creature, as often in the water as out of it. Come, now, will you hire a boat to please me?"

"Of course! I would do anything in the world to please you, my angel!"

"Then engage that little pea-green boat. It is a nice one," she said, pointing to a frail skiff moored near them.

"That, my dearest Mary? Why, that is a mere egg-shell! It could not live in rough water. And if this gentle breeze should rise into a wind—"

"Are you afraid?" she inquired, with provoking sarcasm.

"I say again not for myself, but for you."

"And I say again that there can be no ground of fear for me. I say again I can row like a squaw and swim like a duck. There! Now will you get the boat I want?"

"Yes, my darling, I will. And I will also take the precaution to hire the man in charge of it to help us row, in case of accidents."

"No, no, no; I won't have the man! He would spoil all our pleasure. I want you and myself to go out alone together, and have no interloper with us."

"But, my beloved—"

"I don't believe you love me at all, when you want a great hulking boatman to be in the boat with us, watching us," said the bride, with pretty childish petulance.

"Not love you? Oh, heaven of heavens! You *know* how I love you—how I *adore* you—how I *worship* you!" he whispered, earnestly.

"Will you get the boat I want before it grows too dark?"

"Yes, yes, I will, my darling! I can refuse you nothing," said the infatuated bridegroom as he walked down to the water's edge and forthwith hired the one she had set her heart on.

Then he came back to take her down to the boat.

It was a mere shell, as he had said; and though the boatman declared that it could easily carry six if required, it did not look as if it would safely bear more than two or three passengers at most.

They were soon floating out upon the water and down with the tide past the dingy colliers and the small trading vessels that were anchored there, and out among the coming and going sloops and schooners.

"Let me row toward that beautiful wooded shore. It is so lovely over there!" said Mary Grey, coaxingly.

"'Distance lends,' and so forth," smiled Craven Kyte, as he at once headed for the shore.

But the outgoing tide had left a muddy beach there, and so they had to keep at a respectful distance from it.

They rowed again to the middle of the river.

The afterglow had faded away, but the blue-black starlit sky was brilliantly reflected in the dark water.

When they had rowed an hour longer, back and forth from shore to shore, Craven Kyte drew in his oar and said:

"It is growing late and very dark, love. Had we not better go in?"

"No, no, no!" answered the bride, with prettily assumed authority.

"But, dear love—"

"The night is beautiful! I could stay out here until morning!"

"But chills and fevers, these September nights, darling!"

"Fiddle-de-dee! Are you afraid?"

"Not for myself, love, but for you."

"I never had a chill in my life! I am acclimated to these water-side places. If you are tired of rowing give me the oars."

"Not for the world! What, fatigue your dear arms? I would sooner mine dropped from my shoulders with weariness!"

And he took up both oars again and plied them actively, although his unaccustomed muscles were aching from the long-continued exercise.

"Turn down the stream then and row with the tide. It will be so much lighter work than rowing back and forth across the river."

"But it will take us so far from the town."

"Never mind!"

"And it will make it very difficult, when we turn back, to row against wind and tide."

"Bah, we will not stay out long! We will only go around that point that I see before us. What a fascination there is in a turning point! We always want to see what is on the other side," said Mary Grey, lightly.

Meantime, Craven Kyte had turned the boat and they were floating down stream very fast.

They soon passed the point, and saw on the other side a flat, sandy shore, with the woods at a little distance.

They were still off the point, when Mary Grey suddenly uttered an exclamation of dismay.

"What is the matter?" hastily inquired Craven Kyte.

"Oh, my hat! My hat has fallen off my head and is in the water! If you stoop over quick you can reach it before it floats quite away!" she said, eagerly.

Craven Kyte immediately drew in his oars and secured them, and then bent over the side of the boat to reach the hat that was still floating within three feet of his hands. He bent very far out and endangered his balance.

Mary Grey arose to her feet. Her eyes were glittering like phosphorus in the night, her face pallid in the starlight.

He bent lower down and further out, trying to reach the hat, when suddenly she gave him a push and he fell into the river, and went down before he could utter the cry upon his lips.

The force with which she had pushed her victim into the water had given the little boat an impetus that sent it flying down the stream, and rocking violently from side to side.

It was as much as she could do to keep her place in it. Any other than an experienced boat-woman like herself must have been shaken out and drowned.

She heard her victim's agonized scream for help as he rose the first time to the surface of the water.

But she gave it no attention.

For even if she had repented, and had wished to save him, she could not do so now.

She could, with the greatest difficulty, keep her place in the rocking boat until the impetus that had started it was spent.

Yet again that awful cry for help pierced the night sky as the drowning man arose the second time to the surface; but on this occasion the cry sounded farther off, and the boat, though it had ceased to rock, was flying rapidly down stream.

She took hold of the rudder and tried to guide the flying little shell.

Her situation, self-sought as it had been, was one of almost intolerable horror.

The night sky was above her, the dark waters beneath her, and around her, at various distances, like little dim white specks, were to be seen the sails of the coming and going colliers, and other small trading craft.

She steered down the stream with the tide, pausing now and then and listening. But she heard no more that agonized cry of the drowning man, though she knew it would ring in her spirit's ears forever.

She steered down stream until she heard the sound of oars, and of merry laughter and cheerful talk, and then she dimly perceived the approach of a large pleasure boat crowded with gentlemen and ladies.

Then she, knowing it was too late to save her victim, deceitfully raised a shrill scream, that attracted the attention of the people in the large boat, which was immediately rowed in the direction of the cry.

Soon the two boats were side by side.

"What is the matter?" inquired a man's voice from the larger boat.

"Oh, for Heaven's sake, help! My companion has fallen overboard, and, I fear, is drowned!" cried Mary Grey, wringing her hands in well-simulated grief and terror.

"Where? Where?" inquired a dozen eager, interested voices, all at once.

"Just about here. Oh, look for him, listen for him! Do try to save him!" cried the hypocrite, seizing her own hair, as if she would have pulled it out by the roots, in her pretended anguish of mind.

"Where did he fall? Did he not struggle?" inquired two or three voices, as the oarsmen rowed their boat around and around in a circle and peered over the surface of the water for some sign of the lost man.

"Oh, he sank at once—he sank at once!" cried Mary Grey, beating her breast.

"But he will come up again. They always do, unless they are seized with the cramp and it holds them. Keep a bright lookout there, boys, and if you see so much as a ripple in the water make for it at once! We may save the poor fellow yet!" said the voice of a man who seemed to be in authority.

"How in the world did he happen to fall over, miss?" inquired another voice.

"Oh, my miserable, unlucky hat blew off my head and fell into the water. I begged him not to mind it—told him I would tie a pocket-handkerchief over my head—but he wouldn't listen to me. Oh, he wouldn't listen me! And so, in stooping to recover my wretched hat, he bent over too far, lost his balance and fell into the water. And oh, he sank at once like lead! Oh, do try to find him! Oh, do try to save him! He might be resuscitated even now, if you could find him— might he not?" she cried, wringing her hands.

"Oh, yes, ma'am!" answered a man, in his good-natured wish to soothe who he took to be a distracted woman.

And they rowed around and around, peering into the water and listening for every sound.

But there was no sign of the lost man.

After they had sought for him about an hour the man who seemed to be the chief among them said:

"I am afraid it is quite vain, ma'am. It is not a drowning, but a drowned man that we have been seeking for the last hour. Tell us where you wish to go, and we will take you home. To-morrow the body may be recovered."

But Mary Grey, with a wild shriek, fell back in her boat and lay like one in a swoon.

"We must take the lady into this boat of ours, and tow the little one after us," said the man.

Chapter XXXVI.

AFTER THE DARK DEED.

Mary Grey was lifted, in an apparently fainting condition, from her own little boat into the larger one beside it. She was laid down carefully and waited on tenderly by the sympathizing ladies in the larger boat.

Meanwhile the little boat was tied to the stern of the larger one, to be towed up the river.

"Where are we to take the poor unfortunate woman, I wonder?" said one of the ladies.

"If she does not come to her senses in time to tell us where she lives you can bring her to my house," answered another lady.

"Or to mine," said a third.

"Or mine," added a fourth.

"Or mine," "or mine," chimed in others.

Everybody was emulous to succor this unhappy one.

As they neared the city Mary Grey condescended to heave a deep sigh, shudder and open her eyes.

Then a chorus of sympathizing voices saluted her. But she wept and moaned, and pretended to refuse to be comforted.

It was some time before the persevering efforts of a gentleman succeeded in persuading her to understand and answer his question as to where she lived.

"At the Star Hotel," she said, with a gasp and a sigh, as if her heart were broken.

The boat landed; and the "poor lady," as she was compassionately called, was tenderly lifted out by the gentlemen and carefully supported between two of them while she was led to the hotel, followed by the ladies.

The sad news of the young gentleman's fate was immediately communicated to the people at the hotel, and soon spread through the town.

Ah, the drowning of a man at that point was not such an unusual event after all, and it made much less impression than it ought to have done.

Some people said they felt sorry for the poor young woman so suddenly bereaved and left among strangers; and perhaps they really believed that they did so; but the next instant they thought of something else.

But the ladies who had been present near the scene of the catastrophe, and had witnessed Mary Grey's well-acted terror, grief and despair, really did sympathize with her supposed sorrows to a very painful extent.

After following her to the hotel, they went with her to her room, and helped to undress her and put her to bed.

And two among them offered to remain and watch with her during the night.

The sinful woman, already a prey to the horrors of remorse and superstition, dreading the darkness and solitude of the night, fearing almost to see the dripping specter of the drowned man standing over her bed, gratefully accepted their offer, and begged, at the same time, for morphia.

Her kind attendants were afraid to administer a dangerous opiate without the advice of a physician; so they sent for one immediately, who, on his arrival and his examination of the terribly excited patient, gave her a dose that soon sent her to sleep.

The two ladies took their places by her bed and watched her.

She slept well through the night, and awoke quite calmly in the morning. The composing influence of the morphia had not yet left her.

And with the returning daylight much of her remorse and all of her superstition vanished for the time being.

She thanked the ladies who had watched her during the night, and, in reply to their inquiries, assured them that she felt better, but begged them to keep her room dark.

They expressed their gratification to hear her say so. One of them bathed her face and hands and combed her hair, while the other one rang the bell, and ordered tea and toast to be brought to the room.

And they tenderly pressed her to eat and drink, and they waited on her while she partook slightly of this light breakfast.

Then they rang and sent the breakfast service away, and they put her room in order, and smoothed her pillows and the coverlet of her bed, and finally they kissed her and bade her good-morning for a while, promising to return again in the course of the afternoon, and begging that she would send for them, at the address they gave her, in case she should require their services sooner.

When she was left alone, Mary Grey slipped out of bed, locked the door after the ladies, and then, having secured herself from intrusion, she opened her traveling-bag and took from it a small white envelope, from which she drew a neatly-folded white paper.

This was the marriage certificate, setting forth that on the fifteenth day of September, eighteen hundred and — —, at the parish church of St. — —, in the city of Philadelphia, Alden Lytton, attorney at law, of the city of Richmond, and Mary Grey, widow, of the same city, were united in the holy bonds of matrimony by the Rev. Mr. Borden, rector of the church, in the presence of John Martin, sexton, and Sarah Martin, his daughter.

The certificate was duly signed by the Rev. Mr. Borden and by John Martin and Sarah Martin.

Mary Grey sat down with this document before her, read it over slowly, and laughed a demoniac laugh as she folded it up and put it carefully into its envelope and returned it to her traveling-bag, while she reviewed her plot and "summed up the evidence" she had accumulated against the peace and honor of Alden Lytton and Emma Cavendish.

"Yes, I will let him marry her," she said, "and then, in the midst of their fancied security and happiness, I will come down upon them like an avalanche of destruction. I will claim him for my own husband by a previous marriage. I have evidence enough to convict and ruin him.

"First, I have all his impassioned letters, written to me from Charlottesville, while I was a guest at the Government House in Richmond.

"Secondly, I have those perfectly manufactured letters addressed to me in a fac-simile of his handwriting, signed by his name and mailed from Wendover to me at Richmond.

"Why, these alone would be sufficient to prove his perfidy even to Emma Cavendish's confiding heart! And they would be good for heavy damages in a breach of promise case.

"But I do not want damages—I want revenge. I do not want to touch his pocket—I want to ruin his life. Yes—and hers! I want to dishonor, degrade and utterly ruin them both! And I have evidence enough to do this," she said, resuming her summing up, "for there is—

"Thirdly, his meeting me at Forestville and his journey with me to Richmond.

"Fourthly, his journey with me to Philadelphia.

"Fifthly, the rector's certificate, setting forth the marriage of Alden Lytton and Mary Grey.

"Sixthly, the testimony of the rector, who will swear that he performed the ceremony, and of the sexton and the sexton's daughter, who will swear that they witnessed the marriage of Alden

Lytton and Mary Grey; and swear, furthermore—from his exact resemblance to Craven Kyte—to the identity of Alden Lytton as the bridegroom.

"Alden Lytton can not disprove this by an alibi, for at the very time Craven Kyte personated him, and under his name and character married me, Alden Lytton, in a dead stupor, was locked up in his darkened chamber, and no one knew of his whereabouts but myself, who had the key of his room.

"Nor can Craven Kyte 'ever rise to explain,' for death and the Susquehanna mud has stopped his mouth.

"So this chain of evidence must be conclusive not only to the minds of the jury, who will send my gentleman to rusticate in a penitentiary for a term of years, but also to Miss Cavendish, who will find her proud escutcheon blotted a little, I think."

While Mary Grey gloated over the horrors of her plotted vengeance, there came a rap at the door. She hastily put on a dressing-gown, softly unlocked the door, threw herself into an easy-chair, with her back to the window, and bade the rapper to come in.

The door opened and the clerk of the house entered, bringing with him the house register, which he held open in his hand.

"I beg your pardon for this unseasonable intrusion, madam," he said, as he laid the open book down on the table before her; "but being called upon to report this sad case of the drowning of a guest of this house, I find some difficulty in making out the name, for the poor young gentleman does not seem to have written very clearly. The name is registered C. or G. something or other. But whether it is Hyte or Flyte or Kyle or Hyle, none of us can make out."

Mary Grey smiled within herself, as she secretly rejoiced at the opportunity of concealing the real name and identity of Craven Kyte with the drowned man.

So she drew the book toward her and said, with an affectation of weariness and impatience, as she gazed upon poor Craven's illegible hieroglyphics:

"Why, the name is quite plain! It is G. Hyle—H-y-l-e. Don't you see?"

"Oh, yes, madam! I see now quite plainly. Excuse me: they ask for the full name. Would you please to tell me what the initial G stands for?"

"Certainly. It stands for Gaston. His name was Gaston Hyle. He was a foreigner, as his name shows. There, there, pray do not talk to me any more! I can not bear it," said Mary Grey, affecting symptoms of hysterical grief.

"I beg your pardon for having troubled you, madam, indeed! And I thank you for the information you have given me. Good-day, madam," said the clerk, bowing kindly and courteously as he withdrew.

The next day the newspapers, under the head of casualties, published the following paragraph:

"On Friday evening last a young man, a foreigner, of the name of Gaston Hyle, who had been stopping at the Star Hotel, Havre-de-Grace, was accidentally drowned while boating on the river. His body has not yet been recovered."

No, nor his body never was recovered.

Mary Grey, for form's sake, remained a week at Havre-de-Grace, affecting great anxiety for the recovery of that body. But she shut herself up in her room, pretending the deepest grief, and upon this pretext refusing all sympathizing visits, even from the ladies who had shown her so much kindness on the night of the catastrophe, and from the clergy, who would have offered her religious consolation.

The true reason of her seclusion was that she did not wish her features to become familiar to these people, lest at some future time they might possibly be inconveniently recognized.

As yet no one had seen her face except by night or in her darkened room. And she did not intend that they should.

Her supposed grievous bereavement was her all-sufficient excuse for her seclusion.

At the end of the week Mary Grey paid her bill at the Star, and, closely-veiled, left the hotel and took the evening train for Washington, *en route* for Richmond.

In due time she reached the last-named city and took up her residence at her old quarters with the Misses Crane, there to wait patiently until the marriage of Alden Lytton and Emma Cavendish should give her the opportunity of consummating their ruin and her own triumph. Meanwhile poor Craven Kyte's leave of absence having expired, he began to be missed and inquired for.

But to all questions his partner answered that he did not know where he was or when he would be back, but thought he was all right.

Chapter XXXVII.

GREAT PROSPERITY.

> Fortune is merry,
> And in this mood will give us anything.

—SHAKESPEARE.

Alden Lytton prospered wonderfully. Not once in a thousand instances can a young professional man get on as fast as he did.

Usually the young lawyer or doctor has to wait long before work comes to him, and then to work long before money comes.

It was not so with Alden Lytton.

As soon as he opened his office business came in at the door.

His first brief was a success.

His second, and more difficult one, was a still greater victory.

His third, and most important, was the greatest triumph of the three.

And from this time the high road to fame and fortune was open to him.

The astonishing rapidity of his rise was explained in various ways by different persons.

Emma Cavendish, who loved and esteemed him, ascribed his great prosperity to his own splendid talents alone.

Alden Lytton himself, full of filial respect, attributed it to the prestige of his late father's distinguished name.

And the briefless young lawyers, his unsuccessful rivals at the bar, credited it to the "loud" advertisement afforded by his handsome office and the general appearance of wealth and prosperity that surrounded him.

No doubt they were all right and—all wrong.

Not one of these circumstances taken alone could have secured the young barrister's success. Neither his own talents nor his father's name, nor the costly appointments of his office, could have done it; yet each contributed something, and all together they combined to insure his rapid advancement in his profession.

While Alden Lytton was thus gaining fame and fortune, Mary Grey was engaged in mystifying the minds and winning the sympathy and compassion of all her acquaintants.

From the time of her return from Philadelphia she had exhibited a deep and incurable melancholy.

Everybody pitied her deeply and wondered what could be the secret sorrow under which she was suffering.

But when any friend more curious than the rest ventured to question her, she answered:

"I have borne and am still bearing the deepest wrong that any woman can suffer and survive. But I must not speak of it now. My hands are bound and my tongue is tied. But the time *may* come when a higher duty than that which restrains me now may force me to speak. Until then I must be mute."

This was extremely tantalizing to all her friends; but it was all that could be got from her.

Meanwhile her face faded into a deadlier pallor and her form wasted to a ghastlier thinness. And this was real, for she was demon-haunted—a victim of remorse, not a subject of repentance.

The specter that she had feared to look upon on the fatal night of her crime—the pale, dripping form of her betrayed and murdered lover—was ever before her mind's eye.

If she entered a solitary or a half-darkened room the phantasm lurked in the shadowy corners or met her face to face.

It came to her bedside in the dead of night and laid its clammy wet hand upon her sleeping brow. And when she woke in wild affright it met her transfixed and horrified gaze.

Her only relief was in opium. She would stupefy herself every night with opium, and wake every morning pale, haggard, dull and heavy.

She must have sunk under her mental suffering and material malpractices but for the one purpose that had once carried her into crime and now kept her alive through the terror and remorse that were the natural consequences of that crime. She lived only for revenge—

"Like lightning fire,
To speed one bolt of ruin and expire!"

"I will live and keep sane until I degrade and destroy both Alden Lytton and Emma Cavendish, and then—I must die or go mad," she said to herself.

Such was her inner life.

Her outer life was very different from this.

She was still, to all appearance, a zealous church woman, never missing a service either on Sundays or on week-days; never neglecting the sewing-circles, the missionary meetings, the Sunday-schools, or any other of the parish works or charities, and always contributing liberally to every benevolent enterprise from the munificent income paid her quarterly by Miss Cavendish.

Since her return from Philadelphia she had not resumed her acquaintance with Alden Lytton.

They did not attend the same church, and were not in the same circle. It was a very reserved "circle" in which Mary Grey "circulated;" while Alden Lytton sought the company of professional and scholarly men.

Thus for months after their return to Richmond they did not meet.

Alden Lytton in the meanwhile supposed her to be still in Philadelphia, filling a position as drawing-mistress in the ladies' college.

It was early in the winter when they accidentally encountered each other on Main Street.

On seeing her form approach, Alden Lytton stepped quickly to meet her, with an extended hand and a bright smile; but the next instant he started in sorrowful surprise, as his eyes fell on her pallid face, so changed since he had seen it last.

"My dear Mrs. Grey, I am so glad to see you! I hope I see you well," he added, as he took her hand, but his looks belied his "hope."

"I am not well, thank you," she answered plaintively, and her looks did not belie her words.

"I am very sorry to hear it. How long have you been in the city?" he next inquired, holding her hand and looking at her with eyes full of pity.

"I have been back some time," she answered, vaguely. "I was forced to leave my situation from failing health."

"I did not know that you had returned or I should have called on you before this. But," he added, perceiving her physical weakness, "I am wrong to keep you standing here. I will turn about and walk with you while we talk. Which way are you going? Will you take my arm?"

"Thanks, no, Mr. Lytton. I can not take your arm; and neither, if you will forgive me for saying it, can I receive a visit from you. The world is censorious, Alden Lytton. And in my lonely and unprotected position I dare not receive the visits of gentlemen," she answered, pensively.

"That seems hard, but doubtless it is discreet. However, that will all be changed, I hope, in a little while. In a very few months, I trust, your home will be with my beloved wife and myself. I know it is

248

Emma's desire that you should live with us," he said, still kindly holding her thin hand.

"Is your wedding to come off so soon?" she inquired.

"Yes, in a few weeks, and then we are to go to Europe for a short holiday, and afterward take a house in the city here," said Alden, smiling.

"I wish you every joy in your wedded life. And now, Mr. Lytton, you must let me go," she said, wearily.

"One moment. You do not write to Emma often, do you? I ask because only a week ago, in one of her letters to me, Miss Cavendish wrote that she had not heard from you for nearly three months, and requested me to find out your address, if possible. I wrote back in reply that I believed you to be at the Ladies' College, in Philadelphia," he said, still detaining her hand.

"I am a bad correspondent. My hand is still lame. Just before I left here for Philadelphia I sent Miss Cavendish an acknowledgment of the last quarterly sum she sent me. I told her then that I was about to go to Philadelphia on particular business. I have not written to her since."

"And that was nearly three months ago. That is just what the matter is. She wishes to find out your address, so as to know where to send the next quarterly instalment of your income, which will soon be due."

"Tell her that I have returned to this city, and that my address is the same as that to which she last wrote."

"I will; but do you write to her also. I know she is anxious to hear directly from you."

"I will do so," she replied; "though I am the worst possible correspondent. Now good-day, Mr. Lytton."

"If I may not call to see you, at least I hope that you will let me know if ever I can serve you in any manner," he said, gently, as he pressed the pale hand he had held so long and relinquished it.

They parted then, and saw no more of each other for some days.

Alden went on his office, full of pity for the failing woman, who, he said to himself, could not possibly have many months to live.

But his feelings of painful compassion were soon forgotten in his happiness in finding a letter from Emma Cavendish lying with his business correspondence on his desk.

There was really nothing more in it than appeared in just such letters that he received two or three times a week; only she told him that she had written to Mrs. Grey at the Ladies' College, Philadelphia, and had not received any answer to her letter.

Before doing any other business, Alden Lytton took a half-quire of note-paper and dashed off an exuberant letter to his lady-love, in which, after repeating the oft-told story of her peerless loveliness and his deathless devotion, he came down to practical matters, and spoke of their mutual friend Mary Grey. He told Emma that Mrs. Grey was in the city again, where she had been for some weeks, although he had not been aware of the fact until he had met her that morning on Main Street while on the way to his office.

He told her of "poor Mary Grey's" failing health and spirits and ghastly appearance, and suggested those circumstances as probable reasons why she had not written to her friends during the last three months.

Then he went back to the old everlasting theme of his infinite, eternal love, etc., etc., etc., and closed with fervent prayers and blessings and joyful anticipations.

CHAPTER XXXVIII.

THE MASK THROWN OFF.

As a consequence of this, two days afterward Mary Grey received a tender, affectionate, sympathetic letter from Emma Cavendish pressing her to come down to Blue Cliffs at once and let them love her and nurse her back to health and happiness. And this letter inclosed a check for double the amount of the usual quarterly stipend.

Miss Cavendish, for some coy reason or other, did not allude to her approaching marriage. Perhaps she deferred the communication purposely, with the friendly hope that Mary Grey would visit her at Blue Cliffs, where she could make it to her in person.

Mrs. Grey, who did not dare to let her true handwriting go to Blue Cliffs, lest it should be seen and recognized by Mrs. Fanning, and who could not disguise it safely either, without some fair excuse to Emma Cavendish for doing so, put on a tight glove, and took a hard stiff pen and wrote a short note, full of gratitude and affection for Emma and all the family, and of complaints about her wretched crippled finger, that made it so painful for her to write, and prevented her from doing so as often as she wished; and of her still more wretched health, that hindered her from accepting her dear friend's kind invitation.

In reply to this letter, she got another, and a still kinder one, in which Miss Cavendish spoke of her own speedily approaching marriage, and pressed Mrs. Grey to come and be present on the occasion, adding:

"My dearest, you *must* make an effort and come. Alden himself will escort you on the journey, and take such good care of you that you shall suffer no inconvenience from the journey. You must come, for my happiness will not be complete without the presence of my dear father's dearest friend—of her who was to have been his bride."

This loving and confiding letter was never answered or even acknowledged by Mrs. Grey. It was entirely ignored, its contents were never mentioned to any one, and itself was torn to fragments and burned to ashes.

Two more letters of precisely the same character were written to her by Miss Cavendish; but they suffered the same fate at the hands of Mrs. Grey.

She had a deep motive in ignoring and destroying those letters. She did not wish the world ever by any accident to find out that she had been informed of the approaching marriage of Alden Lytton and Emma Cavendish before it had taken place, or in time to prevent it.

Two weeks passed, and then she received a visit from Mr. Alden Lytton.

She received him alone in the front drawing-room.

He apologized for calling on her after she had forbidden him to do so, but said that he came on the part of Miss Cavendish to ask if she had received certain letters from Blue Cliff Hall, and to renew, in Emma's name, her pressing invitation to Mrs. Grey to come and be present at the approaching wedding.

"Emma wishes me to take charge of you on the journey. And I assure you, if you will intrust yourself to me, I will take such tender care of you that you shall know neither fatigue nor inconvenience of any sort," he added, earnestly.

"I can not go," she answered, coldly.

"Ah, do, for your friend's sake, change your mind," pleaded Alden.

"I can not," she answered.

"But Emma will be so disappointed!"

"I can not help it if she should be. I can not be present at the wedding," she repeated, faintly.

"But why not? Why can you not go?" persisted Alden.

"Man—man," she burst forth, suddenly, as her whole face changed fearfully, "how can you ask me such a question? Do you forget that *we* were to have been married once?—that *we* loved each other once? But you threw me over. Now you invite me to your wedding with my rival! And you ask me why I can not go! Do you take me for a woman of wood or stone or iron? You will find me a woman of fire! I told you not to come here—to keep away from me! If you had had sense to perceive—if you had had even eyes in your head to see with, you would have obeyed me and avoided me! I told you not to come here. I tell you now to go away. I will not be present at your wedding. Make what explanation or excuse to Miss Cavendish you please. Tell her, if you like, that the heart you have given her was first offered to *me*—that the vows you have made to her were first breathed at *my* feet! Tell her," she added, with keen contempt, "that you are but a poor, second-handed article, after all! Now go, I say! Why do you stand gazing upon me? Go, and never come near me, if you can help it, again! For I fancy that you will not feel very glad to see me when *next* we meet!" she hissed, with a hidden meaning, between her clinched teeth.

Alden Lytton was so unutterably amazed by this sudden outbreak that he had no power of replying by word or gesture. Without resenting her fierce accusation, or even noticing her covert threat, he stood staring at her for a moment in speechless amazement.

"Are you going?" she fiercely demanded.

"I am going," he said, recovering his self-possession. "I am going. But, Mrs. Grey, I am more surprised and grieved than I have words to express. I shall never, willingly, voluntarily approach you again. If, however, you should ever need a friend, do not hesitate to call on me as freely as you would upon a brother, and I shall serve you in any way in my power as willingly as if you were my own sister."

"Ur-ur-ur-r-r!" she broke forth, in an inarticulate growl of disgust and abhorrence.

"Good-bye!" he said, very gently, as he bowed and left the room.

Nothing but sympathy and compassion for this "poor woman," as he called her, filled his heart.

Her outbreak of hysterical passion had been a revelation to him; but it had shown him only half the truth. In its light he saw that she loved him still, but he did not see that she hated her rival. He saw that she was jealous, but did not see that she was revengeful.

He reproached himself bitterly, bitterly, for ever having fallen under her spell, for ever having loved her, or sought to win her love, and for thus being the remote cause of her present sorrows.

He had never confided to Emma Cavendish the story of his first foolish, boyish love, and sufferings and cure. For Mary Grey's sake he had kept that secret from his betrothed, from whom he had no other secret in the world.

But now he felt that he must tell Emma the truth, gently and lovingly, lest Mary Grey should do it rudely and angrily.

For Mary Grey's sake he had hitherto been silent. For his own and Emma Cavendish's sake he must now speak.

He went straight to the telegraph office and dispatched a message to Miss Cavendish, saying that he should be down to Wendover by the next train to pay her a flying visit.

Then he hurried to his office, put his papers in order, left some directions with his clerk, and hastened off to the railway station, where he caught the train just as it started, and jumped aboard the cars while they were in motion.

Chapter XXXIX.

A SUDDEN WEDDING.

It was midnight when the Richmond train reached Wendover, and Alden Lytton went to the Reindeer for the night.

Early in the morning he arose and breakfasted, and ordered a horse to take him to Blue Cliff Hall.

Just as he was getting into the saddle Jerome, the colored footman from the Hall, rode up holding two papers in his left hand, and staring at them with perplexity.

"Halloo, Jerome, how do you do?" called out Mr. Lytton, cheerfully.

The boy looked up, and his surprise and perplexity instantly mounted to consternation and amazement.

"Well, dis yer's witchcraf', and nuffin else!" he exclaimed.

"What is witchcraft, you goose?" laughed Alden.

"Look yer, massa," said Jerome, riding up to his side and putting the two papers in his hand, "you jes look at dem dere!"

Alden took the papers and looked as required.

Both papers were telegrams. One was his own telegram to Emma Cavendish, saying:

"I shall be down to see you by the next train."

The other was a telegram from Emma Cavendish to himself, saying:

"Come down at once."

"Well, what of all this? Here is a message and its answer. What is there in this like witchcraft?"

"Why, massa, 'cause de answer came afore de message went, and you yerself come quick as enny. Dere's de witchcraf'."

"What do you mean?"

"I knowed as de telegraf was fast, and likewise de steam cars, but I didn't know as dey was bof so fast as to answer a message afore it was axed, and fetch a gemman afore he was sent for. But here's de answer, and here's you."

"This is all Hebrew to me."

"Which it is likewise a conundrum to me," retorted Jerome.

"Tell me what you have been doing, and perhaps I shall understand you," laughed Alden Lytton.

"Well, massa, this mornin' by daybreak Miss Emmer sent for me, and gave me this," he said, pointing to the young lady's telegram. "And, says she:

"'Jerome, saddle the fastest horse in de stable and ride as fast as you can to Wendover and send this message off to Mr. Lytton. Lose no time, for we want him to come down here as soon as possible.'

"Well, Massa Alden, I didn't lose no time, sar, nor likewise let de grass grow underneaf of my feet. I reckon I was in de saddle and off in about ten minutes. But fast as I was, bress you, sar, de telegraf was faster! When I got to de office and hand de message in to de gemman dere I says:

"'Send it off quick, 'cause Miss Emmer wants Massa Alden to come down right away.'

"'All right,' he says. 'De young gemman will be down by de next train. And here's yer answer to yer message.'

"And sure nuff, Massa Alden, he hands me this yer," said Jerome, pointing to Alden's own telegram. "And here's you too! Now, what anybody think ob dat if it a'n't witchcraf'?"

"It is a coincidence, my good fellow. I was coming down, and I telegraphed Miss Cavendish to that effect. When you brought her message to the office you received mine, which must have been delayed. It is a coincidence."

"Well I s'pose a coimperence is a fine book-larnin' name for witchcraf'; but it's all the same thing after all," persisted Jerome.

"I hope they are all well at Blue Cliffs," said Mr. Lytton, who felt some little uneasiness connected with Emma's telegram.

"Yes, sar, dey's all purty well, 'cept 'tis de ole madam. She a'n't been that hearty as she ought to 'a' been."

"I hope she is not seriously ill."

"No, sar; dough I did leave a message long o' Doctor Willet to come out dere dis morning; but you know de ole madam do frequent send for de doctor."

"Come, Jerome, we must get on to the Hall," said Mr. Lytton, as he rode out of the inn yard and turned into the road leading to Blue Cliffs, followed by the servant.

Emma Cavendish, who was on the lookout for Jerome, was surprised and delighted to see her lover ride up first, attended by her messenger.

"It's witchcraf', Miss Emmer!" exclaimed Jerome, as he got out of his saddle to take the young gentleman's horse.

"It is a coincidence," laughed Alden, as he ran up the steps to greet his beloved.

"Well, dat's de Latin for witchcraf', Miss Emmer; but it's all de same t'ing in English," persisted Jerome, as he led away the horses.

"Jerome tells me that grandma is not well. I am sorry to hear it," said Alden, as he walked with Emma into the house.

"Grandma is nearly ninety years old, and she can not ever be well in this world; but she will soon be very well indeed, for she is very near her eternal youth and health," said Emma, with tender, cheerful earnestness.

Alden bowed in silence as they entered the drawing-room together.

"Grandma told me to telegraph for you to come down at once, Alden. She thinks that she can not be here many days, and perhaps not many hours. And she wishes to see you at once. Will you go to her now, dear, or would you rather go to your room first?"

"I will go to see madam first. I have but ridden from the Reindeer this morning, and so I am neither fatigued nor dusted. I telegraphed you yesterday that I was coming down to see you to-day, and my telegram should have reached you yesterday; but it seems to have been delayed. I left the city by the noon train and reached the village at midnight. So I happened to meet Jerome just after he had taken my delayed telegram from the agent, which he supposed to be a magical answer to your message."

"The whole arrangements of telegraph wires, steam engines, gas-lights and lucifer matches are magical to him," said Emma, smiling. "And now stay here a moment, dear, and wait until I go and let grandma know that you have come," she added, as she went out of the room.

Emma Cavendish found the old lady sitting up in her easy-chair by the sunny window, looking very white and fragile and serene.

"Alden has come, grandma, dear. When Jerome went to send the telegram off for him he found Mr. Lytton in Wendover. Mr. Lytton had just arrived from Richmond and was about to start for Blue Cliffs. It was a coincidence," said Emma, sitting down by the old lady.

"It was a providence, my dear child—a providence which has saved two days in time that is very short. And so he is here?" said the old lady, caressing the golden hair of the girl.

"Yes, dear grandma, he is here and waiting to come to you the moment you are ready to receive him."

"Tell him to come now. And do you come with him."

Emma left the room, and soon returned with Alden Lytton.

"Welcome, my son! Come here and embrace me," said the old lady, holding out her arms.

Alden went and folded the faded form to his bosom and pressed a kiss upon the venerable brow, as the tears sprang to his eyes; for he saw that she was dying.

"Alden, I am going home. I must go. I want to go. I have been here so long. I am very tired. I have had enough of this. I want to go home to my Father. I want to see my Savior face to face. I want to meet my husband and my children, who have been waiting for me so long on the other side. What are you crying for, Emma?"

"Because I can not help it, grandma. I know I ought not to cry, when you will soon be so happy," sobbed the poor child.

"And when I am going to make you and your worthy young lover so happy, my love. Come, wipe your eyes and smile! I shall soon be very happy, and I want to make you and Alden as happy as I can before I go. Now sit down, both of you, and listen to me."

Alden and Emma sat down, one on each side of her.

She was a little tired with the words she had already spoken, and she put a small vial of ammonia to her nose and smelled it before she went on.

"Now," she said, as she put aside the vial and gave a hand to each of the young people, "I want you to attend to me and do exactly as I bid you."

"We will indeed," answered Alden and Emma, in a breath.

"I wish you would be married here in my presence tomorrow morning."

Alden Lytton gave her hand a grateful squeeze.

"You should be married to-day, if there were time to make the necessary arrangements."

"Are there any really necessary arrangements that can not be made to-day?" Alden inquired, eagerly.

"Yes, my son. A messenger must take a letter to Lytton Lodge to explain the circumstances, and to ask your sister Laura and your aunt and uncle Lytton to come immediately, to be present at your marriage with my granddaughter. If the messenger to Lytton Lodge should start at noon to-day, as he must, he will hardly reach the Lodge before night. Nor will your relatives be able to reach here before noon tomorrow. So you see the necessity of the short delay."

"Yes, certainly," answered Alden.

"Another messenger must take a similar letter to Beresford Manors, to summon my son and my youngest granddaughter, and your worthy guardian, Mr. Brent, who is on a long visit there. And it will also take about twenty-four hours to bring them here."

"Yes, of course," admitted Alden.

"I say nothing of the time it will take to get a license and to fetch Mr. Lyle, who must perform the ceremony, because that can be done in a few hours."

"If it were possible, I would like to have Mary Grey summoned by telegraph to attend the wedding," said Emma.

"Ah, yes, certainly she ought to be here; but there is scarcely a chance, the time is so short," said Mrs. Cavendish, as she again resorted to the vial of ammonia.

"Mrs. Grey is in very bad health. She would not come," explained Alden.

"Go, now, my dear children. I am very tired, and I must sleep a while," sighed the old lady.

And Emma and Alden kissed her and left the room.

In the passage outside they met Mrs. Fanning, who seemed to be waiting for them.

She cordially welcomed Mr. Lytton, of whose arrival she had heard from the servants. And then she inquired of Emma how Mrs. Cavendish was getting on.

"She grows weaker in the body and stronger in the spirit with every successive hour, I think," replied Miss Cavendish.

"Well, my dear, I only wished to ask you that, and to tell you that I have had lunch laid in the little breakfast room, if Mr. Lytton would like any," said Mrs. Fanning, who now took equal share in all Emma's housekeeping cares.

But Alden, when appealed to, declined the lunch and hinted that they had better see to sending off the messengers to Beresford Manors and Lytton Lodge immediately.

And that same noon the letters were dispatched.

Alden Lytton had come down to Blue Cliffs for the purpose of confiding to Emma Cavendish the story of his first boyish passion for Mary Grey, and of the violent manner in which it was cured forever. But finding all the circumstances so opposite to what he expected to find them, he changed his purpose. He could not bring himself to add another item to the disturbing influences then surrounding Emma.

That afternoon, also, Dr. Willet came to Blue Cliffs, and Emma had to accompany him to the bedside of her grandmother, and afterward to hold quite a long conversation with him in the library.

A few minutes after the doctor left the house, Mr. Lyle, who had heard of the illness of Mrs. Cavendish, arrived to inquire after her condition.

Emma had to receive the minister and accompany him to her grandmother's chamber, and to stay there and join in the prayers that were offered for the sick woman.

Mr. Lyle remained with the family all the afternoon; and having received from Mr. Lytton a notice of the ceremony he was desired to perform the next day, he promised to be at Blue Cliff Hall again punctually at noon, and then took leave.

Very early the next morning Alden Lytton mounted the swiftest horse in the Cavendish stables and rode to Wendover to procure his marriage license.

He did not stay long in the village, you may be sure; but, leaving his horse to rest and drink at the Reindeer trough, he hurried to the town-hall and took out his license, returned to the inn, remounted his horse, and rode immediately back to Blue Cliff Hall.

As he rode up the avenue toward the front of the house he saw that there had already been some arrival. A large lumbering old family carriage was being driven, empty, around toward the stables.

Alden quickened his horse's pace and rode up to the door, dismounted, threw his reins to Peter, the young groom, who was waiting to take the horse, and then ran up the steps into the house.

He almost immediately found himself in the arms of his sister Laura, who had run out to receive him.

"Oh, Alden, my darling, I am so delighted! I wish you so much joy!" she exclaimed.

"Only the occasion that has hastened my happiness is a sad one to others, Laura, my dear," answered the young man, gravely.

"I don't think so at all. I have seen Mrs. Cavendish. I never saw a happier woman. She is so happy that she wishes to make everybody else as happy as she is herself," said Laura.

As she spoke John Lytton came lumbering into the hall.

"Alden, boy, how do? I never was so astonished in my life! But under the circumstances I hope that it is all right to hurry up things in this a-way. Your Aunt Kitty couldn't come; nyther could your grandmother nor the gals. Fact is, they hadn't the gownds to appear in. But they wish you joy; and so do I. For, though I do think you might a-looked higher, because the Lyttonses is a much older family than the Caverndishers, and, in fact, were lords of the manor when the Caverndishers were hewers—"

"Uncle John," broke in Alden, with a laugh, "pray let that subject drop for the present! And follow Jerome, who is waiting to show you a room where you can brush your coat and smooth your hair, and—"

"Make myself tidy for the wedding? All right, my boy! March on, Jerome!" said John Lytton, good-humoredly, as he followed his guide upstairs.

As he disappeared another carriage rolled up to the front door, and Dr. Beresford Jones, Electra and Mr. Joseph Brent—Victor Hartman—alighted from it and entered the house.

Alden and Laura Lytton stepped forward to receive them.

Electra seized and kissed Laura in a hurry, while the gentlemen were shaking hands, and then she flew to Alden and congratulated him with much effusion.

"Now, Laura, take me where I can change my dress quickly. I brought a white India muslin with me to wear, for I am to be bride-maid, of course! So are you, I suppose. But you haven't changed your dress yet. Where is Emma? What is she going to be married in?"

"Be quiet, you little Bohemian!" said Laura, cutting short Electra's torrent of words. "Don't you feel that this is no ordinary wedding? The occasion, if not a sorrowful one, is at least very serious. Come, I will take you with me to my own room. We are to lodge together in the south-west room, as usual."

"But are you to be a bride-maid?" persisted the "little Bohemian."

"Yes; and to wear my white tarletan dress and white rose wreath," answered Laura, as they went off together.

"Where's Emma, and what's she doing? as I asked you some time ago."

"She is in her chamber, dressing for the ceremony."

"She hasn't got her wedding-dress made yet; that I know. What's she going to be married in?"

"She will wear her white satin trained dress, with white lace overdress, which she had made for the last May ball, you remember."

"Oh, yes! I didn't think of that."

"And she will wear that rich, priceless cardinal point-lace veil that was her mother's. And she will wear her grandmother's rare oriental pearls. There, you little gipsy! Are you answered?"

"Yes. And she will be magnificent and splendid, even if she is gotten up in a hurry," said Electra, as she followed her companion into their room.

Alden Lytton, under the unusual circumstances attending the sudden wedding, and in the surprise of his own unexpected happiness, had not once thought of the necessity of making a proper toilet for the occasion. But when he heard the girls, who never, under any circumstances, forget such a matter, talking of their dress, he glanced down at his own suit, and then hurried off as fast as he could to his room to improve his appearance.

While the younger members of the family party were at their toilets, Dr. Beresford Jones was in the "Throne Room," closeted with his mother.

Madam Cavendish, weak as she was, had insisted upon being arrayed grandly, to do honor to the wedding of the only daughter of the house.

She wore a rich crimson brocade dressing-gown, a costly camel's-hair shawl, and a fine point-lace cap. She now reclined very wearily in her easy-chair, and held in her hand the vial of ammonia, which she applied to her nose from time to time.

After a little while she said to her son:

"Go and inquire if they are nearly ready, Beresford. I fear—I fear my strength will scarcely hold out," she faltered, faintly.

Dr. Jones opened the door to go upon this errand, and immediately perceived that it was unnecessary.

John Lytton and Mr. Lyle were coming up the stairs, and the little bridal procession was forming in the hall below.

Mr. Lyle came in and spoke to Dr. Jones.

"With Mrs. Cavendish's permission, even now, at the last moment, we must make some slight changes in the programme," he said.

"Well?" inquired Dr. Jones, pleasantly.

"I was to have performed the ceremony and you were to have given the bride away?"

"Yes."

"Well, we must change that. Mr. Lytton has but one groomsman. I must act in that capacity also. You will please perform the ceremony, and Mr. John Lytton here will have the honor of giving the bride away."

John Lytton bowed.

"I am quite willing. I will speak to Mrs. Cavendish," said Dr. Jones, who went to his mother's chair and explained the situation to her.

"Certainly; be it as you will," she said.

Mr. Lyle then returned to the foot of the stairs and placed himself beside Laura Lytton, who was acting as first bride-maid.

John Lytton and Dr. Jones remained in the room.

The little bridal procession soon entered and ranged themselves in order before the minister.

Emma, as Electra had said, looked beautiful as a woman and elegant as a bride. Her bride-maids also were very fair to see.

The ceremony was commenced with great impressiveness.

Old Mrs. Cavendish listened with the deepest attention, leaning back in her easy-chair and sniffing at her bottle of ammonia.

John Lytton gave away the bride as if he were making a magnificent present at his own expense.

Emma Cavendish not only wore her mother's bridal veil, but was married with her mother's wedding-ring.

Dr. Beresford Jones pronounced the benediction.

And Alden Lytton and Emma Cavendish were made one in law, as they had long been in mind and heart.

Chapter XL.

AFTER THE HOLY WEDDING.

> The bride rose from her knee
> And she kissed the lips of her mother dead
> Or ever she kissed me.

—E. B. Browning.

The benediction was scarcely spoken before the fair bride left her bridegroom's side and moved softly and swiftly to the side of the easy-chair, where the form of her ancestress lay reclining.

All eyes followed her strange action, as she knelt beside the chair and took the wasted hand of its occupant in her own. And some saw what Emma had been the first to discover—that the happy spirit of the aged lady was even then departing.

She spoke no word more, but slowly raising her hand she laid it gently, as in silent blessing, on the bowed head of her young descendant, and so, with a radiant smile, passed away heavenward.

"She's dropped asleep, my dear," said honest, stupid John Lytton, bending over to look at the closed eyes and peaceful face.

"She has fainted. This has been too much for her," said Mrs. Fanning, catching up the vial of ammonia and coming with the intention of administering it.

"She is neither sleeping nor swooning. She has risen," said Emma.

And, calmly putting aside the useless drug, she arose and reverently pressed a kiss upon the lifeless lips.

A moment of deep silence followed her words.

Then Dr. Jones, the son, himself an aged man, drew near and tenderly took up the lifeless hand and looked into the motionless face, and with a profound sigh turned away.

While this group was still gathered around the chair of death, the door was silently opened and the family physician entered the room and stood among them.

"She is gone, Doctor Willet," said the son, turning to greet the newcomer.

The physician nodded gravely to the sorrowing speaker, bowed to the assembled friends, and passed through them, as they made way for him to approach the body. He felt the wrist, where there was no pulse, looked into the eyes, where there was no light, and then, with a grave and silent nod, he confirmed the opinion of Dr. Jones.

Electra, who had been incredulous all this time about the reality of the death, and was anxiously watching the face of the physician, now burst into violent weeping, and had to be led from the room by Joseph Brent—Victor Hartman.

Emma stood, pale as marble, with her eyes cast down, her lips lightly pressed together, and her hands closely clasped.

"Take your young bride away also, Mr. Lytton. She is exerting great self-command now; but she can not much longer control her feelings," said Dr. Willet.

"Come, love," whispered the bridegroom, as he passed his arm gently around the waist of the now weeping girl and drew her away from the scene of death.

Mr. John Lytton followed them out, with the half-frightened air of a culprit stealing away from detection.

There now remained in the room of death the aged son, Dr. Beresford Jones, the family physician, Dr. Willet, the minister of the parish, the Rev. Mr. Lyle, and the two ladies, Mrs. Fanning and Laura Lytton.

"She passed away very gently, without the least suffering," said Mrs. Fanning.

"I thought she would do so. Hers has been a really physiological death, of ripe and pure old age," answered the doctor.

After a little more conversation the gentlemen withdrew, leaving the remains to the care of the two ladies, while they went to commence arrangements for the funeral.

Four days after this the body of Mrs. Cavendish was laid in the family vault, beside those of her husband and her son, the late governor.

The old lady had been long and widely known, and deeply and sincerely loved and honored, and her funeral was as largely attended as had been that of her son, some years before. After these solemn offices had all been performed the friends assembled to consult and make arrangements for the temporary disposition of the family left behind.

It was settled that Mrs. Fanning should remain at Blue Cliff Hall, in charge of the establishment, with Laura Lytton as her guest and companion.

Dr. Jones and Electra would, of course, return to Beresford Manors. They would be accompanied by Mr. Joseph Brent—Victor Hartman—who had grown to be a great favorite with the aged doctor, and in truth almost indispensable to his comfort and entertainment.

Mr. Lyle went back to the duties of his ministry at Wendover.

And finally, as there was now a vacation of the courts, and the young barrister was temporarily at liberty, Alden Lytton decided to take his young bride to Europe for their bridal tour.

On their way to New York they stopped for a day in Richmond, because Emma wished to see her old "friend," Mrs. Grey, before leaving for Europe.

Alden Lytton, though he felt persuaded in his own mind that Mrs. Grey would not receive them, yet promptly complied with his fair bride's wish.

So, the morning after their arrival at the Henrico House, in Richmond, Alden took a carriage and they drove to the old Crane Manor House and inquired for Mrs. Grey.

But, as Alden had foreseen, they received for an answer that Mrs. Grey was not at home.

Upon further inquiry they were told that she had left the city on business and would not return for a week.

And Alden Lytton rightly conjectured that she had gone away, and was staying away, for the one purpose of avoiding Emma and himself.

So the young bride, with a sigh, reluctantly resigned all hope of seeing her unworthy "friend" before sailing for Europe.

Early the next morning the newly-married pair took the steamboat for Washington, where in due time they safely arrived, and whence they took the train for the North.

They reached New York on Thursday night, had one intervening day to see something of the city and to make some few last purchases for their voyage, and on Saturday at noon they embarked on the magnificent ocean steamship "Pekin," bound from New York to Southampton.

We must leave them on board their ship, and return and look up Mary Grey.

CHAPTER XLI.

MARY GREY'S MYSTERY.

After Mrs. Grey's last interview with Alden Lytton, during which, partly because she lost her self-command and partly because she did not care longer to conceal her feelings, she had thrown off her mask, she sat down to review the situation.

"Well, I have betrayed myself," she mused. "I have let him see how I really feel about this marriage engagement between him and Emma Cavendish. He knows now how I loved him; if he has eyes in his head he sees now how I hate him.

"All right. I have now no further reason to deceive him. He has served my utmost purpose for his own and her own destruction. I no longer need his unconscious co-operation. I have his honor and his liberty, and her reputation and peace, in my power and at my mercy.

"And I have done all this myself, without the voluntary help of any human being. I have used men as the mechanic uses tools, making them do his work, or as the potter uses clay, molding it to his purpose.

"Let him marry Emma Cavendish. I can part them at any moment afterward and throw them into a felon's prison, and cast her down from her proud place into misery and degradation.

"I *could* stop their marriage now, or at the altar. But I will not do that; for to do that would be only to disappoint or grieve them. But my vengeance must strike a deeper blow. It must degrade and ruin them. I will wait until they have been married some time. Then, in the hour of their fancied security, I will come down upon them like an avalanche of destruction."

In the feverish excitement of anticipating this fiendish consummation of her revenge she almost forgot her heinous crime, and ceased to be haunted by the hideous specter of her murdered lover.

It was on the fifteenth of the month, when she happened to take up the morning paper.

She turned first—as she always did—to the column containing notices of marriages and deaths.

And her face grew wild and white as she read:

MARRIED.—On the morning of the 10th instant, at Blue Cliff Hall, Virginia, the seat of the bride, by the Rev. Dr. Beresford Jones, Mr. Alden Lytton, of Richmond, to Miss Emma Angela, only daughter of the late Charles Cavendish, Governor of Virginia.

She read no further that day. There were other marriages following this; but she felt no curiosity now about them. And there was a formidable row of death notices, headed by the obituary of Mrs. Cavendish, but she did not even see it.

The announcement of the marriage had taken her by surprise. She had not expected to see it for a month yet to come. And, as she did not observe the notice of Mrs. Cavendish's death, she could not understand why the marriage had been hastened by so many weeks.

"So it is over," she said. "It is over, and it has been over for five days. They are in the midst of their happiness, enjoyed at the expense of my misery. Theirs is a fool's paradise from which I could eject them at any moment; but I will not—not just yet. The longer I suspend the blow the heavier it will fall at last. They will carry out their programme, I presume; so far, at least, as to go upon their bridal trip to Europe. I could stop them on the eve of their voyage; but I will not. I will let them go and return, and hold their wedding-reception, and then, in the midst of their joy and triumph, in the presence of their admiring friends—"

She paused to gloat with demoniac enjoyment over the picture her wicked imagination had conjured up.

—"Then I will turn all their joy to despair, all their triumph to humiliation, all their glory to shame! And I will do all this alone—alone, or use others only as my blind tools.

"Of course they will take this city on their way to New York to embark for Europe. And they will call on me to show me their happiness, and take a keener relish of it from seeing the contrast of my misery. But they shall be disappointed in that, at least. I will not be dragged at the wheels of their triumphal car. I will not stay here to receive them. I will leave town, and stay out of it until I am sure that they have passed through and left it."

She kept her word.

She went down to Forestville, ostensibly to relieve a poor family suffering under an accumulation of afflictions, but really to be out of the way of the bridal pair, and to get up evidence in the case she intended to bring against the husband of Emma Cavendish.

When she had been but a few days at Forestville she received a letter from Miss Romania Crane—who in her absence kept up a sentimental correspondence with her—informing her of the visit of Mr. and Mrs. Alden Lytton, the bride and bridegroom from Blue Cliffs, who stopped for a day in the city on their way to New York.

Immediately on her receipt of this letter she returned to Richmond and to the house of the Misses Crane.

And she very much surprised and shocked these ladies by assuming an air of grief and distraction as extreme in itself as it was unaccountable to them.

They could not even imagine what was the matter with her. She refused to give any explanation of her apparent mental anguish, and she repelled all sympathy.

The Misses Crane were afraid she was going to lose her reason.

They went to see the minister and the minister's wife on the subject. They found only the lady at home. And to her they stated the mysterious case.

"There is something very heavy on her mind, my dear. I am sure there is something awful on her mind."

"There has been this long time, I think," said the minister's wife.

"Yes, I know; but it is a thousand times worse now. My dear, she keeps her room nearly all day. She never comes to the table. If I send her meals up to her they come back almost untasted. And I assure you she does not sleep any better than she eats. Her room is over mine, and so I can hear her walking the floor half the night," said Miss Romania Crane.

"What can be the cause of her distress?" inquired the rector's lady.

"I don't know. I can't get her to tell me. She only says that 'her life is wrecked forever, and that she wishes only to be left to herself until death shall relieve her.' And all that sort of talk," said Miss Romania.

"And have you no suspicion?"

"None in the world that seems at all rational. The only one I have seems foolish."

"But what is it?"

"Well, I sometimes think—but indeed it is a silly thought—that her distress is in some way connected with the marriage of Mr. Lytton and Miss Cavendish, for I notice that every time the name of either of them is mentioned she grows so much worse that I and my sister have ceased ever to speak of them."

"It can not be that she was ever in love with Mr. Lytton," suggested the minister's lady.

"I should think not. I should think she was not that weak-minded sort of woman to give way to such sentiment, much less to be made so extremely wretched by it. For I do tell you, my dear, her state is simply that of the utmost mental wretchedness."

"I will ask my husband to go to her. He is her pastor, and may be able to do her some good," said the minister's wife.

"Do, my dear, and come to see her yourself," said Miss Romania, as she and her sister arose to take leave.

Now you know all this distress was just "put on" by Mrs. Grey, to give coloring and plausibility to her future proceedings.

To be sure she kept her room, but it was not to grieve in secret: it was to excite the compassion and wonder of her sympathizing friends, while she laid her plans, drank French cordials, and feasted privately on the delicacies of the season, which she would secretly bring in, or dozed on her sofa and dreamed of her coming sweet revenge.

Certainly, instead of going to bed at a decent hour, she would walk the floor of her chamber half the night. But this was not done because she was suffering, or sleepless from grief, but for the purpose of keeping poor Miss Crane awake all night in the room below and making the poor lady believe that she, Mary Grey, was breaking her own heart in these vigils.

And for her want of nightly rest Mary Grey compensated herself by dozing half the day on her sofa; and for her want of regular meals she made up by slipping out occasionally and feasting at some "ladies' restaurant."

But her object was effected. She impressed everybody who came near her with the belief that she had suffered some awful wrong or bereavement of which she could not speak, but which threatened to unseat her reason or end her life.

CHAPTER XLII.

MARY GREY'S STORY.

At length her minister came to see her. He expressed the deepest sympathy with her sufferings, and implored her to relieve her overburdened heart by confiding in him or in his wife, from either or both of whom, he assured her, she should receive respectful compassion and substantial assistance, if the last was necessary.

Then, pretending to yield to his better judgment, she consented to give him her confidence.

And taking him up to her own sitting-room, where they could be safe from interruption, she bound him over to secrecy, and then, with many affected tears and moans, she told him the astounding story that she had long been privately married to Mr. Alden Lytton, who had deserted her within a few days after their wedding, and who had recently, as every one knew, united himself in matrimony with Miss Emma Cavendish, of Blue Cliffs, Virginia, and had gone with her on a wedding trip to Europe.

While she told him this stupendous tale, the minister sat with open mouth and eyes, gazing on her with more of the air of an idiot than of a learned and accomplished gentleman.

He was, in fact, utterly amazed and confounded by the story he had heard.

That Alden Lytton, a young man of the highest social position, of unblemished reputation from his youth up, an accomplished scholar, a learned jurist, an eloquent barrister, and, more than all, a Christian gentleman, should have been guilty of the base treachery and the degrading crime here charged upon him was just simply incredible—no more nor less than incredible.

Or that Mary Grey, the loveliest lady of his congregation, should be capable of a malicious fabrication was utterly impossible.

There was then but one way out of the dilemma: Mary Grey was insane and suffering under a distressing hallucination that took this form.

So said the look of consternation and pity that the minister fixed upon the speaker's face.

"I see that you discredit my story, and doubt even my sanity. But here is something that you can neither doubt nor discredit," she said, as she drew from her pocket the marriage certificate and placed it in his hands.

The minister opened and read it. And as he read this evidence of a "Christian gentleman's" base perfidy the look of consternation and amazement that had held possession of his countenance gave place to one of disgust and abhorrence.

"Do you doubt *now*?" meaningly inquired Mary Grey.

"Ah, no, I can not doubt now! I wish to Heaven I could! I would rather, my child, believe you to be under the influence of a distressing hallucination than know this man to be the consummate villain this certificate proves him to be. I can not doubt the certificate. I wish I could; but I know this Reverend Mr. Borden. On my holiday trips North I have sometimes stopped at his house and filled his pulpit. I am familiar with his handwriting. I can not doubt," groaned the minister.

Mary Grey dropped her hands and pretended to sob aloud.

"Do not weep so much, poor child! Deeply wronged as you have been by this ruthless sinner you have not been so awfully injured as has been this most unhappy young lady, Miss Cavendish, whom he has deceived to her destruction," said the minister.

"And do you not suppose that I grieve for *her* too?" sobbed Mary Grey.

"Ah, yes, I am sure your tender, generous heart, wronged and broken as it is, has still the power left to grieve for her as well as for yourself."

"But what is my duty? Ah, what is my duty in this supreme trial? I can not save my life or hers from utter wreck, but I can do my duty, and I will do it, if only it is pointed out to me. Oh, sir, point it out to me!" cried the hypocrite, clasping her hands with a look of sincerity that might have deceived a London detective.

"My dear, can you possibly be in doubt as to what your duty is?" sorrowfully inquired the minister.

"Oh, my mind is all confused by this terrible event! I can not judge rationally. Ought I to keep silence and go away to some remote place and live in obscurity, dead to the world, so as never even by chance to interfere with their happiness, or to bring trouble on Miss Cavendish? I think, perhaps, he expects even that much from my devotion to him. Or ought I not to make way with myself altogether, for her sake? Would not a courageous suicide be justifiable, and even meritorious, under such, trying circumstances?"

"My child—my child, how wildly and sinfully you talk! Your brain is certainly touched by your troubles. You must not dream of doing any of the dreadful things you have mentioned. Your duty lies plainly before you. Will you have the courage to do it, if I point it out to you?"

"Oh, yes, I will—I will! It is all that is left me to do."

"Then your duty is to lodge information against that wretched man, so that he shall be arrested the moment he sets foot in the State."

"Oh, heaven of heavens! And ruin Emma Cavendish!" exclaimed the traitress, in well-simulated horror.

"And save Emma Cavendish from a life of involuntary degradation and misery. You must do this. To-morrow I will introduce you to a young lawyer of distinguished ability, who will give you legal advice even as I have given you religious counsel. And we will both confer together, so as to save you as much as possible from all painful share in the prosecution of this man."

"It is *all* painful; all agonizing! But I think you and I will not shrink from our duty. Oh, could you ever have believed, without such

278

proof as I have given you, that Mr. Alden Lytton could ever have been guilty of this crime?"

"Never! Never! And yet I know that men of exalted character have sometimes fallen very deeply into sin. Even David, 'the man after God's own heart,' took the wife of his devoted friend, and betrayed this faithful friend to a cruel death! Why should we wonder, then, at any man's fall? But, my child, I must ask you a question that I have been waiting to ask you all this time. Why did you not interfere to stop this felonious marriage before it took place? What timidity, what weakness, or what pride was it that restrained your hand from acting in time to prevent this fearful crime of Mr. Lytton, this awful wrong to Miss Cavendish, from being consummated?" gravely and sadly inquired the minister.

"Oh, sir, how can you ask me such a question? Do you suppose that if I had had the remotest suspicion of what was going on I should not have interfered and prevented it at all hazards—yes, even at the sacrifice of my own life, if that had been necessary?"

"You did not know of this beforehand then?"

"Why, certainly not!"

"Nor suspect it?"

"Assuredly not! I had not the least knowledge nor the faintest suspicion that anything of the sort was contemplated by Mr. Lytton until after it was all over. The first I heard of it was from the Misses Crane, who wrote me at Forestville that Mr. and Mrs. Alden Lytton, the bride and bridegroom from Blue Cliffs, had called on me during my absence. The news, when it was confirmed, nearly killed me. But think of the insanity of their calling on me! But I know that was Emma's wish. And I feel sure that Mr. Lytton must have known of my absence from town or he never would have ventured to bring his deceived bride into my home."

"No, indeed; probably not. Well, my poor child, I have shown you your painful duty. See that you do not falter in it," said the rector, as he rose to take leave.

"I will not," answered Mary Grey.

"I will call at ten o'clock to-morrow morning to take you to Mr. Desmond's office."

"I will be ready."

And the minister took his leave.

Punctual to his appointment, the next morning at ten o'clock the rector called for Mary Grey and took her in his own carriage to the office of Philip Desmond, one of the most talented among the rising young barristers of Richmond.

Mr. Desmond enjoyed a high reputation not only as a professional man but as a private gentleman.

But he was the professional rival and the political opponent of Mr. Alden Lytton. They were always engaged on opposite sides of the same case; and on several important occasions Alden Lytton had gained a triumph over Philip Desmond.

He was, therefore, more astonished than grieved when the rector, after introducing Mary Grey under the name of Mrs. Alden Lytton, proceeded to confide to him, under the seal of temporary secrecy, the stupendous story of Alden Lytton's double marriage.

He expressed much amazement at the double treachery of the man, deep sympathy with the sorrows of the suffering and forsaken wife, and great indignation at the wrongs of the deceived and unhappy young lady.

He readily promised to co-operate with the minister in having the culprit brought speedily to justice.

"You, madam, of course, as his wife, can take no active part in the prosecution of this man. You can not even give testimony against him with your own voice. But you must appear in court, to be identified by the rector, the sexton and others who witnessed your marriage," said the lawyer, in taking leave of his visitors.

The rector took Mrs. Grey back to her boarding-house, and while she was gone upstairs to lay off her bonnet and shawl he told the Misses Crane that their interesting boarder had confided her trouble to him; that she had suffered the deepest wrong that any woman could be doomed to bear; but he could not explain more then; they would know all about it in a short time, when the wrongdoer should be brought to justice.

And having thus mystified the poor ladies, he further recommended Mary Grey to their tenderest sympathy and care.

And so he went home, leaving them in a state of greater bewilderment than ever.

CHAPTER XLIII.

ABOUT BLUE CLIFFS.

Before Mr. and Mrs. Alden Lytton had left Blue Cliff Hall they had made arrangements for the complete renovation of that old ancestral seat, to be carried on under the supervision of the Rev. Mr. Lyle.

And they expressed their intention to purchase and send furniture from London and Paris to refit it.

But the works were scarcely commenced when they had to be suspended for a few days.

Another death had occurred in the family circle.

Dr. Beresford Jones, after a very pleasant evening spent at Blue Cliff Hall in company with Mrs. Fanning, Laura Lytton, his granddaughter, Electra, and his great favorite, Mr. Joseph Brent, arose, saying:

"I will now retire to bed, and I recommend you, Electra, my dear, to do the same, as we have to rise early to-morrow morning to set out on our return to Beresford Manors."

And he kissed her good-night, bowed to the other members of the circle, took up his taper and retired.

The next morning he went away indeed, but not to Beresford Manors.

For when Electra went into his room, as was her custom, to kiss him good-morning before he should get up, she found nothing but his body, still warm, and with the face still wearing the happy smile with which his spirit had impressed it in taking his heavenward flight.

Her screams desecrated the holy room of death and brought all the household to her presence.

When they discovered the cause of the girl's wild grief, Mrs. Fanning and Laura Lytton together forced her from the room and took her to her own chamber, where they set themselves to soothe her.

Joseph Brent, himself overcome with grief at the sudden loss of one who had proved himself so warm a friend, set out on horseback to Wendover to fetch the family physician and the minister.

They were useless to the departed, of course, but they might be of some service to the bereaved ones left behind.

So Mr. Lyle and Dr. Willet returned with Mr. Brent, and remained at Blue Cliff Hall until after all was over.

And thus it happened that within one fortnight there were two funerals at Blue Cliffs.

On the day after that upon which the remains of Beresford Jones were laid in the family vault his will was opened and read to his relatives.

With the exception of a few legacies left to friends and servants he bequeathed the whole of his real estate and personal property exclusively and unconditionally to his beloved granddaughter, Electra Coroni.

And he appointed his esteemed friends, Stephen Lyle and Joseph Brent, joint executors of the will, trustees of his estate, and guardians of his heiress.

And to each of these executors he left a legacy of ten thousand dollars.

Folded within the will was an informal letter addressed to his surviving friends, and requesting that no mourning should be worn for him, no wedding deferred, no innocent pleasure delayed on his account, for that death was only a higher step in life, and that which to him would be a great gain and glory must not seem to them a loss and gloom.

Electra, with her gusty nature, wept vehemently during the reading of this will and letter.

But there was one present who, though he betrayed no emotion, was much more deeply moved than any one present. This was Joseph Brent.

In being appointed guardian, trustee and executor of the will, he had just received from Dr. Beresford Jones the greatest proof of esteem and confidence that any one man could receive from another. And when he thought of this in connection with his own woful past he felt deeply disturbed.

After the reading of the will the assembled relatives dispersed from the room, leaving the two executors to converse together.

When Joseph Brent found himself alone with his friend Stephen Lyle he gave way to his feelings and said:

"My heart is full of compunction."

"Why?" gravely inquired Mr. Lyle.

"Because I should have confided in the dear old friend who put so much trust in me. I should have told him my whole miserable past history. And then, perhaps, he never would have given me so great a mark of his esteem. And Heaven knows I fully intended to tell him before asking him to accept me as a suitor of his granddaughter, even though it had cost me the loss of her who is dearer to me than life. But I put off the painful task, and now it is too late. And I feel as if I had obtained the honors he has conferred upon me by a fraud. No less!" said Joseph Brent, covering his face with his hands.

"My brother, you are morbid on this subject. Certainly you intended to tell him before asking to marry his granddaughter. And most certainly it would have been right for you to do so, had he remained among us. But he is gone. And you are free from blame. If you must tell any one tell the girl you love, and who loves and trusts you, for it is now no one's business but hers and yours. Or, rather, because you would never do yourself justice, let me tell her how, once a poor, motherless boy, left to himself, lost his way in the world and strayed even to the very brink of perdition. And how nobly since that he has, by the grace of Heaven, redeemed and consecrated his life. And then see if she will not place her hand in yours for good and all."

"You always comfort and strengthen me," said the young man, seizing and wringing the hand of his friend.

And then they consulted about the will of the late Dr. Jones, and the arrangements to be made with his estates and the disposition to be made of his heiress.

"We are her guardians," said Mr. Lyle; "but neither you nor I, being bachelors both, have a proper home to offer her. Nor will it be well for her to live at Beresford Manors, with no one but her colored servants. Mrs. Fanning has invited her to remain here for the present, and really this house seems to be the best place for her just now. But, after all, the decision must be left to herself, and she must choose her own home."

Mr. Brent agreed perfectly with the views of Mr. Lyle.

And later in the same afternoon they consulted the wishes of their young ward, who emphatically declared in favor of Blue Cliff Hall as her temporary home.

The next morning Mr. Lyle and Mr. Brent took leave of the ladies and returned to Wendover, where the Californian again became the inmate of the minister's home.

But both gentlemen continued to be frequent visitors at Blue Cliff Hall.

On the Monday following the funeral the work was recommenced on the old mansion and went rapidly on—the three ladies, Mrs. Fanning, Laura Lytton and Electra, moving from one part of the house to another as the improvements progressed.

Six weeks after this they received the first cargo of new furniture for the drawing-rooms, which were ready for it.

And as the work went on, from room to room, they received more furniture to fit them up.

At the end of three months the work was completed within and without.

And the fine old mansion, thoroughly remodeled and refurnished, presented as elegant and attractive an appearance as any modern palace in the whole country.

And then, when all was ready for the returning bride and bridegroom, Mrs. Fanning received a letter from them informing her that on the Saturday following the date of that letter they were to embark on board the steamship "Amazon," bound from Liverpool to New York, and they expected to be at Blue Cliffs two weeks from the day of embarkation.

Yes, the happy young pair were on their way home, unconscious of the horrible pitfall that had been dug to receive them!

CHAPTER XLIV.

WEDDINGS AND WEDDING RECEPTIONS.

What do you think of marriage?
I take it as those who deny purgatory.
It locally contains or heaven or hell:
There is no third place in it.

—WEBSTER.

It was a beautiful day near the last of May, and the scenery all around Blue Cliff Hall was glorious with sunshine, bloom and verdure.

A happy party of friends was assembled at the Hall that day for a double purpose—to meet the returning bridegroom and bride, who were expected to arrive that evening, and to assist at their wedding reception, which was to be further graced by two new bridals the next morning; for it had been arranged by correspondence that Stephen Lyle and Laura Lytton and Joseph Brent and Electra Coroni should be married on that occasion.

All was ready: the house newly-restored, decorated and furnished, the rooms aired and adorned with flowers, and the wedding-breakfast laid out in the long dining-room.

The supper-table for the returning travelers was set in the small dining-room opening upon the garden of roses.

Carriages had been sent from the Hall early that morning to meet the travelers, who were expected to reach Wendover by the noon train from Richmond and to come direct to the Hall, so as to arrive in time for an early tea.

On the delightful porch in front of the house, that commanded a view of the carriage-drive and the forest road beyond, sat a pleasant group, enjoying the magnificent sunset of that mountain region, and watching the road or the first appearance of the carriage that was to bring home their beloved young friends.

This happy group was composed of Mrs. Fanning, Laura Lytton, Electra Coroni, Stephen Lyle and Joseph Brent.

"I hope they will arrive before the sun goes quite down. I should like them to come home in the sunshine," said Laura Lytton, looking anxiously at the glorious orb just then touching the horizon.

No one answered. All were watching the setting sun and listening for the sound of the carriage-wheels until a few moments had passed, and then Electra said, with a sigh:

"You will not get your wish then, for the sun is gone and they are not come."

"They are coming now, however. I hear the sound of their carriage-wheels," said Joseph Brent.

"Yes, indeed, for I see the carriage now," added Mr. Lyle, as the traveling-coach rolled rapidly in sight of the whole party and turned into the home drive.

A few moments more and the carriage drew up before the house, and Alden Lytton alighted and handed out his wife.

Another moment and Alden was in the arms of his sister and Emma on the bosom of Mrs. Fanning.

Hearty greetings, warm embraces ensued, and then they held off to look at each other.

Emma was more beautiful and Alden handsomer than ever.

"What a happy coming home!" said Emma, gratefully. "And you are all so well! And you are all here except those who are in heaven. Stay! I think *they* also are here to meet us, though we do not see them! Come, let us enter the house."

"Let me show you to your rooms. No one shall be your 'groom of the chambers,' Mr. and Mrs. Alden Lytton, but myself," said Laura, playfully, as she led the way upstairs to the elegant apartments that had been prepared for the young master and mistress of the house.

"Come too, Electra. I do not wish to lose sight of you so soon, my child," said Emma, kindly, as they went along. "Is everything arranged satisfactorily to yourselves, my dears, and are you both ready to be married at the same time to-morrow?" she inquired, addressing her two companions.

"Why, of course!" smiled Laura.

Very early the next morning the whole household was happily astir.

The youthful family met at an early breakfast in the little dining-room, and then separated and went to their chambers to adorn themselves for the bridals.

A little later in the morning carriages containing guests bidden to the wedding began to arrive. The guests were received first by accomplished ushers, who took them to handsome and convenient dressing-rooms, in which they could put the last perfecting touches on their toilets, after which they were ushered into the long drawing-room, where they were received by Mr. and Mrs. Alden Lytton.

Emma was beautifully dressed for this occasion. She wore a rich white satin, with a point-lace overskirt, looped up with white roses sprinkled with small diamonds like dew. A wreath of the same flowers, bedewed in the same way, rested on her rich golden hair. A diamond necklace and bracelets adorned her bosom and arms. A delicate bouquet of white roses was held in her hand. Dainty gloves, and so forth, of course completed her toilet.

The two brides were dressed exactly alike, in long-trained, rich white silk dresses, with illusion overdresses and illusion veils, white orange-blossom wreaths, pearl necklaces and bracelets, and dainty white kid gloves, and carried delicate white lace handkerchiefs and white bouquets.

The bride-maids were all dressed in a uniform of white tarletan, trained, with overdresses of the same, rose-colored sashes and bows, and rose wreaths on their heads.

The bridegrooms wore the regulation "invisible blue" swallow-tailed coats and pantaloons, white satin vests, patent leather boots and kids. The groomsmen were got up in precisely the same ridiculous—I mean fashionable—style.

Now, reader, did you ever see a double marriage ceremony performed?

If not, I will tell you how this was done.

The first bride and groom were Mr. Lyle and Miss Lytton. They stood in the middle of the semicircle, immediately facing the bishop. The second bride and groom, Mr. Brent and Miss Coroni, stood on each side of them, Mr. Brent standing next to Mr. Lyle and Miss Coroni standing next to Miss Lytton. The six bride-maids, of course, completed the semicircle on the ladies' side and the six groomsmen on the gentlemen's.

The opening exhortation was made and the opening prayers were offered for both pairs together.

Then the momentous questions were put and answered, and the marriage vows were made, by each pair separately.

Each bride was given away in turn by Alden Lytton. Finally the concluding prayer was offered and the benediction pronounced upon both.

It was over.

Congratulations, tears, smiles and kisses followed. A half an hour in pleasant chatter, in which every one talked and no one listened, followed, and then the doors of the dining-room were thrown open and the company was invited in to the breakfast.

Three long tables stood parallel to each other, the whole length of the room, leaving only space to pass around them.

Each table was decorated with the most fragrant and beautiful flowers, adorned with the most elegant plate, china and glass, and loaded with every delicacy appropriate to the occasion.

But the middle table was distinguished by the "wedding-cake" *par excellence*—an elegant and beautiful piece of art, formed like a Grecian temple of Hymen, erected upon a rock, adorned with beautiful forms, birds, butterflies, flowers, and so forth.

This middle table was also honored with the presence of the brides and bridegrooms, with their attendants and immediate friends, and with that of the officiating bishop.

After the first course Mr. Lytton, who occupied a seat at the foot of this table, arose in his place and made the usual little speech, and proposed the health of both "happy pairs."

This was drunk with enthusiasm.

Then the health of the bride-maids was proposed and honored.

Mr. Brent proposed their accomplished host and hostess. And this toast was honored with an enthusiasm equal to that which had attended that of the brides and bridegrooms.

An hour, every moment of which was filled up with enjoyment, was spent at the table, and then the beautiful hostess, Mrs. Alden Lytton, gave the signal, and the ladies all arose and withdrew.

The two brides, accompanied by Emma, went upstairs to their rooms to change their bridal dresses for traveling-suits, for the two carriages were already waiting at the gates to convey them to Wendover, whence they were to take the train for Richmond, *en route* for the North.

They were soon dressed in their pretty suits of soft, dove-colored silk, with hats and gloves of the same shade.

They went down to the drawing-room, still accompanied by Emma.

The gentlemen had just come in from the breakfast-table, and all the guests were assembled there to see the happy pairs off on their bridal tours.

Emma had left the room for a few minutes to give some orders.

Alden Lytton had just embraced his sister, and was holding the hand of his brother-in-law, wishing him all manner of happiness and prosperity, when the door opened and Jerome entered, saying:

"There's a gemman out here wants to see Mr. Lytton most partic'lar."

"Show him in," said Alden Lytton, smiling, and expecting to see some guest who had come too late for the wedding.

Chapter XLV.

A TERRIBLE SUMMONS.

You have displaced the mirth, broke the good meeting
With most admired disorder.

—Shakespeare.

The servant left the room, and presently returned and ushered in a tall, stout, gray-haired man, whom all present recognized as Mr. John Bowlen, the deputy sheriff of the county.

The new-comer bowed to the assembled company and walked straight up to Alden Lytton, who advanced to meet him.

"You are Mr. Alden Lytton, I presume?" said the deputy-sheriff.

"Why, of course I am, Mr. Bowlen! You know that quite well, don't you?" smiled Alden.

"I thought I did; but I wished to be quite sure in a case like this. You are my prisoner, Mr. Alden Lytton," said the deputy-sheriff, so calmly and distinctly that every one in the room both heard and understood the strange words.

Yet no one uttered an exclamation of surprise. I think they were all too much stunned for that.

Alden Lytton simply stared in silent amazement at the officer, while others, including the two bridegrooms, gathered around him.

"What did you say just now? Perhaps I did not hear you aright," inquired Alden, elevating his eyebrows, for there was something that struck him as unreal, ludicrous and bordering upon the burlesque in the whole situation.

"I said that you were my prisoner, Mr. Alden Lytton," answered the deputy-sheriff, gravely. "I repeat that you are my prisoner."

"Prisoner!" echoed a score of voices, giving expression at length to their amazement.

"Yes, ladies and gentlemen, he is my prisoner. I think I spoke plainly enough; and I hope I shall have no trouble in making the arrest," answered the deputy-sheriff, who, if he were not behaving very rudely, was certainly not doing his duty very courteously.

"Upon what charge, I pray you, am I to be arrested?" inquired Mr. Lytton, sarcastically, still inclined to treat the whole matter as a very bad practical joke.

"You may read the warrant, sir," answered the officer, unfolding a document and placing it in the hands of Alden Lytton, who, with some anger and curiosity, but no anxiety, began to read it.

"What is the matter? What does this person want here?" inquired Emma, in surprise, as she entered the room, came up to the group and saw the intruder.

"He has some business with me, my love," answered her husband, controlling himself with a great effort, as he read the shameful charges embodied in the warrant commanding his arrest. Then, still speaking with forced calmness, he said to the deputy-sheriff:

"I will go with you first into the library, Mr. Bowlen, where we can talk over this matter with my friends."

And turning to the two bridegrooms he inquired:

"Can you give me a few minutes with this officer in the library?"

"Certainly," answered Mr. Lyle and Mr. Brent, in one voice.

"Ladies, you will excuse us for a few minutes?" inquired Mr. Lytton, smiling around upon the group.

"Certainly," answered two or three ladies, speaking for the whole party.

"Follow me, if you please, gentlemen," said Alden Lytton, as he led the way to the library.

There the four men—Mr. Lytton, Mr. Lyle, Mr. Brent and the sheriff—stood around a small table, all with anxious and some with questioning looks.

"Read that and tell me what you think of it," said Mr. Lytton, placing the warrant for his arrest in the hands of Mr. Lyle.

"Think of it? I think it at once the falsest, basest and most absurd charge that ever was made against an honorable man!" exclaimed Mr. Lyle, in righteous indignation, as he threw the document on the table.

"It is all a diabolical conspiracy!" added Joseph Brent, who had read the warrant over the shoulder of his friend.

"It can not stand investigation for one moment," said Stephen Lyle.

"And the wretches who got this up should be severely punished!" exclaimed Joseph Brent.

"Most severely!" added Stephen Lyle.

"But what show of foundation could they have had for such a charge? The warrant accuses you of having 'feloniously intermarried with one Emma Angela Cavendish in and during the lifetime of your lawful wife, Mary Lytton, now living in this State!' Now, who the very mischief is this Mary who claims to be Lytton? Oh, Alden, my son, what *have* you been up to?" inquired Joseph Brent, half in mockery and half in real anxiety.

"Whatever else I may have been 'up to,' I certainly never have been 'up to' marrying two wives at one time," answered Alden, in the same spirit of half banter, half protest.

"But who is this Mary, self-styled Lytton?"

"I know no more than the dead!"

"But are you sure you never had a slight flirtation with, or a platonic affinity for, a Mary or anybody else?"

"Never! Nor do I even know a single 'Mary' in this world, except—"

"Oh, yes!—except whom—except whom?"

"Mrs. Mary Grey," answered Alden, gravely, and with a certain new disturbance in his manner that had not been there before.

Mr. Lyle brought his hand down upon the table with an emphatic thump.

"That is the woman!" he said, with an air of entire conviction. "But surely you never fell under her baleful spell?"

"Ah, who that ever knew her has not fallen under that baleful spell? But for the last two years I have been entirely disillusioned," answered Alden.

"Come, gentlemen, I am sorry to hurry you; but really," said Sheriff Bowlen, taking out his watch, "it is now two o'clock, and we must get on to Wendover."

"Very well," answered Alden Lytton, coldly. Then turning to Mr. Brent and Mr. Lyle he said: "And you, my friends, must be getting on, too, or you will lose your train. And then what will become of your bridal trips?"

"I do not care what may become of *my* bridal trip! I mean to see you safe through this abominable conspiracy—for a conspiracy it certainly is, whoever may be the conspirators!" said Joseph Brent, emphatically.

"Pooh—pooh! Some very shallow piece of malice, or some very poor practical joke upon me or the magistrate! The wonder is, however, that any magistrate could be found to issue such a warrant as this," said Alden Lytton, making light of a matter which he thought the slightest investigation must soon set right.

In the meantime Joseph Brent and Stephen Lyle spoke apart for a few minutes, and then came to Alden Lytton and said:

"Look here; we are going with you to the magistrate's office. We are determined to see this matter through. It may be a trifle or it may not."

"And how about the two pretty girls who are waiting, with their hats on, to be taken on their wedding tours?"

"They can wait. A few hours, which must decide this, can make but little difference to them. Your lovely lady will give them house-room to-day," said Mr. Lyle.

As Alden Lytton was about to reply, urging his friends not to delay their journey on his account, he caught sight of Emma standing in the hall, just outside the library door.

Her face was pale with anguish, and her hands were clasped tightly together, as she said:

"Alden—Alden! Oh, Alden, come to me for one moment!"

"Let me go and speak to my wife. I will not run away," said Mr. Lytton, sarcastically, to the deputy, who was close upon his heels.

And he went up to Emma and said, cheerfully:

"Do not be alarmed, love; there is nothing to fear."

"Oh, Alden, dearest, *what is it*? They are talking about a warrant and an arrest in there. It is not true—oh, it can not be true!" said the young wife, a little incoherently.

"There is some mistake, my love, which would be simply ludicrous if it were not so annoying. I must go to Wendover and set it all right," replied Mr. Lytton, cheerfully.

"Are you certain it is nothing more than a mistake?"

"Nothing more than a mistake or a jest, dear love. But I must go to Wendover to set it right."

"But what sort of a mistake is it? What is it all about?"

"I will explain it all when I come back, my wife. I do not quite comprehend it yet."

"How soon will you be back?"

"As soon as ever this matter shall be explained—in time for tea, if possible. Mr. Lyle and Mr. Brent are going with me. You will take care of the girls during the few hours' delay in their journey. There, love, return to your guests and let me go. This officer is growing impatient."

While Alden Lytton was trying to soothe the anxiety of his wife, Mr. Brent and Mr. Lyle had crossed to the drawing-room to explain to their brides that an unexpected event had occurred which would delay their journey for a few hours, during which they would remain as the guests of Mrs. Alden Lytton.

And before the young ladies could make a comment the deputy-sheriff, with Alden Lytton in custody, passed out.

Then Stephen Lyle and Joseph Brent hurried out and entered the same carriage occupied by Alden Lytton and the sheriff.

During the drive to Wendover the three gentlemen tried to learn from the sheriff more particulars concerning the charges made against Mr. Alden Lytton.

But the sheriff knew little or nothing concerning those charges beyond what was embodied in the warrant that authorized the arrest.

Chapter XLVI.

THE INVESTIGATION.

One is my true and honorable wife,
As dear to me as are the ruddy drops
That visit my sad heart.

—Shakespeare.

In due time they reached the village and were driven at once to the office of the magistrate, Squire Estep, of Spring Hill Manor.

No rumor of the arrest had got abroad, and no crowd was collected about the office doors.

The sheriff alighted first, and was followed out by the accused and his two friends.

They entered the office, where just then no one was present except the magistrate, one clerk and two constables.

The three gentlemen bowed as they entered, and the venerable magistrate arose and acknowledged their presence by a nod and sat down again.

The sheriff laid the warrant on the table before the magistrate and, pointing to Mr. Alden Lytton, said:

"That is the prisoner, your worship."

One of the constables placed chairs, and the gentlemen seated themselves and waited.

"White," said Mr. Estep, addressing one of the constables, "go to the Reindeer and serve this upon the gentleman to whom it is directed, and whom you will find there."

The constable took the slip of paper from the speaker's hand, bowed and went out.

And the three gentlemen waited with what patience they might command, while the magistrate drummed upon the table with his fingers.

Presently the constable returned, ushering in two persons, in one of whom Alden Lytton recognized his great rival at the bar, Philip Desmond. The other, an elderly gentleman in a clergyman's dress, was a total stranger to him.

Both these gentlemen bowed to the magistrate and to the accused and his friends, and one of them—the clerical stranger—came up to Alden and, to his great amazement, said:

"I am very sorry, Mr. Lytton, in meeting you a second time, to see you here in this position; sorrier still that I am here to bear testimony against you."

While he was saying this the magistrate, who was engaged in searching among some documents, drew forth from them a paper which seemed to be a memorandum, which he from time to time consulted, as he addressed the accused and said:

"You are Mr. Alden Lytton, attorney at law, of the Richmond bar, I believe?"

"I am," answered Alden Lytton.

"Attend, if you please, to the reading of this," said the magistrate, as he commenced and read out aloud the warrant upon which the accused had been brought before him.

At the conclusion of the reading Alden Lytton bowed gravely and waited.

"Mr. Alden Lytton, you have heard that you are charged with having, on the fifteenth of February of this present year, feloniously intermarried with Emma Angela Cavendish, in and during the lifetime of your lawful wife, Mary Lytton, now living in this State. Such marriage, under such circumstances, being a felony, punishable with imprisonment and hard labor in the State Penitentiary for a term not less than — — or more than — — years. What have you to say to this charge?" inquired the magistrate.

Alden Lytton with some difficulty controlled his indignation as he answered:

"It is perfectly true that in last February I married Miss Cavendish, of Blue Cliffs. But it is a false and malicious slander that I ever at any time married any one else. It is only amazing to me, Mr. Magistrate, that you should have issued a warrant charging me with so base a crime. You could not possibly have had any grounds to justify such a proceeding."

"We shall see," answered, the magistrate. "You admit that you married Miss Cavendish on the fifteenth of last February?"

"Certainly I do."

"Then nothing remains but to prove or to disprove the statement that at the time of your marriage with Miss Cavendish, at Blue Cliffs, you had a lawful wife then living in the city of Richmond."

Alden Lytton flushed to the temples at hearing his true wife's pure and noble name brought into this dishonoring examination. He spoke sternly as he inquired:

"Upon what grounds do you make this charge? Where are your witnesses?"

"The Reverend Mr. Borden will please step forward," said the magistrate.

The strange clergyman came up to the table and stood there.

The magistrate administered the oath to this witness.

At the same moment Mr. Philip Desmond took his place at the table to conduct the examination.

"Your name is Adam Borden?"

"Yes, sir," answered the clerical witness.

"You are the rector of Saint Blank's Episcopal Church, Philadelphia?"

"Yes, sir."

"You know the accused?"

"Yes, sir. He is Mr. Alden Lytton," replied the rector, bowing gravely to the prisoner.

Alden acknowledged the courtesy by a nod, and then waited with more amazement and curiosity than anxiety to hear what sort of a case they would make out against him with the aid of this man, whom he never saw before, and yet who claimed to know him well.

"State, if you please, Mr. Borden, what you know of Mr. Lytton in regard to this case."

"In the month of September of last year Mr. Lytton came to my house in company with a lady to whom he wished to be married immediately. I conducted the pair into the church and married them there, in the presence of my sexton and his daughter. I registered the marriage in the church books and gave a certificate, signed by myself and the witnesses to the marriage. They then left the church together. I had never seen them before, and I have never seen them since until to-day, when I see and recognize Mr. Lytton, just as I should recognize his bride if I should see her."

"Where is she?" inquired the magistrate.

"Your worship, the lady can be produced at once, to be identified by the witness," said Philip Desmond.

And he wrote on a slip of paper and handed it to a constable, who silently left the room.

Meanwhile Alden Lytton waited with constantly increasing curiosity to find out to whom he had been unconsciously married in the month of September, and in the city of Philadelphia. It flashed upon him suddenly that he had been in Philadelphia about the middle of the last September, and in company with Mary Grey. But he felt certain that he had never gone out with her while there; and he

302

waited with intensely curious interest to hear how they could possibly make out a case against him.

Presently the door opened and the constable returned, bringing with him a gracefully-moving woman, dressed in black and deeply veiled.

"Your worship, this is the true wife of the accused, produced here to be identified by the witness," said Mr. Desmond, taking the hand of the lady and leading her to the table.

"Will you be so good as to raise your veil, ma'am?" requested the magistrate.

The lady lifted the black veil and threw it behind her head, revealing the beautiful face of Mary Grey.

Alden Lytton had half expected to see her, yet he could not forbear the exclamation:

"Mrs. Grey!"

"Mrs. Lytton, if you please, sir! You have taken from me your love and your protection, but you can not take from me your name! That is still mine. You have taken from me my peace of heart, but you shall not take from me my name! When you address me again call me Mrs. Lytton, for that is my legal name!"

"It is false—infamously false!" began Alden Lytton, crimsoning with indignation.

But the magistrate stopped him, saying:

"Mr. Lytton, this is very unseemly. If this lady claims a relation to you that she can not prove she will do so at her own proper peril. Let us continue the examination and conduct it with decent order."

Alden Lytton bowed to the magistrate and said, with what calmness he could command:

"This woman—no, this libel upon womanhood, who is brought here to be identified as my wife, might have rather been summoned to bear testimony against me in any false charge she and her co-conspirators might have chosen to set up, since she is not, and never has been, my wife. Her presence here can not establish one single point in this infamous accusation. Yet I am anxious to know how she and her confederate—as I am forced to regard this witness—will attempt to do so. Let the examination proceed."

"Mr. Borden, will you look upon this lady?" respectfully demanded Mr. Desmond.

The reverend gentleman put on his spectacles and scrutinized the face of Mary Grey, who met his gaze, and then lowered her eyes.

"Can you identify her as the lady whom you united in marriage with Mr. Alden Lytton?" inquired Mr. Desmond.

"Yes, assuredly I can. She is the lady, then called Mary Grey, whom I united in marriage with that gentleman, then called Alden Lytton, and to whom I gave the marriage certificate, signed by myself and two witnesses. Those witnesses can be produced when wanted," answered the Rev. Mr. Borden, with much assurance.

"These witnesses are not needed just now. But I wish you to examine this certificate, Mr. Borden," said Mr. Desmond, putting a folded paper in the hands of the minister.

The reverend gentleman adjusted his spectacles and scrutinized it.

"Is that the certificate of marriage that you gave Mrs. Mary Lytton, the wife of Mr. Alden Lytton, on the day that you united them?" inquired Mr. Desmond.

"Yes, sir, it is," answered the minister.

"Are you quite sure?"

"Quite sure, sir. Why, I know the paper and the printed form, as well as my own autograph and the signatures of the two witnesses," declared the minister.

"That will do. You may sit down, sir," said Mr. Desmond.

"I beg your pardon. I would like to ask that witness a few questions before he retires," said Mr. Lytton.

"Of course that is your right, sir," said the magistrate.

Alden Lytton arose and confronted the witness, looking him full in the face.

"You are a minister of the gospel, I believe, Mr. Borden?" he inquired.

"Yes, sir. I am rector of Saint Blank's Episcopal Church in Philadelphia, as you yourself know very well, having there received my ministry on the day that you then declared to be 'the happiest of your life,'" replied the minister.

"As Heaven is my witness, I never saw your face before I met you in this office! Now then, reverend sir, please to look me in the eyes while you answer my next questions. Being upon your oath, you declare that on a certain day, in the month of last September, in your parish church, in the city of Philadelphia, you performed the marriage ceremony between Alden Lytton and Mary Grey?"

"I do most solemnly declare, upon my sacred oath, that I did so," answered Mr. Borden, meeting the searching gaze of the questioner without flinching.

"This is the most astounding effrontery! But attend further, sir, if you please. Being on your oath, you declare that I am the man and that female is the woman whom you joined in marriage, under the names of Alden Lytton and Mary Grey?"

"On my sacred oath I most solemnly declare that you are the man and she is the woman I then and there united together," unflinchingly replied the minister.

For a moment Alden Lytton was mute with amazement; and then he said:

"Let me look at that paper that is said to be a certificate of this marriage."

Mr. Desmond handed over the document.

Alden Lytton read it, and then recommenced his cross-examination of the minister.

"And this is the certificate you gave the pretended bride?" he inquired.

"That is the certificate I gave your wife, sir."

"And you persist in declaring, under oath, that you solemnized a marriage between myself, Alden Lytton, and this woman, Mary Grey, here present?"

"I do, most solemnly."

"Then, sir," said Alden Lytton, flushing to his temples with fierce indignation, "all I have further to say is this—that you have basely perjured yourself to assist and support an infamous conspiracy!"

"Sir—sir—Mr. Lytton!" said the magistrate, in trepidation. "This gentleman is a most highly respected preacher of the gospel, quite incapable of such a thing!"

"I do not care whether he be priest, bishop, pope or apostle! He has basely perjured himself in support of an infamous conspiracy!"

"Mr. Lytton—Mr. Lytton," said the magistrate, "if you have anything to bring forward to disprove this strange charge we shall be glad to hear it. But vituperation is not testimony."

"I know it," said Alden Lytton, trying hard to control his raging passion. "I know it, and I beg pardon of the magistrate. But this is a foul conspiracy against my peace, honor and liberty—and oh, great Heaven, against the honor of my dear, noble young wife! But this vile conspiracy shall surely be exposed, and when it is, by all my hopes of heaven, no charity, no mercy, no consideration in the universe shall prevent me from prosecuting and pursuing these conspirators to punishment with the utmost rigor of the law!"

"Mr. Lytton, have you anything to bring forward in disproof of the charges made against you?" inquired the magistrate.

"No, sir; not now, nor here. I must have time to look this monstrous falsehood in the face and prepare for its total destruction."

"Then, Mr. Lytton, I shall have to send your case to court for trial. Have you bail?"

"Yes, sir," spoke up Joseph Brent, coming forward before Alden Lytton could speak, "he has bail. I will enter into bonds for my esteemed young friend, Alden Lytton, to any amount you may please to name."

"The charge is one of the gravest; the position of the parties involved in it is high in the social scale; the evidence already elicited is of the most convincing and convicting character; every circumstance would seem to point to the expediency of evading the trial by flight, or any other means. In view of all the circumstances of the case I feel it my duty to demand a very heavy bail. I fix the bail, therefore, at the sum of twenty thousand dollars," said the magistrate.

"It might be twenty times twenty thousand dollars, and I would enter it for him. A man of honor, like Mr. Lytton, falsely accused of a base crime, does not fly from trial. On the contrary he demands it for his own vindication," said Joseph Brent, earnestly.

Alden Lytton turned and grasped his hand in silent acknowledgment of his noble friendship. Then, addressing the magistrate, he said:

"I am ready to enter into a recognizance with my esteemed friend here for my appearance at court to answer this charge—this charge as ridiculous as it is monstrous."

The magistrate nodded and directed his clerk to fill out the proper forms.

When these were completed and signed the accused was discharged from custody.

He bowed to the magistrate, and even to the others, and was about to leave the office, followed by Mr. Lyle and Mr. Brent, when Mary Grey darted swiftly and silently to his side and hissed in his ear:

"I swore that I would take you in the hour of your greatest triumph and strike you down to the dust in dishonor! I have done so! I will send you to the penitentiary yet—felon!"

"I think that you will find yourself there, madam, before many months have passed over your head. There are severe laws against forgery, perjury and conspiracy," answered Alden Lytton.

Outside of the office the three gentlemen consulted their watches. It was now six o'clock in the afternoon.

Then they looked about them.

They had come to Wendover in the deputy-sheriff's carriage. That had gone. And there was no conveyance waiting to take them to Blue Cliff Hall.

"We must go to the old Reindeer and hire their hack," said Mr. Lyle.

"Excuse me, Lyle; let us walk to your parsonage first. You must give me house-room there for a few weeks, for I do not wish to stop at the hotel to be stared at, and—I shall not return to Blue Cliffs, or enter the presence of my pure and noble young wife, until I shall be cleared from this foul charge," said Alden Lytton, firmly.

"Not return to Blue Cliffs? Why, Lytton, you will break your wife's heart if you keep her from you in this your day of sorrow!" exclaimed Mr. Lyle.

"Her heart is too heroic to be easily broken. And a little reflection will convince you that, under the peculiar circumstances of this accusation, it is expedient that I should absent myself from her and from her dwelling until I shall be cleared. Now if the charge against me were that of murder, or anything else but what it is, my wife might be by my side. But being what it is, you must see that I best consult her dignity and delicacy by abstaining from seeing her until after my acquittal. No, I shall neither see, speak, nor write to her while I suffer under this charge."

"I see now that you are perfectly right," said Mr. Lyle.

"Yes, that you are," added Mr. Brent, as the three walked out toward the minister's cottage.

"I only wish you to install me, Lyle, by explaining to your good old housekeeper that I am to be an inmate of the parsonage during your absence, so that she may not take my presence as an unjustifiable intrusion," said Alden Lytton.

"She would never do that in any case," answered Stephen Lyle.

"And when you have installed me I wish you and Brent to return to Blue Cliffs and rejoin your brides at once. And you, Lyle, must break this matter to my dear Emma as delicately and tenderly as you can. She does not need to be told that I am entirely guiltless of the crime that is laid to my charge; for she knows that I am incapable of committing such an one. Nor does she require to be assured of my undying love and faith. She is assured of that. But tell her to be of good cheer, to bear this temporary separation patiently, and to wait hopefully our speedy meeting in happier days. Will you do this, my friend?"

"Most faithfully," answered Mr. Lyle.

"And then I wish you to start at once upon your wedding tours. They must not be further delayed on my account."

"Look here, Lytton," said Stephen Lyle, earnestly. "I speak for myself and also for Brent, who feels just as I do. We start upon no bridal tours until you are out of this trouble. We could not leave you in your trouble. And our girls, I am sure, would not leave your wife in her sorrow. So that is all over. What I have to propose is this: That I bring our Laura home here to-morrow. And that we remain here to keep you company, while Victor—I mean Brent—and Electra stay for the present at Blue Cliffs as the guests of Mrs. Alden Lytton."

"I hope you approve the plan. We talked it over and settled it all while we were in the magistrate's office attending the examination," added Joseph Brent.

They had by this time reached the gates of the pretty cottage.

Alden Lytton stopped, turned around and grasped a hand of each faithful friend. For a moment he could not speak for the strong emotion that choked him.

"God bless you!" he said, at length, in a half suffocated voice. "God bless you both! I have surely found one 'precious jewel' in the head of this 'toad' — the priceless jewel of your friendship!"

CHAPTER XLVII.

HOW EMMA HEARD THE NEWS.

An angel guard—
Chariots of fire, horses of fire encamp,
To keep thee safe.

—MRS. ELLET.

It was eleven o'clock that night when the Rev. Mr. Lyle and Mr. Brent reached Blue Cliffs on their return from Wendover.

Of course all the guests of the bridal reception had long since gone away. The house was closed and all the windows were dark except those of the library, where the gentlemen found the two brides and their hostess sitting up and awaiting their return.

"Where is Alden? Is he not with you?" anxiously inquired Emma, coming to meet them.

"Our friend might certainly have come back with us if he had chosen to do so; but he deemed it better to remain at Wendover to-night, and we agreed with him. He is at my house," answered Mr. Lyle.

"You have something painful to tell me. I beg you will tell it at once," said Emma, turning very pale, but controlling herself perfectly and speaking with calmness.

"Something ridiculous, if it were not so outrageous, I should say, dear Mrs. Lytton. Is there a light in the parlor?"

"Yes."

"Then come with me there and I will tell you all about it," answered Mr. Lyle, speaking cheerfully, as he offered his arm to Emma.

They left the room together and went to the parlor, where a lamp was burning low and shedding a dim light around.

Mr. Lyle led his hostess to a sofa, where he sat down beside her.

And then and there he told her the whole history of the charge that had been brought against her husband, as it came out upon the preliminary examination.

Emma listened in unspeakable grief, horror, amazement and mortification. Yet with all these strong emotions struggling in her bosom, she controlled herself so far as to preserve her outward composure and answer with calmness.

"And Mary Grey claims to be *his wife*? I should think the woman were raving mad, but for the plausible testimony she has managed to bring together. As it is, I am forced to look upon this in the same light that you do, as a base conspiracy, in which she has found some skillful confederates. Of course it must be only the embarrassment and mortification of a few days and then the whole plot must be exposed. Such a plot can not, certainly, bear a thorough investigation," she said.

But though she spoke so confidently, and believed all that she said, yet her face continued deathly pale and her hands were clutched closely together on her lap.

Then Mr. Lyle explained to her the delicate motives that governed her husband in deciding him to remain at the Wendover parsonage, and to absent himself entirely from Blue Cliffs and from her until this charge should be disproved.

Emma flushed and paled again, and clutched her hands a little closer, but made no comment yet. She seemed to wait for Mr. Lyle to proceed.

"He says, my child, and he speaks rightly, that if the accusation against him was of almost any other felony than what it is, you should be with him through all he might have to endure. But the accusation being what it is every consideration for your dignity and delicacy constrains him to absent himself from you until his fair fame shall be cleared. He therefore implores you, by me, not to attempt to see him, or even to write to him, but to let all your communications with him be verbal ones, sent through me. And I, on my part, my child, promise to fulfill my duties to you both faithfully and loyally," said Mr. Lyle.

"I must comply," answered Emma, in a low, restrained voice, that would have faltered and broken had she not possessed and exercised such great power of self-control. "I must comply, although this is the very hardest requisition that my dear husband could make of me—to abandon him in this hour of his greatest need. I must comply, because I know that it is right. Our mutual honor demands this temporary separation—for of course it will be but temporary."

"Very temporary, and lightened by frequent news of each other through me," replied Mr. Lyle.

"But that woman, Mary Grey! The amazing wickedness of that woman!" said Emma, with a shudder, and almost under her breath.

"My dear," said the minister, gravely, "you knew Mrs. Grey intimately for several years. Had you really confidence in her during all that time?"

"N-no. I often doubted and suspected her. And I blamed myself for such doubts and suspicions, and compelled myself to think the best of her and do the best for her, for my father's sake—because he loved her. Oh, the astounding wickedness of that woman, as it has developed itself in this conspiracy against us! But she must have had confederates. The minister who professes to have married her to Mr. Lytton, and who gave her a marriage certificate to that effect, may he not have been a confederate of hers? May he not have taken a false oath—made a false statement and given a false certificate?"

"Oh, no, no, no, my child—a thousand times no! The character of the Reverend Mr. Borden is far above any such suspicion," answered Mr. Lyle.

"Then he must himself have been deceived. Some one must have personated Mr. Lytton at that ceremony—some one who has some resemblance to him—and utterly deceived the minister," said Emma. And she paused for a few moments, with her head upon her hand, as in hard, deep thought; and then a sudden flash of intelligence, like lightning, lit up her face, as she exclaimed: "I know who it was! I know all about it now! Oh, Mr. Lyle, I shall save my dear husband's honor from a breath of reproach, because I have found out all about it now!"

"My dear child—" began the good minister, who thought that she looked a little wild.

But Emma vehemently interrupted him.

"It was Craven Kyte who personated Mr. Lytton at that marriage! Oh, I am sure it was! I am as sure of it as I am of being alive at this time! Oh, Mr. Lyle, don't you remember the wonderful personal resemblance between Craven Kyte and Mr. Lytton? They were counterparts of each other, except in one small particular. Craven Kyte had a black mole on his chin. And he was deeply in love with Mary Grey, and she could have done whatever she pleased with him. She could have persuaded him to personate Alden Lytton at that marriage ceremony; and I am sure that she has done so. I feel a positive conviction that he is the man."

"The explanation of the mystery is a very plausible one indeed," gravely mused the minister, with his bearded chin in his hand.

"It is the true and only one," said Emma, emphatically.

"Where is the young man now? Has he been heard from yet?" inquired Mr. Lyle.

"No; I believe not. He is still missing. He has been missing ever since last September, when he went away for a holiday. That is another link in the chain of circumstantial evidence against him, for it was in September that this marriage was performed."

"This looks more and more likely," mused the minister.

"Mr. Lyle, this is what must be done immediately: Advertisements must be inserted in all the principal newspapers in the principal cities of the United States and Canada, offering great inducements to Craven Kyte, late of Wendover, to return to his home, or to communicate with his friends."

"Yes, that must be done immediately, even upon the bare chance of his being the man we want. But if he *be* the man, there is little likelihood of his making his appearance, or even answering the advertisement. If he be the man he knows that he has committed a misdemeanor in personating Mr. Lytton under these circumstances. And he will not be likely to place himself within reach of justice."

"Then we must also supplement these advertisements with others, offering large rewards for any information as to the present residence of the missing man. And this must be done at once."

"Certainly, if it is done at all. The man must be found and produced in court, to be confronted with Mr. Borden beside Alden Lytton. My dear child, your woman's wit may have saved your husband."

"Heaven grant it!" said Emma, fervently.

Next Mr. Lyle informed her of the proposed arrangement by which the two newly-married pairs were to give up their bridal tour for the present, while two of them, himself and Laura, should go home to the Wendover parsonage to stay with Alden Lytton, and the other two, Joseph Brent and Electra, should remain at Blue Cliffs, in attendance upon Emma.

"Emma is not a queen, that she should require ladies and gentlemen in waiting; but she will be very much comforted by the presence of her dear friends, Joseph and Electra," said the young wife, with a sad smile, as she arose to return to her guests.

Later in the evening Laura and Electra were informed about the state of affairs.

Their amazement was unmeasured and unutterable.

But they at once set down the criminal conspiracy of Mary Grey against Mr. and Mrs. Lytton to its right motive—malignant hatred and revenge for scorned love.

The two young brides most willingly gave up their tours and consented to stay at home with their friends during the time of the trial.

The next morning, therefore, Mr. Lyle took his young wife and returned with her to the Wendover parsonage, where he comforted the soul of Alden Lytton by reporting to him all that had passed between himself and Emma.

"She keeps up bravely, heroically. She is worthy to be a hero's wife!" said the minister, warmly.

"She is—she is! She comes of a heroic race; therefore the deeper guilt of those who seek to bring dishonor upon her!" groaned Alden Lytton.

Then Mr. Lyle said:

"Her feminine intuition discovered what we men, with all our logic, would never have learned—that is to say, who it was that personated *you* at that false marriage."

"Indeed! Who was it?"

"Craven Kyte," answered Mr. Lyle.

And then he told Alden Lytton all that had been said between himself and Emma on that subject.

"I feel sure that her suspicions are correct," he added.

"I think it highly probable that they are. Now there are two or three things that must be done this morning. First, those advertisements for the missing man must be written out and distributed all over the country. Secondly, a messenger must be dispatched to Philadelphia to question the people at the Blank House as to whether any of them entered my room and saw me sleeping there during the hours of eleven a. m. and one p. m., on the fifteenth of September of last year, when I was said to have married that woman. And also to search the registers of that date of all the hotels in the city for the name of Craven Kyte."

"To get up evidence for the defense?"

"Certainly; to get up evidence for the defense."

"Have you thought of employing counsel?"

"Certainly. Berners and Denham are as good men as any I can find. I have sent a note to ask Berners to come here to see me to-day. While waiting for him you and I can write out those advertisements," said Alden Lytton.

These plans were all promptly carried out.

That same day an experienced detective was found and dispatched to Philadelphia to hunt up evidence for the defense.

And that evening advertisements were sent by mail, to be scattered all over the country.

But some days after this, Mary Grey, who was stopping at the Reindeer, saw one of these advertisements in a Richmond paper and smiled in triumph.

"They have scented out a part of the truth," she said. "They have more sharpness than I gave them credit for possessing. They have scented out a part of the truth, but they can not follow the scent. Ha, ha, ha! They may advertise from now till doomsday, but they will never get a response from him! Let them rake the Susquehanna if they can! Perhaps, deep in its mud, they may find what the fishes have left of him!" she said, with a sneer.

But even as she spoke these wicked words she shuddered with horror.

Meanwhile, every day Mr. Lytton and his counsel, Messrs. Berners and Denham, consulted together concerning the proper line of defense to be taken by them.

It is almost needless to say that Messrs. Berners and Denham felt perfectly sure of the absolute guiltlessness of their client, and quite sanguine in their expectations both of a full acquittal of the falsely-accused and of a thorough exposure and successful prosecution of the conspirators.

But as time passed and no answer came to the advertisements for the missing man both counsel and client began to grow anxious.

The detective who had been sent to Philadelphia to look up evidence for the defense returned to Wendover with such meager intelligence that the hopes of all concerned sank very low.

So overwhelming was the evidence against the accused that to gain an acquittal it was absolutely necessary either to prove an alibi or to find the man who had personated Mr. Lytton at the marriage ceremony.

But neither of these most important objects had been yet effected.

No one had been found in Philadelphia, or elsewhere, who had set eyes on Mr. Alden Lytton between the hours of eleven and one on the fifteenth of the last September, at which time his marriage with Mary Grey was alleged to have taken place.

And no one had answered the advertisements for Craven Kyte.

And what complicated this part of the case still more was the circumstance that Mr. Bastiennello, the senior partner of the firm in which poor Craven Kyte was once the youngest "Co.," was absent in Europe, where he had been on a visit to his relations for the last two months, so that he could not be consulted as to the probable whereabouts of his former partner.

Meanwhile Mr. Lyle and his young bride Laura did all that they possibly could to comfort and cheer their unfortunate brother and sister.

One or the other of them went every day to Blue Cliffs to carry to Emma the encouraging news of Alden's continued good health and spirits, and to bring back to him the glad tidings of Emma's heroic patience and cheerfulness.

And in this manner the tedious weeks passed slowly away and brought the day of the trial.

CHAPTER XLVIII.

THE TRIAL.

It was a glorious morning in June. All nature seemed exulting in the young summer's splendor.

And any stranger arriving at the town of Wendover that day would have supposed that the population of the whole surrounding country were taking advantage of the delightful weather to hold a gay festival there.

The whole town was full of visitors, come to the great trial.

Mr. Hezekiah Greenfield, of the Reindeer Hotel, was beside himself under the unusual press of business, and his waiters and hostlers were nearly crazy amid the confusion of arrivals and the conflicting claims made all at once upon their attention and services.

The scene around the court-house was even more tumultuous.

The court-house was a plain, oblong, two-story edifice, built of the red stone that abounded in the mountain quarries of that district. It stood in a large yard shaded with many trees and surrounded by a high stone wall.

In the rear end of this yard stood the county prison.

The court-yard was filled with curious people, who were pressing toward the doors of the court-house, trying to effect an entrance into the building, which was already crammed to suffocation.

In the minister's cottage parlor, at the same early hour, were assembled the Rev. Mr. Lyle, honest John Lytton and his shock-headed son, Charley, Joseph Brent, Alden Lytton, and his counsel, Messrs. Berners and Denham.

John Lytton had arrived only that morning. And on meeting his nephew had taken him by both hands, exclaiming:

"You know, Aldy, my boy, as I told you before, I don't believe the first word of all this. 'Cause it's impossible, you know, for any man of our race to do anything unbecoming of a Lytton and a gentleman. And I think a man's family ought to stand by him in a case like this. So I not only came myself, but I fotch Charley, and if I had had another son I would a-fotched him too. I don't know but I'd a fotched your aunt Kitty and the girls, only, as I said to them, a trial of this sort a'n't no proper place for ladies. What do you think yourself?"

"I quite agree with you, Uncle John. And I feel really very deeply touched by the proof of confidence and affection you give me in coming here yourself," said Alden, earnestly, pressing and shaking the honest hands that held his own.

And at that moment Mr. Lyle placed in Mr. Alden Lytton's hands a little note from Emma, saying:

"She gave it to me yesterday, with the request that I would hand it to you to-day."

Alden unfolded and read it.

It was only a brief note assuring him of her unwavering faith in Heaven and in himself, and her perfect confidence, notwithstanding the present dark aspect of affairs, in his speedy and honorable acquittal.

He pressed this little note to his lips and placed it near his heart.

And then Mr. Lyle told him that it wanted but a quarter to ten, the carriages were at the door, and it was time to start for the court-house.

Mr. Lytton nodded assent, and they all went out.

There were two carriages before the cottage gates.

Into the first went the Rev. Mr. Lyle, Mr. Alden Lytton, and his counsel, Messrs. Berners and Denham.

Into the second went Mr. John Lytton, his son Charley, and Mr. Joseph Brent.

The court-house was situated at the opposite end of the town from the parsonage, and was about a mile distant. The gentlemen of this party might easily have walked the distance, but preferred to ride, in order to avoid the curious gaze of strangers who had flocked into the town.

A rapid drive of twenty minutes' duration brought them to the court-house.

The Rev. Mr. Lyle alighted first, and called a constable to clear the way for the party to pass into the court-room.

The accused, Alden Lytton, was accommodated with a chair in front of the bench, and near him sat his relatives, John and Charles Lytton, his friends Mr. Lyle and Mr. Brent, and his counsel, Messrs. Berners and Denham.

Judge Burlington sat upon the bench to try the case.

After the tedious preliminaries were over the accused was arraigned with the usual formula, and—not without some natural scorn and indignation, for he was still too youthful to have learned much self-control—answered:

"Not guilty, of course!"

As if he would have added, "You know that quite as well as I myself and everybody else does."

Chapter XLIX.

A HOST OF WITNESSES.

Mr. Martindale, State's Attorney, opened the case for the prosecution with a few brief but very severe remarks upon the baseness of the crime with which the prisoner stood charged, and then called his first witness—

"The Reverend Adam Borden."

Mr. Borden took the stand and testified to having performed the marriage ceremony between Alden Lytton and Mary Grey on the morning of the fifteenth of the preceding September, at his own parish church, in the city of Philadelphia.

He was strictly cross-examined by Mr. Berners, but his testimony only came out the clearer from the ordeal.

John Martin, sexton of the church, and Sarah Martin, his daughter, were successively examined, and testified to having witnessed the marriage ceremony between the parties in question.

They also were cross-examined by Mr. Berners, without detriment to their testimony.

"Mrs. Mary Lytton" was then called upon to come forward for identification.

And Mary Grey, dressed in deep mourning and closely veiled, came up, leaning heavily on the arm of Mr. Philip Desmond, assistant counsel for the prosecution.

At the request of counsel she drew aside her veil, revealing a face so ghastly pale that all who gazed upon it shuddered.

Alden Lytton turned to look at her, in order to catch her eyes, but they were fixed upon the ground, and never once raised.

Even he, so deeply injured by her diabolical arts, turned away from her with shuddering pity.

"The woman is at once going mad and dying," he said to himself.

Mary Grey was then fully identified by the three witnesses as the woman who was, at the time and place specified, married to Mr. Alden Lytton.

But she had scarcely stood long enough to be sworn to, when her white face turned blue and she fell swooning into the arms of Philip Desmond.

She was borne out into the sheriff's room, amid the sympathetic murmurs of the audience.

Mr. Martindale then produced and read the marriage certificate, and recalled the Rev. Mr. Borden, who acknowledged it as his own document, presented to "Mrs. Mary Lytton" immediately after the marriage ceremony had been concluded.

The State's Attorney next produced certain letters, purporting to have been written by Mr. Alden Lytton to Mrs. Mary Grey during the period of his courtship.

These letters, he said, were important as corroborative evidence, and he begged leave to read them to the jury.

He then commenced with the correspondence from the earliest date.

And there in open court he read aloud, one after the other, all those fond, foolish, impassioned letters that the love-sick lad, Alden Lytton, had written to the artful woman who had beguiled him in the earliest days of their acquaintance, and before he had discovered her deep depravity.

This was the severest ordeal Alden Lytton had to bear. For he knew he had written these foolish letters in his romantic boyhood, and in his manhood he felt heartily ashamed of them. Under *any* circumstances he would have been heartily ashamed of them. His ears tingled and his face burned to hear them read aloud to judge, jury and gaping crowd.

And then and there he registered a vow never, never, never to write another gushing love-letter so long as he should live in this world; no, not even to his own dear wife.

When the last terrible letter was finished he felt as much relieved as if he had been unbound from the rack.

But his relief was soon superseded by the utmost astonishment when Mr. Martindale took up another parcel, saying:

"The letters that I have just read, your honor, and gentlemen of the jury, were, as you have heard, written from the University of Charlottesville some years ago. Those that I am about to read to you were written from Wendover last year, in the few weeks preceding the marriage of the prisoner with Mary Grey."

And so saying, the State's Attorney proceeded to read, one after the other, all those forged letters which had been executed with inimitable skill by Mary Grey herself and mailed from Wendover by her unconscious confederate, Craven Kyte.

These counterfeits were even fonder, more foolish and more impassioned than the real ones, and every letter pressed speedy marriage, until the last one, which actually arranged the mode and manner of proceeding.

During the reading of the final letter Mr. Alden Lytton beckoned his counsel, who approached him.

"I acknowledge the first batch of folly written from Charlottesville, when I was a boy of eighteen or nineteen," said Alden, between a laugh and a blush.

"Every man has been a boy, and a fool, at least once in his life. I know I have; and I would much rather be hanged than have my letters read," laughingly replied Mr. Berners.

"But, by all my hopes of heaven, I never wrote one of those infernal letters of the last parcel!" added Mr. Lytton.

"I never supposed you did. It will, no doubt, be possible to prove them to be forgeries. If we can do that the whole prosecution breaks down," replied Mr. Berners.

"They *are* forgeries!" said Alden Lytton, indignantly.

But that was more easily said than established.

A score of witnesses, one after the other, were called, and swore to the hand writing of Mr. Alden Lytton in those letters.

Other witnesses of less importance followed—waiters and chambermaids from the Blank House, Philadelphia, who swore to the fact that Mr. Lytton and Mrs. Grey had taken rooms together at that house on the fourteenth of September and had left it on the afternoon of the fifteenth.

The prosecuting attorney said that he might call other witnesses who had seen the parties meet as by appointment at the railway station at Forestville and proceed thence to Richmond, and others again who had seen them together in the Richmond and Washington steamer; but he would forbear, for he felt convinced that the overwhelming amount of testimony already given was more than sufficient to establish the first marriage. The second and felonious marriage was a notorious fact; but for form's sake it must be proved before the jury.

And then, to their extreme disgust, the Rev. Stephen Lyle, Joseph Brent and John Lytton were successively called to testify that they had all been present and witnessed the marriage of the accused, Alden Lytton and Emma Angela Cavendish, on the fifteenth of the last February, at Blue Cliff Hall, in this county and State.

John Lytton, who was the last of the three put upon the stand, came very near being committed for contempt of court by saying:

"Yes, he had witnessed his nephew's, Mr. Alden Lytton's marriage with Miss Cavendish, which he had a perfect right to marry her, never having been married before. None of the Lyttonses were capable of any such burglarious, bigamarious conduct as they accused his nephew of. Everybody knew the Lyttonses. The Lyttonses were none of your upstart judges"—this was aimed directly at the bench. "The Lyttonses was as old as the flood, for that matter!" and so forth, and so forth.

The witness was not committed for this offense, but merely reminded that all this was very irrelevant to the matter in question, and ordered to sit down.

He obeyed, growling at the indignities heaped upon the "Lyttonses" by "upstarts."

State's Attorney Martindale then arose in his place and opened his argument for the prosecution in a very able review of the evidence that had been given by the witnesses examined and the documents presented.

It was while he was still speaking that a little disturbance was heard at the lower end of the court-room.

All who heard it looked around to see what the matter was.

Presently a bailiff was seen pushing his way up through the crowd.

He came up to the counsel for the accused and handed a card to Mr. Denham.

That gentleman took it, looked at it, stared at it, changed color, and, without a word of explanation, abruptly rose and left his seat, and followed the note-bearer through the crowd and out of the court-room.

Mr. Berners and Mr. Lytton looked after him in surprise and curiosity.

State's Attorney Martindale, meanwhile, went on with his argument.

After an absence of about fifteen minutes Mr. Denham returned and resumed his seat beside his senior colleague, Mr. Berners.

He gave no explanation of his abrupt departure and absence, but sat there listening attentively to the speech of the prosecuting attorney and smiling to himself as in silent triumph.

Neither his senior colleague, Mr. Berners, nor his client, Mr. Lytton, interrupted his reflections, considering that it fell to his duty to follow Mr. Martindale's speech with an opening address for the defense.

At length Mr. Martindale brought his argument to a conclusion by a very brilliant peroration, and sat down, saying that there the prosecution would rest the case.

Mr. Denham, giving his client a reassuring pressure of the hand, and wearing the same strange smile of secret mirth and triumph on his face, arose for the defense. He began by saying:

"Your honor and gentlemen of the jury: The prosecution has favored us with some able speeches, and has produced a host of witnesses to prove the truth of a false and malicious charge brought against our client. We of the defense have no speech to make, and only one witness to call. Let Craven Kyte be put upon the stand and sworn."

CHAPTER L.

ONE SINGLE WITNESS.

> This is all true as it is strange;
> Nay, it is ten times true; for truth is truth
> To the end of reckoning.
>
> —SHAKESPEARE.

Every one arose and looked around to catch sight of the expected witness.

But no one was so much affected as the accused. He started to his feet on first hearing the name of Craven Kyte, and then dropped back into his chair, pale as marble.

Evidently he had not expected to hear this man called.

In the meantime a little bustle was heard in the bottom of the hall, as of some one pushing his way through the crowd.

And presently Craven Kyte, pale, calm, handsome and well-dressed in clerical black, came forward and entered the witness-box.

He bowed to the presiding judge and stood ready to give in his testimony.

All eyes within range of them turned constantly from the witness on the stand to the prisoner at the bar.

The two men were perfect duplicates of each other.

The oath was administered to the witness.

Mr. Berners conducted the examination.

"Please to state your name and age, the place of your nativity, and all you know of the marriage performed at the Church of St. — —, in the city of Philadelphia, on the fifteenth day of September last, between the hours of twelve and one p. m.," said the counsel.

"My name is Craven Kyte. I am a native of this town. I am twenty-three years of age. I know Mrs. Mary Grey, one of the parties to this marriage. I was engaged to be married to her. On the evening of the fourteenth of September I arrived in Philadelphia, having followed her there at her request. On the morning of the fifteenth I met her by appointment at the art gallery of Bertue Brothers. It was arranged that we should be married on that day. I took a cab and we entered it. At her suggestion I directed the driver to take us to the rectory of the Reverend Mr. Borden. As we drove along she proposed that I should marry her under the name of Alden Lytton."

At these words of the witness there was an immense sensation in the court, breaking forth into murmurs of astonishment and indignation, so that the judge arose in his place and said that order must be observed or he should be obliged to command the clearing of the court-room.

His words produced the proper effect, and the spectators became "as still as mice."

The examination of the witness was resumed.

"You say that Mrs. Mary Grey proposed that you should marry her in the name of Mr. Alden Lytton?"

"Yes. I was very much astonished at the proposal, and expostulated with her about it; but she was in earnest, and at last she made it an absolute condition of my ever getting her at all that I should marry her under the name of Alden Lytton."

"What reason did she give for this singular request?"

"She said she only wanted to play a harmless practical joke upon Miss Cavendish, the betrothed of Mr. Lytton."

"But her joke was so deep and earnest that she made it the only condition upon which she would marry you at all, you say?"

"Yes, sir."

"And did you comply with that condition?"

"Yes, sir. Sooner than lose her I complied with that wicked condition. It did not seem wicked to me then. It only seemed foolish and purposeless. And, besides, I firmly believe I was half crazy at that time."

"Quite likely," said Mr. Berners, dryly. "What followed?"

"Well, sir, and gentlemen, we drove to the rectory. She took a blank card out of her pocket and with a pencil wrote Mr. Alden Lytton's name on it, and told me to send that in to the rector as if it were my own. When I looked at the name on the card, I exclaimed how much it looked like Mr. Lytton's own handwriting; and she said so much the better."

Again, at these words, a murmur of indignation ran through the court-room, which was, however, instantly suppressed, as every one wished to hear every word uttered by this witness.

He continued:

"I rang the bell at the rectory, and sent the card in by the servant who came to open the door. Presently I was invited into the rector's study. He addressed me as Mr. Lytton, and wanted to know how he could serve me. Then I told him what I had come for. And he consented to perform the marriage ceremony, but said that he must do it in the church, which was just next door to the rectory. I went back to the carriage for Mary—"

"Meaning Mrs. Grey?"

"Yes. But I called her 'Mary' then. I went back for her, and brought her into the church, where, under the name of Alden Lytton, I was married to Mary Grey by the Reverend Mr. Borden, in the presence of John Martin, sexton of the parish, and of Sarah Martin, his daughter. A marriage certificate, signed by the minister and witnesses, was then given to Mrs. Grey."

"What happened next?"

"At her request I drove her back to the Blank House, where she had been stopping. She got out at the corner of the street, however, and walked to the house, while I waited in a neighboring reading-room for her return. After an hour's absence she came back, and we drove to the Asterick, where I had engaged rooms for us both. But she declined staying in town any time, and expressed a wish to go to Havre-de-Grace. So we only stopped at the Asterick long enough to pay my bill and gather up my effects, and then we took the train for Havre-de-Grace, where we arrived the same afternoon."

Here the witness suddenly became so much agitated that he could not go on for some moments.

Mr. Denham brought him a glass of water.

He drank and seemed somewhat revived.

"Tell us what occurred at Havre-de-Grace."

"We took rooms at the Star, had tea there, and after tea she proposed to take a walk down by the water-side, as the evening was so delightful. When we had walked a while she proposed that we should hire a boat and go rowing. I objected, being but an indifferent oarsman. But she insisted, declaring that she had been brought up on the water-side and could row like a squaw and swim like a fish. I was her slave, and I obeyed her. We hired the boat of her choice—a mere shell of a boat—"

Here the judge, who had been growing a little impatient, inquired of the counsel for the defense:

"Pray, Mr. Berners, what has all this about the boat to do with the case on trial?"

"It has a great deal to do with it, your honor, as tending to prove that this woman had a deep design upon the peace and honor of the gentleman whom she claims as her husband, and that she did not hesitate at any crime to carry out that design to a successful issue," respectfully replied the counsel.

"Let the witness proceed then," said the judge.

"What happened next?" inquired Mr. Denham.

"Murder happened next—at least, an attempt at murder. We got into the little shell of a boat, and I took the oars and rowed out into the river and down with the tide. We rowed about for more than two hours. It grew very dark and I then wished to come in; but she objected, and asked me to row around a certain point that I saw dimly down the river. I rowed to the point and around it, when suddenly she made an exclamation that her hat had fallen into the water, and she begged me to get it for her. It floated about three feet from the side of the boat. I drew in my oars and secured them, and then leaned over the side of the boat and reached out my hand to get the hat, which was floating further off. I had to lean so far over, and stretch my hand so far out, that it was as much as ever I could do to keep my balance. But just as I touched the hat she gave me a sudden and violent push from behind and sent me into the water."

At this a murmur of horror and indignation passed through the court-room. And on this occasion no one attempted to enforce silence.

But soon the deep interest of the audience in the story of the witness closed their lips and opened their ears again, and they became silent and attentive.

"Do you mean to say that Mrs. Grey pushed you into the water purposely?" inquired Mr. Denham.

"Yes, sir. She could not have done it accidentally. She waited until I had leaned so far over that the least jar might have made me lose my balance; and then suddenly, with all her strength, she pushed me, and I dropped into the water and sunk like so much lead. I could not swim at all. Twice, in my struggles for life, I rose to the surface and cried for help. Both times I saw her boat whirling round and round from the impetus given it by the violence with which she had pushed me over. The second time I sank I lost my senses. When I recovered them I found myself stretched out on the deck of a collier, with several people rubbing and rolling me. But I was weak in all my limbs and sorely confused in my head."

"Witness, can you not shorten this?" inquired the judge.

"Yes, your honor, I can shorten it, if they will permit me. The schooner that picked me up was the 'Sally Ann,' trading from Havre-de-Grace, and other coal depots, to Washington and Georgetown. They were outward bound then, and, as I could give no account of myself, being so nearly dead, they took me along with them. They carried me to Washington, where I lay ill in the free ward of the Samaritan Hospital, under the care of the good Sisters of Mercy, for two months. When I recovered sufficiently to know where I was I found out that I had been registered there under the name of Albert Little. I don't know how that happened, but I suppose somebody must have found in my pocket the card with Alden Lytton written upon it, and perhaps blotted with the river water, and had misread it Albert Little. But that is only a conjecture."

"Confine yourself to facts, witness, and leave conjectures," said the judge.

"Well, your honor, the fact then was that my name was registered Albert Little, however it came to be done. I did not care to set the good Sisters right about my name, and so I let the matter go. As soon as I was able to write, and before I was able to walk, I wrote to my senior partner, Mr. Bastiennello, a private and confidential letter, asking him to come and visit me at the hospital, and to inquire there for one Albert Little. Mr. Bastiennello, who had suffered great anxiety on the subject of my long protracted and unaccountable absence, came at once to see me. I told him of everything that had befallen me, especially as to Mary Grey's insisting on my marrying her under the name of Alden Lytton, and afterward attempting to get rid of me by murder. He was dreadfully shocked, of course, but in a subsequent conversation with me suggested that Mrs. Grey had some ultimate purpose in the perpetration of these crimes, and he advised me to lie perdue for a while until we should see what her purpose was and foil her in it. Some days afterward he proposed that I should take a commission from him to go and purchase goods for him in Europe. As soon as I was able to travel I left the country on this business. I was absent several months, and only arrived in my native country five days ago. On the day after my landing at New York, in looking over some files of newspapers, I read the advertisements for me. I guessed at once that I was wanted for business connected with the secret of my own life, and so I packed up and took the first train to Washington, and the next boat to Richmond, and the train to Wendover, without stopping an hour on my journey. I reached this place at noon to-day; found the town full of people, as if a fair or a festival was going on; asked what was the matter, and was told about this trial. Of course then I had the key to Mary Grey's mysterious crime, and I knew where I was wanted. I came at once to the court, wrote my name on a card and sent it in to Mr. Lytton's junior counsel, who came out to meet me and brought me here."

"That will do, Mr. Kyte. Gentlemen of the jury, you have heard the testimony of our witness, the only and all-sufficient witness for the defense; but we will recall one who appeared here as the most important witness for the prosecution. The Reverend Mr. Borden will please to take the stand once more," said Mr. Berners.

The rector of St. —— came forward and took his place in the witness box.

"Mr. Borden, will you be so good as to look at these two gentlemen and tell me, upon your oath, which of them you married to Mrs. Mary Grey?" politely requested Mr. Berners.

The rector looked from Alden Lytton to Craven Kyte, and from Craven Kyte back to Alden Lytton. And his face paled and flushed as he exclaimed:

"May the Lord of heaven forgive me, for I have made an awful mistake! It was *that* gentleman whom I married to Mrs. Grey;" and he pointed straight to Craven Kyte.

A murmur of great excitement passed through the court-room.

"A while ago you swore it was the other man," said Mr. Desmond, with an ugly sneer.

"So I did! May Heaven forgive me for the awful, though unconscious perjury; for so I thought, with all my judgment, until I saw this last man! And certainly they are perfect duplicates of each other. Any one, under the same circumstances, might have made the same mistake," meekly replied the minister.

And certainly every one who saw and compared the two men agreed with the last speaker.

"Will you be so good, reverend sir, as to explain by what test you now know these perfect duplicates, the one from the other, and are enabled to identify the particular one whom you married to Mrs. Grey on the fifteenth of the last September?"

"Certainly, sir. I can distinguish them by a certain indefinable difference which I can perceive while I see them together, but which I might fail to perceive if they were apart from each other. Also I can identify this last man, who calls himself Craven Kyte, by that small mark or scar that he bears on his temple near the corner of his left eye. I noticed it at the time I performed the marriage ceremony, but I thought it was a fresh scar. And I never remembered it at all when called upon to identify Mr. Alden Lytton, or indeed until I saw it again upon Mr. Craven Kyte."

"That will do," said Mr. Desmond; and the minister was allowed to retire.

John and Sarah Martin were recalled in succession, and each, when confronted with the two men, recanted from their late testimony, and swore pointedly to the person of Craven Kyte as the man whom they saw married to Mary Grey.

At this point the foreman of the jury arose in his place and asked permission of the bench to render their verdict at once, as they had all quite made up their minds upon the case.

After a few moments' consultation, the requested permission was given, and the jury, without leaving their seats, rendered their verdict of—

"Not guilty!"

The accused was formally discharged from custody. And then the judge did an almost unprecedented thing. He adjourned the court, came down from the bench and warmly shook hands with Mr. Lytton, congratulating him upon his complete vindication.

And friends crowded around him, rejoicing with him in hearty sympathy.

Among them came Craven Kyte, saying, as soon as he got a chance to speak:

"Mr. Lytton, I have come to implore your pardon for the great wrong I unconsciously did you. Heaven knows I never meant it!"

"I do not believe that you ever did," said Alden Lytton, kindly, taking his hand.

"I was mad and blind. She told me it was only to be a practical joke, and made it the only condition of our marriage, and I complied because I was her slave," continued Craven Kyte, not very clearly.

"Say no more about it. Forget it all as fast as you can. I shall," answered Alden, gently pressing and relinquishing the hand that he had held.

"Your carriage waits, my dear Lytton. And I am sure you are anxious to get back to Blue Cliffs and be the first to convey this good news to your wife," said Mr. Lyle, with a view to help Alden to get rid of his well-meaning but troublesome friends, who, in the earnestness of their sympathy with his triumph, forgot they were keeping him from her whom his soul most longed to meet.

Friends took the gentle hint, shook hands with him and released him.

And very soon Alden Lytton, with Mr. Lyle and Laura, were on their way to Blue Cliffs.

As the carriage rolled into the yard, Emma ran down the steps, her face radiant with joy, to meet the beloved husband from whom she had been separated for so many weeks under such trying circumstances, and whose face she had been the first to see through the glass windows of the carriage.

A moment more and they were locked in each other's arms, fervently thanking Heaven for their happy reunion.

Later that evening the six friends were all assembled together in the drawing-room.

John Lytton and Charley, who were the guests of the house for the night, had just bid them good-night and retired to their room.

And then and there two little confessions were made.

Alden Lytton related the whole history of his foolish boyish love for the fascinating and unprincipled widow who had so nearly effected his destruction.

Emma listened in full sympathy, with his hand clasped in hers; and no retrospective jealousy disturbed the serenity of her loving and trusting spirit.

And at the close of the story she silently raised his hand and pressed it to her heart. That was her only comment. And the subject was never afterward mentioned between the two.

Then it was that Joseph Brent made his identity known to Alden Lytton, Emma and Laura, as it had long been known to Mr. Lyle, his friend, and to Electra, his wife. And Emma and Laura wept anew over the long past sorrows of poor Victor Hartman.

Alden grasped his hand in earnest gratitude and friendship.

"And it is to *you*," he said, "that my sister and myself owe all our present happiness. You thought for us, planned for us, toiled for us, made us even as your own children, simply because you were falsely accused of having made us fatherless!" he said, as the generous tears filled his eyes.

"I did all this because, but for the mercy of Heaven, a mad blow of mine *might* have made you fatherless, as it nearly did," answered Victor Hartman.

"Do you know who really struck the fatal blow and why it was struck?"

"No; I know neither one nor the other."

"Then you shall learn, for now is the time to speak," said Alden Lytton.

CHAPTER LI.

WHO KILLED HENRY LYTTON—FATE OF MARY GREY.

In pursuance of his promise to tell who killed his father, Alden Lytton said:

"One hardly knows how to begin so painful a story. But here it is. You may have heard of a wild, handsome ne'er-do-weel who kept the White Perch Point hotel and married a relative of the Cavendish family?"

"Oh, yes, of course! He was the husband of this widow lady who lives here."

"The same. They had one child, a daughter, said to have been as beautiful as the mother, and as wild and reckless as the father. Out of pure deviltry, as it would seem, this girl ran away from her boarding-school in company with an unprincipled young play-actor, who afterward abandoned her. Soon after this my dear father, who had known her parents and herself, too, met and recognized her under the most painful circumstances. He was deeply shocked, and almost with a father's authority he insisted on taking her home to his own house and sending for her friends. She was but a child. She knew, also, that, being a minor, she was liable to be taken in custody, upon complaint made, and forcibly restored to her family. But she was full of duplicity. She affected to consent to return to her parents, and allowed my father to bring her back as far as his own house, whence he wrote a letter to her father telling him of the whereabouts of his daughter, and asking him to come and receive her at his hands. But the very day upon which this letter was mailed two events occurred to frustrate the good intentions of the writer. Ivy Fanning ran away from Fairview, my father's villa. And Mr. Fanning, having heard from the principal of the school from which his daughter had eloped, came furiously to town in search of the fugitive. Most unfortunately, he ascertained beyond a doubt that his daughter was living at Fairview, whither she had been taken by the master of the house, Mr. Henry Lytton. Mistaking altogether the situation, believing my dear father to have been the first abductor of the girl, he waylaid him and struck that fatal blow which caused his death, and which had so nearly cost you, also, your life.

"After committing this dreadful deed, the guilty man fled to his own home, where he found awaiting him the letter from Mr. Lytton explaining everything.

"After this his remorse knew no bounds. But ah, he was a coward! He dared not meet the penalty of his crime. He saw another man condemned to die for his offense, yet he dared not confess and save the guiltless. He tried indirect ways. He wrote anonymous letters to the governor. And when at last he found that these had no effect, and the day of execution drew very near, he came by night to this house, and in a private interview with Governor Cavendish, after binding him to a temporary secrecy, he confessed himself the murderer of Henry Lytton and related all the circumstances that led to the tragedy.

"This confession, made as it was under the seal of temporary secrecy, placed the late Governor Cavendish in a false position.

"He could not permit an innocent man to be executed for the crime of a guilty one. Nor could he, being bound to secrecy, expose the guilty. He was, therefore, compelled to pardon the supposed murderer, without giving any explanation to outraged public sentiment for the strangeness of his action. Such was the explanation made to me by the late Governor Cavendish, with the stipulation that I should keep the secret during the natural life of Frederick Fanning—which he felt sure could not be of long duration—and also that afterward I should reveal it to you, if ever I should happen to meet you. That is all, my dear friend and benefactor. And some day, when the poor old lady upstairs shall have passed away to her heavenly home, this story, which is your vindication, shall be published to the world. And the name of Victor Hartman, which you have renounced and declared to be dead and buried, shall be rescued from unmerited reproach and crowned with merited honor."

While yet they spoke together, there was heard a loud knocking at the hall door. And the next moment Jerome, the hall footman, who had immediately opened the door, entered the drawing-room, saying that there was a messenger from the Reindeer with a note for Mrs. Fanning on a matter of life and death.

Mr. Lytton immediately went out to see the messenger, who proved to be no other than Mithridates, or Taters, once the slave of Frederick Fanning, some time the hired servant of John Lytton, and now the hostler at the Reindeer.

"Well, Taters, what is it? Mrs. Fanning has gone to bed, and we don't like to disturb her at this hour of the night," said Mr. Lytton.

"Oh, marster, you'll have to 'sturb her nebbertheless and notwivstandin'," said the weeping boy, "because my young missis, which wasn't a ghost after all, but was a libbin' 'oman when I see her here, is a-dyin' now, at the Reindeer, and wants to see her mudder."

"What on earth are you talking about, boy?" inquired the bewildered man.

"Miss Iby Fannin', sir! My young mist'ess as used to was! She be a-dyin' at de Reindeer and wants to see her mudder, Missis Fannin', my ole missis, wot libs here," explained the boy, bursting into fresh sobs and tears.

"Ivy Fanning, the long missing girl, supposed to be dead—dying now at the Reindeer?"

"Yes, sir—yes, sir! And if you don't make haste and tell my ole missis she'll be dead before her mudder can get to her," sobbed the faithful boy.

"Sit down here and wait," said Mr. Lytton, who now understood the emergency.

And, leaving the boy seated in the hall, he went into the drawing-room and told Emma the surprising news that Ivy Fanning, the long-lost, erring daughter of Frederick and Katharine Fanning, and the unworthy cousin of Emma Cavendish—Ivy Fanning, whose faults had caused so much misery to all connected with her—Ivy Fanning, supposed to be dead long ago, was now lying at the point of death at the Reindeer Hotel, and begging to see her poor, wronged mother!

"What a terrible thing to tell Aunt Katharine, when we rouse her up at the dead of night!" exclaimed Emma, with a shudder.

"And yet, my dear one, it is your duty to do that very terrible thing. Go bravely and do it, my love, while I go and order the most comfortable carriage in the stable to convey the poor lady to Wendover," said Alden Lytton, encouragingly.

Emma went to Mrs. Fanning's room and waked her up, telling her at first, very gently, that she was wanted.

The poor woman, jumping to the conclusion that some one of the household servants was ill and in need of her ministrations, got up at once and inquired who it was.

"It is a friend of yours who is ill at the Reindeer Hotel at Wendover, and desires to see you," said Emma, beginning gently to break to the poor mother the news that it was her dying daughter who had sent for her.

"Friend? I am sure I have no friend who is near enough to send for me, at dead of night, to come sixteen miles to see him, or her, as the case may be," said the widow, looking very much perplexed, as she hastened to put on her clothes.

"I should have said a relative—a very near relative—a long-lost—" began Emma, but her voice broke down in sobs.

"It is Ivy!" exclaimed Mrs. Fanning, as a swift intuition revealed to her the truth.

"Yes, it is Ivy," wept Emma, throwing her arms around the afflicted woman. "And oh, is it not better so—better at once to know her fate, even to know her safe in the peace of death, than to go on enduring this dreadful uncertainty about her?"

"Oh, my child, my child! Oh, my child, my child!" wept the poor mother, scarcely able, through sobs and tears, and failings of heart and frame, to complete her simple toilet.

Emma, with great sympathy and tenderness, assisted her to dress, pinned the shawl around her shoulders, tied the bonnet strings under her chin, and brought her her gloves and pocket-handkerchief.

"I will now run and get my hat and sack, Aunt Katharine. I will go with you to Wendover," she said.

"You go with me? My dear child, you have been so long parted from your husband, and only received him back to-night, and leave him to go with me? No, no! I can not permit you to do so, Emma," said the weeping lady.

"But you need me, Aunt Katharine, and I should be utterly unworthy of my dear Alden's love if I could fail you in your time of trouble. Besides, I think Alden, also, will go back with you to Wendover."

"Heaven bless you both! You are the solace of my sad old age," said the widow, earnestly.

Emma ran out, and soon returned prepared for her sudden night ride.

Then she took her poor aunt's arm within her own and supported her as they walked down-stairs together.

In the hall below they met Alden Lytton, also prepared for the journey.

He did not seem at all surprised to see Emma in her hat and *paletot*. He understood her too well for that. He merely inquired if the ladies were both quite ready. And being answered in the affirmative, he took them out and put them into the carriage, that was immediately started at a rate that astonished the usually steady-going horses.

The journey was made almost in silence. Mrs. Fanning wept quietly behind her pocket-handkerchief, and Alden and Emma sat with their hands clasped in each other's in mute sympathy.

It was some time after midnight when the carriage entered Wendover and drew up before the old Reindeer Hotel.

Lights about the house at that hour showed that something very unusual was transpiring within.

Hezekiah Greenfield himself came out to meet the party from Blue Cliffs.

With much gravity he greeted them, and to Mrs. Fanning's agonized inquiries about her daughter, he answered:

"I can't well tell you how she is, ma'am. But I will call Sukey, and she will take you to her."

He then conducted them into the parlor and went out in search of his wife.

Very soon good Mrs. Greenfield came waddling in.

Mrs. Fanning arose and hurried to meet her, eagerly inquiring:

"How is my child? How is she now? Does she still live?"

"Yes, ma'am, she is alive, and when she sent for you she was still in her right senses; but now she is wandering, poor girl, and imagines herself still to be living at Peerch P'int," answered the weeping woman, as she took the poor mother's hand to lead her to her daughter.

She led her to a spacious upper chamber, dimly lighted by a single taper, where on a white bed lay extended the form of the dying girl.

"Ivy, my darling! My darling Ivy, do you know me?" tenderly whispered the poor mother, taking her erring daughter's wasted hand and gazing into the fading face, nothing but love and sorrow and forgiveness in her heart.

"Is that you, mamma? Is it near morning? I'm so glad!" said the dying girl, panting as she spoke. "Oh, I've had such a dreadful dream, mamma—such a long, dreadful dream! I dreamed of doing such horrible and wicked things—that I never could have done in my waking hours. I have lived long years in last night's dreadful dream. I am glad it is morning. Kiss me, mamma."

These were her last words, panted forth with her last breath. The mother's kiss fell upon "unanswering clay."

Katharine Fanning was borne in a fainting condition from the death-bed of her daughter and conveyed to another chamber, where she received the most sympathetic and affectionate ministrations from Emma and Alden Lytton.

But it was not until Alden and Emma saw the face of that sinful child of passion in her coffin that they knew Ivy Fanning and Mary Grey to be one and the same person.

Her remains were laid in the family vault at Blue Cliffs, where, before many weeks had passed, the body of her brokenhearted mother was laid beside them.

Craven Kyte was never clearly certain whether he was himself a widower or a bachelor. But in either character he was free. And the first use he made of his freedom was to go to White Perch Point and propose to the brave little maiden of the light-house, who was his last love, as she had been his first.

And soon he made her his wife, and brought her and her aged relative away from their bleak home and dangerous duties and settled them in a pretty rural cottage within easy walking distance of his own thriving place of business—the fashionable bazaar of "Bastiennello & Kyte."

The two young brides, Laura and Electra, were taken to Europe by their husbands, and reached Paris in time to be present at the great World's Fair. And before they returned Victor Hartman's story was published to the world, and his fame was fully vindicated.

THE END.

Lightning Source UK Ltd.
Milton Keynes UK
UKHW010636230721
387648UK00001B/18